For

B L A I R C L A R K

tenens res
multorum veterum, leges divumque hominumque,
prudenter qui dicta loquive tacereve posset.
hunc inter pugnas Servilius sic conpellat.

THIS IS A BORZOI BOOK
PUBLISHED BY ALFRED A. KNOPF, INC.

FIRST EDITION

Distributed by Random House, Inc.
Published simultaneously in Toronto, Canada,
by Random House of Canada Limited.
Library of Congress Catalog Card Number: 67–18597
Manufactured in the United States of America

Portions of this book originally appeared in slightly different form
in the September 1967 issue of PLAYBOY *magazine,*
as a short story entitled "A Small Buffet in Maldita."

A

QUIET

PLACE

TO

WORK

HARRY BROWN

ALFRED · A · KNOPF · NEW YORK · 1968

A Quiet Place to Work

BOOKS BY HARRY BROWN

A Quiet Place to Work   (*1968*)

The Stars in Their Courses   (*1960*)

The Beast in His Hunger   (*1948*)

A Sound of Hunting   (*1946*)

Artie Greengroin   (*1945*)

A Walk in the Sun   (*1944*)

These are Borzoi Books

Published in New York by Alfred A. Knopf

SOURCES OF THE EPIGRAPHS

DEDICATION PAGE: *Ennius,* Annales, *VII (fragment).*

PART ONE: *A slight rephrasing of a clause in Tacitus,* Agricola, *30.*

PART TWO: *Shakespeare,* Antony and Cleopatra, *IV, 3.*

PART THREE: *Mrs. Alfred North Whitehead, in conversation, as recorded by Lucien Price in* Dialogues of Alfred North Whitehead *(Boston: Little, Brown; 1954).*

PART FOUR: *Plautus,* Pseudolus, *35–6.*

The four lines on page 215 are a mild reworking of Robert Graves's interpretation of a nursery rhyme, as developed in his essay "Mother Goose's Lost Goslings" in The Crowning Privilege *(Garden City, N.Y.: Doubleday; 1956).*

*** *Maldorado* Pop. 24,475, Alt. 6,588

Built in a long ravine, through which the lovely ***Río Maldorado*** courses, among the western foothills of the Sierra Cansada, Maldorado lies in the southern quarter of the State of Nuevocegado, 13.5 miles over a good paved road that branches off Highway 69 at Km. 316, the turnoff (not well marked) coming 8.1 miles south of **Fuerte*.

Once fantastically wealthy in gold and silver deposits, in the 1700's Maldorado was called "the richest place on earth," with a larger population, at the time, than Mexico City itself. Early in the last century, however, the veins of precious metals began to be mined out; and as the gold and silver dwindled the great refining haciendas, one after another, closed their doors forever. At Maldorado's height of prosperity there were 27 of these haciendas (they used the mercury process) stretching west for 3 miles, where some of them made up the heart of ****MALDITA,*** the so-called Lower City of Maldorado. By the final half-decade of the 19th century, however, only 6 were still in operation.

Late in the afternoon of September 5, 1896, Nature struck a severe blow to Maldorado, meanwhile giving Maldita a mortal wound. An earthquake, which otherwise was considered minor, opened a crack in an old dam in the hills SE of the city. It had been a summer of heavy rains, and within a half-hour the weakened dam gave way to the water pressure. Fortunately there had been time to warn the inhabitants, so the loss of life was small (Maldorado—3 dead, 12 missing; Maldita—8 dead, 10 missing).

Although considerable damage was done to the rich houses and elaborate public buildings of Maldorado, it was Maldita that received the full force of the flood. The entire center of the place, including the last of the silver-refining haciendas, was either swept away or left in water-soaked, uninhabitable ruins. In fact, to all intents and purposes, Maldita ceased to exist: its population, over 20,000 in 1801, was less than 300 in 1901. And so it remained for more than 40 years.

Then, in 1938, Fredrich Frueling (died 1949), a rich Austrian refugee who was also an amateur architect, passed through the vine-covered ghost town of Maldita and was intrigued by its possibilities. He forthwith bought one of the old ruined haciendas and reconstructed it in a fascinating and unusual combination of architectural styles. His example was followed, after World War II ended, by a number of other people, most of them Americans, and most of them holding faithfully to Frueling's style of architecture. Today, nearly 20 years after Frueling's death, Maldita is a unique showplace, and well worth an excursion from Maldorado (although tourists should be warned that the reconstructions are privately owned and occupied, and that trespassers are *not* welcomed).

Maldorado, too, has long since recovered from the effects of the catastrophe, and although a handful of the beautiful old mansions of the ennobled mine supervisors were wrecked beyond repair, the majority of them, refurbished and kept up by the Mexican government, are open to visitors daily. Others remain in private hands, and are still occupied by the descendants of the original builders. Probably no other city of the same size in all of North America holds so many delightful public buildings. They are, in general, small (befitting Maldorado's own smallness) but exquisite (befitting the city's onetime wealth that built them); and, since Maldorado is now more or less what in England would be called a National Trust, the entire city might be considered as a Grand, Open-Air Museum. Among the major sights of Maldorado, architecturally speaking, are: (1) the ***Palacio de las Montañas.* Built in 1714-19 as a residence for the Conde del Arco, this was the most expensive structure to be . . .

From Benson J. Bolling: *Mexico for People Like Us*
(New York; 1963), pp. 195-6.

Contents

Defiéndame Dios de mí

PART ONE

THE SHORES
OF LAESTRYGONIA

ubi solitudinem reficiunt, pacem appellant

❧ One

I Could've Gone Back
to Poe's Mug,
of Course

I was sitting under an old pepper tree in the patio, at one of those round, hide-topped tables whose design hasn't changed since before stout Cortez hit the beach, trying to put down some ideas about the thing I wanted to do. There was an open notebook on the table, but my mind was shut and locked. I felt ill at ease and uncomfortable, and I was damned if I knew why.

A big black bird, with a tail that I could've sworn had been designed by a drunken Blériot, beat through the air over my head and set up shop in another old pepper tree at the far corner of the patio. For a bird that looked like a crow's idiot cousin it had a distressingly well-stocked sound department. I listened to squawks, trills, ripples, whoops, a rattle like distant snaredrums, and the cut-short gurgle of somebody making the Deep Six the hard way. Then it broke off, in the middle of what I took to be the French alphabet as recited in the elementary schools of Dahomey, and flew toward the river, swearing.

A girl came in through the open mesquite gates.

She might have been a lanky, awkward boy. A pair of gray-flannel trousers, long out of style and perhaps still in mourning for the death of Calvin Coolidge, was held up to a certain extent by a scuffed belt, over which a frayed pink Brooks Brothers shirt drooped like untrimmed piecrust. Her auburn hair was cropped much too short, her face was a problem in solid geometry, and she stood, God help her, over six feet tall. The lace of one dirty white tennis shoe was untied, flopping along on the patio tiles as she shuffled up to the table and lurched to a halt.

"I know you," she said. Her voice resembled someone walking on gravel toward a badly played French horn.

"All right," I said. "You know me."

"But you don't know me. I'm Lalage Delmore."

My mouth, which often leads a life of its own, let its corners turn up a little. "Lalage," I said pointlessly. I nodded. The nod had no point, either.

"L-a-l-a-g-e. La-la-*gay*." She spelled it out, then pronounced it, expelling the last syllable as though it had a bad taste. "It's a fool name, I know. I hate it. Go on and laugh."

"Why should I?"

"You started to."

I closed the notebook and brushed a few pepper leaves from the table. "I never *start* to laugh, Lalage," I said. "I either laugh or I don't. And as far as your name's concerned, I've heard it before and I like it."

I guess that nobody had ever said such a thing to her about her name, because she stared at me in surprise and disbelief before she got around to asking: "Did you know a girl named Lalage?"

"In a way, yes."

"Where is she now?"

"Long gone, I'm afraid."

Instead of pursuing the matter as a normally curious female might have done, Lalage went off at a tangent. "You don't look as old as I thought you would."

The remark shouldn't have cut, but it did. "That's nice," I said, bleeding a bit. "In spite of your disappointment."

"What?"

"How old did you think I was?"

"My mother says you're over fifty."

I should've stayed away from Hollywood: the price of fame, like that of almost everything else, is slightly higher west of the Rockies. "In that case, the back of my hand to your mother."

Lalage frowned at the table. "It doesn't matter," she said.

"It does to me," I told her, "not to mention my wife. And my son. He takes age very seriously, my son does. How old are you, incidentally?"

"That doesn't matter, either." She went over to one of the rose-bushes along the wall and lightly batted a bud around. "Twenty-two," she said. Her back was toward me and I could barely hear her. "A horrible age," was her afterthought, spoken to the rosebud.

"Want to swap ages?"

"If I—" She treated the bud to a fast left hook and spun about clumsily. "My father's dead. Is yours?"

"No, he lives in Boston. Amounts to the same thing, though."

"Is he nice?"

"My father? He's a dirty old man."

I had shocked her. "Oh, he isn't!"

"No, he really isn't, Lalage, when you come right down to it." I grinned at her. "But he would be, understand, if I didn't send him soap."

Now, for the first time, she smiled. I drank it in quickly, but not so fast that I couldn't taste a jigger of bitters in it. "*I* know," she said. "You're teasing me."

"That's the way we men in our fifties are, always teasing girls in their thirties."

"I don't mind teasing, not that kind." The smile went back where it came from. "I'm used to being teased. I live with my mother, and—"

"And she likes to tease you morning, noon and night."

"No, I didn't mean that. I meant—" Her teeth calipered her lower lip. "It's sometimes I'm thinking of lots of things at once and the wrong words come out."

"You're not alone there, Lalage. I do it myself. Sit down."

She sighed and folded into the chair across from me like a dropped pawnshop accordion. These chairs, which are made of the same materials as the tables, are called *equipales* by the Mexicans. I've never yet found out what they call the tables, not that it makes any difference, one way or the other. "How old are you, Mr. Culloden, honest?" she wanted to know, leaning her weight on her thin forearms. "Or shouldn't I ask?"

"On the contrary, Lalage, I've been hoping for weeks that somebody'd ask me. I'm forty-five. And on August nineteenth I'll be forty-six."

"You don't have birthday parties, do you? Not any more, anyway. They're for small children. You know, very small children."

"That's where you're wrong, Lalage," I said. "Believe me, I'm a man who has fantastic birthday parties, a man who hasn't been told he's not a very small child any more."

"Oh, I *do* believe you!" she exclaimed, and waited eagerly for me to go on. It was then that I realized how desperate she was for someone to talk to her, even if what she heard was nonsense or bombast or merely a ten-cent tinsel lie.

"One birthday a year," I said, speaking as carefully as I could, making it up from clause to clause. "And sometimes two. And with the strangest guests, and in the strangest places."

"Who'd you invite last year? Where did you have the party?"

"Last year? Let's see—" I lifted my eyes unto the sky, from whence cometh my help. "Oh, sure, *last* year. Well, last year, you might say, I mixed business with pleasure. Maybe 'business' isn't the right word, though, it was more like research. Anyway, Lalage, I'd run into this old argument about how many angels can stand on the point of a pin. So I threw a wild bash for the whole Host of Heaven. On the point of a pin, naturally. Don't bother to R.S.V.P. Dress optional. Well, when they started to fly in, I—"

She laughed. I have heard loons on northern lakes make nearly the same noise, strident and startling. "Oh, you're teasing again," she managed to say among her ululations.

"Now, that's a mighty un-Christian attitude to take," I told her. "Incidentally, it was a safety pin, not a common one." I pushed myself lower in my chair, stretching out a leg on each side of the table. "Remember, Lalage, always hedge your bets. The Mohammedans could be right."

"Whatever that means." The laughter, slowed by a steep grade not far from Mecca, tried to shift into low gear and stalled.

"It doesn't mean a thing. Nothing I say before noon ever means a thing. Didn't your mother tell you that about me, too? Why should it?"

"I don't know."

"Neither do I. Any more than I know why you came calling."

My tone was casual, but the pitchout caught her ten feet off base. She swallowed and said: "Why, I came—I thought I—it's about the party my mother's giving you. She said to—"

"What party?" It was my turn to dive back to second, safe by a whisker.

She flushed and sagged away from the table, letting her big hands drop into her lap. "*Wants* to give you, I should've said." She blinked at her hands. "Yes, that's it, she wants to give you a party, my mother does, and she sent me over here to tell you. *Ask* you, I mean."

"That's very kind of your mother," I said. "We've never met, though."

"But you're best friends with the Weatherbys." She was still paying attention to her hidden hands. "And they're best friends with my mother, sort of. That ought to count for something, my mother'd say."

We knew the Weatherbys very slightly indeed, and mainly because they owned the country house, the *finca,* we had rented in Maldita. "Count for what?" I asked.

Now she seemed to be twisting her fingers. "At least, I guess that's what my mother would say."

"Can't you tell what she's thinking?"

She shook her head. "When it doesn't matter, maybe."

"And it matters now?"

Lalage's reply could have been the memorized opening of a set speech: "Naturally, everybody in Maldita—from the foreign colony, that is—won't be invited. Only the ones who are most interesting and who have something to offer, the ones you'd be most apt to like. It would be a pleasant, small buffet dinner outdoors, weather permitting, with not more than ten or twelve other people, none of—"

"None of whom I know." I spoke more sharply than I'd intended. Her shoulders twitched. "I guess not," she said. "I'm sorry. I could've told her. People don't."

Her voice was so low that I thought I'd missed the end of a sentence. "Don't what?"

"Invite somebody they haven't even met. To their houses, I mean." She stopped whatever the latest thing was that she was doing to her fingers and lifted her eyes to mine. They had become wet somehow. "It's not the same thing, don't you see? It isn't the same thing at all."

I was out of my depth. The air in my tank was nearly gone, and Lalage Delmore was still a hundred fathoms below me, where the light had faded completely and the fish, glowing and grotesque, ran on their own private generators. I decided to make for the surface, get out of the water fast, and try to dry off in the sun.

"Listen, Lalage," I said, "I came down to Mexico to work. Not to eat. Not for love. Not even to glide. I expect to meet your mother, and everybody else who's around, but I don't want to commit myself to the people who live in Maldita when I haven't even had time to commit myself to the place where they live. So please thank your mother for me, tell her that I appreciate her invitation, and ask her if she won't give us a rain check. That make sense?"

Lalage stood up as though I weren't there and went over and paid attention to the roses again. Her left hand banged away at the same old rosebud. It was beginning to look shopworn.

After a while she cocked her head and her body stiffened as if she were being summoned by a whistle pitched too high for my ears. Then she made for the gates, ambling loose-jointedly like some giant marionette—manipulated, perhaps, by an apprentice god.

Halfway down the patio she stopped and turned. Under her eyes the flesh had become damp all the way to the jawline, and at least one friendly neighborhood teardrop had left its mark on the old pink Brooks shirt, above where her insignificant breast must have been. "Whatever you're thinking," she said in a flat voice, "I'm glad you can't come."

She spun around and went out the gates. I wouldn't say that she ran, since her progress more resembled a horizontal fall. Her arms flapped like the featherless wings of some monstrous fledgling. Of the chick of a Roc, for instance.

Lalage's departure left me with an intensified feeling of malaise. I didn't open the notebook again. Instead I took a therapeutic turn around the patio, walking counterclockwise along the bougainvillaea-covered, rose-bordered wall. I went around and behind the second of the two exterior staircases that led to the balcony off which all the main rooms were reached, then strolled back to my chair through the portico whose columns supported the long balcony above, and whose cool stones were almost always in shadow.

When I heard our Ford station wagon being eased down the narrow cobblestoned road to the house I got up, walked to the gateway, and watched the car crawl into the patio. My son was driving and my wife sat beside him. Concepción, the cook-housekeeper-laundress who came with the house, was in the back seat, flanked by a big pair of baskets I had never seen before. Each of them held enough food to take care of a team like the New York Mets on a month-long road trip.

I opened the door on Polly's side. Her lap was hidden by a mass of wet flowers. "Why didn't you lasso the whole market and drag it home with you?" I said.

Polly's upper lip had tiny drops of sweat on it and her hair had been much neater an hour before, but she was glowing. "Oh, Sam, it's a wonderful market, truly. You've got to go in with me tomorrow."

I sized up the baskets in an unfriendly way. "You mean this stuff won't feed us all summer?"

"It's mostly staples. Here, hold these." She shoved the flowers at me, four bunches of them, and got out of the car. I didn't recognize any of the flowers, which wasn't surprising. Sometimes I know a daisy when I see it, but even then the wind has to be right. This is a dangerous and negative talent for a writer, but it's a talent I'm stuck with, *pace* Carolus Linnaeus.

"I suppose this means we can't pick any of the Weatherbys' flowers," I said.

"Aren't they lovely?" was all she answered. That took care of me.

Luis, the gardener, came through the arched tunnel that ran under the house to the river terrace and helped Concepción drag the baskets out of the car. These two bedded down, presumably in wedlock, in an adobe house, painted blood-red, about twenty yards upstream from our rented *finca*. Each lugging a basket, they staggered up the exterior staircase opposite the gates, then a few feet along the balcony to the kitchen door.

Polly gathered up the flowers from my arms and took them over to the nearest table while I watched my son drag his long carcass out of the car. Jock had turned seventeen in Yuma, Arizona, while we were driving to Mexico. He was already two inches taller than I and, although he was gawky enough to make a newly foaled colt look like Seabiscuit with a tailwind, he would be a big and graceful one when he got his growth. He came around the front of the station wagon and held out the ignition key. "You want this?" he asked wearily.

I shook my head. "Not today, if my luck holds. How was driving in town?"

"Okay, I guess. But this heap's too wide for some of those narrow streets. You ought to turn it in for a stable of Vespas."

"I will," I said, "as soon as my hearing starts to go. That sixth-form Spanish of yours work?"

Jock shrugged. "Polly did all the talking. I just lurked around and watched the game from the sidelines. But Polly was good."

"Your mother's a born linguist," I said. "She proposed to me in three languages, plus a private one of her own."

"I heard that, Sam Culloden," Polly said over her shoulder.

"Stands to reason you did." I went to where she was and watched her do the usual things that women do to waterlogged, untrimmed bouquets they've bought in a market.

While she was stripping away some dead leaves she asked: "Did you get anything done, Sam?"

"Not exactly," I said. "I had a visitor. Young. Female. Presumably nubile."

"Oh?" said Polly. It was a small, round *Oh?* Hardly noncommittal.

"Pretty?" This was Jock, reacting like Pavlov's dog.

I was amazed at how quickly he'd reached my side. "Oh, *you* might find her pretty, Jock," I said. "She was tall for a girl, scrawny, all elbows, unreasonably shy, and—well, a little brainwashed, say. Yes, Jock, I think you'd find her right down your alley."

"Wait a minute," Jock said. "She didn't have on one of those pink shirts, did she?"

"She did."

He clapped his hands and bellowed like a lost calf. "Oh, man, we *saw* it! Walking down the road about a couple of hundred yards from here. I tell you, if all the local stuff's like that, this child is shipping out."

"That's enough, Jock," Polly said quietly. "From both of you, as a matter of fact. What did she want, Sam?"

"Seems like her mother wanted us to come to dinner. No date set—but a command performance, so to speak. Small buffet, outdoors, weather permitting. Ten or twelve other people, none of whom, it was made clear, could be called Maldita riffraff. Their name's Delmore. And I said no."

"Any particular reason?"

"Several, if I needed to dredge them up. But what shivered my timbers was the idea of Mrs. Delmore rushing to put her *imprimatur* on us. Besides, I don't want to suffer the slings and arrows of outrageous fortunes, Maldita variety—not right off the bat, anyway. Or is this belief of mine out of date as of this morning?"

"Don't be silly," Polly said, then went on in an abstracted way: "A woman came up to me in the market, a Mrs. Gage. She knew all about us: who you are—her husband's a writer, too, according to her— and how long we're staying, and—" She assembled the flowers, which she had improved considerably from their natural state. "Oh, well, I wasn't paying *too* much attention to what she said. I was trying to make sense with Concepción about the marketing, and Mrs. Gage had a couple of little girls clinging to her who kept shrieking that they wanted to go to the toilet or get married or something even less attractive. They live across the river somewhere and, according to her, hold continual open house, for what that's worth. She insisted that we drop over there within the next twenty-four hours, but I didn't let her pin *me* down, either." She glanced at the top of the table, covered with moist brown leaves and moist dead blossoms. "I'll send Luis to clean up this mess," she said, speaking more to herself than anyone else. Then she went up the stairs and into the kitchen.

Jock followed me to the table where I'd left my notebook and slumped into the chair Lalage had used.

"Well," I said, using the brilliant conversational opening gambit that had put the Versailles of Louis XIV at my feet, "how do you like it where you are?"

"It'll do. Except—" He yawned. "Except it's full of foreigners." The wink he gave me was upstaged by another yawn.

"Charles Lockridge Culloden, you should go far," I said. "You are sensitive and perspicacious, and the stethoscope of your mind is placed firmly upon the wheezing right lung of the world. The State Department needs men like you, not to mention the Peace Corps, the War Corps, the CIA, the P.T.A., the F.F.V., NATO, the UN, and, in good time, some philosophic woman."

"You can't use language like that to your own truly begotten son," Jock said languidly. He yawned a third time. "Is it the altitude that's making me sleepy?" he asked, stretching. "Or old age?"

"It's the altitude. And I don't know where you get the idea you're my own truly begotten son. Your mother and I found you under a gooseberry bush. And we may very well put you back there."

"Okay. But make it the shady side, will you?" He closed his eyes.

He didn't go to sleep, but he might as well have, for all the fatherly companionship he'd've had from me at that moment. I lit a cigarette and tried to sift various thoughts through the sieve of my brain, but all the holes turned out to be clogged. The black notebook, finally aware that my brain was as blank as its pages, sneered at me. I sneered back.

I did have some ideas, certainly; but the ones that were limping around inside my skull had nothing to do with those I'd hoped would come to me earlier, when the patio noises were, however briefly, as muted as a mortician's belch.

For instance, I found myself visualizing the clumsy black bird that had heralded Lalage Delmore. After a slow dissolve from this shot, I drifted into a sequence dealing with Poe and his pinchbeck-Gothic poem about the Raven.

I have nothing against ravens. They are very smart, as birds go, as smart as many politicians and smarter than most actors. But I've always considered Poe to be as cacophonous as a peacock in heat and with about as much depth of feeling. No good ever came from pondering on that weak and weary man.

I fought myself clear of him. As I did so, the raven became an owl, and the owl gradually changed into an enormous pair of eyes. I couldn't connect them with a person at first, and then it hit me that they belonged to Lalage Delmore. A pailful of ice-cold water, unexpectedly heaved in my face, would have been less of a shock than the absolute zero of realizing that this gauche beanpole, this travesty of a female, had the most beautiful eyes I had ever seen. If a woman of merely average features and figure had owned such eyes she'd've been able to write herself a ticket to Anywhere in this kowtowing, scarecrow world. But to discover them—and in retrospect, oddly enough—burning out of Lalage Delmore's spare-shanked, puppet-loose body struck me as being a sick joke, of dubious decency, on the part of Almighty God. I therefore tore myself away from the vision of Lalage Delmore.

It wasn't easy. I could've gone back to Poe's mug, of course. I may not have liked him, but the poor devil did at least have a definable nineteenth-century face. Instead, I did my best to think of reasons for being smack-dab in the middle of Mexico, doing rather less than the mental equivalent of counting my toes, in an uneasy year of a murderous century.

◉ On the night that followed Lalage's morning visit, which was our second night in the *finca,* I was lying beside Polly in the Weatherbys' oversize antique bed, all fancy dowelwork and Spanish Colonial creaks, while I listened to an enfilade of wind-encouraged rain ricochet from the tiles of the roof. I was still brooding about where I was and growing less partial to it with every clatterbone raindrop. On my chest lay a paperbound guidebook to Maldorado and Maldita, a local product which I'd picked up from the night table, but which I was too sullen to open. "We've been taken, Polly," I said. "Weatherby told us it never rains during the rainy season except between six and eight p.m., and then for only half an hour. That's a perfect name—Weatherby. 'Haow be the weather, Old Retainer?' 'Aw, the weather be dorty, Missus.' It's now ten minutes to eleven. Five hours straight, Polly."

"Didn't rain at all last night," Polly murmured. She lay facing me, half asleep, her knees slightly drawn up.

"Merely fattening us for the slaughter," I said. Then: "Oh, hell—!"

Polly's eyes opened part way. "Now what, Sam?"

"Another one." I got out of bed and went over to the iron-grilled glass door that opened on the balcony. I used the guidebook to kill a scorpion that had come from behind one of the drawn drapes. It was a clean kill, too: he died, but he kept his shape. "How many does that make since we got here?" I asked as I strode, a sulky Achilles, back to the tent of my bed. "Eight? Nine?"

"It's because the house hasn't been lived in for months," Polly said drowsily.

Three-hundred-year-old wood wailed below and behind me as I settled back on my pillow. "What makes you think it's being lived in now?" I regretted the words as soon as I'd said them.

"That brings the total to eleven." Polly spoke with deliberate slowness. "I killed two I didn't bother to tell you about." She raised herself on one elbow. "And I'm glad I didn't. You're bad enough as it is. You've been impossible ever since—oh, ever since noon. What's the matter with you, anyway?"

"The altitude," I said.

"You're the one who started this, Sam, don't forget. You wanted to get away to a quiet place, a place where you could work. But you also said you wanted it to be—"

"I know. A place you'd like yourself."

"Well, I *do* like Maldita. And Maldorado. Or I will, if you'll let me. Please let me, Sam."

I couldn't hold out in the fortress of my mood any longer. The walls were all at once breached in a dozen places, at weak points betrayed by my own treacherous thoughts. I surrendered. I came out with my hands up. "I will let you, Polly," I said, offering her, hilt-foremost, the best smile I could forge on short notice. "Sure, I'll let you." I leaned over clumsily and kissed her pretty nose. "I'm sorry, darling, really I am. And I'll feel better about things tomorrow. That Delmore girl threw the whole damned day out the window, don't ask me why. I should've gone into town with you instead of drawing a blank in the patio. So how about seeing the sights together in the morning?"

She ran her hand along my upper arm and gave my shoulder a gentle pinch. "The sights of Maldorado will keep," she said. "What I'd like you to do in the morning is take a long walk around Maldita. You could go back to the turnoff that crosses that bridge with the statues on it, the headless ones. We saw it from the main road on the way here, remember? And then you could come back along the other side of the Río Maldorado, on that old dirt road we can see from the river terrace."

"All the way into Maldorado? Is this supposed to be a casual stroll or a Bunion Derby?"

"Oh, there must be another bridge you can cross, before Maldorado."

"Did you see one when you and Jock drove in?"

"No, but the river curves away from the main road and goes behind some little hills. You can't see it for a long time."

"Never mind, I'll—what's the Spanish for 'scorpions'?"

"*Alacranes.*"

"When I want to get back across the river I'll lay down a pontoon bridge of today's bag of *alacranes.* Eleven ought to turn the trick very neatly. They're big as lobsters."

"If I'd realized how grotesque your imagination was, Sam Culloden, I wouldn't've married you, ever."

"I tried, time and again, to show you that this handsome hide hid a monster," I said, "but you were too far gone in adoration. And that's how it's always been. Whenever a woman becomes infatuated with me, which has happened hundreds of times, my fair face invariably blinds the poor creature as to the wickedness lurking within."

I gave her another clumsy kiss. "Dr. Frankenstein has spoken. Good night, dear Polly."

"Good night, poor old silly Sam."

She went to sleep then as a child does, on the instant and empty of all regrets. One moment she was saying my name, and the next she had left that particular day, puzzling, exciting and strained, behind her forever. I watched her calm face and listened to her calm breathing, and after a while I felt a new calmness myself because she was there beside me. I put aside a desire to stroke her cheek and sighed, to my surprise, with contentment. Then I took up the guidebook.

It was a prize package, and no mistake, consisting of photographs taken by one madman, captioned by another, and bound into the approximation of a book by a third. It was printed with shoeblacking on corn husks: the caption writer had been fathered by *Finnegans Wake* on a bowl of alphabet soup; and the photographer obviously had no recollection of the single lesson he had been given, on an extremely overcast day, by Daguerre's most backward pupil. They were a lunatic, charming trio. Right off the bat I liked them all.

There was, for instance, a photograph of a marble woman, holding up what might have been a cow's horn or a tired length of sugar cane, who turned out to be Liberty herself. According to the caption, which, like the photograph, was out of focus: *Our Statute to Libberty is by all meams smaller then that of Nueva-York, but it rises her revolucionary torcht in one of the Aristocratidad boroughs of Maldorado!!*

I didn't get the significance of the exclamation points, although I sensed levels of meaning beyond my rustic gringo comprehension. Yet I was delighted with the proud assertiveness, the upright determination, of those two impassioned exclamation points. Because of them I went greedily through the guidebook, cover to cover. It was like eating peanuts, only more so.

I was informed that the City Hall, known as the Palacio de las Montañas, was *the most notorius bilding of the city,* and that the carefully restored house of a grandee of the 1700's was a *gorgous resident wort of being admired in River, Sidedrive, N.Y.* The main plaza was—well, *surrounded by trees, the olden place records the pusle of the town, it's band playes beautiful romanzas, for our famous brass-band gathers lovin couplers, gosipp and sumpathetical romances.* Under an overexposed shot of the Maldorado Normal School, a caption told me that *when enterring this place we feet the sencation of going back to our riotous and worried of scholar days— or going to church, as the buildig has too facades wich was taked away from some colonial and Ruinous temples.* One of a pair of streets, so narrow as almost to require people to pass through them sideways, was called *very suggesting for every Gay visitor;* and the other, *rumantic, tipical and full of ocal calor.*

As for Maldita, I learned it had *once been notted for the sadist ruinas in México, but of lately it has undertakened many pimprovements, some of wich has inceased it's caracter.*

When I returned the book to the night-table it was after midnight, and for the first time since our arrival I felt at home. There even seemed to have been a lessening of the noisy, wretched rain. The nightmare gales that had raged through my head all day were gone— to the Cave of the Winds, I hoped, never to be freed again. But they'd stayed around me too long. I was very tired.

So I put out the light, after taking a last dim look at the lovin coupler beside me. And then I sank like a two-ton anchor down through estranging depths of sleep.

✠ Two

If You Ever Find
Yourself in Naples,
Giuseppe

It must have been a good bridge in its day. It had stood up to earth-quake and flood, one hard on the heels of the other, and yet here it was, still a fair bridge, spanning the Río Maldorado.

There were ten female statues—five on either side, and each slightly askew on her pedestal outside the carved stone railings. Every marble head had been knocked off, with the exception of one lady's lower jaw; but this was certainly the work of local misogynists, full of mescal and whooping it up for *machismo,* rather than combined operations on the part of shaken earth and a river gone crazy. From the stance of the headless torsos and the cut of their pitted draperies, they were, I thought, put up previous to the American Revolution, before the discovery of what a few men with much resentment and a fair amount of firepower could do had made its ineradicable impression on the Mexican mind.

I'd planned to ask Jock to come with me, but as soon as he'd shoveled in enough breakfast to hold a squad of starved doughfeet he'd loped out of the house and into the private country that's only yours when you're seventeen. So here I was at midmorning, alone on the Maldita bridge and staring down a river valley whose flanks were wrecked haciendas, all the way to the small breast-shaped hills behind which Maldorado nestled. The sight was so impressive that I could've dawdled the whole day in that one spot; and I certainly would've lounged around for another half hour if a car with Illinois plates hadn't come bumping down from the main road, to stop as it reached the bridge.

After nearly a week of leisurely driving from the border I was able to divide American tourists, by their carfuls, into two types. The first consisted of a man in his early thirties with rumpled clothes, a rumpled face, and a lot more paunch than he needed; accompanied by a little pudding wife, with a little pudding head and a voice like an egg beater; and she, in turn, would be serving as a flabby trapeze for several seagull-lunged children under ten, who had the raucous civility of a rout of winter-starved wolves. Then, driving in cars that somehow managed to look as unhappy as the people in them, came the second type, the Senior, God save us, Citizens, the goddamned turkeynecks, all frowning as though they were victims of a face lift in reverse by some mixed-up Midwestern plastic surgeon, and all bewildered to be in the Land of the Night-Blooming Dysentery.

The six people who creaked out of the Illinois car, a 1964 Oldsmobile, were of the second type. While the males, recognizable because of their trousers, took snapshots of the bridge, pointing their exposure meters like death rays, their females glared in hard-shell outrage at a bare chipped nipple on the nearest statue.

I stepped back from the middle headless lady on the upstream side, whose voluted buttocks I'd been inspecting, did a right face that would have brought a grunt of approval from the toughest D.I. on Parris Island, and, double-timing away from the turkeynecks, swung off the bridge and clattered down a pebble-dotted bank to the left. Somewhere during my descent I nearly took a header over a debased young pig that was practicing truffle hunts, an ocean away from truffles, below an overthrown column drum.

When I got to level ground I was on the old dirt road to Maldorado, so I did the sensible thing and stopped running. When you're forty-five it's a risky business to stay at a full gallop, nearly seven thousand feet above sea level, unless somebody with a loaded gun and a grievance is drawing a vindictive bead on your short hairs.

The first ruin I came to wasn't far from the bridge. It had been a hacienda, and its walls, with their water-darkened stones enclosing the ghosts of murdered rooms, ran a hundred yards up a hillside to disappear among some huge jacarandas. The carved façade of what had been the hacienda's main entrance was weather-worn but intact. Where the original doors had been, however, were two shoddy, ill-mounted affairs that offered a silent comment on the present state of Maldita carpentry.

One of these cheapjack things hung ajar, and as I passed the entrance I glanced in that direction, hoping for a glimpse of what was inside. I was jolted to see a lean old man in the narrow doorway. He wore a clean white shirt, open at the throat, and neatly pressed threadbare black trousers. His body was erect, his figure trim, and he was well above average in height. Iron-gray hair, cut short, lay forward on his brow in the style of the Roman Republic, before a bald and sensitive Caesar made gold wreaths fashionable. His mouth was bracketed by the lines proper to a man in his early sixties, which I supposed he was. His eyes, blue and interested, held steady on me.

I smiled at him and, merely for the devil of it, threw him an arm-out salute. " 'Morning, sir," I said.

He literally stiffened with surprise. It was as though he'd recognized me as someone he'd known for years, but I was the last person he'd expected to meet in this place and at this time. Slowly his mouth came open. I was ready to stop, under the impression that he wanted to speak to me.

Then a woman's banshee voice screeched Spanish from beyond the slatternly doors. The old man's lips snapped shut at the sound. He stepped out of sight. The door remained ajar. And I ambled on my way.

The only newly reconstructed ruin I passed on this, the south, side of the Río Maldorado wasn't far upstream from the Weatherbys', as the crow flies, but it couldn't be seen from there. A low, fingerlike hill was responsible for a minor bend in the river, and the new *finca* was on the Maldorado side of this bend. At least, I took it for a *finca*. It also could've been a miniature and selective penitentiary for those happy few, the richer breed of felon. All that was visible from the road was a long stone wall, twice as tall as a man, with heavy, padlocked gates at dead center. Faint sounds, as of steel striking stone, came from somewhere inside.

Several hundred yards beyond this chill place a battered Volkswagen bus was parked in front of an architectural oddity that had nothing in common, to put it euphemistically, with the rest of Maldita. The road made a lazy swing at this point, which meant that the layout was approached at an oblique angle. A rusting wrought-iron fence ran along the top of a stuccoed base about four feet high, which was set back five yards or so from the road. Beyond the iron fence was a raised area, flat for the most part, that was screened from the road by some kind of dense thorny shrub and shaded by unkempt pepper trees whose branches drooped so low that it was hard to make out the rambling one-story structure beyond them. Enough of the house could be seen, however, to convince me that the pepper trees were doing a service to human vision. The grim thing seemed to consist of jerry-built pustules, each the size of a single room, jutting from a long and narrow core with no rational plan whatsoever. Maldita, I reminded myself, had certainly undertakened a lot of pimprovements of lately.

What could have been a caterwauling of children came from the concealing pepper trees, but when the racket abruptly stopped I blamed it on one of the big black fan-tail birds, most likely yesterday's virtuoso who, believing I'd disliked his previous performance, had pounded off in silent anger when he saw me. I grinned at the thought until, as before, the image of the bird became an image of Lalage Delmore's eyes, after which my grin pounded off, too. By then I was abreast of the Volkswagen bus, but not really seeing it. I'd absorbed all I wanted, on an empty stomach, of that lackadaisical tittle of the Maldita landscape.

"Hel-*lo*, there! You're going by us!"

Through a gap in the shrubbery I could make out the head and upper torso of a very tanned, very thin, somewhat bearded young man who was standing under a pepper tree on the other side of the wrought-iron fence. He had the face of a tatty wolverine and his narrow chest was like badly coiled rope.

As I stopped he raised his right hand, in which was a nearly full bottle of Carta Blanca beer, and made a nervous summoning gesture. "Come on up, come on up," he said. "The steps're behind the Bug. I was getting ready to throw in the sponge, even though Rose told me it wasn't honest-to-God definite, but women never did know what they're talking about or why. Come on up, Culloden, it's the shank of the evening."

The cheetah in me suggested that I head for Maldorado at an eighty-mile-an-hour clip, instead of which I listened to a hamster, peeking from behind the cheetah's twitching tail, who was a nut on politeness and who started me toward the bruised front bumper of the Volkswagen as though I were his own private zombie. A man never knows, I was thinking. When he's on the verge of sleep the bed collapses. Or a forgotten cigarette sets the mattress on fire. Or he discovers a cobra between the sheets. Or he opens his eyes to find he's run smack into the writer named Gage.

He didn't introduce himself, of course. That would be cheating. "Your wife couldn't get away, hey?" he asked as I started up the steps.

I was resigned to losing this game of Half-upmanship. "No," I said glumly. "And actually *I* wasn't plan—uh—merely taking, I mean, a walk."

The hiatus in my speech was caused by my having to catch my breath. And I had to catch my breath because three naked girls were standing by Gage's shorts-and-sandals-clad body, studying me with X-ray eyes.

The oldest, who'd lost her baby upper incisors, was about eight; the youngest, about six. I'd been momentarily startled because I hadn't expected to run into three naked girls that morning *anywhere*, let alone on the old dirt road to Maldorado. Otherwise, when all's said and done, I'm a neat, clean quarter-century away from finding females of that age, and especially in their natural state, attractive. "We thought we'd drop by later sometime," I said off the top of my head to Gage as I joined the jolly family group. "After we'd gotten—you know, more used to Maldita."

"Ah, it doesn't take twenty minutes, getting used to Maldita," Gage said. "But getting the town used to you, especially if you're a writer, that's another thing. They don't trust real writers much in Maldita." He pinched the oldest girl's neck. "Right, Alpha?" he asked her.

"Right!" Alpha yelled. "*Left!* Right! *Left!* RightLeftRightLeft-RightLeft*Right!*" Her voice rose higher, the words came faster, until she cupped a dirty little paw over her mouth, convulsed by giggles. Her sisters began to giggle, too.

"Crazy," Gage said. He shrugged. "Kids," he added. He held up the bottle of Carta Blanca. "How about a brew, hey? Or something stronger, if you want. Shut up, Gamma! Beta! All of you—*shut!*"

"No, thanks," I told him. "I never have a belt before lunch. Or noon, anyway."

"I never drink before lunch, either," he said. "Know how I manage it? Simple. I have my lunch at eight a.m. You call it breakfast? Okay, I call it lunch. That's using the old semantics, hey?"

"When do you work?" I asked. "At night?"

"Oh, I work," he said vaguely, "I work." He gulped down some Carta Blanca, an action calculated to change the subject. "Ah, and incidentally, I knew who you were, soon's I saw you walking on the road. I saw a picture of you in some Book Section four, five years ago, and I knew who you were from that. Pretty sharp, hey?"

I remembered the photograph, which Bachrach made at my publisher's expense. It had been used for publicity in connection with my last novel—and over my dead body, so to speak. My face was a study in mild wonder mixed with faint disgust, quite what Trelawny's expression must have been as he stared at the braised heart of Shelley in his hand. The fault wasn't Bachrach's, though; it was mine. I have never yet sat for a satisfactory picture.

"Sharp as a tack," I told Gage. I was too bored to avoid the cliché. But then, in case he should open a debate on how photogenic I was, I retired to a previously unprepared position: "How is it you named your girls after the letters of the Greek alphabet?"

The question set Alpha to giggling again, God knows why, until her father dummied her up with a dispassionate box on the ear. "There's another one someplace," he said. "Delta, she's only five. She's out with her mother—and you've got to meet her before you go. Rose, I mean, my wife. It was her idea, Rose's, to give the kids those names. Me, I didn't care one way or the other. Come to think of it, I didn't care about kids at all for a long time, especially having 'em, and neither did Rose, much. You'll be meeting her, Rose, in a minute, she's hanging out the wash now. So when we got—"

"Don't you have a maid?" I broke in. "To do things like laundry? I thought everybody in—"

"Ah, the *muchachas* around here don't see things the way they ought to, what with the Catholic Church and all. Anyway, when we got married, Rose and me, we made a deal to stay off the kid kick. But then, I don't know, all of a sudden it was bangbangbangbang, every year one damned kid after another. So we quit. Smart move, hey? Trouble is, girls run in Rose's family, it's the genes, her family's genes, so I figure if you can't have a little pecker-proud boy every so often, well, the hell with it. Not that I don't love these bare-assed babies to distraction. I do. Right, ladies?"

"*Right!*" The three girls shouted as one, then doubled up with laughter, clutching their fat brown bellies.

When the laughter had lessened I said: "If you *did* have a fifth and it turned out to be a boy, you couldn't call him Epsilon, could you? That '-on' ending's neuter."

A wolverine that had fouled every trap line north of Vancouver couldn't've been any happier than Gage when I gave him this lead. "You hit it, Culloden, you sure did," he said. "This other guy told me the same thing, had me worried every night about that Epsilon tag. And it wasn't just the neuter bit, except that was what worried me the most. Economics come into it, too. Four kids was all we could afford to feed then, and it's all we can afford to feed right now, at least till I hit that old jackpot. And we travel all over the place, besides, and four kids in a beat-up car is hell enough without trying to go for five. So, you want to know how I beat the Gage population explosion? Simplest thing in the world. One morning, out of a clear blue sky, I went to this clinic and had myself tied off. And that day in the clinic, I swear, put ten years onto my life. I tell you, Culloden, there's nothing like sterilization to really *relax* a man. Why don't you give it a whirl, hey?"

"Well, " I said, "I guess I'll stay the way I am for the time being. We always like to keep a little potency around the house—you know, for emergencies." I glanced at my watch. "And speaking of emergencies, this posse's supposed to head the bad guys off at the pass. I'd better get going."

"Ah, you can't yet," Gage said, "not until you've met Rose. She'd never forgive me, Rose wouldn't, if she found out you'd dropped in and I didn't bring you two together." He grabbed my left arm above the elbow. "Like I said, she's out back with the wash. Won't take a minute, come on."

I let him steer me toward the hideous house. The bare little girls didn't trail after us but skipped off to do God knows what at the base of a pepper tree. "Rose liked your wife a lot," Gage said. "They met in the market, but your wife must've told you. What's her name?"

"My wife? Polly."

"Short for Pauline, hey?"

"Short for nothing. They named her Polly."

"Well, let's face it, why not?" Gage said, frowning.

He pulled me through the front door, into a corridor that formed a crossroads with another corridor after a few feet, then continued on to a second door. The junction of corridors was obstructed by several broken toys, a dead scorpion, a moribund beetle, and the yellowed front page of a Mexico City *News* on which an impressionistic skull and crossbones had been done in red watercolor or, just possibly, blood.

Gage freed my arm, hopped over the debris, and pushed open the rear door. Beyond was a king-size bathtowel, hanging wet and limp from a clothesline. There was a knave-size hole in it, dead center. Gage leaned around the doorjamb. "Honey, you listening?" he called. "Culloden's here. Polly couldn't make it, but no matter, *he* stopped by and he's dying to meet you."

"Oh, I want to meet him, too," I heard Rose Gage say. "Bring him out, Jeff, I'm almost through."

"Let's go," Gage said over his shoulder. I did some broken-field walking to the rear door, then followed him down a line of damp sheets that cut off my vision well above eye level. Another bare little girl, evidently Delta, peered from under one of the sheets and made a Gorgon face at me. I stuck out my tongue at her, a logical response, and went on to the end of the jam-packed clothesline.

Gage was waiting, and as I reached him again he grabbed my arm, the right one for a change, and swung me around a clothespole. I caught hold of the pole just in time to avoid a head-on collision with his wife. And if I'd been talking at the moment I saw *her* there'd've been much, much more than a mere hiatus in my speech.

For Rose Gage was stark-naked too.

The nakedness of a woman of thirty is somehow more disconcerting, especially at half past eleven in the morning, than the nakedness of a legion of little girls. No man in his right mind has anything against a naked woman, if her figure's good, but he does like to be given a few seconds' warning before he finds one facing him in full sunlight and smiling at him in the friendliest possible way. An un-expected view, full-rigged, of a stripped-down female hull can bring on serious physical or mental disturbances: heart failure, for instance; or an upsurge of the Why-Wasn't-Mother-Ever-Nice-To-Me-On-Mondays syndrome; or a decision not to put off any longer that girded-loin Call to spread the Gospel; or even, in extreme cases, a sudden and fatal attack of marriage.

"Welcome to Maldita," Rose Gage said, tossing some clothespins into a shredding wicker basket at her feet. "I got through just in time. Did your roof leak last night? Ours did, something awful. Jeff's always climbing up there with tar, but it doesn't seem to help. There's a leak someplace else the next night it rains. But the mornings are worth it, aren't they? Oh, I *do* love this Mexican sun, don't you?" She closed her eyes, raised her head, spread her arms wide and arched her body backward.

I tried to stare at an imaginary object somewhere between her rib cage and the sky, but it was a lost cause. St. Anthony might've been able to swing the deal on one of his good days, but I was merely Sam Culloden and my last couple of days hadn't been good at all. The only way I could've avoided an inspection of Rose Gage's flesh would've been to tell the officer commanding the firing squad that I wanted my blindfold *now,* please, and never mind the cigarette, old chap. But the firing squad only visits Maldita on the last day of every month, so I had to give in to my male hormones. I inspected.

Rose was bare even of cosmetics. Her eyes, nose, and mouth, each a bit larger than necessary, added up to a pleasantly vacuous Earth Mother face; the rest of her added up to a sun-darkened, well-constructed Earth Mother body, also a bit larger than necessary. Her figure, except for a slight insecurity around the pectoral muscles, belied the bearing of four children—bangbangbangbang, as Jefferson Gage had so delicately put it. There was also a strange crouched-to-spring sensuality about her, lurking with bared fangs behind every curve.

She was blonde all over, so I supposed that she came from Scandinavian or Germanic stock. The fact is, if a spasm of coughing had racked Gage right then, visions of two sugarplums called Frieda and D. H. L. would've instantly danced in my head. But Gage didn't cough. He gurgled instead, as he took a long pull at his bottle of beer.

The sound had a sobering effect on me. I drove my male hormones back to their steam room with whips and scorpions, then returned to the amenities. After all, *si fueris alibi, vivito sicut ibi;* or, as they say around the Baths of Caracalla these days, *If you ever find yourself in Naples, Giuseppe, play it* their *way.*

"I haven't seen enough of it to know whether I'll love it or not," I said. I had taken so long to answer Rose's question about the Mexican sun that I sensed an ambiguity in the words. I should've realized that Rose Gage and ambiguous statements were poles apart.

"When can you come back with Polly?" Gage was asking. "Only one of us, me or Rose, ever goes to the market, with maybe a couple of the kids, so somebody's always here with the kids who didn't go. People drop in all the time."

"Many people?"

"You'd like them." It was a faded echo of Lalage's "ones you'd be apt to like," as she recited her mother's Royal Command. Mrs. Delmore, I was sure, wasn't among the people who dropped in on the Gages.

"He'd like a beer or something, too, Jeff," Rose said. "What's got into you? Where're your manners?"

I'd managed by unadorned will power to concentrate on Gage while we were talking, but now my eyes broke their chains and scampered back to Rose. She'd dropped her arms and unbent her body and was standing relaxed. "He's already offered me a drink," I said. "I didn't want one. That is, I'm only passing by on my way into town. I have to go to the—the post office, whatever it's called. I'm expecting a package, and—"

"Car on the blink?" Gage interrupted to ask me.

"*La Oficina de Correos,*" Rose said. "Oh dear, and the package section closes at noon. You'd better let Jeff drive you in."

"The car's fine," I told Gage.

"Or I'll drive you myself," Rose went on. "I haven't been in today."

It was an intriguing offer. I could picture her, stark-naked, tooling me into Maldorado. I could picture the delight of the Mexican policemen who'd arrest her, too. Certainly a score of cops would find it necessary to pile into the Volkswagen bus for that long, long ride to jail, like as not via Guatemala. "That's kind of you," I said to her, "but I've got to walk. Doctor's orders."

Gage studied me with morbid interest. "What's the trouble?"

"Nothing serious, really. My plethora's been acting up, that's all."

"Ah, sure, the *pleth*ora." An entire wing of the Mayo Clinic couldn't have nodded as solemnly as Gage did. "Those things're always getting out of whack."

"That's the truth," I said. "Goodbye, Mrs. Gage. I'll tell my wife."

"Oh, yes, you *do* that. And remember, we're expecting you and your family to drop in any time. Day or night, it doesn't matter, just any old time. The kids're never asleep, anyway. And they'd love to play with that boy of yours. I know they would." She held out her hand and I shook it. As soon as our moist palms had parted she picked up the empty clothesbasket and undulated out of sight around the nearest pustule of the house.

"I'll walk with you, far as the steps," Gage said from behind me. When I turned I saw that he had taken off his shorts and, except for the sandals on his feet, was as naked as the rest of them. I was beginning to understand why the Gages had a servant problem.

The girls were gone from the front of the house, which was a change for the better. "Next time I want to talk to you about writing for pictures," Gage said. "It's tough going, hey?"

"Nothing to it. Especially if you leave the ribbon off your typewriter."

"No, I mean getting a *job* out there. Well, we'll talk, hey?"

"How can we help it?" I said.

He stayed where he was, listing slightly to loo'ard, watching me walk down the road. When I was sixty feet away I could hear a final gurgle as he polished off the beer.

There was no bridge across the river between Maldita and Maldorado, of course, and I was a fool to have imagined there'd be one. By the time I'd slogged all the way into Maldorado the only local point of interest I wanted to see was a taxi that would take me home. At a cab rank outside the market I stumbled into the first in line.

When I got back to our *finca* the station wagon was gone, and in its place a Mercedes 600 sat in gleaming black arrogance. At one of the patio tables Polly was sipping rum with a good-looking, raven-haired woman whose racehorse legs were crossed under a Mondrian print dress. I thought she was about thirty-five, but as I limped toward the table I saw that I'd flattered her by fifteen or twenty years. The face had been lifted, the hair dyed, the body kept trim by ruthless dieting. The clues were subtle, but I'd been in the company of too many aging actresses, too many times, not to recognize them.

"Sam," Polly said before I'd made it to the table, "this is Mrs. Delmore. She was—"

"*Marian* Delmore," the woman said, smiling up at me. "I'm so glad you put in an appearance before I had to leave. I've been wanting to meet you for years, ever since I read *The Flowers of the Forest,* and when Jack Weatherby wrote that you'd taken his house—I can't tell you how excited I was. Especially since I was in New York in April and saw the revival of your play that they did in Greenwich Village."

I was having a great day, all right—first the naked Gages and now the Widow Delmore. "I saw it, too," I said. I didn't bother to add that I'd met Weatherby on the plane back to Los Angeles.

"Oh, I did love it, that play," Marian Delmore said. "Didn't you think it was beautifully done, considering how tiny the theater was, and all?"

"Unusual, anyway," I said.

"Oh? You wouldn't give it higher marks than that?"

In 1955, during a six-week run on West 47th Street, my only play had been that Pyrrhic victory, *a succès d'estime;* in 1966, put on within spitting distance of Washington Square, it was a prancing fiasco. *The Shooting Gallery* called for seven male and five female parts, but there wasn't a single heterosexual in the off-Broadway cast which, during an interminable evening, dragged the corpse of the play, feet first, back and forth across a quivering Lilliputian stage. The drill-sergeant dykes made violoncello declamations above the footlights; the upstaged fruits fluted happily as they tried to flutter up the walls of the set. I'd been stupid enough, for no ascertainable reason, to cross a continent to watch twelve footnotes to Havelock Ellis make a wreck out of what had been a fairly well-timbered drama. "I thought your daughter was charming," I said to Mrs. Delmore.

I could've answered her question a hundred ways, but she never expected to get the answer I gave. When she recovered she said hurriedly, "Oh, no, no, *no!* She was very rude to you. I made her tell. And she was very stupid, besides."

"I'm sorry," I said, "but I liked her."

"You made a mistake, my dear man, believe me." Mrs. Delmore was no longer smiling. "The girl's impossible, and in every possible way. I've just about made up my mind that she and I would both be better off if I sent her to—"

"Marian's invited us all to a buffet tonight," Polly broke in. "And I've accepted," she went on sweetly—so sweetly, in fact, that I didn't think to throw a table at her. "Isn't that *nice*, Sam?" She was spooning out the words like vanilla junket.

I seemed to be caught in a circle of glass from which there was no immediate escape, so I briefly became a vanilla junket myself. "*Terribly* nice!" I said, which is the way vanilla junkets talk. Then I took the bottle of rum in my vanilla-junket hand and poured myself a stiff belt.

After all, I could throw a table at Polly later. Mrs. Delmore's buffet table would be ideal for the job. And as a captive audience I'd have the only ten or twelve people in Maldita with something to offer, the ones I'd be most apt to like.

Three

Poor Me! I Think
I'm Becoming a God

I spent the afternoon sprawled on my back across our bed, until a little after five o'clock when, even over my own sodden snoring, I could hear Concepción's chatter and Polly's level voice. I dragged myself out of sleep to find my brain pan full of cotton, my throat full of phlegm, and the room full of two women. "What's all the damned racket?" I said. At least that's what I tried to say. I was using a borrowed voice at the time.

Concepción started to toss vowel sounds at me as though they were rice at a wedding. Then Polly cut her off and sent her packing with a grandiose wave of the hand that would have warmed the heart of Catherine the Great. "Some woman came with a message for you," she said. "From a man named—well, it sounded like Flay-a-*chair*. Anyway, he wants you to come and see him tomorrow sometime."

"The hell with him," I said, "whatever his name sounds like." I went into the bathroom and shut the door. At that fretful moment I'd've been happy to sign a contract never to meet another human being, let alone one whose name sounded like Flay-a-*chair*.

"You'd better clean up and change, Sam," I heard Polly call. She'd used precisely the same phrase a couple of thousand times since our wedding.

After the bedroom door had closed behind her I confronted myself in the mirror over the washbasin. The reflected face was that of a bug-eyed monster, ultragalactic for sure. A lot of work would have to be done before it would again resemble the control panel of a sapient, carnivorous biped. I thereupon went to work. It was malleable stuff, thank God.

I shaved. I massaged my head. I took a hot shower. I took a cold shower. I rubbed my body with a towel until the terrycloth felt like sandpaper, then covered what was left of my flesh with fresh clothes. When I finally stood in front of the full-length mirror in the bedroom the man I saw seemed vaguely familiar. I'd met him before, somewhere. Perhaps at an embalmers' convention, where he was the door prize.

As I stepped out on the balcony I nearly collided with Polly, who was coming to take possession of the bathroom and dressing table for her usual ninety minutes. She gave me a sidelong glance without breaking her stride. "That's better," she said. "Somewhat." And shut the door behind her.

I stomped along the balcony and down the stairs. What remained of the bottle of rum was still on the table in the patio, along with the glass I'd used. I lugged these objects through the tunnel to the river terrace, eased myself into a canvas butterfly chair, and began to liquidate the liquid. There was less than a quarter-hour to wait before the appearance of pretty, punctual Polly when I squeezed a last two fingers of eighty-proof into the glass. Then I tossed the dead soldier into the river.

The dead soldier's buddy disposed of his effects.

◎ The Delmore party sequence might as well start with a close shot of a stoned Samuel Fraser Culloden, standing alone by a wooden column at the end of one of several Delmore loggias, gloomily watching the ice cube melt in his second rum-on-a-rock. He had decided that it was time for another drink. He also reckoned that it was time to find Polly, since the St. Bernards had obviously lost her in all that snow.

It was a sleeper jump across the Delmore patio from my column to where the liquor hung out. I use the word "patio" because I can't come up with a more precise one. It certainly covered an acre; it may have covered two. Anyway, more trees than I felt like counting were lost in it. Most of the area was lawn, through which a confusion of tile paths meandered. Close to the geographic center of all this earth the remains of a small building had been polished and landscaped. I was reminded of the artificial ruins that the richer landowners of England used to have in their great private parks, until the twentieth century showed up and spoiled all the fun.

The main house sprawled along better than half of one side of the patio. French doors gave on a terrace the size of a basketball court, where garden furniture was strewn helter-skelter like a crowd leaving after the game. Running parallel to this terrace was a swimming pool in which the *Niña,* the *Pinta,* and the *Santa María* could have been anchored, with enough open water left over to rebaptize every backslid white inhabitant of the state of Mississippi.

Ten miles away, on the side of the patio opposite the main house, were two indifferently matched buildings; and although there shouldn't've been a loggia between them, that's where another loggia was. The newer of these constructions was a shambles of glass-brick Modern Design; and the less said about it, the better. The older, a tower which had a room at its top that was reached by a beautifully graduated exterior staircase, was charming and full of interest. The proportions were good, and the stones had certainly been in place for centuries. Compared to this tower, both the loggia and the out-of-place glass-walled job seemed merely giant versions of the Put-Them-Together-Yourself-Buster cardboard construction kits that Woolworth's sells for one forty-nine to lazy ten-year-old architects.

No hard knot of guests was on the terrace; in fact, the only living thing there was the liquor table. As I paid my devoirs to the Genteel, by plopping an ice cube into my glass before dumping in the rum, I tried to locate Polly and couldn't. I saw Jock, though, sitting under the grandfather of all jacarandas with a family named Young, about as far from me as second base is from home plate. The Youngs, who'd arrived in Maldita a week before us, were also still holding to American punctuality and had driven up as we were approaching the Delmore door.

Young was a full professor of American history at one of those large, economy-size Midwestern state universities, his particular field being the 1840–70 period, which included the Causes, Waging, and Aftermath of the Last War Between Gentlemen. I liked the cut of his jib, if only because he was handsome in an ugly way, or vice versa, and was about my own age, give or take a year. His wife—well, his wife was attractive, in the same way that a suit of Gothic armor is attractive. She struck me as being compact, useful, and steel-hard—which also describes the U.S. Army helmet. Undoubtedly she had more to do with getting that full professorship, with tenure, than Professor Young himself.

Their daughter, Nancy, was compact like her mother, but fresher and prettier; and in her the steel had become blancmange. She was Jock's age, or a year younger, and she was the only reason that he was sitting where he was. I couldn't blame him. Nan Young was the prettiest little lily-light to have come tripping down his pike in a good many months. Of course, this made her more than he could handle, at his age and in his dubious state of grace and confidence. Whenever Jock, wrapped in his mute seventeen-year-old longings, his neither-child-nor-man pains, finds himself nose to nose with a new and utterly desirable girl he could give lessons in silence to a Trappist monk.

As I lit a cigarette I found myself feeling sorry for poor old silent, worshipping Jock. So, with an ulcer in one hand, lung cancer in the other, I was set to make the Young & Co. foursome a five, if only to do a touch of backstopping for my tongue-tied son, when I saw Lalage coming down the stairs from the tower.

I recognized her, in spite of distance and the dying light, by the ridiculous way she moved. I thought she might be walking that last mile across the patio to the terrace, but when she got to the bottom of the stone staircase she sat down and became a breathing stone herself. I decided to join her. Jock would have to do without a backstop for a while.

By the time I reached the tower I felt as though I'd been my own

porter on a safari from Capetown to Cairo. "Room here for two?" I
asked.

Lalage's marvelous eyes were having a private twilight. "You
don't have to talk to me," she said. "Not after what I—" She stopped
and gnawed her lower lip. But she also shifted her body to make a
place for me. I sat down.

She was wearing a dress. Her calves, which I'd've thought would
be pipestems, and which I now saw for the first time, were in excellent
shape. "After you *what?*" I asked.

"I was rude."

"Not to me. Want a drink? Cigarette?"

Lalage shook her head. "I don't like parties," she said, as though
this explained the double refusal. "It's going to rain, too. Good."

"What *do* you like, Lalage?"

"What do you?"

"Right now, sitting where I am."

"That's a waste of time, sitting with me."

"I'm over fifty years old, remember? I ought to know what I like."

She smiled, but as though she were smiling at someone in Duluth,
Minnesota. "Yes, you do," she said slowly. "And I only wish I did,
too. I mean, the things I like don't count. They don't have importance,
my mother says."

I flipped my cigarette at the glass-walled What-is-it. "Such as?"

"Who was she?"

I should have known. To sail with Lalage Delmore was to risk un-
charted shoals. You thought you were on a true course until you
looked at her compass and found the needle pointing west-south-
west. "She?"

"The girl. The one with my name."

"Oh, *that* Lalage." I guzzled the rest of my rum and set the glass
against the balustrade on the lowest step. "Weren't you ever curious
about your name before?"

"No," she said. "And I don't know why I am now. But please tell
me about the girl. And my name. Only—" She was ready for tears.
"Only, don't tease me. Please don't."

I felt such pity for her that I was embarrassed. "No, I won't," I said, my eyes fixed on Nowhere, "but I'll have to tell it in my own way. If you get the shell open, though, the nut'll be inside."

"Thank you." A whisper.

No, I wouldn't tease; but, yes, I'd have to tell it in my own way. And if that wasn't a properly serious way, it was because I wasn't a properly serious person—even when I was at my most serious. That was the form my character—flattered, confused, mishandled, tricked, loved, and deplored—had taken. I've always warmed to old Vespasian, so long in the Roman army, so long in command of bloody men in an especially bloody time, who could have been a cold and cruel presence on the Palatine—except for a sense of humor, which really means a sense of the unimportance of almost everything; and who, when he faced up to the fact that he was dying, could stick his coated tongue in his cheek, and wink, and whisper: "Poor me! I think I'm becoming a god."

The sad, awkward girl beside me wasn't becoming anything, except more perplexed and lonely. As she moved into each fresh morning, hand in hand with her only friend—a wasted, dying Hope —she found that the doors of the day were locked against her, and that under the gorgeous sylvan scenes painted on their surface they were made of tempered steel. She might be grateful, in her fatal progress, for any light words that could make her pause, if only for a moment, on the path that led to the quicksand. I may even have discerned that both of us ought to rein in for a while, but I don't see how I could've done anything for myself. The Good Samaritan always dies alone and of a rattlesnake bite, a hundred miles from help or even a highway.

But I'd wasted enough time playing patty-cake with my own baby thoughts. "Well, the original Lalage," I began, "the Real McCoy Lalage, was a beautiful Greek girl, last name unknown—which isn't surprising, since the Greeks didn't go in much for last names in her day. She was probably a high-bracket slave, and her life must've been like the top of the bottle, all cream and no curds. A good-looking female slave, if she played her cards right, had it made—as we used to say around the Christian Endeavor Society. She'd have more fun than the emperor's wife—"

"What emperor?"

"Man named Augustus. An interesting character. He had all the virtues except the right ones, which means that the present world would be made to order for him. However, fifty corporations, several cartels, the Mafia, and God knows how many emerging governments'll have to struggle along without his services, since he's been unavailable, together with your lovely namesake, for a couple of thousand years. But while the first Lalage was on this side of the one-strand river, kicking up her little pink heels, Horace went plumb off his rocker for her. He even—"

"Horace? Who was he?"

My jaw dropped. After it finally drew itself back up against the rest of my skull I asked, "Where'd you go to school, for God's sake?"

"The wrong ones, I guess. All over the place."

"Well, you might not've heard of him even if you'd gone to the right ones. They've blown the whistle on teaching the classics in American schools, bless their little technological hearts. Anyway, Horace was a pretty fair country poet, with only one bad habit: he wrote a Latin that was, and remains, almost untranslatable—due to the subtlety of the word order and various other matters which I needn't go into. Still, he couldn't very well have written those odes in English, because England hadn't been invented then, in spite of what some British historians say."

"Odes? Are they poems?"

"Poems, Lalage, and in spades. And it just so happens that I can quote his comments on Lalage Number One, because I got my education a whoop and a holler before Science lowered the boom on the Humanities. Let's see, now—"

I intended to recite the last Sapphic strophe of the great ironic ode beginning *Integer vitae,* lines I had once known as well as my own name, if not better. I stared up to where darkness and leaves were blending together to form the equivalent of $\sqrt{-0}$ while I eased out of a deep, reclusive alcove of my memory the words that had waited there, unspoken, for so long.

"*Pone sub curru nimium propinqui,*" I heard myself droning, "*solis in terra*—uh—*terra*—" Something was wrong. "—*in terra*—*in*—" Nothing more remained. Nothing. The rest, whatever was left, was gone, all gone, utterly gone, the resounding fine lines dissolved like leaf smoke in late October, gone like the young Sam Culloden who'd loved them. Something was indeed terribly wrong—much, much more than a mere forgetfulness.

I felt a thinning of the air, grabbed the balustrade, and pulled myself to my feet. When I relaxed my grip I damned near fell headlong. I clutched the chill stone again and clung to it until the world made sense, more or less. As Lalage gradually came into focus I saw that she was standing, too. And she was asking, "You're not sick, are you? You're not sick?"

"It's the altitude," I mumbled.

"Yes, the first few days," she said. "Somebody should've told you."

"I'm all right now, though." I gulped air. "I'm fine. I mean it."

"Sure?"

"Sure. And no teasing." It was true, too; the air had thickened.

"Then—what was it, what you said?"

"What I—? Oh, the Latin. Look, Lalage, I'll tell you tomorrow. Sometimes my memory—" I flapped my right hand in a silly and meaningless gesture and grinned in a silly and meaningless way. "'Bye, Lalage," I went on. "Got to track down those St. Bernards. Jock, too. He's the brain. You ought to meet him. Meanwhile, darling, hold fast." I took maybe six steps, then stopped and looked back at her. "Your eyes—" I said. "Your eyes are the most beautiful on any living woman. In case nobody ever told you."

With another ridiculous flap of my hand I bade a fond farewell to kohl-orbed Cairo and began my return trek across the endless plain, pointed in the general direction of Capetown. It goes without saying that the rum hadn't had the slightest effect on me; that mile-high air, indecently thin, was what had done the damage. Yet now, against my will, I was being made to imitate Lalage Delmore, the high-pockets puppet. The apprentice god who controlled her movements, and who was now handling my strings from the rain clouds overhead, was certainly working overtime. Like as not he was caching the extra money with the idea of cornering ambrosia before the next Olympic Games.

Somewhere on the patio I almost rammed a man and woman who bore in on me without running lights. They were both Mexican. The man was handsome in an overdone way; but the woman, who hadn't been a woman very long, had the rich and soothing beauty of a very good liqueur. I supposed they were fellow guests, but I had no intention of halting my safari to say: *"Buenas noches,* you friendly aborigines. I'm Imperator Sam Vespasian, the famous but forgetful Latin poet and author of the well-known line, *Vae! puto deus fio."* I therefore continued my advance, flanks unprotected, toward the upper reaches of Lake Victoria.

Behind me the man called out, in a New York City accent: "Head for the roundhouse, buddy, they'll never corner you there!" People're seldom what they seem at first sight. *It says here.* Which is, of course, another catch-phrase that was bandied around Christian Endeavor in, oh, 1944.

When I finally got to Capetown I sent the apprentice god to his time clock, then counted noses. Several people were looking up at me, the way a fox and two vixens might drool over some out-of-competition grapes. "Where's old Jock?" I demanded. "My son, my son. He used to be here, just before the battle. *Mother!"* I counted muzzles again: Mother Young, Father Young, luscious Miss Young. But no Master Culloden.

"Why, he went looking for you," Young said. "Some time ago."

"Everybody's looking for somebody," I said. "Except the St. Bernards. Always exclude *them* when making blanket statements. All right to sit down?"

"Please do." Mrs. Young was smiling.

"Where's your drink?" Young asked.

To sit is amazingly easy. All you have to do is withdraw support from a few joints here and there among your knees and hips and —plop!—down you go. Of course, it helps if you have a coccyx like whitleather, and if what you land on isn't harder than concrete, and especially if you're feeling no pain to begin with. Suddenly there I was, arranged in comfort on the grass. To sit, I repeat, is amazingly easy.

"Must've left it someplace," I said, filling the lower part of my face with my new clownish smirk. "St. Bernards must've swiped it."

"What were you drinking before the robbery?"

"Huh? Oh, rum. Straight. Three thick fingers. And one ice cube. One lonely, meltable, opaque ice cube. Lonely: that's the countersign in this camp tonight. Gen'l Hooker's orders."

"Get Mr. Culloden what he wants, Nan," Young told his daughter. She scrambled to her feet and made for the terrace. Didn't say a word.

Mrs. Young hadn't yet sent her smile to the armorer's for repairs. "What are these St. Bernards of yours, Mr. Culloden?" It was a tricky smile, done with the corners of the mouth drawn southward, and capable of being interpreted in a number of ways, which probably pleased her no end. She must've spent years in front of a mirror, getting that smile down pat. I could have done without it.

"Oh, just some dogs I know," I said, then turned to her husband. "What's growing in the Groves of Academe, Young?"

"Why, the mixture as before. When we're not reading we're writing something for someone else to read. Never a dull moment."

"Never an exciting one, either," Mrs. Young said.

"That's because we're a balanced lot, Helen," Young said. "Followers of the golden mean." He added, wryly: "On a pinchbeck standard."

"*Domibus negata!*" The forgotten phrase of Horace had broken loose in my brain. Before I could catch myself I'd said the words aloud.

Young was amused. "Your charm against inflation?"

"No, the countersign for the camp tomorrow night. Gen'l Meade's orders."

"Too bad, I'll be on pass."

"So will the camp."

"You two sound like an Ionesco first draft," Mrs. Young said. "Not that I can imagine such a thing." Her tone had dropped a fast forty degrees but the curled-down smile was evidently being held over for a second week, by popular demand.

Young ignored her. "And what's new in the, as it were, entertainment business?" he asked me.

"Very businesslike, Mr. Bones. Not very entertaining. But we have to draw the line somewhere, don't we? After all, it's these bleeding hearts, who think audiences ought to be entertained, who cause—" I heard someone closing in on me from the direction of the terrace, undoubtedly a pretty St. Bernard named Nan bearing rum to succor the lost traveler. "Well and good," I said aloud to myself, "and not a moment too soon." My arm was extending, by its own volition, before its out-of-control possessor had himself caught sight of the relieving draught and the blessèd creature who bore it.

"You're right, Sam, not a single moment." Polly was looking down at me, sober-faced.

My arm sank while Young was rising. "Were you talking shop, Professor Young?" Polly asked pleasantly.

"In a way we were, yes," said Young.

"Non-union shop," his wife added. "Non-U shop."

Polly's gaze came back to the upturned flower of my face. "Aren't you hungry, Sam? The clans're beginning to gather."

"I didn't hear any pipers," I said sullenly. "Besides, Nan's bringing me a drink."

"No, she isn't. I saw her on the terrace and told her never mind."

"Taking a lot on yourself, weren't you?"

"No more than what I hope *you'll* take on now." Polly glanced quickly at Helen Young. "Or have you given up handling my plate at buffets?"

"Ah, no, Polly," I said. "I'll handle your plate. Sure I will."

There was guile in my guilelessness. Cunning old Sam saw several ways by which he could toss off another rum while Polly thought he was filling her plate with ham hocks and collard greens or whatever else the Widow Delmore might have placed on the altar of the Great God Buffet. "Wait here," cunning old Sam said, taking care that his voice didn't show how sly he was. "I'll be back in two shakes." And cunning old Sam climbed to his feet, only to discover that several of his legs had lost a lot of their own cunning. A new instability was abroad in the land. "Shakes of a lamb's tail, I mean," he muttered.

"No, it's nicer when we're together," Polly said, slipping her arm through mine. "*I* mean, I feel lost without you."

So we set out abreast for the table of vittles, cunning Polly and unstable old Sam.

It started to pour before we got anywhere near the terrace. And the hell of it was, I'd left the Ark in my other pants.

Four

Everything Had Begun to Resemble Ratatouille

Two maids scuttled twittering out through the rain. They snatched up whatever came to hand from the buffet table, then tottered into the house again under loads of earthenware and food. Their failure to distinguish between full platters and empty plates was too subtle to have been entirely due to instinct; each girl must've taken a course in Applied Carelessness at the Maldorado Normal School.

My chore was to salvage the liquor. There was so much headless-chicken confusion going on at the time that eight or so ounces of it found a home in the Culloden belly, unperceived. After all, Polly couldn't be everywhere at once; and she was then helping the Widow Delmore and her *muchachas* to arrange another buffet table inside. Anyway, my chug-a-lugging was a reward for the three trips I made to and from the liquor table. My exterior got pretty wet too.

On my last slosh through the deluge a couple of slim Juggernauts swept past me in tandem. Their brows were lowering, their nostrils dilated. Their lips were pressed tightly together and their eyes fixed on an imaginary point directly ahead of them and maybe a week away.

The first man's angry mask was topped by a mop of curly chestnut hair. The mask of the other, also angry but more insecurely in place, was set beneath hair that was long and lank and black and greasy. Both wore what amounted to a uniform. Their Adam's apples rested on foulard stocks, their skimpy torsos were enclosed by mauve form-fitting shirts, and the rest of them had been poured into much-too-tight black jeans that made their buttocks stick out like sore thumbs. On their feet were canvas, rope-soled shoes. They were both about thirty years old. A talkative raindrop, trickling down my ear lobe, said in passing that they weren't what you might call heterosexual, that they were in the middle of a fearful tiff, and that they would never again be on speaking terms, or not for a whole hour, anyway.

As they stalked stiff-legged into the house I hoped they were on their way to a climactic scene. If anyone deserved a scene, it was Marian Delmore; and if the scene deserved to have witnesses, then the ten or twelve people in Maldita I'd be most apt to like were the people I'd be most apt to like see placed within range of flying fur.

Twenty minutes later, when I'd come back from the buffet that had been set up indoors, juggling Polly's plate and my own, I floated damply down into a chair across the rectangular table from her to find that Curly Chestnut had made a place for himself and some chicken *mole* at the end of the table nearest the terrace door. Two other couples were between us. The table-crasher's name was Francis St. Albans and he dabbled in, as it were, painting. He also had a British accent that he must've learned through some correspondence school, since the nearest he had ever been to England was thumbing through the pages of *The Queen*.

His fellow tiffer, Philip Payne, who was, as it were, a poet, was seething in the Coventry of Marian Delmore's table, the middle of three that had been hurriedly set up in a living room that was only a few inches lower and a few degrees colder than the main chamber of Mammoth Cave. Payne, who looked several days dead himself, came from a moldy mansion that stood across from the decaying courthouse in the rotting county seat of Upper Piraeus, Alabama. I had never seen any of his poems in print. I don't think he had, either.

A pair of oddly shaped women, one a polyhedron, the other an isosceles triangle, were also at the Widow Delmore's table. They lived in a little *finca* and made little post-pre-Columbian pots without the use of a little potter's wheel and decorated them with little gruesome designs that could only have come from their little personal, primary-color nightmares. Elizabeth Piper and Barbara Saltus would never see forty-five again, even on a TV rerun. They were known, up to several kilometers away, as "Pepper and Salt." Beyond this cheery crew the Youngs were breaking bread with a WASPish elderly couple named McDermott. He was a dry-brained retired lawyer with a dripless-candle face, and his wife was a tiny, bejeweled ruin of a woman. Next to the nubile daughter of the Youngs, his hide as silent as the rind of the expanding universe, but with a clanging brain and kettledrum heart making loud music in his core, huddled Charles Lockridge Culloden, as miserably happy as any boy could be.

This was something that couldn't be said for his father. On any given occasion I prefer the company of a familiar devil to that of an unknown saint, but there I was—doomed to spend an hour or more in small talk with Curly Chestnut and Sr. and Sra. Salvatierra and Sr. and Mrs. Gutierrez. The only satisfaction I got out of being introduced to them by my occasional social secretary, Polly Lockridge Culloden, was that during the nods and becks and introductory wreathèd smiles I was able to fill my glass with wine—my water glass, that is, which was impressively bigger than the wine one. Polly objected in the only way she could, by kicking me high on my shinbone. The objection wasn't overruled; merely ignored.

I'd run into the Salvatierras before, or nearly. Her name was Luz, and she was the lovely midnight-haired girl-woman who'd reminded me of a rare liqueur; and he—José Salvatierra—was the man who'd talked New York when he told me to head for the roundhouse. He was a lot older than his wife. I put him down as being between thirty-five and forty.

The other couple, whom I purposely called Sr. and *Mrs.* Gutierrez, were, in their mating, as ancient as the human race and as modern as tomorrow afternoon at five o'clock. Marriages like theirs will be part of life, I suppose, as long as a certain type of young man is handsome and willing and a certain type of aging woman is desperate and rich.

Angela Ammon DeKalb Pierce Gutierrez, *née* Wade, had burst from her chafing girlhood as a lusty rip-snorter out of Pittsburgh who might have been used as a character by Rabelais, had she been French and born not too many years before her actual birth. You knew she was rich because she banked a great deal of her money on her fingers and neck. Around 1928, when she bounced into the bed of the late DeKalb, the second and richest of her four husbands, she was a damn-the-torpedoes, full-speed-ahead heller, with a wide, painted mouth and a broad, uncolored viewpoint. Now, however, the jazz-age body had been caught up in a fleshly inflation, the mouth was no longer so painted or so wide, the lip-rouge hues were muted, and the broad viewpoint was narrowing, against her will, with the passage of each anxious month. The anxiety came from her having to do un-relieved guard duty against the various Dianas who kept trying to slip into the preserve for a shot at Lorenzo Gutierrez, her tame unicorn.

He was known as Lencho, which is the Mexican nickname for Lorenzo, and he was the only *beautiful* man I've ever seen. If every above-ground Mexican male were one quarter as stunning as Lencho Gutierrez, there wouldn't be an unmarried woman to be found in the rest of this bloated, beef-cake world. They'd all be flat on their backs, love-drunk and goggle-eyed, somewhere between the Río Grande and the Guatemala border.

Yet, for all that, into each love a little brain must fall. This is a fact of life implicit in the old complaint which men apply indis-criminately to very tall girls and very stupid ones: *You can get on, all right, but there's nobody to talk to.* Accordingly, if there were a place where the beautiful Lencho might come a cropper, it would have to be in the soft, porous terrain between his ears.

When we were introduced he gave me no more than a glum nod, which struck me as peculiar. Among the few things I'd learned about Mexicans was that, as heirs of the Spanish language and culture, they have a fantastic jargon for use in daily social intercourse, with elaborately polite formulae for such major events as introductions and, like as not, for such minor ones as shooting you dead in the street. I let his lack of courtesy pass, though. There had to be impolite

Mexicans now and then, just as there had to be Mexicans who didn't own a pistol. There even had to be an occasional Mexican who couldn't play the guitar.

"I'm surprised, *señor*—" I started to say to Lencho, whose bored stare should've stopped me, but didn't, "surprised that Hollywood hasn't snapped you up."

He turned empty eyes away. Anger was getting a hammerlock on me, not only because of the man's seeming rudeness, but also because I'd let myself come out with such a ridiculous cliché.

Then Angela W. A. DeK. P. Gutierrez broke the hammerlock. "Mr. Culloden," she said quietly, "my Lencho's twenty-eight years old. He's been married to me for three years. During those three years he's heard English being spoken constantly, and he's had every chance to learn it. But as of right now, his entire English vocabulary consists of three words. 'Yes,' 'No,' and—" A small, strange smile showed up on her lips. "—and 'Don't.'"

"But they're mostly used for answering questions, aren't they?" Polly asked. "Then he must understand some English, or he wouldn't be able to answer an English question. How could he?"

"It's the tone the speaker uses," Angela Gutierrez said. "The *tone*, dear. And I honestly don't think he understands the meaning of the tiny vocabulary he has. He uses 'Yes,' 'No,' and 'Don't' whenever the spirit moves, and sometimes the results are funny and sometimes they're shocking. So mostly when he hears English being spoken he —well, you'd have to call it *withdraws*. Lencho knows what's best for Lencho." And Angela went back to eating.

"Good," I said, "and let's keep it that way. I'll stick to Urdu from here on in." It hadn't crossed my mind, of course, that anything but Spanish might be beyond Lencho, even after Angela had rubbed off on him for three plump years. With his beauty, he may not have needed a vocabulary in any living tongue; but I wouldn't have given odds on the idea. I was seeing him not as a man but as a pet—a Grand Champion poodle, say, made noddle-witted by inbreeding, whose kennel, grooming, and diamond-studded collar bills were enormous.

"Ah, *does* he, Angel?" St. Albans drawled. "Does he cross-his-pretty-red-heart *truly* know what's best for Lencho? Or do *you*?"

"I think so." She was concentrating on her plate.

The lackluster response irritated St. Albans, who'd evidently expected a verbal Roman candle. "Well, all *I* can say, Mrs. Den Mother, is that my *finca*'s a hotbed of English being spoken, so he can come and withdraw with me just any old time that tickles his fancy."

"That'll do, Saint." Angela's glance was like a fishhook, blue-steel and barbed. "Don't bring your dirty linen to any table *I'm* at."

"No fear, ducks," St. Albans said almost gaily. "It's at the next table and it's going to stay there." He called to Mrs. Delmore: "Marian, I'm depressed, and it's because that grotesque daughter of yours isn't around to *amuse* me. Don't you let her appear in public any more? Do you keep her caged these days? And if she is in a cage, doesn't she have feeding hours, the way the rest of the rare animals do? I tell you, Marian, I miss that Questing Beast. The zoo's simply *nothing* without our Ugly."

"Ugly eats in her tower now, Saint," Marian Delmore said. "Either that or she creeps into the kitchen at some ungodly hour and nibbles things like cheese."

"Like a great ungainly mouse—yes!" St. Albans crowed. "And she lives in a *mouse* tower. Oh, so *per*fect!"

"I'll be content if she never shows her face in the main house," the Widow Delmore went on, "and especially if I have guests. It's so easy, you know, to get the wrong impression—not about her, but about her mother. It's really reached the stage where I can't do a thing with her, not that I ever could. She's become so silly and so willful—the most willful, silliest creature in Christendom."

"Ah, not quite," St. Albans said, "not *quite,* lovey. I know a *person* who's far more willful." His smile, as friendly as the working end of a wasp, darted toward the pallid Payne. "And infinitely sillier."

Pepper and Salt, strangely, were shaken into a defense of the poet. "Oh, that's not *fair,* Saint!" exclaimed Pepper.

"And its *not* true!" cried Salt.

St. Albans went cold on them. "When you're speaking to me of truth," he said, each word an icicle, "please remember to address me by my real name—Pontius Pilate. And remember, too, that I don't suffer little women to come unto me." He then decided that the subject was closed, and, wiping everybody at the next table from the slate of his interest, sprinkled a pinch of attention on what his plate contained.

It was an unconsciously wise move. My hope that he and Payne would start a ruckus was dying, gradually giving way to a desire to shove St. Albans' face into his food. After all, Marian Delmore was owed a scene; and he who scened this night was quit for the next. I closed my eyes and had fun seeing St. Albans, publicly brown-nosed at last, with his thin and contemptuous snoot dripping warm chocolate *mole* down that torso-molding Ah Men–Village Squire shirt.

Unfortunately the rain kept intruding on my private slapstick film. Nature was carrying on as though she'd been given a handful of minutes in which to make up for aeons of drought. If I'd been standing at a window, watching it, the rain would have been a fused and furious mass; but to a man sitting with closed eyes it became a form of hypnosis, untouched by human hands. Then, filtered through an immensity of bone and an opiate of water, I seemed to hear my name being spoken on a mountaintop in Tibet. It was so far away, so faint, that I—

"*Sam—!*"

I opened my eyes, to see someone who looked like Polly peering at me from the other side of a thousand bead curtains.

"—Sam, Sra. Gutierrez asked you a question."

"Did she? From Tibet? And in the rain?" I was still treading water when a strange woman floated by. I grabbed her by the neck and held her head above the current until I recognized her as Angela Gutierrez. "Sorry," I said. "Thinking of something else."

"I asked you, Mr. Culloden, how many films you'd written."

"Never counted them. Enough to kill a more sensitive man."

"Fifteen," Polly said.

I gaped at her. "Don't tell me you kept count?"

"I did," she said firmly. "And so did Jock."

"Well, I'll be damned. My own wife and son."

"Did you ever write a film that Robert Taylor was in?" Angela continued. "Lencho's a great Robert Taylor fan." As the actor's name was mentioned Lencho nodded, with more vigor than I'd thought he had in him.

I had no choice but to run through my credits mentally. "Let's see, now—there were three, I think, altogether. There was *Whaler,* and *The Hunters of Kentucky,* and—and—oh, sure, *Falaise Gap.*"

The Gutierrezes spoke rapid Spanish to each other, after which Angela said to me: "Lencho liked them all very much, very much indeed. And he'd like to know, were you—*are* you—a friend of Robert Taylor?"

"Too bad, but I only met him once, on the set of *Whaler.* The way it is, by the time the actors get around to working on a film the man who wrote it is either two studios away or, if he's smart, in some other business."

After Angela had translated what I'd said Lencho paid no more attention to a man who'd written three pictures for Robert Taylor and yet had only met him once.

"He used to be an utterly *gorgeous* thing." St. Albans appeared to be talking to a gold I.D. bracelet on his right wrist. "Years and years ago, of course. Now he's got too much *character* in his face." The bracelet, like the people at the table, didn't reply.

"Well, Culloden, when Joy Durwood gets here," Salvatierra said, "you two'll have plenty to talk about."

I wasn't swinging at curves that night. "Joy? Durwood? Why should we?" I refilled my glass of wine, which had cleverly emptied itself, to the tune of another kick from Polly. This one landed on my instep. "Did she meet Robert Taylor on the set, too?"

"Sure, hundreds of times. She was married to one of the top boys at M-G-M."

"Never heard of M-G-M.," I said.

"He was in the New York office."

"Never heard of the New York office, either."

Salvatierra's laugh was a dry run. "Well, you'll hear about Joy. She's taking the Matthews *finca.*"

"A little way up the river from where you are," Luz Salvatierra said in a careful, spaced English. "Toward Maldorado."

I ran through the landmarks of my morning walk. "A little up-river? Is that the place that looks like a prison?"

Salvatierra laughed again, but for record this time. "Yeah, like a prison. I always say it ought to be a maximum-security convent for habitual nuns. But that's what Joy wants, a couple of months in solitary, to think a few things out. She's had a tough time lately. Yeah, they gave her a rough time." He didn't mention who "They" were.

"She is a childhood friend of José," Luz said without much enthusiasm.

"That's right," Salvatierra said. "I met her in Washington, D.C., when I was a kid. Her grandfather was a senator from Georgia, and she lived with him and her grandmother in a big apartment. We went to the same dancing school, Joy and me."

"What were you doing in Washington?"

"Oh, my father was with the Mexican Embassy. My mother came from New York, though. They met at some horse show in New York."

That took care of Salvatierra's American accent. "Are you something in the Mexican government now?" I asked him.

"Me a *politico?* Hell, no! I've got the Volkswagen agency in Maldorado."

"Better than nothing," I said.

"Yeah, it keeps me off the streets." Salvatierra winked at Luz. "You and Volkswagens, *querida,* eh?"

"The Volkswagen's a box," St. Albans said.

"If there's anybody in Maldita who doesn't know what a box is, Saint," Salvatierra said quickly, "it's you."

"I know enough to keep out of them."

Angela Gutierrez struck her knife against her plate. "That's enough *cantina* conversation," she said, then switched to a milder tone: "José, somebody told me this Mrs. Durwood was supposed to come last week."

"No, day after tomorrow. And it's *Miss* Durwood."

St. Albans snorted but kept his mouth shut.

"Oh, did she take her maiden name?" Angela asked. "Funny, I

never did. I was always Mrs. Angela So-and-so, depending on who was the last husband."

"More dignified that way," I said. "Right, Polly?"

"Let's not go into dignity now," Polly murmured.

Angela had only heard me. "I don't know about dignity," she said. "*I* wasn't dignified between marriages. God forbid! It never really pays. No, I think I kept the 'Mrs.' because I thought it was something I'd earned the hard way and through my own talents, like being made a Dame on a British Honours List."

"Pooh!" said St. Albans.

Salvatierra spoke in Spanish to Lencho, and Lencho's reply made Angela laugh. Salvatierra, too, was laughing as he turned to me: "I asked Lencho if he'd call himself *Señor* Gutierrez after he and Angela were divorced—and Lencho said, she was the expert, he'd have to find out from her."

Angela's laughter had come to a boil, and now she drained it off. "He won't ever be in such a position," she said. "Still, José, there's nothing wrong with your friend going back to being a Miss, as long as she doesn't try to keep her divorce a secret from the next piece of male perfection she meets. He'll find out about it, she can bet. They always find out about it."

"This is her third divorce," Luz said in her slow, precise English. Disapproval dripped from the roof of her mouth.

"Oh, Lord, another one!" Angela exclaimed. She wasn't jumping for joy, either.

"Cheer up, Angela," Salvatierra said placidly, "she's not going after your record. I'm not worried about it, so you needn't be. All I'm worried about is if the Matthews house'll be in shape when she gets here."

"I walked past this morning," I said. "Heard hammering. Lots of hammering."

"The men were chipping new stones," said Luz.

"Yeah, that Matthews place's always on the edge of falling apart," Salvatierra said. "When they built it they used cheap out-of-town labor and cheap crumbly concrete and cheap sandy mortar and cheap everything else. Why, they even built the walls with stones that were so weathered they were flaking away, and that's a corner-cutting the stupidest *campesino* wouldn't do. And it wasn't because they didn't have much money—God, no! They're both loaded. Matthews owns a couple of newspapers and a bunch of warehouses, and her father's the president of a big bank. A Canadian bank. They're Canadians."

"Is she coming alone, your Miss Durwood?" Angela asked.

"Far as I know, yeah—but don't put a Bible under my hand. Or if you mean, does she have any children? the answer is *No*. No kids."

"I didn't mean children, but never mind."

"I have not met Miss Durwood," Luz said in her deliberate voice, "but I feel she could be a person not to like Maldita very much. There is so little excitement here."

"Now, that's something I can't believe," I said. "Surely there must be ten or twelve people in Maldita with something to offer her, people she'd be apt to l—*ike!*" Another kick from Polly, which hurt, raised my pitch. Her earlier salvos had merely bracketed the target. This one was zeroed in, and she was firing ten-inch Delman shells.

"Sorry, Sam, an accident," she said. "Incidently, you haven't eaten a bite, and everybody else is nearly finished."

"I'm saving my strength for dinner," I told her, and drank some more wine. As I peered over the rim of my glass I saw the unassuaged eyes of a feather-boa constrictor named St. Albans fixed on a helpless baby bird named Sam Culloden. I stopped scratching for bugs in the gravel, cocked my downy head at him, opened my tiny yellow beak and chirped: "Something bothering you, Buster?"

"Why did *you* come to Maldita, or don't you remember?"

There was no clean-cut explanation for his turning nasty and choosing to pick on me instead of Philip Lank-Locks at the middle table, but the remark was just what the doctor ordered. While I placed my glass on the table I sent the baby bird scurrying behind a big rock, from which he popped back immediately with a companion—a razor-beaked, needle-taloned golden eagle that considered any snake up to, and including, a feather-boa constrictor as a kind of

sinuous caviar and, oddly enough, was also named Sam Culloden.
The golden eagle spoke very softly to the snake: "What would you
like me to say, Mary?

"Something sensible. Unless you're beyond that."

"Now, Saint—" Angela's voice trailed off in a semiwarning.

"I came to Maldita," I said, my tone still level, "because they told
me, Heraclitus, they told me the town was awash with people I'd be
apt to like, ten or twelve hundred of them. They also swore on a
stack of André Gides that there wouldn't be any Fruits of the Earth
in Maldita, because they preferred the arsier-crassier places, or maybe
the bell-bottom hangouts like Acapulco. They also told me—"

"*Sam!*" It may have been only a whisper, but it was Polly's god-
damnyoutohellsamculloden whisper, which is never hissed around
Hook & Ladder No. 7 unless the fifth alarm has rung. I had enough
sense remaining for it to stop my slide when I wasn't quite halfway
down the pole.

"And what can I do for you, my dear old Carian guest?" I asked
her.

"You can go to the buffet and bring me some more ham, not much,
a nubbin maybe, and a little of that wonderful salad, and one piece
of bread, no butter."

"No feather-boa constrictor caviar?"

"What?"

"Forget it." I took her plate and rose to my feet, delighted to find
that there wasn't as much instability around as there had been. The
quadruple shot of eighty-proof vaccine, plus the twelve per cent
boosters, had helped the old stability a lot. "All right with you,
Mary?" I asked St. Albans.

I must've slipped into one of my more unattractive faces as I got
up, since he was suddenly too busy counting his fingers, all fifteen
of them, to take the trouble to answer me. So I hauled anchor, put
on sail, and pointed my bow for the buffet table.

I had just reached port when the loudest clap of thunder that the
world has heard since Sodom and Gomorrah got their comeuppance
shattered the air above the house, so close that it arrived simultaneously with its lightning.

The room shook, as did everything and everybody in it. A terrified wail came from Mrs. McDermott and a variety of caterwauls from the other guests. Hot on the heels of this exclamatory period followed a Moment of Awful Silence, honoring the Unknown Thunderbolt. During this Quiet Time I bowed my head at the buffet table Cenotaph and tried to find the ham and the salad and the bread. I wasn't having much luck. Everything had begun to resemble *ratatouille*.

Then I heard St. Albans cry: "*Well,* Miss Payne, that was your *real* Big Daddy cursing you. He *hates* you, Miss Payne, because you're *disgusting,* the way *everybody* hates you because you're disgusting. And later tonight, Miss *Payne,* yes, later to—"

"Oh, *stop* it, Saint, for pity's sake!" Payne squealed. His voice cracked on "pity." He was a very frightened unpublished poet.

There was another thunderclap, not quite overhead and not quite as loud as the first, but a mighty substantial citizen for all that. Before its rumbles had run their course St. Albans was back in the side-saddle and riding an octave higher. "—tonight, and I *mean* it!" he was shrieking. "If you *dare* to come back to the house, if you *dare* to try to come in, if you even dare so much as to *knock* on the door, I'll take my letter opener with the jade handle and—Oh, damn damn *damn* it—!"

The lights had gone off.

"Now please sit right where you are," I heard Marian Delmore say. "The candles're in the *cocina,* and I'll have the girls bring them in. Please stay right where you are."

While I was staying right where I was she shuffled past me, using a corner of the buffet table to guide her. I set Polly's plate at a tilt on a platter of some mysterious slime-mold pastry and swung around toward the guests—not that I could see them, of course.

However, nobody was going along with the Widow Delmore's Last Request. Invisible people were pushing invisible chairs back and standing up and talking to other invisible people with invisible cheerfulness. "When they *do* go out," an unseen McDermott said, "they invariably choose a time when you're at dinner, or when you're shaving."

"In-*vair*-iably," replied a deep, Pepperish voice. Somehow I was glad to learn that the Pepper not only ate dinner, but shaved.

Then Hysteria returned, at a gallop and on a fresh nag. "Now they can't *see* you, Miss Payne!" St. Albans screeched. "How lucky for them! How lucky for *them!*"

For a millisecond lightning made it midday in the room. At our table everyone was standing, even Polly, who'd felt her way to the terrace door—everyone, that is, except St. Albans. He was lounging in his chair and, by God, while he was shouting at Payne he was calmly picking at his chicken *mole*.

That lightning-fathered glimpse of him, making cool little stabs with his fork while doing his best to destroy another human being, was what made me open the ball. Actually, my decision to act sprang from quite another source—the rude remarks that St. Albans had made about Lalage earlier. For all I knew, making rude remarks about Lalage when she wasn't around—or, if one wanted to try for a double-point score, when she *was* around—might have been the favorite indoor sport of Maldita. But I'd begun to feel inexplicably protective toward that sad young mock-up of a woman. Vengeance is mine, saith the Culloden. I headed back to the table I'd started from.

I couldn't've crossed the room more precisely if I'd been escorted by a kennel of seeing-eye St. Bernards with arc lights in their mouths. And when I had my hands on the table I wasted no time. There was a slop and sliding of earthenware, a clatter of crockery and a crash of smashing glass, and one scared yelp from St. Albans as he and his chair tumbled backward to land hard on the indiscriminating floor. "Compliments of the Ones, you Third bastard," I said.

I let the table drop. When the legs slammed down on the tiles it sounded as though they cracked a few. Then, while a babble began among the unseen and unseeing witnesses, I groped my way out of the room and out of the Delmore house. The rain faded and died as I stumbled toward our *finca,* and all the lights of Maldita came on again as I passed through the Weatherby gates.

I'm at a loss as to how I got home in an obsidian night, over unfamiliar terrain, but I did, I swung it somehow. Prince Samuel the Navigator was what they used to call me around the Tagus River taverns, in the days when I taught Zen archery and New England navigation to Vasco da Gama, but without ever letting him handle my arrows or borrow my trot of Bowditch.

As soon as I switched on the night-table lamp I spotted an *alacrán,* the size and weight of a short lobster, brooding on the wall above the bathroom door. I suppose I should've sent it to join its ancestors, but in the long run you can't kill everything—even with a license. So all I did was strip, drop my soaked clothes on the floor, and crawl into the old complaining bed. I left the light on, and I left the scorpion where it was—a brown, disgusting, poisonous, mindless, antedeluvian horror.

Just like the drunken gringo who'd let the critter live.

✪ Five

The Morphine Packet
Has Been in Shreds

Polly froze with her cup of coffee a foot above the saucer, and a spoonful of sugar Jock was taking from the bowl halted in midair, along with his whole nervous system. It was like a breakfast visit to a domesticated Madame Tussaud's, except that *I* was today's Marat, and a wax Charlotte Corday now had a seventeen-year-old wax apprentice.

But Marat's fatal bathtub was still in the wings, so I sat down and poured myself some coffee while the Living Picture dissolved. "All right," I said, "let's get on with it. Who's first?" The sip of coffee I took seared my throat.

"First for what?" Jock asked blandly.

"The old 'Oh-how-could-you?' speech. The cozy little kangaroo court. The invention of the guillotine. Polly, you want to start?"

The straight face she'd been keeping exploded like a small, pretty sun as she began to laugh. Then Jock got into the act with his lost-calf bellow, letting every adolescent stop out.

This was the third unusual thing that had happened to me in what was still a very young morning. To begin with, I ought to have been squirming, in a hangover fog, through the most exquisitely horrible of Bosch's Hells—yet my head was as clear as an apogee view. Secondly, I should've looked like Hector after a few of those heel-drawn trips around the walls of the old home town, instead of which I was as bright-eyed and rosy-fleshed as a seventeenth-century preacher consigning some unbaptized infant to a fire-and-brimstone Limbo. And lastly, although I'd expected to find myself in a barbed-wire stockade of incriminatory silence, here I was being laughed at by the wife of my bosom and the issue of my loins. I felt as confused as a blindfolded bee.

The laughter ended, as all laughter must. "I'm waiting," I said patiently.

"Poor old Sam," Polly said. "What do you want us to say?"

"Beats me. I'm not writing your dialogue."

"Maybe you wrote yourself out last night," Jock said. He tried to laugh again and ended up choking, as he deserved.

"Never mind the literary criticism," I said. "The conversation can get along without frills."

Jock, who'd been playing the scene by ear, decided he was off-key. "Yes, sir," he said.

"*Poor* old Sam." Polly patted my cheek. "Feel awful, don't you?"

"No, pretty good. Don't forget, the Devil takes care of his own." I sucked in some air. "Sometimes," I added.

"*Buenos días, señor.*" Concepción had come in from the kitchen.

"*Buenos días,* Concepción," I said. "*Quiero jamón y huevos fritos y pan tostado, por favor.*"

"Your vocabulary's improving," Polly said. "There's a lovely papaya."

"I believe it," I said. "*Nada más,* Concepción."

She returned to the kitchen and I amused myself by concealing as much of my face as I could with my coffee cup. The coffee was cooler now.

"Nobody's mad at you, Sam," Polly said, "if you're worried about it."

I wasn't worried about it, but I also wasn't being lulled into thinking I'd get off scot-free. However, I came out from behind the cup. "Nobody?"

"Oh, some people, maybe. But not Jock and me."

"And who cares about the others?" Jock added.

"That's a worthy thought," I said, "but it's too early in the morning." I was keeping my guard up, but my shield arm was getting tired.

"Of course," Polly started to say, "you *didn't* behave very well—"

"To put it mildly," I said.

"—but if you *had* to behave badly, and I can see why you felt you had to, you couldn't've picked a better time or place, or a more deserving person to—to—"

"Up-end?"

"'Up-end' will do. Thank you."

"But why didn't you wait till the lights came on?" Jock asked. "Then I could've seen it. Maybe next time, maybe?"

"There won't be a next time," I said.

"Let's hope not," Polly said. "Anyway, Marian told me—"

"I know. To take yore white-trash chile an' git yo'se'fs outuh thar an' don' you nevuh dargen her do' no mo'."

"Oh, Sam, don't be silly. She told me, and this was later, when we were leaving, she said she honestly didn't blame you a bit, that every so often St. Albans likes to get out of hand and runs on and on and *on* until everybody else is as miserable as he is. She was sorry, she said, that it had to happen at her party instead of somebody else's, but she thinks it served him right, what he got—what you did to him, that is—and she doesn't even want you to pay for the things you broke."

"Too bad," I said. "I was looking forward to giving her a bad check. How about St. Albans? Anything broken on him?"

"Now what do *you* think, with the Devil taking such good care of his own? And—Oh, Lord! Wouldn't you know?—after all that disgusting cross-talk he and his friend went home together, draped around each other's necks. And crying, mind you, *crying*."

"Bawling like babies," Jock said cheerfully.

"Poor old Sam," Polly said for the third time. "I shouldn't've said yes to Mrs. Delmore, should I?"

"Why not? I'm glad you did, in a way. It may've cleared the decks."

"For action?"

"Of a boarding party, at least."

"In that case, then, I'm glad, too, in spite of—oh, never mind. Will you be working today?"

"I wouldn't put money on it."

"What're your plans, then?"

"Well, I think it's about time I went into Maldorado and cased the joint. Want to come?"

She wrinkled her nose at the kitchen door. "It makes no difference if I want to or not. I promised myself that today I'd get the house wheels greased and turning smoothly once and for all. Besides, you always get around better by yourself, you know you do."

"Not necessarily. How about it, Jock? You want to come?"

"Aw, I'm sorry, but there's this ten a.m. date with Nan. But I won't need the car. You can take it."

"Gee, thanks, Dad," I said. "Gosh, I was hoping you'd let me."

He poked the top of the table. "Aw, you know what I mean."

"Perish the thought. But someday I'd like it if you and I spent an hour together. Forty minutes, anyway."

"We will, Father, we will."

"I'll believe it when it's in writing," I said.

"Sometime this morning," Polly said absently, "you might look in on that Flay-a-*chair* man, too."

I'd forgotten about Flay-a-*chair*. "Listen, I feel good, but not that good," I said. "He'd probably turn out to be St. Albans' maiden aunt."

Then Concepción brought in my breakfast, and in my hunger I forgot Flay-a-*chair* again. I didn't know it at the time, but I would never be allowed to forget him after that sunny morning.

◉ The one-way street called Calle Santa Amarga, which mounted at a twenty-five-degree angle all the way through Maldorado, was, in places, narrower than an Edwardian trouser leg and everywhere had a tendency to twist like a snake with the hives. The town itself stopped, abruptly and absolutely, at a reservoir about two miles from where it had begun, between a motel and a cemetery, on the road coming in from Maldita. This reservoir, or *presa,* was the fanciest of several that had been constructed after the Maldita debacle to tame the Río Maldorado, which had been using the higher gorges of the neighboring mountains as a lethal roller coaster. The *presa*'s dam was concealed from the eyes of nervous tourists by an Aztec architectural student's idea of a Chinese pavilion.

After Calle Santa Amarga had run parallel to the dam it made a U-turn through a scrubby park. Then, remaining one-way and keeping a couple of hundred feet distant from itself coming up, it went back through Maldorado, meanwhile having changed its name to Calle B. Juárez.

I drove slowly. When I wasn't threading the eye of opposite curbs or braking with some violence to avoid doing even greater violence to a jaywalking Mexican national, I saw a number of delights that had been photographed and reproduced, as though through a curtain of chocolate milk, in the wild guidebook. For instance, in the middle of a traffic circle of sorts, surrounded by large, tattered town houses, I came upon the Statute to Libberty, rising her revolucionary torcht. I leaned out the window of my tired, my poor station wagon while I paid mute homage to an abused and misused abstraction.

Later I went by the Maldorado Normal School so slowly that the car almost stalled. I hoped to feet the sencation of going back to my riotous and worried of scholar days, but the only sencation I feeted, or footed, or fote, was that of nearly stalling the Ford in front of the Maldorado Normal School on a fine July morning. I therefore didn't bother to drop in and ask about taking their short summer course in Applied Carelessness.

A stretch of Calle Juárez flattened out and the main plaza appeared off to port. The bandstand was visible, but I could see neither hide nor hair of any lovin couplers. They all must've gone home to do exercises for improving the circulation of the blood, making themselves fit for the famous brass-band's next recording of the pulse of the town.

On the opposite side of the plaza was the façade of a neat bijou theater, done in the classic style. Marble steps, laid across the entire front, led up to a porch from which six slim Corinthian columns rose to support a rectangular entablature, where TEATRO ALLENDE was set in bronze letters two feet high. Along the edge of the flat roof stood a series of classical female figures, decently draped, but each one looking as though she wished she were as naked as a jaybird. I put them down as being the Muses until I counted them and got only eight. Perhaps Clio, the Muse of History, had sneaked off to the Ladies' Room. She couldn't've picked a better century for the trip.

I decided to take a gander at the interior of the theater and then poke around Maldorado for a bit, so I parked on the south side of the plaza, across the street from a painfully Spanish Colonial hotel, La Posada del Conde Azul, that was doing about as much business as a sun-lamp salesman in the Sahara.

The doors between the porch and the foyer of the theater stood open, but the three inner double doors, leading from the foyer to the orchestra seats, were locked. I tried them in turn, shaking the last pair until they rattled, on the chance that the racket might wake up a janitor or a cobwebbed impresario or anyone else with a key and the authority to use it. Nobody appeared, not even the ghost of Lope de Vega. I crossed the foyer to the box office but it, too, was closed. Judging from the amount of dust on the tiny counter outside the ticket-window grill, it hadn't been in use since a road company of *La rosa irlandesa de Abie* played a split week in Maldorado during the dry season of 1930.

I felt dizzy as I came out on the porch again. The attack wasn't as bad as the one I'd had while sitting with Lalage the night before: at least, I didn't think it was—although at the time I was in no condition to undertake a comparative study of the Culloden vertigos. Of course, it had to be the altitude again, playing games with my balance. Oh, of course. Meanwhile, five minutes flickered by.

I did nothing more strenuous than lean against a column and glower at a newsstand outside a restaurant on the nearest corner of the plaza. I'd been so intent on the theater that I'd walked blindly by restaurant and newsstand both. So, when I finally felt steady enough to ease myself, foot by foot, down the Teatro Allende steps, I no longer wanted to explore any more of Maldorado. All I cared about was learning what had happened to the Red Sox, and not necessarily what passed for the rest of Western civilization, during the days since I'd last read an English-language newspaper in a Guadalajara motel.

There was one copy left of the Mexico City *News* of the previous day, and I roved around the front-page headlines while the dealer made change for a twenty-peso note.

The headlines were, simply and boringly, More of the Same. The sandpapered Lincoln who'd be calling the shots for the next couple of years was quoted as saying that things would get worse, in Vietnam, before they got better. This, while not being news, was certainly inaccurate. The truth is, as any old doughfoot could tell you, that no war ever gets better. It merely gets less worse—and not very goddamned often, either.

A bad taste was in my mouth when I finally got my change in the form of a fistful of Mexican coins. I went into the empty restaurant, whistled up a waiter, and had a bottle of Carta Blanca brought to a table in the corner. I'd lit a cigarette, taken a couple of swallows of the beer, and was about to open the *News* to the sports page when the Headache hit me.

This was no hangover, delayed and concentrated, but the third such crashing pain I'd had since late April. A railroad spike was sledge-hammered across my brain from ear to ear, then another was driven through my forehead at right angles to the first. These simultaneously copulated and gave birth, casting a spawn of smaller but sharper spikes at every dark millimeter of my skull.

A scream was in order, but during the second of these Headaches, early in June, I'd applied for a Screaming License and been turned down. So I squeezed my eyes shut, pressed my hands against my head, and gritted my teeth—until suddenly the agony was over, the unbearable spikes were blunted, and my knuckles were grinding into my temples. Sweat was running from my scalp to my shoulders, and I seemed to be breathing air that was as warm and thick as blood.

I sat quietly, quite motionless, until I was sure that the seizure was over and the patient checked out as ambulatory. Then I left some pesos with the undrunk beer and the unopened *News,* made it to the car, and headed for home.

As I wound downhill I wasn't being as careful of my fellow men as when I'd first driven into Maldorado. Since my immediate concern was with my post-Headache self, any Mexican nationals who were indulging themselves in their usual four-hour, slew-foot crossings of streets had a choice of skedaddling to the sound of my horn or hearing a Different Klaxon. They all stepped to the music they heard.

My self-concern didn't last, of course; it never does. A capital-H Headache, they tell you, is not only a preview of Hell but even a warning of sorts. A more logical man than I, after being tortured by three of these rip-snorters over a ninety-day period, would've raced to a seat near that dog-eared stack of 1926 *National Geographic*s in the waiting room of the nearest migraine specialist. But my strength lies in my illogic as well as my hair; and rationality is what you toss to mice when the cupboard's plumb out of cheese. Thus I worried about this latest skull buster until I'd driven between the graveyard and the motel and so was out of town. And when I came to where the old dirt road to Maldita branched off from the main highway I veered left and got on it, an action that might be taken, only too logically, by a Master of Illogic.

Before I'd gone a hundred yards I found that the old dirt road wasn't as I'd remembered it from the day before. The cloudburst had made a morass here, water-filled potholes there, and everywhere a subtle and distinctive type of muck, unknown to the average gringo, which I hope the Mexicans never bottle and ship north. By the time I was aware that I ought to turn the station wagon around and splash back to the highway it was too late. I could only go forward to disaster, like an ice skater on a ski jump or the Wehrmacht after it had clanked across the easy Ukraine.

I don't remember whether I passed three ruined haciendas and four bends in the road or four ruined haciendas and three bends in the road, but I do know that after much too long in the molasses I saw a very large man striding toward Maldita as though he'd invented Outdoor Exercise twenty minutes ago and was in a hurry to tell the Olympics Committee all about it. As a matter of fact, he was moving so fast that, with the dirt soup I was skidding around in, he stood a six–five-and-pick-it chance of beating me into Maldita. When the chips are down, however, eight cylinders will beat a full house of ligaments every time. I gained on him, cylinder by ligament, inch by millimeter.

When we were neck and neck he turned and looked at me. His face, in spite of being bent in places, was a pleasant one. Above thick eyebrows his forehead receded to where a sketchy fringe of hair made an unbarbered curve from one ear to the other, slightly above the nape of his neck. The basic man was covered by heavy workman's shoes, faded chinos, and a wool shirt in an impossible plaid that would've made any tartan-conscious Highlander puke in his haggis.

I didn't dare stop, since I was certain that the car's forward motion was the only thing that kept if from sinking into the muck forever. But I pointed my index finger at the road ahead and bawled at him through the closed window: "Maldita?"

He got into the moving car with the agility of the King of the Goats. "Thanks," he said. "If you were driving a duck you'd be on the perfect road for it."

"*Eh*-uh, or a brace of herons," I said automatically, the "*eh*-uh" being the down-East version of "yeah" or "yup" or "yus," in case the California plates on the station wagon might have made him think I was from Pomona or New Orleans or San Luis Potosí. Then I realized that he had to be talking about the amphibious truck of the last war but one—or two—or three—which we called a Duck and whose official Army nomenclature was DUKW, give or take a few letters and numerals. I figured I'd better get away from the subject before it got away with me. "You live in Maldita?" I asked.

"Five years now. My name's Simmons. George Simmons." He stuck out his hand.

"Sam Culloden." I took it.

"Sure. And you're on your way to see Tom Fletcher." He wasn't asking a question; he was giving out information. He was also confusing me with another Sam Culloden. You can always find eight or nine of us in the telephone directory of any small city. The

Cullodens breed like rabbits, and all their children, male or female, are named Sam.

"I'm on my way home," I said. "No place else. I never heard of Tom Fletcher."

"Didn't you get a message from him yesterday?"

I was shaking my head when certain names and such fell into place. "Yesterday? Wait a minute. They told me the name was Flay-a-*chair*. When you said 'Fletcher' I didn't—"

"Oh, that'd be Dolores' fault," Simmons said. "Fletcher's maid. She has a lot of trouble with names, including 'Tresguerras,' which happens to be her own. She's well over seventy, Dolores. Hasn't got a tooth in her head. No wonder she can't pronounce names. She calls me Sr. Sins."

I occupied myself by swerving to avoid a rock pool of particularly sinister appearance. "This freeway could use some work," I said, after I'd jounced the car back into the familiar slop. "Where's he live, this Fletcher? I may drop by."

"Just this side of the bridge."

"The beat-up hacienda with the orange-crate doors?"

"That's it." Then Simmons pointed at the Gage house. "Been *there* yet?"

"Yesterday," I said. "For fifteen minutes." It wasn't enough that I had to fight the wretched road; I had to pass where the Gages lived, too.

"Fifteen minutes're about long enough," Simmons said. "Twenty can be destructive." He didn't elaborate on his statement, and I saw no reason why he should.

The road improved after we got beyond Gage's weird acre. This might have been due to the soil being more porous, but I wouldn't've made book on it. I reminded myself to ask Nature for an explanation the next time she took me to a cloudburst.

In front of the Matthews *finca a* Jaguar Mark VII sedan, painted British racing green, was blocking the road, while the driver, a woman, bore down angrily on the horn. Nobody inside the high, harsh wall was paying any attention to the noise, which could have been that of a burro in heat; and meanwhile neither the horn-tooting woman nor the swarthy young man beside her was paying any attention to the approach of my Ford.

"I guess she got in a day early," I said.

"You know her?" Simmons asked. "That woman in the car?"

"Only indirectly. She's a former dancing partner of a man named Salvatierra."

"José? That makes sense. You know him, too?"

"Only directly." Neither of us was elaborating on our statements that morning.

I stopped the station wagon. There wasn't anything else I could do except plow into the Jaguar amidships. The man saw us and spoke to the angry woman, who left off leaning on the horn. The volcano within her subsided as she gave her attention to Simmons and me; and where lava had bubbled there was all at once a lovely smooth meadow, packed with roses and daisies and caroling birds. "There's not a *soul* here to let me in," she called over. "Could you *possibly* help me?"

It was the voices of all the Sirens, the way they must have sounded to Odysseus, but rolled into one. It was the whisper of oil-hipped Delilah, sprawled glistening on that painted couch and reaching up for Samson, to bring him down upon her. It was the purr of Cleopatra as she stretched in lubricate nakedness for Caesar, on her back on the unrolled rug. It was a very dangerous voice indeed.

My hair didn't warn me by standing on end, as Samson's mop should've done and failed to do; but at the same time my body, unlike that of sun-dark Odysseus, wasn't lashed to the mast of an ancient Greek coaster. I got out of the Ford and walked toward the Jaguar. So did Simmons.

"The goddamned gates're *locked,* poor babies," Miss Durwood said. It was the only greeting she gave us, but as good as any, I suppose.

What the boys around Christian Endeavor used to call a million-dollar wound, the kind that laid a dogface in a nice warm bed for a nice long while, doesn't hurt to begin with. It's only after the shock wears off that you grope for the morphine—to discover, like as not, that the morphine packet has been in shreds for the last two hills or six hedgerows.

Joy Durwood, at first sight, didn't hurt at all. Her black hair, hinting of russet, hung nearly to her shoulders, its carelessness so studied as to suggest an unstudied care. Under starless-night lashes fantastically long her eyes were a strange green. The unconfirmed rumor of a tilt was at the tip of her nose, and her mouth was a marvel. The small amount of make-up on her face could have been applied merely to demonstrate that she had no need of make-up. Her throat and shoulders were bare, and what I could see of her light summer dress was a darker green than her turquoise eyes. A plain gold bracelet on her left wrist was her only piece of jewelry. I made up my mind to keep the old morphine packet visible and handy at all times. "You're a day early, aren't you?" I asked.

Her stare dove into mine, touched bottom, and surfaced. "I don't know *why* you should know that," she said, "but I'm glad you do."

"José Salvatierra said you were coming," I told her. "And I'm glad you did. I'm Sam Culloden, by the way, and this is Mr. Simmons." I hadn't meant to say I was glad she'd come, because I wasn't, especially. As far as her being in Maldita was concerned, I had no reason to be glad or sorry or anything else. Maybe, I thought, it might be a good idea to salvage an ancient Greek coaster and lash Culloden of the Many Wiles to the mast for a few years.

"—is Joy Durwood," she was saying as I returned from Ithaca. "But you knew *that,* too, didn't you?"

"Not until now," Simmons said. "How long are you staying, Miss Durwood?"

"It all *depends,* doesn't it?" She put a smile on the stove for Simmons, then turned the burner up for me. "*You're* a friend of Joe's, Sam Culloden. Well, where *is* he?" She'd made no effort to introduce the sullen, handsome Mexican who sulked beside her, which was fine with me. He had the insufferably superior air of a *mariachi* who's serenading the rich people at the next table.

"In town, I guess," I said. "And I'm not exactly a friend of his. I met him at a party last night."

"Well, he's not important right *now,* anyway. But what *is* important is to get *into* this sweet little goddamned place." She tried another blast on the exhausted horn. "There's *got* to be a maid or *somebody* around. Joe *promised* there'd be a maid."

"Juanita," Simmons said, "she's the maid. I know where she lives,
too, and if you can be patient for a little while I'll send her along with
the keys."

"Oh, I can be *very* patient, Mister—" She wrinkled her nose. "Formality's so *boring.* What's your first name?"

"Fa—that is, George. George Simmons." He was flustered.

"I can be very patient, *George,* when it's only for a little while."
She spoke to Simmons but her eyes were on sun-dark Sam. If the
next thing on me had been her sullen companion's throttling hands,
I'd've understood.

"I'll drive you to pick up the maid," I told Simmons.

"No you won't, Sam. I live just the other side of the bridge, and
Juanita's house is only a couple up from mine. There's no need."

"Suit yourself."

It was not until we were sitting in the station wagon, waiting for
Joy to maneuver the Jaguar out of the way, that I realized Simmons
had already put me on a first-name basis.

As I squeezed the big Ford past the Jaguar Joy blew us a kiss.
"Christ Almighty!" Simmons said to the dashboard, a remark I
accepted at its face value. We rode a short distance in silence, then
he said: "I hope José Salvatierra's aware of what he might be doing."

"About what, in case he isn't?"

"If you'd lived here longer, Sam, I wouldn't have to tell you. But
Maldita's not so much a town as it is a passenger rocket on a launch-
ing pad. A lot of people are aboard who've bought tickets, but the
tickets don't say what the destination is—whether it's the Moon or
Mars or Hell or Venus or Heaven or an everlasting orbit around
the Earth. The passengers're getting very restless, because all systems
seem to be Go, but they've been waiting, strapped in their seats, for
a long, long time. What they haven't been told, poor wretches, is
that all systems are Go except one: there's no fuel in the rocket. And

that, of course, is why they're still earthbound. Well, something's given me the idea that the solid fuel *may* have arrived this morning. I could be wrong, however—and I pray to God I am."

Neither of us said anything more until I pulled to the side of the road across from Fletcher's hacienda and cut the engine. "Are you going to work on a book while you're here?" Simmons asked as we got out of the car. "Somebody mentioned that you wrote books."

"I'll work," I said, "with luck."

"You'll need it. Not much writing gets done in Maldita."

I grinned at him. "Don't tell me you're a writer, too, George."

He compressed his lips and frowned at the mud-spattered hood of the car. "At the moment," he said slowly, "I'm nothing. I'm *less* than nothing." He started to walk toward the bridge. "But I used to be a Catholic priest," I heard him say.

✠ Six

I'm Rumantic,
Tipical and Full
of Ocal Calor

The face of Dolores Tresguerras, photographed in extreme close-up, might have been mistaken for the Himalayas as seen from a yawing weather satellite, and the crackling noises coming out of her had a lot in common with what radiotelescopes keep picking up around the Crab supernova. Simmons had flattered her when he'd said she was well over seventy. She looked old enough to be her own grandmother, and very likely was.

We stood just inside the shoddy orange-crate doors, between two buildings that flanked the main entrance of the Fletcher hacienda as though pulling a kind of architectural interior-guard duty. They were one-story former ruins, solidly rebuilt and obviously lived in—which was more than could be said for the rest of the tumbled-down rock piles that I could see from where I was. A narrow street, originally cobblestoned, ran through the middle of the shattered hacienda to end halfway up the hill at a wide gap in the rearward wall. Most of the pavement had long since gone to glory, and the street was now no more than a strip of groin-high yellow grass, sprouting thickly from where the cobblestones had been. A path, well-trodden, went all the way to the hillside wall, holding to almost the dead center of the grass. On either side of this ex-street the hollow shells of a variety of roofless buildings were rotting into black and jagged stumps, the smashed teeth of that earth-imprisoned ogre, Human History.

The cacophonic mish-mosh emerging from Dolores was so loud that I decided either she herself or Fletcher must be deafer than a dead waiter. It was the infinitely amplified sound of several dozen walnuts being rolled around inside a rough wooden bowl, and it made about as much sense. While the nuts careened she was waving this arm, flopping that one, and occasionally jabbing a petrified finger toward the street of grass. I translated her body movements, and especially her fingerwork, as meaning that Fletcher, rather than hang around whichever of the two repaired houses he lived in, had wandered off to some hill or other for the sake of its lulling cicada song. It occurred to me to track him down, if only for physical reasons. Anything was preferable to the burst ear drums that would shortly belong to Henry M. Culloden, the African explorer. So I quietly slid around Mount Kilimandolores and started up the path in a search that would end, I presumed, in my stumbling over a lost Dr. Livingstonedeaf. Behind me the old trout kept on talking. The decibel count stayed high.

I glanced into each ravaged building as I passed it, but without leaving the path and without much hope of spotting Fletcher. At that distance he'd've had to be exceedingly deaf not to hear the Music of the Spheres, as interpreted by Dolores Tresguerras, even if the ruins had acoustical problems beside which those of the New York subway system were as child's play.

The slope was deceptive, as I soon found out, and by the time I got to the gap in the upper wall I was winded. I waited until my lungs and heart quit pretending to be a calliope and a tom-tom, then climbed over some rubble to the goat-worked hillside of cactus clumps and morose evergreens. On my right, and not far off, were the gigantic jacarandas I'd seen before; and to my left another path ran close to the outside of the crumbling wall, vanishing when the hill dipped beyond the corner of the hacienda that was nearest to Maldorado.

While I was trying to make up my mind about the direction I should take in my hunt for Fletcher, the head of the hunted appeared above the dip of the hill, followed by the rest of him. He looked as he had when I'd first seen him, except that the white shirt had been changed to a light blue one. He held out his hand even before he reached me. "Sorry, Culloden," he said. "But that's what I get for hiking around these hills every morning. I should've set a definite time."

"It doesn't matter," I said.

"It does to me, son." He spoke in a dry, nasal way, half twang and half drawl, that was very familiar. His hand was big, and his grip, when we shook hands, was steady and strong—surprisingly so for a man well over sixty. "I saw your car coming, the other side of the Matthews *finca*," he went on. "I had a feeling you'd stop here, so I started back. But I'm not as spry as I used to be. Been waiting long?"

"No, sir," I said. "There was a little delay at the Matthews place."

"Well, I wouldn't've known that. You can see the back of the house from the hills, and most of the grounds, but that wall on the river side cuts off any view of what's going on in front of the gates. When they're closed, I mean. Well, never mind. How about you? Done any walking in these hills yet?"

"I had all I could do to walk through this hacienda of yours. And I don't know how I'll ever—"

"You'll get around to it," Fletcher said. "Everybody does." He was studying me. "What's the matter? You look like you'd been sent for and couldn't go."

The matter was that I'd been doing some mental calculation. Barely fifteen minutes had passed since I'd been roadblocked by Joy Durwood's Jaguar, and it was a good three quarters of a mile, on the level river road, from the Matthews *finca* to here. By the up-and-down hill route he'd taken it might conceivably be twice that distance to cover and certainly twice as exhausting. Yet the old man didn't have a drop of sweat on him. He wasn't even breathing hard. "Nothing," I told him. "Except that it struck me you made mighty fast time, considering—" I didn't finish the sentence. Some men don't like to have their age brought up.

"Considering that I'm so old?" Grinning, he finished thought and sentence for me. "I suppose it is hard to believe. I can't believe it myself sometimes. Nor much else, either." He tapped me on the chest, lightly. "Come on, son, let's go down where it's comfortable. It's the time of day when people ought to strike a blow for liberty."

I followed him over the rubble to the downhill path through the yellow grass. "Thought you had your boy with you," he said over his shoulder. "There was somebody else in the car."

"That was a man named George Simmons. I gave him a lift."

"Oh, George, was it? That was thoughtful of you."

"Was he really a Catholic priest?" I asked.

"Ah, he's told you already, has he? George must've been feeling down in the mouth about something. Yes, he was a priest."

"What happened?"

Fletcher glanced back at me and chuckled. "Didn't you ever hear of St. Judas Iscariot?"

"Judas Iscariot? Since when was he a saint?"

"I think it's best that George tell you himself. He's planning to, I guess, since he didn't waste any time in letting you in on his being an ex-priest. In here, son. After you."

We had reached the on-guard houses and Fletcher pushed open the door of the one on our right. As soon as he'd shut it behind us he made a beeline for a huge cabinet, leaving me free to look over the place where he lived. As a matter of fact, I think he wanted me to look it over.

Not that there was much to see. The interior of the house consisted of a single room. I'd expected it would contain at least a couple, so the one that took up all the space probably seemed larger than it was. Be that as it may, it was bright and clean and neat—and completely impersonal. The walls, which might have been whitewashed within the past hour, were bare of everything except a little wooden shelf, set on cast-iron brackets and placed at eye level near the door, where five books leaned on each other. The whiteness of the walls was interrupted, now and again, by undistinguished pieces of furniture—the cabinet, an armoire, a massive iron chest whose padlock alone must've weighed ten pounds, and a heavy four-poster bed, uncanopied. The chest, I daresay, had been around for a couple of centuries; the other articles might have been made a week ago Tuesday.

The bed was at the opposite end of the room from the door, and at its foot was another chest, smaller and wooden, with a big old iron key. Between me and the bed was a round table, hemmed in by six chairs. I gathered that one of these, with a higher back than the others, was where Fletcher eased his old bones when company came.

As soon as I'd done a quick survey of the room I went over to the shelf and read the books' titles. This is something I always do, if I get the chance, when I enter a strange house. A man may appear to be this or that, but he *is* what he reads. In every collection of books a human soul stands naked.

Fletcher's five were: the Bible; Shakespeare and Montaigne in one-volume editions; a translation of the *Iliad;* and a Spanish *Don Quixote.* The collection was what a tolerably smart high-school senior might list as Gems of Literature I'd Most Like to Have with Me on a Desert Island. But the covers of Fletcher's tiny library were worn and scuffed, and the bindings had taken a beating. He either had read them again and again or had picked them up, fifth-hand, in bookstores where they'd been dumped by brutal owners.

Fletcher brought a bottle of rum, along with the glasses in which to pour it, from the cabinet to the round table. I was still studying his books when he clattered the makings down on the wood. "It's all there," he said, nodding at the shelf while he uncorked the bottle, "all you want—or need—to know about your fellow man. As you can see, I finally learned to travel light. Perhaps not as light as I could, though. I wish I'd bought smaller editions of some of those—Montaigne, for instance—but then the type would've been smaller, too, and I'd end up wearing glasses before I was ready for 'em."

I put on my sent-for-and-couldn't-go face for the second time. "You don't wear glasses, not even for reading?"

"Son, I've got the eyes I started with, and they've held up better than most." He had filled each glass with rum, and they weren't shot glasses either. "And everything else I started with, too—if you're willing to disregard a few teeth." He handed me a full glass of rum. "And half a dozen illusions," he concluded.

We raised glasses silently to each other and took swallows of what turned out to be the best rum I'd had since Captain Kidd paid me off and I turned middling honest. Then Fletcher sank into the high-backed chair and I settled down opposite him. We smiled at each other and swallowed some more good rum. As it trickled, warm and golden, along my gullet I felt sorry for the lower animals and the simple pleasures they had to do without.

"How old are you, Sam?" Fletcher asked suddenly. Then he added: "Do you mind if I call you Sam?"

"No, sir, I don't," I said. "And I'll be forty-six, middle of August."

Sadness appeared in his face, but it was a short-term sadness and he drove it away with a laugh. "That's funny," he said. "My birthday's in August, too. August eighth.

"Great. Mine's the nineteenth." I had the warmest, most soothed gullet this side of the nearest side-show fire eater. "So why don't I give us both a party? On the—the—on the thirteenth, say?"

"I'd like that, Sam," Fletcher said, "but I don't think I'll be here after the first of August. Got to make a trip. Can't get out of it, either."

"Going back to the States?"

He gulped some more good rum. "If you've got to cross the border, summer's as good a time as any other, wouldn't you say?" he asked.

"Depends on how you travel. Will you fly? Planes're something I can do without."

"Well, your generation's more up on those things than mine," he said, "so maybe I'll bring up your rear." He winked at me. "How about if I took the subway?"

"That's the best way to travel," I said. "The worst that can happen to you is having those empty faces across the aisle. But you can always keep your eyes closed." The rum in my glass was nearly gone.

"Reckon I will," Fletcher said. He pushed the bottle toward me. "Help yourself."

I did. As I replaced the cork I browsed over the label. The rum was called Azteca. "I've never seen this brand in the States," I said.

"It's made by the damnedest, smallest distillery on the face of the earth. None of it leaves the country, far as I know."

"Because it doesn't travel well? That's how the French'd explain it."

"No, because they've got more customers than they can handle, right here in Mexico. You never even see it in the stores. But I once did a favor for Chávez-Trueba—his family distills the stuff—and whenever I want rum a case of Azteca turns up on the doorstep."

"Is there any favor I can do him, so that a case'll show up on my doorstep once in a while?"

"I'll write him a letter." He reached out and took the bottle. While he was putting a head on his own drink he said: "I thought you'd be more curious about things."

"What things?"

"Well—like my asking you to come and see me."

I considered the matter for a moment. Actually, his asking me to come and see him didn't strike me as unusual. The Widow Delmore had done it first, and offered to feed me in the bargain. "No, sir," I said. "The old inhabitants're always more anxious to see the new arrival, and size him up, than the new arrival is to see and size up the old inhabitants." I probably shouldn't've been quite so frank with a particularly *old* old inhabitant, but my gullet, as I said, was very warm.

He smiled at me. "I know a lot about you, Sam. A lot more than you believe I know."

"But I *do* believe it, sir," I said with cheerful disinterest.

He frowned. Evidently he found my offhand manner unattractive. I guess I would've found it unattractive, too, if I'd held it up to a mirror. But I was too busy admiring the reflection of my warm gullet; and, besides, there wasn't a mirror anywhere in the room.

"I wasn't talking about last night," he said, and the frown went away.

Not very far, though. It ended up on my face as I asked: "How'd you hear about that?"

"Sam, if anything happens in Maldita it takes about twenty minutes for the news to be all over town. In this case, Mrs. Delmore's cook is Dolores' niece. The niece told her father, and he told Dolores when he brought his goats by here this morning. The natives're always gossiping about the gringos. It isn't evil gossip, though, because the natives think the gringos're funny and handle them the way monkey-cage keepers handle the monkeys. They have to feed them, sure, and clean out their cages—but they enjoy it, because meanwhile the monkeys are talking monkey and doing monkey things and making damned fools of themselves in general. Including me, I suppose."

"Me, too," I said. "Although I never fancied monkeys much."

"Well, you'll find a good many different species in this Maldita cage—spider monkeys and marmosets and chimpanzees and God knows what. You ought to meet George Simmons—"

"I met him," I said.

"Then there's Jim Inskilling, and Hy—Hy—" He leaned toward me. "What'd you say?"

"I said I'd met Simmons."

"That's right, you did, didn't you?" His eyes seemed to have clouded over and his cheeks were taking on a doughlike quality. He pushed his glass to one side, leaned closer to me, and spoke with great intensity, as though he raced against time: "I wanted to tell you something about yourself, but now I've got to tell you something else instead. I'm not as strong as you think I am, understand? These spells come. More and more often. The current gets shut off and I'm like a dead battery. But then somehow I recharge myself, inside me somehow, and I'm all right until the next spell. And now I'm going—"

"Have you seen a doctor?" I asked. It was a question that properly should have been raised by a six-year-old kid with two heads.

"Jim Inskilling's a doctor. But there's damn-all can be done about it, son. It's pure and simple senility, that's what it is, and so I take the spells in my stride and reckon I'm getting off terrible easy. It could've been a crippling ticker or cancer of the guts or whatever else there's around that's worse." He lay back in his chair and his gaze locked on the beamed ceiling. When he spoke again the words came in little dry spurts. "Please—do favor—leave your—leave drink —go, please—see soon—you—talk—we'll—" Without going quite rag-dollish and limp, all of Fletcher relaxed. I would've thought it impossible to relax like that and live. His breathing slowed, slowed and lessened, and his eyes became like frozen cream. I'd been listening to an old man; I was looking at a vegetable.

Twice that morning I'd left a drink unfinished. I went outside and knocked, not too hard, on the door of the opposite house. When Dolores opened it, I put a finger to my mouth and pointed back where I'd come from.

She nodded to show that she understood, pressing her lips together until I thought she'd jam her chin into a nostril. As soon as I went through the miserable semi-gates I heard her bolt them behind me. I'd not have imagined that they could be bolted. Or, for that matter, that the silence of Dolores Tresguerras could sometimes be deafening, too.

I sat in the car for a while: having been to Nether Hither, I was in no hurry to get to Further Yon. I'd achieved nothing since I left the house and headed for Maldorado—with the exception of a murderous Headache, a fortuitous meeting, a near view of senility, and a slug of excellent rum. Fletcher had asked me to come and see him. *Why?* Then he'd said he wanted to tell me something very important. *What?* And what was a man who was less than twenty years older than I doing with a ten-twent'-thirt' version of senility? Hell, I'd've been better off standing in the foyer of the Teatro Allende and pounding on the box-office window until the ghost of Lope de Vega damned well *did* show up. But that, alas, was the story of my life: I'd never had the patience to wait until the ghosts got around to appearing. And the subplot of my life's story was that I somehow always got sucked into paying visits to the wrong people. Especially in Mexico, where a week ago I hadn't known a soul, which meant I'd been very well off. "Ouch!" I said.

I had forgotten I'd lit a cigarette until the damned stub tried to set fire to a finger. I snuffed it out in the ashtray, together with any additional thoughts about Fletcher the Unrecharged and Dolores of the High Decibels. Then I started the motor and took off from Cipherville for what I hoped would be forever. It wasn't, of course. A cipher can be a very binding oval, if a man finds himself inside one.

As I swung up from the old dirt road I saw Lalage on the bridge. I suppose I should've kept rolling, but I was so resentful of senility and its side effects that anything human and under thirty looked pretty good *pro tem*. I drew up alongside her and cut the switch.

"I've been waiting for you," she said as I pulled myself free of the plastic seat of the station wagon. "I saw your car at Mr. Fletcher's as I came by."

"Came by from where?"

"Walking. And I wanted to talk to you."

"Okay, but you'll have to get in line. This is Dr. Culloden's day to listen, and the waiting room's jammed with logorrhea patients."

"I'm glad. I want you to listen." She was wearing a dress again, I noticed.

"I've done nothing else for hours, Lalage—all the way from here to the Mountains of Hitzedam, where the lion roareth and the whangdoodle mourneth for her first-born. So now *you* listen a minute, and I'll relax your mind for you. The English of it is: 'Put me under the Sun's chariot, someplace where it gets so close to the earth that nobody can live there. Because no matter how hot it is, I'll still love that sweet-talking Lalage of mine, that Lalage who laughs so sweetly.' The translation's rough but comprehensive—just like me. Happy now? Satisfied?"

"Come look at the river," she said. She was beginning to sound like Polly.

We leaned on the cold balustrade of the bridge and considered the Río Maldorado. It was perhaps an inch lower than when I'd picked up Simmons, but I couldn't've cared less.

"I like Mr. Fletcher," Lalage said slowly.

"No reason why you shouldn't."

"But I love," she went on, even more slowly, "you."

"No reason why you—" was coming out automatically when Something, from Somewhere, hit me a Judo blow just under my jawline. My first reaction was inwardly to murmur: Oh, *Jee*sus!. My second reaction was inwardly to murmur: *Why?* And it was "Why?" that I said aloud. After all, self-control was invented by a Culloden. The fact that he also ran naked over the heather when he wasn't painted line-of-battle blue is neither here nor there; he lived, let us remember, the day before the day before yesterday.

"It's not a question of 'why,' " Lalage said. "I just know, that's all."

"Child, please don't kick the word around. I have a son nearly as old as you are, and if I'm not old enough myself to be your grandfather, I've certainly got a leg on it. A spavined leg, at that."

"I don't care," she said. "It'll come to you."

"What? Love?"

"Yes."

"Oh, *Jee*sus!" The name had found an off-tackle hole in the line of my self-control. It served me right for neglecting spring practice.

"He'd understand."

"Jesus?"

"Somebody."

"Lalage—" I might as well have been saying "Nice pussycat" to a lion I'd met on the Colosseum sands. "Do you know what love is, Lalage?"

"What I'm feeling. Warm and steady and calm."

"You can feel like that any summer afternoon, as long as nobody gives the hammock a shove. No, love's not a dead calm. It's an apex."

"Apex sounds right," she said. "I don't know the word, but I'm apex."

"God!" I said. I'd now taken two thirds of the Trinity in vain; only the Holy Ghost was left. "Another thing you don't know," I went on, "is that after the apex it's downhill. All the long, long way."

She decided then that perhaps she'd better look at me, and I nearly drowned in those eyes. While going down for the third time I remembered a smooth side-overarm I used to do, and I made for the edge of the pool.

"Prove it," said Lalage.

I was nowhere near the edge yet, but the nymph of the pool had grabbed my ankle and the smooth side-overarm was going to waste. "I can't," I said. "Nobody can, or ever could. But maybe I can give you an idea of what happens during the rise and fall of that particular barometer. So listen very carefully, Lalage. When *two* people are in love, each with the other, and beyond all thought or caring, they're given this one perfect moment. It may not be longer than a few seconds, and it's never longer than a few hours; maybe, with very great luck, it might last through a whole afternoon, or part of a summer night. While it's happening, of course, neither the man nor the woman knows it; but it's *perfect,* and that's the important thing. And sooner or later, if you've been one of the lovers, you'll discover that those few seconds, or those few hours, were the most magnificent seconds, or the richest few hours, in your entire life. But—" I stopped. I didn't like the turn that my thought was about to take.

"But what?"

I let my thought take the turn, every tire screaming. "But there's a catch to it," I went on. "And the catch is: once you're over the shock of knowing how perfect that one moment was, you get the sustained and killing shock of knowing that everything since has been imperfect and, no matter how long you live, nothing will ever be perfect again."

"Oh," said Lalage, very quietly.

I touched her hair. "I love you, too," I said. "As I would a daughter."

"That's all I want," she said, and started to cry.

"Now don't do that."

"I wish my own father were here."

"So do I." My reason had to be different from hers.

She was leaning over the balustrade and letting her face droop in the direction of the river. Tears trickled down her cheeks and dropped off to let their salt merge with the passing detritus of Maldorado. "He named me Lalage, you know," she said.

"Bully for him," I said. Now we both were leaning over the balustrade again.

"He was very tall and very thin and he wasn't handsome at all. He gave me his worst features, my mother says. But he couldn't have, because he had to wear glasses all the time, and I have very good eyes. His family owned a big department store in Cleveland, Delmore and Company, but everybody called it just Delmore's. My mother says my father didn't want to work there, all he wanted to do was sit around and read. But he was an only child, like me, and my grandfather'd had a stroke and died, so my father worked there for a while until he died, too. Until he was killed, I mean—"

"Killed?"

She nodded absently. "Yes, and on my sixth birthday. He'd left the store early to be at my party, and the phone call came right in the middle of this game we were playing. And then all the children went home." She was speaking more and more quietly, and it wasn't easy to hear her over the sound of the water. "I remember how hard I cried, but I don't know whether it was because of what happened to my father or because they stopped the party before the ice cream and cake. I had a funny pink paper hat on. Six years old. You don't understand things when you're six years old. Or any other time, I guess, not really. But I kept that funny pink hat for years. And then one night, when I was alone in the house, I took it from this special secret place and tore it into little pieces and flushed them down the toilet in my mother's bathroom. That was in Pennsylvania, in this house she'd rented for the summer."

The Jaguar was coming much too fast along the old dirt road, heading for the bridge. If Joy Durwood were still in the driver's seat she was bucking for a broken neck, let alone a broken axle.

The tears seemed to have stopped, but Lalage went on talking in a rapid but listless monotone: "My mother used to keep a picture of him around, and I'd sit and study it for hours. And my mother says I kept asking why couldn't the picture have been killed and not my father. Then one day the picture was gone. Maybe my mother wanted me to ask what became of it, but I never did. Maybe she burned it. She was always telling me my father never cared about me or anybody else. He only cared for himself, she said. I never believed her, though, not when she talked about him that way. His mouth was very gentle, in the picture, and his eyes were, too, under the glasses. He was loving and kind to me, but he wasn't happy. My mother says she told him a thousand times not to drive so fast, but he never paid her a bit of attention, she says. And I think he was unhappy because he hated her, and maybe he got this fantastic idea that if he drove fast enough, and closed his eyes real tight while he drove, then he'd leave her and everything else he hated behind him forever—and there'd be just him and me. Do you suppose that's what he was trying to do, at the end there?"

"Yes," I said, "and I wish he'd been able to bring it off." I had turned slightly away from her, because I was watching the Jaguar, which had reached the bridge. Joy was driving and the Mexican sat beside her. He was still handsome, but his sullenness had deepened enough for the Mindanao Trench to seem, beside it, like something a baby might gouge in wet sand.

"But you could say he killed himself, couldn't you?" Lalage asked.

"Not with conviction, I couldn't," I told her. "No."

Lalage became aware of the Jaguar as it pulled up behind my Ford, and her first reaction was to pay more attention to the river than it deserved. As I walked to Joy's window I sensed the flames of Etna behind the Durwood façade, although her manner was pleasant enough. "*Sam!*" she exclaimed. "I'm simply the *luckiest,* running into you this way. Otherwise I'd've gotten lost *millions,* trying to *find* it. But you can tell me how to *get* there, can't you?"

"Depends on where it is you want to get to."

"The bus station, Sam, the *bus* station."

"They've a lot of funny things in Maldita," I said, "but I don't think a bus station's one of them."

"I mean in Maldorado."

"Then your guess is as good as mine. I've only been around here a couple of days myself."

"Only *two?* Oh, damnation of *pigs!* Now I'll have to try and find the Volkswagen store, and I *hate* to. I didn't want Joe to know I was here, since he didn't bother to—"

"I'll show you. I have to go into town." Lalage was at my shoulder. Her cheeks had been dried and it was hard to tell that she'd been in tears within living memory.

The Durwood reaction to the Delmore eyes was instantaneous, as opposed to the delayed fuse, patent pending, which is part of the Culloden anti-eye armament. "Oh, *would* you, darling? It won't put you to any *trouble?*"

"No. Honestly."

"That's *unbelievably* sweet of you, darling. Hop right in back. And my name's Joy Durwood, but you'll call me 'Joy,' *won't* you?"

"Yes, if you want. I'm Lalage Delmore."

"What a *lovely* name! Is your Spanish good, Lalage?"

Lalage was entering the Jaguar and she wasn't being awkward at all. "I think so, yes. Although my mother says—"

"*Won*derful!" Joy put the car in reverse. "And mothers say too' goddamned *much,* the whole smothering *crew* of them."

I stepped away to let her get past the station wagon. "Only one of you's taking the bus, is that it?" I asked as the Jaguar started forward.

"That's right, only one *male,*" Joy said cheerfully. "See you *soon,* Sam dear. Maybe we'll get a Merry going, just the *two* of us." The Jaguar leapt growling across the rest of the bridge. Meanwhile the Mexican hadn't opened his handsome, resentful yap. Something very serious and very sudden must've taken place between him and Joy in the short time since I'd last seen them. Well, buddy, I thought, it's back to the *mariachis* for you. Just stay away from the Culloden table, that's all.

As I settled myself on the Ford's burning seat it occurred to me that something sudden and serious also had been only a hair's breadth from taking place between Lalage and me—from her point of view, anyway. It was sensible to have chopped *that* beanstalk before it had soared all the way to the giant's house. "Well, Holy Ghost!" I said aloud to the steering wheel. Then I properly should've headed for the dugout. Three strikes is all they give you; and I'd used up the Trinity.

Polly was writing a letter at one of the patio tables when I eased the car through the gates. I could barely see the leather top for stationery and an ice bucket and a bottle of rum and several of Peñafiel and more tall, opaque highball glasses than she could possibly use without my help. She ran her eyes over me as I came toward her, found that I was still in one piece, and returned to her writing. I poured myself some rum, honoring her creativity meanwhile with the silence that working writers and men with thirty-five-foot putts to make deserve.

"I'm telling Sarah Weatherby how much we love her house," she said.

I tipped some Peñafiel in on top of the rum, but not enough to make the drink dishonest. "How about the neighbors?" I asked. "We love them, too, don't we? God wants us to, according to what trickles down."

"And they love us," Polly said. "Here." She passed me a sheet of blue notepaper that had been lying at her elbow. "From Sra. Gutierrez."

> *Dear Mrs. Culloden,* a bold hand had scrawled in oversize letters, *You're a delightful woman and your husband's only fault seems to be waiting until the lights are out to enjoy himself. Don't you dare let him do that at home in more attractive circumstances! Not that I think you do. Can you both come (with son) for drinks tomorrow at 6? Please let me know today. Informal, completely. My warmest, Angela Gutierrez.*

"I'll write a 'Thanks, but some other time' answer and send Concepción over with it," Polly said. "I could've done it before, but I wanted you to see the note first."

"Tell you what, Polly," I said, slumping into the *equipál* opposite her. "You put down on paper, in real, live grammatical words, that I don't do anything but enjoy myself every minute in this house, lights or no lights—and Mrs. Gutierrez can check on this statement any minute she wants, and even bring a photographer. But until she finds one with a strong stomach—"

"*Sam—!*"

"—but until she finds a photographer with a strong stomach, we'll be delighted to have drinks with her, not to mention Hers, tomorrow it eighteen hundred hours, Greenwich Mean Time. Better find out where she lives, though. I shot all my seeing-eye dogs."

The way Polly was staring at me, you'd've thought I'd used the last bullet on Santa Claus. "You mean you want to *mingle?*" she said. "My God, whatever made you change your mind?"

"You're a backward and unobservant woman, Polly Culloden," I said. "Here you've been married to me for sixty-odd years and never found out that I'm the Chameleon Prince, traveling incognito as a Man." I paused to taste the rum. It didn't make me wince, but it did make me dream of Azteca. "Besides," I continued, "the gringos here like to have me around. And you want to know why? Because I'm rumantic, tipical and full of ocal calor."

"Silly old Sam," Polly said, "what *are* you talking about?"

"Exactly," I said.

She sighed. "Oh, never mind. Did you do the grand tour of Maldorado?"

"*Eh*-uh."

"And saw everything?"

"I guess so. And what I didn't see I visualized."

"And had fun?"

"Not as much as if I'd had on a pair of roller skates," I said. "You could sure work up some speed going down through that town. *Hoo* boy!"

"How about that Flay-a-*chair* man? Did you see him, too?"

"No," I said, and I meant every word of it.

PART TWO

THE UNBURIED
HELMSMAN

Musicke of the Hoboyes is under the Stage.

2 SOL. Peace, what noise?

1 List, list.

2 Hearke.

1 Musicke i' th' Ayre.

3 Under the earth.

4 It signes well, do's it not?

3 No.

1 Peace I say: What should this meane?

2 'Tis the God *Hercules,* whom *Antony* loved,
Now leaves him.

✣ One

It Was Only
a Baby Earthquake,
Not Even Weaned

I was sitting under the same old pepper tree in the patio, at the same round, hidetopped table, glowering at the same black notebook, and getting nowhere at a gallop. The table was damp from the night's rain, the big multivoiced bird had taken the morning off to record some hard-sell commercials for a Mexican radio network, I hadn't quite managed to open the notebook, and my brain was as a barren doe.

A few men have prehensile minds, wonderfully adapted for moving among the higher branches of thought but not worth much in the swamp of day-to-day existence; although existence for most of mankind is no more than the nuzzling of damp, infertile acorns in protective shade. I neither snuffle under the safe oak nor carom from bough to bough. Any ideas that I have, and that I feel are important enough to be passed on to other people, come to me in my little gray home in the west—a soundproof lead coffin, six feet down —a place where nothing is important, let alone impartable, and where nobody listens to me except myself. Even *I* don't listen most of the time. I'm too busy trying to send an SOS to a sequoia root, as I was on the morning in question.

A comedy is merely a tragedy that has come out to take the sun for a couple of hours, after which all the characters will have to go back in the house. Such, at least, had been my theory; and such was the basic attitude I wanted to take in the work I'd come to Mexico to do—a novel about Hollywood. Originally it had seemed to be a project that would be pleasant to develop and simple to carry out. I knew a great deal about what a person might call either the Art of the Cinema or the Film Industry, depending on whether he reads *Sight & Sound* straight ahead or upside down. Setting nomenclature aside, though, Hollywood shaped up to me as an ingrown society of performers, mechanics, craftsmen, and double-entry bookkeepers, some of them competent, all of them frightened, and most of them sad; a society built on piles of play money that were too often swept away by the treacherous breakers of public taste; a society in which you couldn't keep up with the Joneses because you yourselves *were* the Joneses; a tigerish society that even as it leapt unsheathed toward its prey was apt to have its belly laid open from below. For years I had been challenged by, and had responded to, this commercial-diamond society of clever Jukes and cute Kallikaks, and most of its flawed facets had glittered around me at one stage of the game or another. I was sure that all I had to do was assemble what I'd seen and heard, invent some characters who'd do and say the remembered things, wrap characters and incidents in a sturdy manila-paper plot, and then hold the package up to a mirror of mercurial readers.

Unfortunately, a stampeding herd of second thoughts was driving my shorn flock of first thoughts completely out of the pasture. The more I brooded on my subject, the more I realized that the society that had been my concern for so long wasn't a tiger at all; it was merely the uncured skin of some P. T. Barnum predator, beneath which a terrified ass was braying. Any novel written about the place would only be holding one distorted Fun House mirror up to another, with a crazy series of images shrinking within themselves to ultimate invisibility.

In my head the novel was well on the way to invisibility, too, growing smaller as my frustration swelled—a diminishing will-o'-the-wisp that capered in a mad marsh-gas dance, always inches beyond my clawing fingers. I wasn't even finding it easy to recall the way life had been in Hollywood. The faces of friends were nebulous; and something was never exactly right, or was oddly off-center, in whatever setting I tried to bring to mind. To dredge up a mental picture of a specific house—in Beverly or Holmby Hills, say—was to dredge up a minor nightmare, in which the furniture turned out to be breakaway Louis Quinze while strange people who'd wandered in were being sick on the Aubusson.

Extraneous anecdotes kept popping up like targets at a turkey shoot, and I was so busy with them that I wasn't able to create a single and definite character, let alone round him or her out. I once more ate salad with a beautiful young English actress, barely out of her teens, at a buffet around a Bel-Air pool while she told me, with her angelic mouth full of hearts of palm: "Some Wogs want me to make a film called *Salammbô* over in Rome, but I've had it up to *here* when it comes to those corseted seventeenth-century costumes. Do you see my point, luv?" I heard again the producer, for whom a sense of humor was something that was taken off the train, in custody, at Pasadena, explaining that his new Cadillac Fleetwood was really an economy: "Pound for pound, you know, it's cheaper than steak."

These blackouts may've had point, but they'd never add up to a novel; and maybe the abacus named Samuel Culloden wouldn't add them up to a novel either, no matter how long he flipped the brittle beads along the wires of his brain. All I was getting done that morning was sitting in the Mexican sun nearly seven thousand feet above sea level, breathing rain-washed air without much enthusiasm, and losing badly to a notebook in a staring match, which, like chess by mail and the life of a man, is a game that has no time limit. I could've won, of course, by tearing the notebook apart; but that was a form of cheating, and later, in the locker room, I'd be sorry for what I'd done.

I decided instead to use psychology to confuse my opponent, so I opened the notebook and set about covering some virgin pages with funny faces. None of them turned out to be very funny—with the exception of a head that rose from twin necks, one broken. And even that was about as funny as a giggle from a gallows.

Above me a select cortege left the kitchen, came along the balcony, and, beneath no flags or banners, clattered down the exterior stairs— Polly the van, Concepción bumbling behind her with one of the huge new baskets, and Jock bringing up the rear.

"We're going to the bank, then the market, Sam," Polly said as she strolled toward me, "picking up the Youngs on the way. They want some money, too, but it's a waste to take both cars. How about you? Want some travelers cheques cashed?"

"I'm not traveling. I'm a homebody."

"What's that you're doing?" She twisted her torso and cocked her head in an effort to see the comic masterpieces that Sam the Sidewalk Artist had done.

"Oh, just some sketches for that nonsense they want me to put on the Sistine Chapel ceiling," I said, and shut the notebook. "But I told the Pope he'd have to get another boy unless I can lie face down while I'm painting—you know, with my stomach on a mirror. I refuse to let azure drip on my chin. Do you see my point, love?"

Polly didn't. She's apt to be very solemn during the hour before she enters a bank. "Are you working?"

"Sort of."

"Wouldn't you like your typewriter?"

"Want me to bring it down?" Jock called from the bottom of the staircase. "And some paper, too?" He was poised to take the stairs three at a time if I gave the word.

I gave it, all right, to both of them and smack between the eyes. "What was mankind's greatest invention?" I asked.

"Rubbing two dry sticks together," Polly said quickly. "Wasn't it?"

"No, the wheel, the invention of the wheel," Jock said. "Right, Father?"

"Mankind's greatest invention," I said, "was the interrogative sentence, although it'd be useless for me to explain why the hairy Edison who uttered the first one was instantly killed out of hand. Now all of you go rob a bank, please, and leave Old Werther to his sorrows."

"You must be working," Polly said, and stalked off to the car.

Then, almost before I knew it, the three of them were on their way to Maldorado, via the Youngs, and I was left alone with my very worst enemy, a cannibal with bow ribbons of bone in his barbed-wire hair, who clacked his teeth and licked his chops when addressed as Cully Sambo.

He spoke excellent English, old Cully did. As we strolled toward the long-pig pot he was chock-full of those newly discovered interrogative sentences, especially a chic number that he kept repeating: *Why did you say 'No,' bwana, when your pretty wife asked you if you'd seen Fletcher?*

I couldn't answer him because the sight of the long-pig pot, surrounded by seventeen salivating assistant chefs, was making me tongue-tied when it came to a simple declarative sentence. But I was getting more and more curious about Fletcher, and at last *I* began to ask questions of Cully Sambo: *Who was Flay-a-chair? What was he, that all good cooks commend him? And if so, why not?*

Then, having unlocked the secret of the interrogative sentence, I huddled over my closed notebook and waited to be killed, instantly and out of hand, by my little paleolithic friends, who appeared to be in no hurry. Finally, though, I was lowered into the pot and left to stew in my own juice. It was warm in the pot, and the encircling stones and trees and flowers became very still as they watched me. And after a while I began to sway back and forth.

I supposed this was due to the bubbling of water as it came to a boil, but it wasn't. I had become a human rocking chair because somewhere below me a fault in the earth's crust had been having an incestuous affair with itself. As a result, a newborn earthquake was going about its business.

◎ "But of *course* it did, Jim!" Angela Gutierrez exclaimed. "How can you sit there and say you didn't notice?"

Dr. James Winters Inskilling, whose face would have felt quite at home on one of the tougher emperors of the middle Decline-and-Fall period, pointed his graven-image profile at the beautiful Indian girl beside him on the sofa and spoke Spanish like lightning bolts to her. She lowered her lashes and answered, very softly: "*Nosotros bañábamos.*"

This girl, whose name I hadn't caught, had a beauty that was left over from at least a thousand years ago. Had she been around while Cortez was still casing the joint, before he stepped up to scratch, that bloody-minded man wouldn't have laid a glove on the New World if, in return, he were given a month alone with her. The dominant colors of Mexico were in the costume she wore. Her jet hair hung in two braids through which red ribbons were entwined; and the tip of each braid rested delicately on a nipple that was sensed, without being seen, through the dead-white cloth of her blouse.

"I suppose we were in the pool," Dr. Inskilling said.

"Bathing?" Angela asked. The blueprint for a smile was on her lips.

Inskilling's cold-fish mask was part and parcel of his humor, and he used it to good effect. "I presume we were," he said, "if you'll allow for a certain amount of latitude in what you mean by 'bathing.' Then again, we might've been rinsing dishes, or even behaving badly. Mornings have a tendency to run together, you know, along with what's done in them. Anyway, we missed it. Pity."

Angela compressed her lips. "Does water absorb earth tremors?"

"Except for, I think, the teeth of sharks, it absorbs everything it gets," Inskilling said. "Eventually."

"What earth tremors?" Polly and the Youngs, who'd been having a second look at the Gutierrez collection of *santos,* were back in the living room, jumpy with excitement after reviewing Angela's heavenly battle order, rank upon rank, file after file, lined up on a gigantic carved sideboard that took up as much space as the dining-room table. Polly's voice was louder than usual.

"We were talking about the earthquake," Angela said.

"Oh." Polly relaxed. "I'm glad I wasn't living here then. It must've been horrible."

"What?"

"Why, that earthquake in 1896. And the flood that came after."

"We were talking about the one this morning," Angela said.

Polly's coloring ran and hid. "An earthquake this morning? You're not serious!"

"We try to be, off and on," Inskilling said. "If this were a well-run planet the things'd send out invitations. But Angela doubles as the Maldita seismograph and, according to her, it took place around ten o'clock."

"Oh, my God!" Polly gasped.

Angela said: "Where were you, Polly dear? Not bathing?"

"I—" Polly, confused for once, made an audible signal change and the ball was centered directly to Professor Young: "Did you feel an earthquake, Bruce?"

"I don't think you can, in a car," Young said. "We were driving into town then." He'd made a nice gain, but was inches short of a first down.

Polly glared at me, still unsatisfied. "Did you feel an earthquake, Sam?"

"I tried to," I said, "but she kept pushing my hand away."

"It's not a joke!" Polly said. "And you know how I hate any natural disasters. Why didn't you tell me?"

She was frightened and she was angry, but as far as I was concerned she was carrying her after-the-event terrors a longer distance than they deserved. "It slipped my mind, for God's sake," I said. "And anyway, it was only a baby earthquake, not even weaned."

I pushed myself away from the section of wall I'd been holding up, and the conversation I hadn't been holding up, and walked out of the house with the dignified stride that I always use whenever the talk gets around to earthquakes. Nobody clutched my ankles to stop me. Nobody asked me where I was going.

The fountain in the patio was full of orange fish, swimming in drowsy circles near the surface. Their dorsal fins stuck listlessly out of the water and their mouths hung open in boredom. I leaned over and immediately they all came to gape up at me hungrily, as though I were Wackford Squeers and it was time for worm soup at Doth-boys Hall. One of them looked like an ex-Pop Art painter called Andy Warhol.

These gaudy gluttons had learned to connect a sight of the god with a fall of manna, so it didn't take them long to get restless when there was no edible fallout from the mushroom cloud of godhead looming above them. Restlessness led to irritation, and soon they were snapping at each other's gills in a swirl of pink underbellies. "That's the way to go, boys," I said encouragingly. "That's the way to be in this week's swim. Yessiree, until the galleries open on Monday good old cannibalism's the In Thing, the nexus-sexus-plexus of Campy Pop. Or maybe it's Poppy Camp. No matter, boys—either way there's a hip gold tank, full of hep gold water right up to its hup gold gunnels, in that hop 57th Street future of yours. Ain't it so, Andy, you old fingerling, you?" I waited for Andy the Fish to endorse this latest product of my mind, but when he didn't I walked away.

Poppy Camp, I thought, might make a fine *nom de nudité* for a stripteaser of the 1960's. She could begin her act wearing a Roy Lichtenstein silk-screen print, cut like a hostess gown, of a single homey panel of the French comic strip *Barbarella*. With a John Cage arrangement of "Oh, Tell Me, Pretty Maiden" for background music, she would remove this garment, thread by thread. The performance would take precisely nine hours, sidereal time. And instead of a G string, now that G strings had become more *kitsch* than Camp, one narrow black vertical line from a Mondrian abstraction would sustain, when she took those dozens of curtain calls, her inherent modesty. My only problem was to get word to the man who dreamed up fancy names for strippers. More than likely he was the great-grandson of the man who used to name Pullman cars, so it might be possible to reach him c/o The New York, New Haven & Minsky Railroad. The N.Y., N.H. & M., flattered to learn that somebody thought they were still in business, would of course forward the letter. And then I'd never have to work again.

Darkness was coming down earlier than it had to, helped by a heavy layer of rain clouds that had rolled in and tipped its hand with a short preliminary shower just after Polly and Jock and I arrived. The Youngs were already there, and when the shower came we all carried the cocktail impedimenta back inside the house. The cook and housemaid, who lived somewhere in Maldita, had already gone home. Their working day ended at five thirty, even when guests were coming. This was Angela's decision, and one which I approved. Servants talk; and if the people who employ them do nothing that makes good gossip, then the servants have to invent, and what their limited imaginations produce is, for the most part, appalling stuff. I have always liked what a friend of mine, a writer-director named Pike Gata, once said to me: "Sam, I wish I were rich enough so I could afford not to have servants."

Angela's house was remarkably small, considering that the woman herself was, as they say, loaded. Everything in it was expensive, though, and in surprisingly good taste—with one exception. The house formed a compact L, as had the ruin on whose filled-in stone walls it stood. At the top of the L was the master bedroom, which was also the only bedroom in the house. It had as its center of attraction a monstrous bed, Angela's sole lapse into vulgarity. This satin monument to fun-and-games was big enough to engulf, quite comfortably, a squad of six-footers from a Heavy Weapons Company, along with an 81mm. mortar, a recoilless rifle, ammo for both, rations for ten days, and several general-purpose WACs.

Next in line was a Puebla-tiled bathroom with a sunken tub of a size sufficient for swimming meets of aquatic dwarves. After this came a library-study that Angela called her "office," and correctly; most of the space on the shelves was taken up by folders and portfolios and cardboard files, and the few books were either teat-swinging historical novels or examples of the easier types of nonfiction. The office led into the living room, a comfortable rectangle that was half the length of the L's base, with the other half given over to the dining room and kitchen.

The flagstone-paved patio was like an arcade, because its wall, on the highway side, was as high as the house and rose a mere ten yards away. At each end of the patio broad staircases along the sides of the house descended to a walled garden beside the Río Maldorado. In the garden were a scattering of flower beds around a young grove of fig and avocado trees, a trim stone guesthouse, and a swimming pool whose surface, the one time I saw it, was dimmed by a film of pollen.

I'd nearly come to the kitchen end of the patio when low voices, barely heard but speaking from the staircase around the corner, brought me to a listening stop. More than a minute passed before I realized that I was eavesdropping on Jock and Nan Young, mainly because Jock was doing most of the talking. I decided that if Jock were leading with his tongue for a change, instead of his toenails, his father wouldn't be the man to jump into the ring and throw him off balance. I quietly reversed my field and began a slow-motion stroll back toward the starving fish.

Lencho Gutierrez erupted through the front door, which opened directly on the living room, hurried across the patio without seeing me, and darted through a narrow double-doored gate in the exterior wall. Seconds later a motor leapt into overaccelerated life in the parking area. Then tires spun noisily, like pinwheels in pain, throwing off a sparkless gravel, after which a car hurtled up toward the highway. Angela kept two cars in the parking area—a hulking Buick station wagon and a Mexican-assembled Ford 200. To judge by the sound of the motor, Lencho had taken the Buick.

As of that moment, I couldn't say that I had Lencho Gutierrez pegged. An hour before he'd greeted me with a grin, a prolonged *abrazo,* and a flood of Spanish trills and liquids so overwhelmingly joyful that I found myself gawking stupidly over his shoulder at a laughing Angela and feeling like someone in the sixth hour of a ten-child day at Disneyland. For a man who'd only met Robert Taylor once such a welcome was Just Too Much.

Later, while we were being shown through the house, and Polly and the Youngs were getting their first look at the *santos,* Angela whispered to me: "Lencho likes you, you know, for what you did to Saint—and that's very unusual, because he doesn't often take to men. I've never seen him take a shine like this to anybody before. Aren't you pleased?" I answered her by raising one shoulder an inch and a half, thus demonstrating my admirable command of the English language.

Now, however, Lencho had driven off, for better or worse, and darkness had all but taken things over. I didn't bother to stop at the fountain again; the fish and I had entertained each other enough for one evening. Thunder was flexing its muscles off to the black east. In the living room the lights had been put on. I sighed and went inside again, glumly.

They'd dropped the subject of earthquakes, thank God, although the topic that had taken its place—the care and feeding of *santos*—wasn't much of an improvement. Still, it was a lot easier to illustrate. A flock—or group—or perhaps worship—of these battered wooden holy men had been brought in from the dining room. Polly, the Youngs, and Angela sat in a rough circle on the floor, and while the latter gave a breathless lecture on what, other than termites, made the figures tick, her captive audience, gurgling appreciatively, passed the flaking, worm-eaten saints from hand to hand like so many religious hot potatoes. Dr. Inskilling and his gorgeous Companion of the Bath hadn't left their sofa to join in the *santos*-shuffling, I was glad to see. She undoubtedly held back because she drew the line at committing herself to any god or servant thereof who was later than Quetzalcoatl; and Inskilling, like as not, thought of all religions as bootleg brands of sodium pentathol, cheaper than the regular, AMA-advertised stuff, but with potentially dangerous side effects.

"—simply won't rest until I have my very own," Polly was saying as Raffles Culloden, the Gentleman Thief of Time, immaculate in white hopes and black thoughts, his Mask in perfect order, came in from the patio. "When can we go there, Angela?"

"Whenever you want," Angela said. "But don't forget, Tepectlán's an overnight trip. It's between Guadalajara and Morelia, and driving time's over six hours—because why go if you can't stop for a nice, leisurely lunch?"

"I'll go any time," Polly said.

"We'll go any time," said Helen Young.

"Go where?" I wanted to know.

Polly, who'd been facing the other way, swung around. "Oh, you're back, are you? To Tepectlán, to buy *santos*."

"A man there has the market sewed up," Young said.

"Not sewed up, exactly," Angela said. "But he does manage to get his hands on the best ones. You're interested too, aren't you, Sam? We can all fit into the Buick."

"Reckon I'll stay here until I'm sure General Motors'll last out the summer," I said. "They gave the little old ladies a rough spring. Where'd Lencho go?"

"Oh, in town, to check on any mail and pick up the papers. He does it every day around this time. Don't you like *santos,* Sam?"

"Well, I'll tell you, Angela. Once upon a time I went to this Billy Graham revival. It was one of his early whoop-de-dos, after he found out that if he ran *real* fast the ghost of Billy Sunday couldn't throw him out at second, but before they got around to letting him and Jesus through the front door of the White House. Up to then, you remember, Billy and Him had to come in by the Saviors' Entrance. But that fresh-from-Rah!-Rah!-Bob-Jones-U, five-ring Ringling prayer-fest—Ah mean tuh say, Angela, ever'thin an ever'budduh in thuh *ree*-ligion business, since Ah come out alive from that git-saved-by-a-lovin-Gawd-or-burn-in-Hell-damn-yuh moment of pee-*yew*-ah an simpul blessèdness has been nothin but dross—Yay, bo, Angela!—nothin but ah-*pawker*-fill damn-a-nation *drawss.*"

"Don't be ridiculous, Sam," Polly said.

"Whut Ah'm bein, Miz Cullyden—and it hoppens tuh be a thang you never unnerstood—is in a Jawjaw-Billy-Graham-cracker, come-tuh-Jeepers mood. All us Bapidists slups intuh them moods when thuh fit's upon us, which it most of thuh tahm *is.*"

"Sam, for God's sake, what've you been up to?" Polly demanded.

I shrank into myself and became a cherub, all innocent wings and lovable head. "Out there? Not much. Trying to remember a song this photographer I knew used to sing, 'Jesus is a Safelight in the Darkroom of my Soul.' Reckon it's Bapidist. Sure as hell ain't High Church, is it, Angela?" I favored the woman who was my hostess with the smile that we Thirty-third Degree cherubim are taught to use on the women who are our hostesses. "And now that that's over, can I have a drink? This thing's been ice and melted glass for the last fifteen minutes."

"Of course, dear, I'll fix—" Without making arrangements to finish her sentence, Angela made arrangements to get up.

"Sit still, Mistress Quickly," Inskilling was on his feet. "Every man's a born bartender, and I need some freshening myself."

I joined forces with Inskilling where the liquor had been stashed, at a square table by the door to Angela's office. "Those *santos* bore me too," he said quietly as we went to work getting ice out of a silver bucket. "I go along with pre-Columbian bits and pieces, but those Inquisition Raggedy Andys make me shiver." He shivered, to show how it was done in medical circles, while he pulled the cork from a bottle of rum.

"Is that your wife you're with?" I asked without thinking.

Inskilling glanced at the lovely girl on the sofa. "Inés helps me with the housework," he said. "Rum?"

"Thanks. You're not married, then?" I must've used up my conversational brilliance on the fish.

"Hmmm. If the idea's occurred to Inés, she's been very good about keeping it to herself. I found her in a town called Chalco, not that it matters. South of Mexico City, though not very far. She's pre-Columbian too."

"No argument there. She speak English?"

"You know, I'm not sure. Let's hope not." He shook his head when I offered him an opened bottle of soda. "Incidently, your wife's an immensely attractive woman. But you're aware of that, aren't you?"

"If I'm aware of anything," I said. I poured an ocean of soda into the duckpond of rum in my glass. I was now doing no more than going through the motions of drinking. I'd put away more booze in the few days I'd been in Maldita than I ordinarily would in a month. "What's the pre-Columbian situation here? Any sites in the neighborhood?"

"Supposedly not. Have you met Hy Levinson?"

"No."

"He's a nice old man. He's also unique—in my experience, anyway—because he's the only retired Jewish boilermaker I've ever run across. Well, Hy's always stomping over the hills with pick and shovel. He's convinced he'll turn up a site someday. It'll be quite a trick if he does. This was Chichimeca country, you know. They never stopped long enough anywhere even to bury their dead."

"*Hy* Levinson? I met Fletcher yesterday, and he used a name that sounded like 'Hy.' "

"It was. I saw Tom Fletcher yesterday too."

"Professionally?"

Behind us the *santos* lovers clucked over a San Ysidro who'd lost his angel and oxen. "No, I wouldn't put it that way," Inskilling said slowly. "I go to Tom's often, when the day begins to drag."

I wasn't able to tie up draggy days with the demure and beautiful Inés, but they were Inskilling's days, not mine. I also saw no reason to do a Lalage and march off at a left oblique so I held to the course we were on: Thomas Fletcher. "How can a man in his early sixties be senile?" I asked.

Inskilling was, for him, startled. "Who told you he was in his early sixties?"

"Nobody. I guessed."

"You make bad guesses. Tom Fletcher'll be eighty-six next month."

"Eighty-six!" My astonished hand held on tight to the edge of the table. "I don't believe it."

"You would if you were Tom."

"And you can't help him?"

"Help?" Inskilling's eyes found Inés briefly, then paid attention to the floor at his feet. "To tell the truth," he murmured to the tiles and, incidentally, me, "I've given up the practice of medicine, what with one thing and another." He sighed and went on, semiprofessionally: "Nobody can help Tom, worse luck. Now, I'd be the first to admit that he's deceptive in a physical sense. Good Lord! that body of his is worth a whole chapter in a textbook. But mentally—even though I'm speaking, understand, about a field in which I'm the man in the corner, wearing a dunce cap—mentally, mind you, I'd say he's been not lost but gone before, the poor old fellow, for a good twenty years."

"In laymen's terms, off his rocker," I said.

"I never fail to express myself badly, do I?" Inskilling shook his head. "No, Culloden, Tom's not crazy. Call him a sleepwalker, and you'd be close to the bull's-eye. Not that you can blame him, after what happened to the sons and—"

"Sons? I hadn't heard about any sons."

"Oh—hadn't you?" Inskilling concerned himself with the floor again. "Well, the really terrible thing is—"

The terrible thing, whatever it was, stayed in Inskilling's voice box. Three ponderous knocks on the door had cut off whatever he'd been going to say.

The grown-up children quit playing with their saintly soldiers. "Now who can that be?" Angela exclaimed. "It can't be the Salvatierras. José wouldn't knock, not when he could yell 'Boo!' through the window and scare everybody out of her skin. Oh, well—" She began to pull her mass off the floor. "—we'll know in a minute."

"Stay there," Bruce Young said, getting up. "I'll go."

He crossed to the door and opened it, poised to step back gingerly in case it opened on Hell. Evidently it didn't, because when he did step back he was in no hurry. It took a long time for him to get the door open.

When it was open enough to be at a right angle to the wall Joy Durwood glided into the room.

At her heels, his eyes like two burned holes in a blanket, came José Salvatierra. "Surprise!" he shouted. "She couldn't wait to meet you, so I brought her uninvited. Ladies and gentlemen, I give you— Miss Joy Durwood!" The unpaid M.C. for a terrible amateur talent show in Topeka might have made a worse botch of it, but not by much.

The Durwood head managed to rise above this alien corn, inclining slightly, as Salvatierra presented us to her, one at a time. Angela, who'd somehow hoisted herself erect, shook hands. Polly and Helen Young, who remained on the floor, legs tucked under them, nodded warily. Inskilling and I were the farthest away, so we were the last to be introduced. The distant Durwood smile that I was given was no different from the smile she gave the others, so the Samuel Culloden smile was equally remote. If she chose not to let people know that we'd met before, that was all right with me. Especially since I'd forgotten to mention our meeting to Polly.

Joy pouted at Salvatierra as soon as the introductions were over. "Oh, Joe, if you'd only *told* me!" she said. "If I'd known there were so many simply *beautiful* women in Maldita, I never would've *come*. They make me feel *dowdy*, Joe—so dowdy I could *cry!*" None of the simply beautiful women, I noticed, made even a token protest about this self-deprecation.

"How about handsome men?" Salvatierra asked. "Some of those are around. Where's Lencho, Angela?"

"I've had my fill of handsome men for a while, thank you," Joy said, coming up with a new formula for a rueful smile: Remembrance^2 + Rue^2 = Woman (Disillusioned)^n.

"And she has, too," Salvatierra said heavily.

"Lencho's in town," Angela said, adding in a cool voice: "Where's your Luz?"

"She's got the car," Salvatierra said. "I thought she'd be here, as a matter of fact. But if she isn't—well, Joy'll drive me home."

"If I can bring myself to leave this *delicious* room," Joy said. "The earthquake didn't hurt it at *all,* did it? My bedroom's simply a *mess,* with plaster and these nasty little *pebbles* everywhere."

"The Matthewses' ceilings again, Angela," Salvatierra said. "The plaster was still damp."

"Oh, let's not talk about plaster," Joy said. "Mrs. Gutierrez, I just *know* the rest of your house is every *bit* as exquisite."

"Whether it is or not," Angela said, "people seem to think that daylight's the best time to see it in."

"And it's not going anywhere," Salvatierra said. "We can only stay for a minute anyway, Angela. We only came—"

"Perhaps tomorrow, though." Joy's words, half question, half plea, were spoken to no one in particular.

"—came by to make some arrangements," Salvatierra finished.

"Arrangements?" Angela frowned.

"Sure. To go to the fiesta."

"Fiesta?"

"My God, don't tell me you forgot, after all the talking we did about it? Listen, Angela—fiesta—tomorrow night—at La Presa de las Abejas. Any bells ringing for you now?"

"Oh, Lord, that Dam of the Bees thing!" Angela exclaimed. "It's true, José, I did forget."

"It doesn't matter. Anyway, Joy's dying to see it, so I thought we'd all join forces and go up together. Then we could—"

Angela cut him short, laying her hand on his arm: "José dear, I *am* sorry, but we've made plans to go to Tepectlán in the morning. And we won't be back until Sunday night. You should've reminded me sooner."

"Just you and Lencho?" Salvatierra asked.

"No, the Cullodens and Youngs're coming. We'll be a carful."

This snap decision must have surprised the Youngs and at least one of the Cullodens, but nobody batted an eyelash, including the Culloden *paterfamilias,* who knew danged well he weren't going to no consarned Tepectlán, not with the South Forty laying there unplowed and the Dog Days close to hand.

"How about you, Jim?" Salvatierra hated to go down swinging. "Interested in the fiesta?"

"I detest fiestas," Inskilling said. "And dams. And bees."

"Well, then—" Salvatierra's shoulders were drooping as though he'd blown a sure-thing Volkswagen sale. He looked glumly at Joy.

"Then I can't see the house tomorrow," she said.

"But of course you can, honey," Angela said. "The maids'll be here. I'll tell them to show you around."

"But without *you*," Joy said, "it wouldn't be the same."

Angela thought about this, then said calmly: "It never is." Coming from her, it struck me as an extraordinarily cryptic remark. But perhaps the remark was an ordinary one, and it was Sam Culloden who was—

Oh, forget it, I told myself.

But I couldn't. There had been undercurrents in the small talk that I didn't like. They made me damnably restless. I wished I were home in bed.

◎ Jock had been invited by Nan for supper at the Youngs, so Polly and I walked by ourselves to the *finca*. The rain was still holding off. As we cut across the parking area I thought I saw the tall shadow of Lalage competing with a short tree on the other side of Joy's Jaguar. I didn't tell Polly, though. More than likely it was a trick of the inefficient light bulbs that flickered above the cars they were watching.

Polly broke the silence of our walk three times.

The first time she said: "Wasn't that the Delmore girl cowering behind that Jaguar?"

I said: "I didn't see anybody."

The second time she said: "We're going to Tepectlán tomorrow mainly because Angela doesn't want Lencho to run into *her*."

I said: "The Delmore girl?"

She said: "The Durwood woman. And as soon as we get back from Tepectlán Angela'll take him off someplace else. Wait and see."

And I said: "I'm not going to Tepectlán. Get that straight."

The third time she said: "Did you meet the Durwood woman before?"

I said: "What put that in your head, for God's sake?"

And she said: "It was the way you looked at each other. Never mind."

Then later, when we were in bed and it was raining hard and I thought Polly had gone to sleep, she said: "Can you get along all right alone here while we're gone?"

I said: "Any reason why I shouldn't get along all right alone here while you're gone?"

And she said: "I don't know. It's just that you—Oh, *nothing*. Good night, Sam."

"Good night, Lady, good night, sweet Lady, good night, good night."

Nothing, my foot.

✸ Two

Some Fool Had Left
the LSD Running All Night

There he sat, St. Samuel Stylites, on his dear little pillar in the desert place known as Patiodelafinca. A single note, belled forth from Nadita's fane on the near hill, marked each hour; and when he heard the hollow clang he exercised his holy body by lowering his eyelids and then, with superhuman effort, raising them again. Every night he let down a full hamper of his thoughts, and every morning the disciples at the base of the pillar hauled the hamper aloft—the thoughts burned to ashes but otherwise unharmed. Months droned by while in blessèd fascination he beheld his flesh-and-bones carcass becoming One with the wood-and-hide platform on which he sat balanced between Earth and Heaven. Year after year two oddly matched birds, a phoenix and a turtle, came back to his bosom and remodeled the nest they'd once built against his breastbone, and there they sang and mated and sat on eggs and raised their timorous half-breed young. And after forty-five years had run their course, the forty-sixth was a Sacred Year. Then in tents put up around the dear little pillar the disciples prayed and held orgies, held orgies and prayed—at the same time, more often than not. And St. Samuel Stylites felt the Spurt of the Load descend upon him, and his eyes

were as lightning and his tongue as thunder, and while the mountain-
tops danced in the distance and the grasses of the field became
bristling darts, he opened the immortal mine shaft of his mouth and
said: *How ya gonna keep 'em down onna farm, after they've seen
Saint Me?* And then he shut his notebook with a mighty noise, that
was like unto the breaking of cities.

Actually, I'd been within an inch of slamming the damned thing
into the roses; but I wasn't especially keen on busting a couple of
plants, and later I might want to heave an undamaged notebook at
a worthier target, such as my own head. If space really were curved,
and if my throwing arm still had the old power, I might be able,
when the time came, to put a dent in my skull merely by heaving
the notebook at the nearest galaxy. And the time was indeed coming.

After Polly and Jock had been gathered in and driven off toward
Tepectlán I was certain I could break my writer's block; alone for
two days, with no distractions, I was going to race my carload of
ideas over the thwarting mountains and down to the easy plains
beyond. But as soon as I let my brain's clutch out I discovered that
not only had the steering assembly gone haywire but also the gears,
no matter how they were shifted, always meshed into reverse. I'd
spent two gray and overcast morning hours going around in circles,
backward. At the moment I had a choice of staying on the same
mental Snap-the-Whip until it was time for *comida,* in which case
I'd do well to whistle up some stretcher bearers now, or of quitting.
So, since q-u-i-t is a four-letter word and I was in a four-letter mood,
I quit.

I slouched through the tunnel to the river terrace, leaned on the
wall, and did a little plain-and-fancy spitting into the rain-swelled
Río Maldorado, whose surface had become a turbulent miscellany
of trash. A cloudburst or a steady, all-night downpour not only
augmented the river but also sent a town dump's worth of castoff
oddments and soggy refuse swirling through Maldita.

A dead mongrel dog bobbed past me, its belly swollen, drum-taut,
and on the point of bursting. "I know just how you feel, boy," I said,
"seeing as how I'm the Club Librarian." I hung over the wall a while
longer, rather hoping that the dead dog's dead master might pass in

review, too. The parade of garbage and culch went on and on, however, like May Day in Moscow, with no further surprises, so I decided to go on and on myself—in any direction but the one that led back to the notebook and the damp table and the futile rat-tat-tatting on my swollen, drum-taut, point-of-bursting brain.

As soon as I turned away from the wall I knew my destination— Mrs. Weatherby's small collection of books.

Jack and Sarah Weatherby had individual workrooms on this quieter side of the house, with windows overlooking the river and the old dirt road. A shared bath was between the rooms, but each had a private entrance from the terrace. I hadn't been in either of them since Polly and I peeked in during the quick survey we made before dark on the day we arrived, but I did remember seeing some shelves of books in Sarah Weatherby's room. There would certainly be a few that would tempt me, in spite of the seven I'd brought from California and which had yet to be cracked. The books you bring with you are never the books you read.

I would've sized Sarah up as a Book-of-the-Month Club type, so it was disturbing to find that most of those she kept in her workroom were volumes of poetry. The others were nonmovement novels in the Robbe-Grillet style, turned out by that shrewdness of young writers, of various sexes, who consider a vacuum to be the best of all possible worlds.

The only poet on the shelves who was fairly far removed in time was Byron; nearly all the rest had slithered into print since 1950. That year, of course, the Muse was being held, not to mention kept, at arm's length by those polite sell-outs, the poets who'd latched on to a doctorate. They could hardly wait, after the war, to skitter back into the womb of Alma Mater Magna, where a poem wasn't a poem without four footnotes to the line, and where the best fun of all, admittedly cutthroat and certainly dour, came from writing up each other's obscure daisy chains for the sports pages of the quarterlies. But then, I remembered, as the fifteen years that followed 1950 disappeared slipshod into the past, poetry was taken over by a jump of clowns who looked like used condoms and smelled like Times Square on a Saturday night. They were loud and they were manic; and as soon as they'd enticed the Muse up to their communal pad they'd stripped her, painted some dirty words on her belly, slugged her a few times, lathered against her in a gang shag, and finally booted her out half-dressed, bawling, rubbed raw, ready for the nut house, and full of as pretty a dose of clap as ever left San Francisco. It seemed reasonable to ignore Sarah Weatherby's modern poets—Academic or Beat—so I ignored them, and gladly. The hell with modern poets.

I did diddle around with a fictive thing, though, which was avant-garde as all get-out. "There is a rumor," the thing's dust jacket said, "that today's novel is the unlaid ghost of an art that has been dead for a century—but to read this book is to reaffirm that the *pure* novel is alive and vivid and dwelling in many mansions; and that Jean-Baptiste Rappaporte, the exciting new author of *The Deserted Painting,* is a great major-domo as well. His subtle prose will lead you into—"

Well, I left the blurb on the sidewalk, chattering to itself, and knocked on the door of the book. Jean-Baptiste Rappaporte, the exciting new major-domo, immediately led me into a high-ceilinged reception room. Or maybe it was a garage. Or an unflushed toilet. I couldn't be sure, because some fool had left the LSD running all night, and the kitchen sink was hip-deep in crystallized scenes of one hand clapping. *Eh*-uh, wherever Jean-Baptiste took me was square and misty, like the center of a sugar cube. Pretty soon I wasn't conscious of being in a room. Or a house. Or, for that matter, a novel. So I put the book back where I'd found it, and after that it didn't bother me at all. It didn't even sniffle. The hell with avant-garde novelists, too.

Nothing was more therapeutic than a calm cussing-out of some of my less attractive confreres. I felt so relaxed that if there'd been a telephone in the *finca* I might've called Pleasantville, New York, and ordered a lifetime subscription to the Nahuatl edition of the *Reader's Digest.* But since there wasn't even a blanket and a fire of green wood for the sending of smoke signals to Pleasantville, I thought it would be equally nice to take a not-quite-so-modern volume of poetry around to the patio and skip here and there in it while I tossed off a little civilized rum. I scanned the shelves casually, not so much reading the titles as looking for bulk. A thick book with a green dust jacket seemed vaguely familiar. I tucked it under my arm and toted it out of the room. It was, I was positive, Robert Frost's *Collected Poems.* Not until I'd plopped it down on my table in the patio did I learn that the poems in the book, although collected, were those of Thomas Hardy.

Hardy is hardly a cheery old card. I didn't lug the book back where it came from, but I wasn't in any great hurry to rummage through it, either. I made myself a drink upstairs in the kitchen, brought it down to the table, smoked a cigarette, and sipped around the edges of the rum while I watched a rear guard of gray Confederate clouds being put to rout by an ubiquitous Blue cavalry. When I felt I was warmed up enough to face a few lines of cold Hardy, I flipped the book open near the middle and then did one of the neatest mental double-takes of my long career as a prat-fall comedian on the Id & Ego Circuit. For the poem I'd turned to, bang off, began:

> *Lalage's coming:*
> *Where is she now, O?*
> *Turning to bow, O,*
> *And smile, is she,*
> *Just at parting,*
> *Parting, parting,*
> *As she is starting*
> *To come to me?*

The hairs on my nape were at a bristling attention as I finished the first stanza. Whoever wrote about the long arm of coincidence must've been browsing in the wrong biology. It so happens that coincidence has eight thick and muscular tentacles, all of which at that moment were encircling my throat. Meanwhile coincidence's parrotlike beak was pecking away at my ears, not very playfully. Millions of books have been published since Gutenberg found himself fooling with fonts—but I had to choose this one and open to that page.

There had to be a purpose behind my acts and decisions, such as they were, during the three quarters of an hour since I'd walked to the river terrace. I examined the sky, hoping to catch a glimpse of—well, of the apprentice god who, I suspected, was behind the whole affair. But the sky was an empty, uniform blue. I hadn't seen a communiqué, of course; but possibly the apprentice god, wounded in the rout of the rain clouds, had limped off only a moment ago to pick up his Purple Heart. Typical of him, I thought. Typical of all apprentice gods.

On the other hand, Troop-Sergeant-Major Culloden had definitely been wounded, which was also typical of him. He hadn't been put out of action, however. At the Battle of Hardysville he'd stood his ground, fighting dismounted, until relieved by the end of a very bad poem. As usual, nobody thought to slip him a Purple Heart; he didn't even get a morphine packet. Instead, Troop-Sergeant-Major Culloden was ordered to appear before a summary court martial, which sentenced him to spend the rest of the day.

Sentence was immediately carried out.

◎ At six o'clock I escaped from the stockade in a Ford station wagon that a careless guard had left lying around, and made for Maldorado and the fiesta, wherever it was. All that the loony-bin guidebook could tell me, in a caption to a photograph that must've been taken under water, was that the Dam of the Bees was in the hills to the southeast. Still, I didn't think I'd have any trouble finding it; there were only thirty miles of hills to the southeast of Maldorado.

At the main plaza in town I parked a few yards beyond the restaurant where my Headache had given me so much good, clean, American fun. The newsstand had a surfeit of that morning's Mexico City *News;* and this time I gave the dealer the correct amount instead of another twenty-peso note. I didn't want a second fistful of hard money. I'm perfectly capable of wearing my own holes in my own pockets, without any help from the Mexican Mint.

A woman swung around the corner, high heels clattering, and slammed into my shoulder. I caught her by the arms, kept her from a fall, and found that I was holding Luz Salvatierra. She broke into out-of-breath Spanish, then recognized me, blushed, and slipped into equally out-of-breath English: "¡*Ay*, Sr.— I mean Mr.—Culloden I am—sorry!"

"I'm not," I said. "And if you're not hurt, I'm twice as not."

Luz put the tricky phrase through her translating machine and chose to like it. "No, I am not hurt," she said, "but I am becoming very *norteamericano*, walking so fast." She had caught her breath. "Especially when I am not going anywhere," she added.

I didn't know how to interpret that last clause, which on the face of it seemed to be part of an unnecessary apology, but which also could be taken as a fragment of a confession or as an oblique invitation or merely as an ingenuous remark by a lovely, not too worldly, girl-woman. "Yes, you are," I told her. "You're coming in here and have some coffee with me."

"No, I—" she began, then: "That is—I mean, yes. Of course. I would like very much to have coffee with you in this place. Why not?" And she led the way in.

We both ordered coffee, and as the waiter wandered away through the empty restaurant I offered Luz a cigarette, lit it for her, and then lit my own. "I did not think to see you," she said, turning her head slightly and blowing out smoke. "I thought you had gone to Tepectlán. Angela told José you were going with her."

"My wife and son went. I was hoping I could get some work done."

"You are writing a novel. ¿*Verdad?*"

"Trying to."

"What is the title?"

"*How to Raise Women for Fun and Profit,*" I told her, and dropped an ash on the floor.

The translating machine promptly blew up from overwork. While fragments of circuits rained down on us she brooded over that spur-of-the-moment title. "I do not think it is very good," she said finally, "if it is for a novel. Please excuse me for saying this, but it does not make sense."

"What does make sense to you, then?" I wanted to know. Her side could have the ball for the next series of downs.

"Every day it is less," she said. Unhappiness tugged at her lovely face. "And there are things, too, that make sense when they should not make sense." She made tiny invisible circles on the top of the none-too-clean table, using one long red nail. I was about to go on to another subject, before her mood infected me, when she came out with a low, lirruping, and incongruous laugh. "What you did to that man at dinner should not have made sense," she said, "but it made sense to me because I do not like that man."

"Neither does he," I told her. "And I don't like him much myself. What I do like, though, is your laugh. I don't think I've heard you laugh before."

"But I have always laughed," Luz said. "Until not long ago I cannot remember when I—" Two women waddled into the restaurant and Luz nodded coldly at one of them, a begirdled and stockingless lump in a black dress, who reminded me of an ottoman in mourning, and whose calves could've used a haircut. "—when I have not laughed," Luz concluded, returning her eyes to mine. The two women sat heavily at a table across the room. As long as we were in the restaurant they paid more attention to us than to the pastries they ordered.

"Too bad you weren't at Angela's last night," I said. "I'd've wallowed in that laugh of yours."

"José did not want me to come, I am sure of it. So I did not. And I do not think I would have laughed if I had come." Her eyes left me again. The unhappiness was back.

"Weren't you supposed to meet him there? He said you were."

"He was not telling the truth. I told him he did not need two women around him to show how *macho* he was, and then I went away in the automobile. I am the wife of José. I am not a medal for him to wear. But I think he wants very much to wear his childhood girl as a medal."

"Don't worry about it," I said. "She's just an old friend who took a house in Maldita on his advice, and he's merely showing her around." Anyone who knew me would also have known, from the casual way I spoke, that I didn't believe a word of what I was saying.

Luz's tongue flicked out and along her upper lip. "I know what he is showing her," she said. "He speaks English, excellent American English, like his mother, but he is Mexican, *muy macho,* like his cavalry father. I do not think you know how different a Mexican marriage is from your own. It is different in the way the husband and the wife act. The husband does what he likes. He comes home, if he likes, and he visits other women—which he always likes. But the wife is expected to stay in her house, like an nun in a convent, unless she goes out to shop with women who are her friends. She has only one duty in life and that is to bear many children, and that is the thing that makes her different from a nun. And she must always be quiet and modest and humble, and she must never be seen alone in a public place with a man who is not her husband or a member of her family. Those women over there have been talking about me ever since they sat down. Not about you and me, but about the wicked Sra. Salvatierra, who has no shame. By tomorrow everyone in Maldorado will have heard that I was drinking coffee with a handsome *norteamericano,* and by tomorrow night they will be saying that we were drinking coffee because we had much thirst from making love in some secret place all afternoon."

"For once, and I'm sorry to admit it," I said, "appearance has it all over reality."

"I do not know what that means," Luz said. "But I do know that José can take his childhood friend to parties and fiestas and even secret places for making love, and people will do nothing but laugh and shake their heads and say how *macho* is José Salvatierra. We have been married now not even two years. It is not a fair world."

"Isn't, wasn't, and never will be," I said. "Is he taking her to the fiesta tonight?"

"At La Presa de las Abejas. Yes."

"And you're not going?"

"I would go with him alone. But he wants also to take his childhood friend. I will not make a three."

"Tell you what, Luz. I'm going up to the dam, but I don't know how to get there. So why don't you come with me and show me the way?"

She gave a slight gasp. The thought of our going together obviously pleased her, but that was as far as it went; twenty-one years of being a female in Mexico stops many a pleasant vision cold in its tracks.

"I will tell you the way," she said, "which is very easy. But I will not go with you."

"Why not? Afraid of more talk?"

"Yes," she said, and paused a moment before continuing. "More talk by me. I have told you too much already, and I am already sorry. If I went with you I might tell you more things, and then we would both be sorry, and sorrow is a dangerous supper when two people share it. I think you perhaps understand a little what I am trying to say."

I didn't. I did understand her directions on how to get to the Dam of the Bees, though. The way was, as she'd said, very easy.

◎ Night had fallen, clear and fine, on La Presa de las Abejas, but it hadn't yet fallen far enough to affect the Mexican stomach. That general hunger was still some hours away, and so the canvas roof that called itself a restaurant was all mine to play with: my private, herb-scented toy. Along with two huge glasses of draft beer I had a plate of roast kid, *cabrito al horno,* which contained enough ribs to outfit a xylophone-playing anaconda, but which was very good eating once I got between the rib bones. And meanwhile I did what I'd begun to think was impossible. I read the Mexico City *News.*

The Red Sox, a remarkably consistent nonteam this year, had blown another game. No one, it seemed, had been able to convince them that you can't get base hits with a swizzle stick or that little pitchers don't necessarily have big years. I digested the day's box scores and the leagues' standings of the moment until my usual bitterness about the customary Boston defeat had faded in a fog of statistics. Not a real fog, though. Taken all in all, sports statistics are the only truth to be found in any given newspaper. And when I'd finished with them, of course, I had to run through the pages of so-called straight news, where havoc was being cried and the dogs of war let loose in a score of forms and places. In a world as frequently blooded as ours, the only contented creatures are leeches and the only cool ones dead men.

More and more people were dawdling past the restaurant. Many of them had walked the three miles from Maldorado, over a bad dirt road that sneaked into the hills near the Chinese-Aztec pavilion at the high end of town. Long after midnight they'd be trudging home again, but it didn't bother them. Their faces were full of somber delight and their voices were as soft as their shuffling feet.

I was ready to stop reading about the world's follies and to become a living part of them. I paid the round and happy waitress, who also did the cooking, what I owed her, left a tip and the discarded *News* on the table, and shuffled into the slow-flowing crowd.

It was more a carnival than a fiesta, and it was taking place in a wide-floored ravine fifty yards or so up from the road that ran along the top of La Presa de las Abejas. Tents, booths, simple counters, and canvas-roofed restaurants were set up opposite each other on the bottom of the ravine, forming a valley for the human glacier. Pitchmen's filed voices worked abrasively on eardrums, coming and going, from either side. You could fire a .22 rifle, throw a dart, toss a coin, or have a wheel spun for you; and you might even end up winning the last thing in the world that you, or anyone else in his right mind, wanted.

The Dam of the Bees, dedicated in 1900 by Porfirio Díaz himself, got its name because during its construction five different hives of wild bees, on five different occasions, had laced into five different foremen, leaving them somewhat the worse for wear. Since only members of the boss class had been stung, the common workmen had good reason to believe that the Divine Hand was in it somewhere; and since no better way has been found to worship God than by getting drunk outdoors, at night, and with friends, the first fiesta began as soon as old Porfirio had been helped aboard his train and gone puffing back to Mexico City. For many years a Bee Dance had been the high point of the carryings-on, performed by men from Maldorado who invariably were drunk. The dancers, year by year, increased their liquid intake, their roughness, and their bad manners. They eventually did very little dancing, preferring to use their stingers, which were their bunched fingers, to sting women not their wives in places not their privilege, for the greater glory of God, and all that. So a paper covered with many fine seals and many elaborate signatures was issued from the Palacio de las Montañas, officially ending the Bee Dance forevermore.

Now and then I'd shuffle myself out of the crowd for some private entertainment. I fired .22 shorts at a line of stationary metal ducks, using a rifle with no front sight and a barrel that wasn't even fit to catch rain in. I didn't hit any ducks. Come to think of it, I was lucky I didn't hit somebody standing behind me. Next I threw a dozen darts at some small and droopy balloons that were fastened to plywood, popping four and winning a prize—a gruesome plastic *mariachi* doll with a sleazy plastic guitar sewn on the front of its skimpy jacket. Then I tried to toss twenty-centavo pieces into circles painted on oilcloth. As the circles were slightly smaller than the coins, I didn't win anything, but I at least got rid of a kilogram of twenty-centavo pieces. I bought the number Forty-five for a spin on a Wheel of Fortune: Sixteen was the number that came up, of course, which was hardly a secret to me. Old Sam the Soothsayer always knows what the winning number's going to be, but he prefers to let the other slobs, who flunked their ESP, walk off with all the goodies. Besides, Old Cagliostro Culloden already had won a doll on which a black mustache was painted and a brown guitar sewn—certainly a richer acquisition than any seer has a right to expect.

I was drifting with the crowd, trying to locate a myopic female child on whom I could foist the doll, when I saw the perfect foil for a quick doll-foisting con. She was a far cry from being a child, and she wasn't myopic, but she was female and she liked *mariachis*. Indeed, she was listening to a *mariachi* group when I spotted her. Joy Durwood, her name was.

The musicians were not so much putting on a performance as taking the kinks out of the repertoire that they'd be strumming through after midnight, when the action would have shifted to the restaurants. Joy had José Salvatierra on her left; and a step behind her, looming over her right shoulder, was Lalage Delmore, who seemed to have taken up the wearing of dresses as a permanent thing.

The *mariachis* blew a couple of wrong notes in the number they were playing, stopped the music, and started an argument. "Wouldn't you like a nice Mexican music man for your very own, Miss Durwood, ma'am?" I asked the back of Joy's head.

They all turned to see who had spoken, Salvatierra with considerable annoyance, and Lalage somewhat frightened; but Joy rolled around like a ball bearing, cool and smooth. "I *knew* that was you, Sam," she said. "I don't think I *want* one, though, not right now. Listening's all I can handle and all I care to. But what're *you*—?" Her eyes became turquoise question marks. "Why, you're supposed to be in—Oh, *you* know the place I mean, that *What*'s-its-name."

"Tepectlán," Salvatierra said.

"That's the place," I said. "Old What's-its-name. Hi, Lalage."

"Hi," Lalage said. She spread her fingers and drew them clumsily through her cropped hair.

"How come you didn't go?" Salvatierra asked.

"South Forty needed plowing."

"Huh?"

"The trouble spot," I said. "The South Forty." I brought the doll from behind my back and held it up. "He's easy to handle, Joy. No trouble spot there."

She grabbed him. "Ah, isn't he *sweet?*" she cried. "A baby *mariachi!* Oh, *Sam*—you really and *truly* don't want him?"

"Reckon not," I said. "I still like girls. So he's all yours."

"And such a *sugar*-doll thing!" She fondled the little horror. "Thank you *ever* so much, you Sam dear." She couldn't leave off her fondling. "And his baby mustache! Isn't he the *dearest* dear you ever saw, Lalage?"

Lalage never got a chance to say "Yes," "No," or "Don't" because Salvatierra was now sitting up and taking nourishment. "You should've let us know you were at loose ends, Culloden," he said. "We could all've come up together. Although Luz—that's my wife— she's feeling lousy. Not well at all."

"I guess my ends are in tight enough," I said, "and maybe my guards are, too. Incidentally, I bumped into your wife this afternoon, late, and she told me she didn't intend to take in the fiesta. So I asked her if she'd come with me."

"Did you?" Salvatierra hesitated, then continued: "And she

wouldn't? Well, I said she was sick. And she should've been in bed, not out."

My turn to hesitate had arrived, and I took my time on the mound. The way the umpires watch you these days, it's hard as hell to get the spit on the ball. "That wasn't how it came through," I said easily. "According to her, the reason she couldn't come with me was because she had another date. She told me his name, too. But, damn it, I'm not good on names. It's gone from me. A friend of yours, I suppose."

A solid backhander might have put more red in Salvatierra's face, but it wouldn't've colored a quarter of the area that my casual words had. He didn't start to get pale again until after he'd said: "Of course. A friend."

"*Eh*-uh, I thought so." I poked the hideous doll. "And meanwhile, take care of *your* friend, Joy, hear? I'm off to where I came from."

"You're not leaving?" Joy said. "You just got here."

"I've been here since before bees had stingers," I said cheerfully. "I've eaten here, I've drunk here, I've even won a doll here—and now all I want to do is crawl home and close my eyes and live my memories over again. Go with God."

I went back the way I'd come. I stuck close to one line of tents, but I still had to fight the crowd more than I felt was necessary for a fine old distributor of dolls called F. A. O. Culloden. Pretty soon, though, the tents ended and the crowd thinned and I was in the open, close to where the cars were parked and the buses dumped their passengers. I was somewhat confused as to where I'd left the Ford; a great deal more parking had been done since I'd tucked it away. But when I saw Rose Gage walking toward me with two of her daughters I wasn't so confused that I didn't regret my lack of a cloak of invisibility. The girls were small enough to be thrown back, so I guessed they were Gamma and Delta. As the trio was fully dressed, in a manner of speaking, by the time I'd recognized them Rose had already recognized me, and it was too late to get out of there.

"Well!" Rose said. "I was wondering where you were."

"When?" I asked. If I hadn't been caught unaware I might've been able to come up with a more stupid remark. The "When?" would have to do.

"Why, you and Polly were coming over, weren't you? That's the impression you gave. Where is she?"

"Polly? She went to Tepectlán."

"Alone?"

"Oh, I wouldn't say that. There were some other people. And our son. And a big stick, of course, to beat off the bandits."

"I've brought these creatures here for an hour," Rose said. "That'll be long enough to wear them out. Then I'll take them home and put them to bed, and Jeff will come back with the other two." As she gave me this unwanted information she was taking me in, and twice, from cowlick to leather soles, like a lascivious, slow-motion, nodding *magot*.

"That's something I'd never've thought of," I said.

She inspected my fair, white, but clothed body for the third time. "Where are you off to now?"

"Oh, home. Or the post office. Or Heaven. I haven't made up my mind. But probably home."

"What time is it?"

"It's—uh—nine seventeen."

"Why don't you come around to my—*our* place—at quarter to eleven, say? These'll be asleep, and Jeff'll have the other two up here."

"Quarter to eleven," I said slowly. "What'll we do at quarter to eleven?"

Rose stared at me as though she'd been insulted. "Why, screw each other," she said. "What else?"

Gamma and Delta giggled so hard they probably wet themselves. They were getting quite an education, those babies, at their full-blown mother's knee.

"Rose, I'm sorry," I said, "but I can't. It's Saturday night."

"What's that got to do with it? Leave your underpants alone, Gamma."

"When you ask what Saturday night has to do with it, Rose, you've answered your own question."

"I simply don't know what you're talking about. But listen, Jeff won't dare come home till two or three o'clock if I tell him not to. It'll be Sunday then."

"So it will. And I'll be asleep. Some other time, hey?" I saw my car and started toward it. " 'Night, Rose."

"Listen, Jeff doesn't mind," she called after me. "Honest he doesn't."

"And he's got a point there, too, by God," I called back. "I'll tell Polly you asked after her."

As I felt for the ignition lock I said to the Self I couldn't see in the rear-view mirror: Buddy, you're on the way to being an old inhabitant, because the *old* old inhabitants are beginning to let you in on what's happening, and why, and who's making it happen. But you're not enough of an old inhabitant yet to be part of a Happening yourself. And I want you to know, buddy, I *admire* you for it. You are the Alpha and Omega, the first and the last, the pride and joy of the centuries, and the apple of the only focusing eye that Mother Eve has left.

Forty minutes later, as the night-table lamp in the bedroom found itself put to work again, I saw a hefty scorpion on the wall above the antique bed. While he was mistily trying to fathom how Darkness could so abruptly become Light I belted him a good one with the crazy guidebook. He was dead before he hit the sheets.

I wasn't.

❀ Three

He Was Pigeon-Dropped
by the Holy Ghost

I awoke in a creaky but unshared bed. I blinked at an enemy brilliance.

Outside in the patio a calculating sun was deploying its rays with great cunning, as though their deceitful yellow curtain could keep me from seeing the Sunday that was huddled in sackcloth beyond the glare, waiting to bore me stiff.

I was in no hurry to meet that sad and leaden day, so I lay with closed eyes and listened to the howling silence on the other side of the wide-open balcony windows and tried to get a little thinking done.

But my mind is like a playful dog. I throw it the stick of an idea and off it gambols, barking, in pursuit. Sometimes it comes prancing back with the stick, but more often, forgetful of what it's chasing, it veers away toward a nest of imaginary field mice. Yet on rare occasions it will return without the stick, its jaws gently closed on a ruby, a pearl, a gold pendant, or a diamond that covers my thumbnail—and when that happens I am the very proud master of that fool dog, my mind.

On this day, however, the dog chose to dart aimlessly all around the field, snarling at nonexistent mice and worrying their nonexistent nests. It made me so angry that when the beast finally lumbered up to heel, tail a-droop, tongue lolling, I let it slink exhausted to the kennel without bothering to tell it that the field, for once, had been nonexistent too.

And then I got out of bed.

In the echo-chamber kitchen Brillat-Culloden made himself a modest gourmet breakfast—ham and eggs, so cleverly mangled that only a connoisseur could say where fowl left off and flesh began; a couple of pieces of toast, burned to precisely the proper blackness; and coffee, with that delicate aroma of brown water that only Brillat-Culloden has been able to achieve in this century.

Half an hour later I had shaved, showered, and dressed and was going down the exterior staircase nearest the gate, bound for absolutely nowhere except the river terrace—which was, in the long run, Absolutely Nowhere—when I noticed something peculiar about the car. Peculiar and, in a way, unnerving.

Lalage lay asleep on the front seat, slumped against the closed window.

My first thought, the one that unnerved me, was that "asleep" might be the wrong word. Lalage was such a desperately unhappy girl that it would take very little to persuade her to hop a fan jet to Oblivion instead of trying to walk there, moving at night, through stony country.

I went around the front of the Ford very fast and yanked open the door by the driver's seat. Lalage's torso jerked erect, her eyelids went up almost audibly, and she goggled at me in terror. Then, as I slid onto the seat beside her, reason took over from instinct; she saw who I was, and embarrassment usurped the place of the fear that went scampering back to its crypt. She remained ill at ease, though, and there was great tenseness in the way she sat bolt upright in a wrinkled dress that was drawn several inches above her knees.

I could relax, however. She might've been tense, but it wasn't *rigor mortis*. I reached in my jacket pocket for a cigarette. "What happened?" I asked. "House burn down?"

"I don't know," she said. "I haven't been home."

"I can see that," I said.

She licked dry lips. "It doesn't matter how I look. I don't care how I look."

"You look all right to me," I told her, "but I wasn't talking about your appearance." I lit the cigarette and let down the window. "I meant that if you slept here you obviously didn't go home—unless you blew the joint after you cut your mother's throat."

Lalage stared fixedly at the tunnel that led to the river terrace. "It was because of the roof," she said. "I haven't seen my mother in two days."

"The roof." I nodded to myself as I repeated the words in a flat voice. Lalage Delmore, All-Pro quarterback of the Maldita Non-sequiturs, had just thrown me a sixty-six-yard forward pass, a breath-taking all-the-way-in-the-air spiral. The only thing wrong with it was that the sixty-six yards it covered were vertical, straight up. "The roof," I said again.

"Yes," said Lalage.

Naturally, I had to find out which of the hundred million or so roofs under which mankind lurks could have caused her to tuck away in my station wagon. "What roof?" I asked impatiently. The only suspense I enjoy being in is designed and built by the Culloden Cliffhanger Company, an organization that, although small, is also undercapitalized; whereas the models brought out by competing firms tend to be shoddy, overpriced, and without disc brakes as standard equipment. "Or whose roof, for God's sake?"

"Why, Joy's roof," Lalage said. "Joy *Dur*wood's. You knew that."

"Sorry," I said, "but I quit second-story work, and sold my tools to a picket fence, a long time before I met Joy. So her roof's a stranger to me. What'd it do, anyway? Sign on as second guitar with a *mariachi* combo?"

"You mean she didn't *tell* you what the earthquake did?"

Snippets of conversation are apt to slip my mind, perhaps because the world is so full of a number, as the phrase-lopping Miss Durwood might say. Now, however, I recalled Joy's chatter during her brief visit to the Gutierrez living room. "Yep, Lalage, now that you mention it, I did hear her say something about plaster and pebbles, and that her bedroom was a mess. But why should that—"

"It's *ever* so worse now," Lalage broke in. "The night before last, when it *rained* so, the water poured in every nook and *cranny*. There must've been *hundreds* of leaks."

"Hundreds?" Lalage, I noticed, had started to imitate the Durwood emphasis on single words.

"Well, enough so that Joy had to lie on a *sofa* all night. And then yesterday the men were sup*posed* to come and fix the roof, and I was going to spend the night with Joy, but the men never showed up at *all*. Joy was *fur*ious and she went into Maldorado to stay at one of the hotels. I let them drop me off near the bridge, and then—"

"Them?"

"You know, Joy and *José*. He drove out with us after the fiesta because he wanted to check on the *bed*room, and then he was going to find the *fore*man of the men who didn't fix the roof and give him a good bawling-*out*. Not today, though, I guess—all the workmen'll be sleeping off being *drunk* last night. Anyway, when Joy and José started back to town I let her drop me off. I should've gone with her, I guess, but I can't *stand* hotels. But it was *very* late, and I didn't care to go to my mother's house, either. So I slept in your car."

"Poor Lalage," I said. "And poor Joy, ending up in some cold, gray, lonely hotel room." The projectionist in my head laughed contemptuously when I asked to see some footage of a willing Joy driving a uxorious José Salvatierra home to his waiting wife; but I made no comment to Lalage concerning the phantom projectionist's attitude. Instead I said: "Ah, you women lead difficult lives, bouncing between cars and hotels."

"Oh, Joy doesn't mind ho*tels*," Lalage said. "The thing she *really* can't stand is hotel *food*. But I told her when she came home I'd make us a *real* breakfast. I'm a good cook, did you know that? I cook for myself all the *time* in the tower. And I'm to go over to Joy's at ten *thirty*, she told me. Is that clock on the dashboard right?"

"It's six months fast," I said. "You've got plenty of time. But about that Matthews place—doesn't it have more than one bedroom?"

"There're three in all, I think. But the Matthewses are *ter*ribly tight with money, considering how much they *have,* my mother says—and she may be right, for once. Anyway, the only bedroom the Matthewses furnished is the one they use them*selves.* They *really* act rich, don't they? For Ca*nad*ians, I mean."

"I wouldn't know, Lalage. As Scott Hemingway once said, 'The very Canadian are different from you and me.' "

"Who was Scott Hemingway? A Ca*nad*ian?"

"No, he was a Figment. First-generation Figment, as a matter of fact. But he died an American citizen and an ex-resident of the Garden of Allah, which is a clean, well-lighted hotel in Ketchum, Idaho. How about some coffee?"

"No, thank you. But I *would* like to walk around the patio for a few minutes. I never slept in a *car* before."

"You haven't missed much," I said. "Help yourself to the patio."

We left the car by opposite doors and I leaned over the hood and watched Lalage stumbling back and forth across the tiles as she worked the stiffness out of her joints. When I was twenty-two, Lalage's age, I occasionally slept—or something—in automobiles; but when the sun came up I didn't have to lubricate my ball bearings by doing Scouts' Pace for fifteen minutes, any more than the girls had to oil their sockets with a bit of hopscotch. Either the mold for car sleepers was melted down a year or so later, and the metal used to kill a lot of wide-awake people in foreign-made tanks, or the new generation of Americans was made of such soft gold that all fondling now had to be done indoors, in wall-to-wall jewel cases.

If there'd been rain during the night Sarah Weatherby would've owned one book of poems less; Hardy had been forgotten on the table. Lalage eventually spotted him, approached him sideways as a crab would, opened him in the same way someone else might disarm a land mine, and riffled the pages without fainting from excitement. "I think you only read *po*etry," she said.

"On the contrary, Lalage, I've been caught with my nose in the *Old Farmer's Almanac.* I've even been seen browsing through the book reviews in *Playboy.*"

In the 1850's Lalage would've made a first-class Mississippi riverboat gambler, the way her thumb worked those somber pages. "This man wrote a *lot* of poetry, didn't he?" she asked.

"That reminds me," I said. I went over and took Hardy away from her. "There's a poem I want to show you."

"Funny, but I always feel weak before breakfast," Lalage said sullenly as I handed her the book; but then she got a look at the first line and her eyes became very wide. "Why, it's my *name!*" she exclaimed, and proceeded to read the whole dreary poem. When she finished she said: "Do you suppose *this* is where it came from, and not that other man, *you* know, Mr. *Hor*ace?"

I suddenly regretted that we'd gotten on the subject of nomenclature again, so I did some rapid tangenting on my own time: "Coffee'd do you good, then."

"I'd *love* to show this to Joy. Didn't I say 'No, thank you' before? *May* I show it to Joy?"

"Sure." Whatever coffee might do for Lalage, tangenting didn't help Samuel Fraser Culloden one iota. But since my bluff, as it were, had been called, I showed her the cards I held. "And if you always feel weak before breakfast, what I'm going to do is take this fine figure of a Ford and ferry you over the river."

"You don't have to. I can walk."

Aces and eights, that's what I was holding. "So could Satan," I said, "according to the Book of Job. And we know what happened to Satan, don't we?"

"What?"

Such ignorance in any other woman would've brought water to a boil on the top of my head, but annoyance was the last thing I intended to demonstrate to Lalage. "Well, he—let's say he had to go into business for himself."

"Unless *you* have a reason to go across." The "What?" had been automatic: Lalage probably hadn't even heard me speak of the Devil.

"Oh, I do, I do," I said with a sigh. "The grass is always greener on the other side of the river."

"*Is* it? *Really?*"

I gave up the struggle. "Come on, child," I said.

It wasn't until I was backing the station wagon through the gates that Lalage thought to ask: "I'll get there too early, won't I?"

"Oh, you'll maybe have time to brew a cup of coffee and spoil your breakfast. You cooks have all the luck."

"Not so much," she said and settled back in the seat. "But it doesn't matter. I think I'm happy now." She was smiling. "*So* happy"

She kept the Hardy volume clutched tightly in her lap. Every so often I'd give her a quick in-and-out sidelong glance. I thought that she was merely taking in the familiar landscape until suddenly I noticed that her face had become changed by a mixture of disbelief and fear. My next glance, a few seconds later, showed that these had been replaced by a visitor more grim. Lalage was in a black tunnel somewhere, mining an untouched vein of misery. And then, when I glanced at her again, her expression had become normal, although a trace of bewilderment still hovered around those marvelous eyes.

"End of the line," I said. I stopped the car in front of the Matthewses' gates.

Lalage stayed put. "You want to know something?" Her voice was quiet and a little unsure. "Just now I had this feeling I was living in my own past. There was one Me here, doing what I was doing, and another Me away in the future someplace, *watch*ing herself do it."

As fantasies go these days, Lalage's seemed harmless enough. "Which was the nicest You?" I asked. "The one here, or the one up ahead?"

After a while she said: "The one up ahead was terribly sad about something. Something I don't think has happened yet. She was sadder than I've *ever* been." Lalage took a deep breath. "Or ever could *bear* to be."

I'd been wrong about the fantasy; it was anything but harmless. However, before I could come up with some dialogue that might take her mind off it, Lalage reached for the door handle, turned to me, and said in a completely normal voice: "Thank you for the ride, and for where I slept last night. Are you going on into Maldorado?"

"The other direction, I reckon. Have yourself a good day, Lalage."

"Oh, *yes!*" she whispered, and got out of the car.

There wasn't room to make a U-turn, so I had to do some fancy back-and-forthing to put the Ford's nose where its tail was. I swung off the road and almost up to the gates while Lalage was unlocking a small door in one of them: Joy must've given her a key. As she stood and watched my maneuvers she let the door swing open by itself, permitting me a brief but comprehensive glimpse of part of the Matthews house.

My hand was on its way to the automatic shift when a man's head and bare left shoulder popped into view between a pair of drawn but ill-hanging curtains in the nearest window. His features were in shadow, but the shadows weren't deep enough for me not to recognize the higher portions of George Simmons when I saw them.

I inadvertently dropped my eyes when I shifted into reverse. When I raised them again Simmons had vanished. And I was carefully backing across the road. And Lalage was closing the small door behind her. And Joy Durwood was in line to be given a very nice breakfast indeed—if she hadn't already eaten, in bed.

I suppose I should've been glad, in a backhanded way, that Sr. Sins had latched onto some solid fuel and had put himself in orbit, even though he was out of uniform. All the other rocket riders I'd seen in photographs were, to put it mildly, dressed in the height of fashion. But Maldita, of course, is a town that's neither *au courant* nor especially partial to changes. And, after all, no No. 1 sack suit that Brooks Brothers ever cut is quite as conservative as the human skin.

Yet I wasn't in the least glad.

◎ Fletcher was outside his hacienda, talking to a regular old crag of a man whom I recognized on sight as Hy Levinson. His body was slightly bent, but he still stood half a head taller than Fletcher. A wealth of curly gray hair sheltered the face of the kind of man who's always being caught in the middle of the street when the traffic light changes to green; it was also the face, somewhat the worse for wear, of a trusting and gullible boy. His hands were those of Michelangelo's David forty years later, and in one of them he held, balanced as lightly as if it'd been a five-cent piece attached to a length of chicken wire, something that resembled a mine detector, as designed by a chap with Abercrombie & Fitch on the advice of a gentleman from Tiffany's.

Fletcher waved at me to stop. I was already slowing down and preparing to pull off the road. It's not every day that a man gets a chance to meet a Jewish boilermaker, active or retired.

Levinson's handshake was a brief but memorable visit with five steel bands, but I don't think he was aware of the power of his grip, any more than a large and loving dog that leaps on a child realizes the child will be knocked sprawling.

"Hy's been showing me his new toy," Fletcher said, with a nod at Levinson's strange device. "Took him six eggs and a *filete* as long as your arm to explain how it works. Thank God he doesn't come to breakfast very often. What do you think of that hell tool he's toting?"

"Why, it's just like Mother used to make," I said. "I didn't know Maldita was mined, though. Who're we fighting this time?"

"Oh, this isn't a real Army mine detector," Levinson said. "Maybe the principle's the same, but this is a purely commercial product. An improvement. And for civilians, like miners and people hunting for old things and treasures. The name is—see it here?—the Treasure Tracer. It's all these new electronics in it. This instrument can even locate gold and silver under the ground, deep as much as five feet."

"Coins or veins?"

"Either one, it's of no importance."

I let out a low whistle. "Suppose it gets a message from a twenty-dollar gold piece, say—what does it do then? Ring a bell? Send up some rockets?"

Levinson grinned. "That I'd like to see. No, it clicks. It gives notice by clicks. And this needle jiggles—this one, under the glass here. When you buy it, the Treasure Tracer people, they give you a real gold nugget to practice on. It's back at the house, or I'd show you the workings."

"Better not walk past Fort Knox," I said. "The Treasure Tracer'd blow sky-high."

"No, this is for here only," Levinson said. "Forty-seven dollars and fifty cents a month I paid, for ten months. And it only was delivered yesterday, an acquaintance brought it driving from Chicago to see his uncle in Veracruz, the Israeli consul. But now I can prove that high-class civilization was around Maldorado before the Spaniards came. The books say not, but because it's bound up in a book don't make it true. I read lots of archaeologies, and mostly the big finds come in places where all the books said was nothing. Around here's going to be another of those places. Care to come along, Mr. Culloden?"

"Very much," I said, "but later, when I'm clearer about what I'm trying to find myself. My son, though—he's seventeen—would be pleased as Punch if you'd take him out. He likes archaeology, and he'd be crazy about that detector."

"Any day he wants, he would be welcome," Levinson said. "It's nine o'clock, every morning it don't rain, and it usually don't. Maybe he'd bring us luck, your son." He squeezed Fletcher's shoulder with his free hand. "You take life easy, Tom, I mean it. As for about the breakfast, it was far from my intention to eat you out of house and home." He patted my arm. "And I enjoyed it to meet you, Mr. Culloden."

Fletcher and I watched him walk away. When he reached the end of the hacienda wall that was nearest the bridge he swung left, heading up the hill toward the huge jacarandas; the wall's weathered stones cut off our view of him. Fletcher made a clucking sound with his tongue. "Poor Hy," he said, "spending all that money to get himself some more disappointments."

"You mean the thing doesn't work?"

"Oh, it works, Sam, it works too well. But I'll bet you there isn't an inch of ground within a ten-mile radius that doesn't have a little metal doodad in it, something that was either lost or tossed away during the last fifty years. Hy'll hear his machine clicking at the top of its lungs and he'll get all excited and begin to dig—and what do you think he'll come up with? Maybe a rusty hairpin that some girl lost in 1922. Or perhaps a 1935 centavo that fell out of some kid's pocket when he was running. Because the books're right, you know. There was nothing alive here except a few grasshoppers until this Spaniard named Juan de la Cuerva tripped over a rock in 1541 and broke his nose on half a billion dollars."

"Have you ever suggested to Levinson that he's barking up the wrong tree?"

"Why should I? He's a happy old dear, so why spoil his life, or try to? He's even happy in his disappointments."

"Then he's a rare bird."

"He is. And you're talking to another." Fletcher winked at me. "Sorry we were cut off the other morning."

"So am I." I was mildly surprised to discover I meant what I said. "You look fine, now. How're you feeling?"

"Sufficient unto the day, I reckon. You busy?"

"No, sir."

"Good. Come on inside. Dolores isn't back from church yet, so the place is a mess. But it's seldom the fog rolls in before noon, and there was something I wanted to tell you."

"So you said." I followed him through the jerry-built entrance and into his one-room house.

Plates, platters, saucers and cups, a coffee pot, and various other after-breakfast odds and ends made a litter on the round table. Fletcher pushed some of them to one side, clearing a space between us as we sat down. "I think Dolores hangs around for three or four Masses in succession," he said. "The nearer she gets to that last on-her-back lie-down, the more time she spends on her knees."

"Can't blame her for that," I said.

"But the old fool overdoes it," Fletcher said mildly. "Why, when she goes to Confession—which is every ten minutes, it seems like—she rambles on so that she's finally taken to splitting her sins down the middle. Half go into one priest's ear and half into another's. And of course the silly old cow hasn't done ninety-nine per cent of what she mumbles about. Hell, all the sins that bag of yelling bones commits from one year's end to the next don't need a confessional. They could be absolved from a matchbox. There ought to be some coffee left. You want it?"

"No, thank you."

He shook the pot. "Just as well. It's all gone. Well, in that case—how's to a dribble of Azteca?"

"You're talking music."

"Thought I was." He brought a bottle of rum and two tumblers from the cabinet. "You got any opinion about a man my age boozing at ten thirty on a Sunday morning?" he asked as he started to pour.

"The other day I didn't know you were eighty-five," I said.

"Oh? I supposed you did."

"No, I figured you to be a mere child of sixty-two or -three. Anyway, a man going on eighty-six has been around long enough to call his own shots."

Fletcher finished filling the tumblers and put the cork back in the bottle. "Sam boy," he said, "I know I'm older than it's decent for a man to be. But my time's coming, and pretty soon now. I'm not sure I couldn't even pinpoint the day, if I had a mind to. Meanwhile, I'm ready to meet it, and the idea doesn't bother me a bit. You see, I've been dead, in a manner of speaking, once or twice in my life, so I've had a kind of advanced look at what I take to be a mighty reasonable state of affairs. Still, until they turn my boots around in the stirrups I intend to do all the living I can fit in. Being alive, Sam, is the errand we're apt to remember a little too late, the errand we were sent on and forgot all about while we stopped to watch the steam shovel. Well, I've left the steam shovels behind me. And the excavations've been filled in long since. And here's the rum you didn't finish—" He pushed a full tumbler at me. "And here's to Ethan Allen." He raised his tumbler.

I raised mine. "Why Ethan Allen?"

"Because when he was dying, and the parson told him. 'General Allen, the angels're waiting for you,' old Ethan said, 'Waiting, are they? *Waiting,* are they? Well, God damn 'em, let 'em wait!' "

So we toasted the Green Mountain Boy with a deep one, and when I put my tumbler down again my gullet was covered with languor and coated with gold, and I could've laughed my way through a month of wet Sundays, with a brace of Lents thrown in.

Fletcher fixed his clear eyes on me. "Now, about this something I want to tell you—" he said. "I guess I'll come in on it from the flank by asking a question: How's Jamie?"

"Jamie?" I'd never met anyone named Jamie in my life.

"Jamie, that's what I said. I—" The old man's gaze flicked from my face to the open door behind me, a fraction of a second before I heard a footstep. "Oh, hello, George. Enter and grow in wisdom." I didn't bother to turn around. I heard George Simmons say: "'Morning, Tom. Only for a minute." As he walked past me Simmons touched my jacket with the tips of his fingers. "'Morning, Sam," he said, then sagged into the second chair to my right.

I nodded, rather curtly, "George," I said.

Simmons' eyes were noticeably bloodshot, his rearward frieze of hair cried out for a combing, and a day's worth of beard darkened his jowls. His breathing, faster than normal, was proper to a man who, as I fitted it together, had gone out the Matthewses' back door as Lalage came in the front one, who had enlisted the aid of a convenient tree in getting up and over the high rear wall, and who had then hurried across the hills to reach the chair he sat in.

"What in Tophet've you been doing?" Fletcher demanded. "You look like something the cat dragged in. Or tried to."

"Walking," Simmons said. "Since before sunup."

"Walking in the dark?"

"Until it got to be daylight, sure."

"This a new idea of yours?"

"I was restless, that's all." Simmons managed to focus on me. "You're up and about on the early side yourself, aren't you Sam?"

He was obviously trying to learn whether or not I'd seen him in the window. "*Eh*-uh, and I'm over on the restless side, too," I said. "My wife and son're in Tepectlán and won't be back until late today sometime. And since I'm out of practice when it comes to being alone, I thought I'd drop in here." I sipped some rum, having carefully passed over my leaving of Lalage at the Matthewses' gates; I never offer clues on Sundays, among other things. "Ever tried this Azteca, George? It's great."

"George doesn't drink," Fletcher said. "All he does is feel restless."

"I can't help how I feel," Simmons said. He'd stopped his scrutiny of Closemouth Culloden, the D.A.'s Despair, and was glumly taking into consideration the contours of his hands, which he'd folded on the table before him.

"Neither can Judas Iscariot," Fletcher said, giving me a split-second grin. "Imagine how that poor bugger's been feeling for two thousand years."

The old man, for reasons of his own, seemed to want to get Simmons started on a subject that was dear to the latter's heart, but Sr. Sins wasn't having any. Nothing existed for him at the moment except his big folded hands. Therefore, Seven-Foot Sam Culloden, the fouled forward, accepted the ball from the referee and made his free throw on the rum-slippery floor. "How does Judas Iscariot fit into the picture?" asked good old Seven-Foot Sam.

The ball bounced around the rim of the basket, but it didn't drop through until Simmons slowly raised his eyes to mine. "He should've been a saint," he mumbled. After I'd taken this in my stride, and made no comment at all, Simmons said: "Did you hear me, Sam?"

"Sure, I did, sure, George," I said, while across the table Fletcher reached, beaming, for his rum. "And I'm still listening. I'm all ears, George."

"Then—just what do you know about Judas?"

"Not too much. Only that he betrayed What's-his-name for what amounted to seven fifty. But then he chickened out, and was last seen as his own one-man lynch mob. And he never even got to spend the dough—or did he?"

A snort from Simmons blew my question to smithereens in midair. "Judas Iscariot," he said with great deliberation, "is the undeserving scapegoat of Christianity." He spoke through clenched teeth, and each word had a private emphasis. "He is the most maligned human being, the most abused innocent creature, since God brought Adam from the dust. Do you believe what I'm saying, Sam?"

"Well," I said, "I can't recall ever hearing anybody put in a good word for him. Of course, I hang around with a backbiting crowd, so—"

"Never mind, Sam, never mind. We all know Judas's been cursed and reviled down through the centuries. Because he betrayed his Lord—that's what they've always claimed. But—and listen carefully, Sam, because this is a serious matter, so serious, in fact, that if all its hidden ramifications were shown in their true light it might mean the death of the Christian religion—" He sucked in his breath and went on: "*But*—Judas Iscariot wasn't responsible for the selling-out of Jesus, and he *must not be held responsible*. Why, in the legal sense of the term, he wasn't even an accessory after the fact. Judas could no more stop that betrayal than you and I can stop ourselves from dying. And do you know why? Because he wasn't in *control* of himself that night in Gethsemane. He hadn't been in control of himself for days, and he never was in control of himself again. No, sir! *Never again!* And do you know what was wrong with him? I'll tell you. He was—"

"Mainlining, maybe?" I suggested.

"Ah, it wasn't drugs!" Simmons exclaimed. "Not *drugs*. What happened to Judas was far worse than drugs. He'd been turned into a lamb—a *hypnotized* lamb—a *brainwashed* lamb—and then they led him to the slaughter. Don't you *see,* man? The betrayal of Christ, that *great* betrayal, was absolutely prearranged—and in *Heaven,* of all places! Judas had no say in the matter. Judas was helplessly carrying out the Will of God!" Simmons's voice rose; his words smoked with resentment. "Yes! Judas Iscariot was *used!* He was set up by the Father, he was the Son's fall guy, and he was pigeon-dropped by the Holy Ghost. I tell you, Sam—Christ couldn't've died for the sins of man if it hadn't been for Judas Iscariot. And without that so-called betrayal by Judas every last one of us would've been damned, right down the line to the dead of Armageddon. And *I* say that because Judas was the *chosen instrument* of God, because he was considered *worthy* to betray God's Son, he should, by all that's holy, be the very first of the hagiarchy of saints—greater than Peter, far greater than Paul, and more highly honored than either. Ah, my *poor* Judas!" There was a rasping sigh, some of the bitterness left him, and he continued more quietly: "But the Church has never let up on her betrayal and hounding of that guiltless man, and she never will stop until an astute member of the College of Cardinals, who'll be not only a future saint but a smart politician in the flesh, and who'll be capable of a knock-down, drag-out fight against the entire Host of Heaven, gets himself elected Pope and has the guts to call himself

Pope Judas Iscariot Primus. How does it sound, Sam? What do you think?"

"I think I'll go along with you, George," I said, getting off the hook as fast as I could. "But meanwhile, tell me—did you leave the priesthood because of a knock-down, drag-out over Judas?"

"I'm no longer a priest, Sam, because I lost my faith. It's as simple as that. I began with a single small doubt, but it grew. Over quite a long time, it grew—until I became a complete atheist. God didn't exist for man, I felt, except as a *convenience* for man. And man had to invent God, to explain man's own mistakes. Well, when I'd reached a state of theologic nihilism I had no choice but to—oh, I won't go into it further. Here I am, though—in this place, and in these clothes." He rose to his feet abruptly. "Which I must go home and change. Be seeing you, Tom."

"Soon, George, soon," Fletcher said. "I enjoyed our talk."

On his way to the door Simmons paused by my chair. "Sometimes it's not easy to be me, Sam. Understand?"

"Sure I do, George," I told him. And I did too. What I didn't quite understand was what he meant by the remark, unless that somewhere during his Judas spiel he'd come to the conclusion that I'd spotted him in the window.

"Good man." He tapped the back of my chair with his knuckles and went on to the door, where he halted. "Oh, I forgot to tell you, Tom," he said. "I think I'm getting my faith back. And it's hell, Tom, sheer hell."

"Are you?" Fletcher was genuinely, but briefly, surprised. "How'd that happen?"

"Oh, you might say I've been rearguing my loss of faith in the direction it originally came from. I'm now where I'm able to believe that perhaps God had to create man, if only to avoid later, and worse, errors on His own part. I'm also fairly close to convincing myself that He did make man in His own image, instead of the other way round. But I'm not yet in a position where I can say 'God help me,' because as things stand I'd merely be asking a favor of an image in a mirror. And mirrors never help." With that, Simmons went out the door.

A moment later he stuck his head in again. "This means, of course, that I'll cut myself shaving," he said.

Then he was gone for good.

"Thus endeth the first lesson," Fletcher said. "Live and learn, Sam boy, live and learn. And now that we've settled Judas' hash—*how's Jamie?*"

❧ *Four*

Did You Drag Me Down
on This Unmade Bed?

Having returned to his native haunches after a twenty-minute anti-eternity spent distracting around in the Dodgem Car concession of an antimatter universe, S. Neutrino Culloden, the wall-none positive electron and whirled trammeler, informed Antisocial Notes From All Over that the rest of the Simmer planned to remain a house with him in Moll Ditis, which he had rendered for ever so why, a coozy ex-priesthole known as Finger Gamy. Frérot Culloden also told From Notes Over All Antisocial that his lass core of hexistences had nayfair been bofficially minuted, dew too a suite for malformation of porrigor brought by a hardboled gras window from Primus Stove, Va., and the georgeous ardoress of the shirt stirrup "My Cundim for a Cabalhero," both of whom were pussing whimselves off as the Contessa Giòia Inguina delle Peccati, *née* Lupe Naríz y Méntula, doughtear and knees of the Porgian Cynocephalite at Iscaria in Judaea, and flamiliar to the jot-sot of nyeteem incontinents as a gland no blagger than a moan's cod. ETAOINSHRDLU or knot to ETAOINSHRDLU, Misstore Killerden said, that is the question. Or was, until—

We were back where we started. "Jamie?" I said again. Whoever Jamie was, the old man seemed to be dead set on settling his hash, too.

"Jamie," Fletcher repeated, in a voice like the rustle of distant leaves.

A sneak right by Comprehension, who happened to be wearing a knuckle duster, caught me smack between wind and water. I sucked in more air than I needed. It came out as a whisper: "My father." When I was a very small boy and when my parents were young themselves, my mother had called him "Jamie." Later, when they were not so young, she'd said "James," and then, much sooner than it should have been, she lay in her coffin and had no name for him at all.

"That's right," Fletcher said. "Your father." His voice became hesitant. "How is he?"

"Father's fine and dandy," I said. "Last time I saw him he looked better than he had in years. Lots of color. You used to know him?"

Fletcher had relaxed on "dandy"; now he chuckled. "Why, Sam, if it weren't for me you wouldn't be sitting here drinking good booze, and if it weren't for Jamie Culloden I wouldn't be watching you drink it."

"I'm mighty glad you ran into each other, then," I said. "I'd've hated to have missed out on this rum." I let a mouthful of the stuff slide south, just to be sure it was holding its flavor. It was. All of a sudden, though, my mind was no longer on Azteca. "Well, I'll be hung for a sheep!" I said in awe, and gaped at the old man for about as long as it takes to fall ten stories in Detroit.

The footlights rimming the stage of my memory had come up. The curtain rose on a scene laid in 1928, in which an ex-buck sergeant of the Yankee Division was spinning yarns about some far-off war or other to a little boy who was like a son to him and who had always been a civilian. "You're *Captain* Fletcher, by God!" I exclaimed.

"Don't it beat the Dutch?" Fletcher said with a grin.

I shook my head in amazement, grinning myself. "Isn't it funny—the way things come back to you? Things you've forgotten for years? Like a flood, sometimes. I'm flooded with them now—except I can't connect your face with the stories Father told me. He didn't have any pictures of you, you know. And I always—I was around eight, nine at the most—I always thought of you as an old man with whiskers, like General Grant. Or maybe white, like Lee's."

"It figures," Fletcher said. "Let's see, I was thirty-eight in '18 and Jamie was—oh, twenty-three, maybe twenty-four. So he probably put the whiskers idea in your head, without being aware that he was doing it. To someone just getting into the swing of his twenties, a man thirty-eight is downright long in the tooth. And I acted older than I felt, anyway. No, as *old* as I felt. If you're handling a company of infantry in the kind of war we whip up nowadays, Methuselah in his dying hour seems about as ancient as a trickle-pants kid on a tricycle."

"I learned that first-hand," I said. "Diamond-and-rockers was as high as I got, but there were ten days when every officer was down and I had the company. Or what was left of the company."

"Weren't you pretty young to be a top sergeant?"

"Sir, there wasn't a hill in Italy as old as I was."

"You've seen the elephant, all right. Sorry I asked the question. Were you ever with a British outfit, by the way?"

"Not when I was sober, no. Why?"

"When you walked by here the other morning you gave me one of those quiver-me-armpit British salutes."

"Oh. Well, we used to throw those once in a while as a gag. I'm damned if I know why I slipped one to you, though."

"Tell you something, son. I'd never seen you before. Didn't know you from Adam. But when you brought your arm up like that all I could think of was 'Culloden'—because sometimes your father'd salute me that way. I call it mighty odd, your doing the same thing, almost as though you were a ghost of the living. Not that you're Jamie's spit and image, not by a long chalk. A little around the eyes, perhaps. He was a fine figure of a man, Jamie Culloden. Still is, more than likely."

"Better-looking than I ever was, or will be," I said.

"Maybe, maybe not," Fletcher said. "I never saw you at twenty-three, or Jamie at forty-five."

"At any age," I told him. "Take my word for it. Or my grandmother's—my mother's mother. She wasn't very fond of my father, but she often said he was the handsomest man she ever set eyes on."

"Why didn't she like him?"

I shrugged. "Why did Father throw you British salutes?"

"Devilment. You see, I was a lance-jack in the British Army from 1915 until the fall of '17, when the Americans put in for me. They gave me a commission and made me an instructor in trench warfare. But I'd been with the Limeys so long that most of the time I forgot where I was and saluted like an old sweat, even after I'd gone to the 312th as a company commander. They really drill you, the Limeys do. Didn't Jamie ever tell you that I'd been with them?"

"I'm not sure," I said. "If he did, I've forgotten."

Fletcher scowled and rubbed his chin. "Well, it's over and done with now, Sam. Long ago and far away. And we're tired of wars and all that goes with them." He pushed the bottle toward me. "Put a head on it, son."

"No, thank you, sir. That'd be too much of a good thing."

"Suit yourself. Incidentally, I wrote Chávez-Trueba to send you a case. So if you should have a birthday party, my advice is: don't serve it to your guests. Don't even let one of 'em smell a cork—unless you're bucking for twelve empty bottles by midnight."

"Speaking of birthdays—you're still planning a trip across the border?"

"Got to be with my boys once in a while. Sure."

He had touched upon something I wanted to learn more about. Dr. Inskilling had been on the point of describing a terrible event in which Fletcher's sons were involved when Joy Durwood made her entrance at the Gutierrez *finca*. I hesitated, then asked: "Can't they come and visit you?"

"They can't get away, either of them. But I don't mind the trip. I'm footloose. Always have been."

I found myself wondering if the sons couldn't get away because they were serving twenty-years-to-life sentences in some maximum-security prison. It was a mean thought. I hated it as soon as it sidled up and introduced itself; and when I refused to shake hands it slunk away. I slunk away, too—as far as I could get from the subject of Fletcher's sons. "Do you mind if I let Father know I met you? I haven't written him since we came down here."

Pleasure lit up the old man's face. "Would you now, Sam? Why,

I'd like that. Lord! It's been nearly fifty years. You in touch with him often?"

"Well, I answer his letters, if and when I get them, and he does the same for me. Neither of us ever went in much for family correspondence. How'd you happen to settle in Maldita?"

"Oh, for one reason or another. Or maybe for no particular reason. It doesn't mean much any more. But you do, Sam. Let's hear about you."

"There's nothing to tell."

"I'll be judge of that. It took forty-five years to get *you* here, and I'd like to know what went into the getting."

The only thing I could do was defer to him, so I crowded on as much canvas as my life would take without the sticks snapping off at deck level, and gave him three quarters of an hour of myself. I held back on a few people and incidents, of course, and skipped over certain periods where the world I recalled was a world in fog, and where things done were seen as though through a frost-rimed window. Still, the picture I gave the old man was certainly as complete as the one my handful of friends keep under lock and key, even though I wasn't especially keen, at the moment, on poking among the shards of that smashed black-figure masterpiece, the Culloden Calyx.

When I finally wound down I could see that Fletcher had wound down, too. He seemed more interested in studying the texture of the table than anything else. I didn't think he was slipping into the kind of spell that had engulfed him on my previous visit, but I certainly was overstaying my present welcome. "Well, sir, I'll be on my way," I said, standing up. "You look a little tired. Why don't you stretch out on the bed for a while?"

Fletcher nodded listlessly. "I'll take a short nap," he murmured. "The damned old woman ought to be back. You trot on home, boy."

"Thank you for everything, sir," I said. He paid no attention.

I met the damned old woman, who was clutching a missal and several rosaries, as she came scuttling, purged of sin, through the hacienda's awful entrance. She gibbered what I guessed was a greeting at me and darted into the house I'd just left. As I reached the road I could hear her yelling at Fletcher. When I heard him yell back I felt easier in my mind.

It was hot inside the car. I opened every window I could reach without slipping a disc, lit a cigarette, and frowned through the windshield at Sunday while I considered where to go. I could've returned to the Matthews *finca,* of course, and perhaps watched Lalage redo the breakfast dishes while Joy and I added up the times we'd met Robert Taylor. But I'd had my day's ration of George Simmons, and he too might be returning to the scene of the crime, his clothes changed and his face smooth from shaving, except for one small cut below the nose. I could even have dropped in on the Gages, which at least one person had told me was what people constantly did. Unfortunately, the Gages would also be there, which spoiled that prospect. Or, as a last resort, I could traipse home and spend the afternoon feeling as depressed as a one-eared sow that'd just been given a synthetic silk purse. As I'm a sucker for synthetics, I decided to let depression turn the grindstone for what remained of Sunday. Home I went.

In the kitchen I made a *cordon bleu* ham sandwich, washed it down with cold vintage coffee, and then attempted to take a nap myself.

I won't say that I woke up so refreshed that I went around smashing Coca-Cola bottles. I tossed and turned while a twitching clutch of predatory fancies ranged my head and snarled and spat and bloodied their claws on the flanks of the bovine depression I'd planned to milk dry. If I'd been aware of them earlier I'd've heaved them, unborn, into the Río Maldorado as I crossed the bridge from Fletcher's. But I was mother as well as father to them; I'd've had to hit the drink with my own creatures. And now it was too late. They prowled through my skull and made sleek, evil plans, while they schooled themselves in loathing.

Most of all, they loathed their parents—both of me. No wonder I couldn't sleep, with a spawn like that loose in my brain pan.

◎ Although the bathroom and balcony doors were open, the Gutierrez horn was muffled by the noise cold water makes while being transferred from a tap to a human face. It was a quarter past five, and I was groggy from an afternoon of playing Laocoön with my kindle of hell cats in a messy bedroom. The status of my depression had improved, too; it was no longer interested in simple squatter's rights, but was erecting a skyscraper where its shanty had been.

As soon as I could I plodded out to the balcony and headed for the patio below. The sky was beginning to go gray at the temples, and the Gutierrez station wagon appeared to be sinking by the stern.

The tail gate was down, and Lencho and Jock, under Polly's direction, were pulling out what belonged to the Cullodens from a jumble of luggage, cardboard cartons, and newspaper-wrapped bundles. Almost everyone seemed tired but triumphant. The exceptions were Jock and Nan Young, who were acting surly and seven miles apart.

I did my damnedest to be cheerful when I reached the dust-dimmed Buick. "Well, Angela," I said to a front-seat window full of earrings and necklaces, "did you leave anything for next week's gringos?"

"Not a splinter," Angela said. "We couldn't've got there at a better moment. My little man'd been on a buying trip and he wasn't even unloaded. Scads of the most beautiful *santos* you ever saw."

"Cheap, too," Helen Young chimed in. "Considering what they'd bring in the States."

"Tepectlán's a lovely old town, Sam," Polly said. "And the motel we stayed at is the best motel I've ever been in, bar none. Instead of rooms they have guest cottages, with a fireplace and free wood in each one. There's entertainment every Saturday night, too. Last night they had some folk dancers."

"That's nice." I kissed her cheek. "I've been wondering what went on in motels these days, now that they've stopped calling themselves tourist cabins and've started putting two beds in a room."

"You came to Mexico by car, Sam," Bruce Young said. "Didn't you stay in motels on the way?"

"Of course we did, Bruce," Polly said. "Sam's talking through his hat."

"Sombrero," I told her. "And I do like a motel, Bruce, if it's got one of those vibrating beds. You know, you put a quarter in the slot and lie down and the thing begins to shimmy like your sister Kate. It relaxes the hell out of me after seven or eight hours on the road. But I don't think a sombrero full of provincial buck-and-wingers, yipping through the Mexican hat dance, would have the same effect, somehow."

"The trouble with my husband," Polly said as she squeezed my arm affectionately, "is that he was too young for the turkey trot and now he's too old for the Watusi. A terpsichorean washout, that's my Sam."

"I guess I got everything, Mother," Jock said. He finger-counted what had been dragged from the Buick. "Yeah, that's all." *All* consisted of a suitcase, an overnight bag, four cardboard cartons, and a couple of whatever was wrapped in newspapers. Jock lifted the two biggest cartons by the cord that secured them, said, "Thanks for everything, Sra. Gutierrez," and made for the exterior staircase at the far end of the patio, the one that led to the living room. At the same time Lencho slapped me on the back and gave me a smile that would've blown any woman under sixty sky-high. He slid into the driver's seat while Polly was telling Angela and the Youngs what fun it had been. Women have fun in funny ways.

"I'll be in touch, Polly dear," Angela said. The Youngs added something that my poor ears missed.

After the Buick had chugged off Polly turned to me and let the starch go out of her.

"Tired?" I asked.

"*Dead.*" Her eyes strayed to the cartons that remained. "Wait'll you see what I bought, darling. Where's Concepción?"

"You gave her and Luis off till Monday, remember?"

"So I did. Be a sweet and bring that other big carton and the two parcels up to the living room, will you? Jock can take care of the suitcases. And the little carton's his." She started for the staircase.

We trailed her, me and my load. "What happened between Jock and Nan?"

"Oh, Lord! He wouldn't tell me. Perhaps he'll tell you."

Jock trotted down the staircase as we ascended. "Did the saints come marching in for you, too?" I asked as he squeezed past us.

"That guy doesn't sell only *santos,*" he said. "I'd like to show you what I got, Father. Later, if you can find a minute."
"There ought to be one stashed away somewhere. Stick around."
Polly did her own unwrapping of *santos,* sitting cross-legged on the living-room floor with her shoes off. She hauled them out into the light, fondled them, discussed them, and then laid them delicately on the hand-woven wool *tapete* that took up most of the floor space. I sprawled on the sofa, secretly holding hands with my depression.

From time to time I vented mild grunts of approval, whenever they were indicated, but without being able to work up a real lather over Polly's busted acquisitions. She surprised me, though, with her no-nonsense knowledge of who each saint was, and where in Mexico the little Tepectlán man had found him, and what the approximate resale value would be in New York. Women practice economics in funny ways, too.

Things reached the point where I had to ask her: "Did you buy them as an investment?"
"Not really. But I'd be a fool not to know what they're worth. Want to know what I paid for them? The whole collection?"
"No."
"Three hundred and eighty-six dollars."
"Didn't hear a word."
"Angela spent over a thousand."
"What else could she do? She was born in Pittsburgh."
"You like my *santos,* don't you, Sam?"
"I like them because you like them. Besides, every red-blooded American man ought to have a home that looks like a wrecked church."

Polly came over and sat beside me on the sofa. "Did you miss me?" She rested her head on my shoulder.
"You know it."
"What did you do while I was gone?"
"Well, yesterday, I went into town around six. I bumped into Luz Salvatierra at the newsstand and had a cup of coffee with her, and after that I went up to the Dam of the Bees to—"

"Alone?"

"Yes, alone. And I came home alone. And I woke up alone. Any other pertinent questions?"

Polly left my shoulder. "All I meant was that you might've gone to the fiesta with the Salvatierras."

"Don't worry. Even the Salvatierras didn't go with the Salvatierras."

The strings of her curiosity had been plucked. "Translation, please."

"Well, this little Salvatierra went to lark it, this little Salvatierra stayed home, this little Durwood had long-pig, this little—"

"Are you trying to say he took the Durwood woman to the fiesta and left his wife home?"

"Not trying to say. Saying. Except that he didn't leave Luz home. She didn't want to go in the first place."

"Did she tell you that?"

"She practically hit me over the head with it. The Durwood woman, as you call her, is not making the Salvatierra woman very happy."

"Is José Salvatierra having an affair with the Durwood woman?"

"Lalage Delmore was playing *dueña* for them at the fiesta, so I'd say yes."

"Oh, you saw them up there?"

"Let's say they saw me. The few words we exchanged had no importance whatsoever. I was on my way back to the car."

"Did you see anyone else?"

"Only our friend Mrs. Gage. She was taking fifty per cent of her brood to where the action was, and managed to throw a last-minute block into me. She had clothes on, incidentally. So'd the kids."

"Where was her husband?"

"Back in the dressing room, I suppose, waiting for the half to end. They were two-platooning the fiesta." I didn't bother to mention Rose Gage's invitation to a refresher course in contact sports. "And my last act of the day was to murder a scorpion. According to my lawyer, I can beat the rap on a plea of self-defense. I was in bed, with the lights out, by ten thirty."

"And today?"

The question period was going on too long; the referee was about to blow his whistle. "Today I listened to voices, and finally I—"

Her eyes lit up. "You started the book, didn't you?" I thought she was going to hug me.

"I listened to voices, that's all," I snapped. "I didn't start anything. So don't *you* start anything, Simone Legree." It was a cruel and stupid thing to say, but self-pity had slithered into my melancholia; I resented being the only depressed person in the room.

Polly quietly left the sofa. She began to rewrap her *santos,* working on her knees with a pallid deliberation that meant she was seething inside. We were both unhappy now, in our different ways. When she at last had something to say she avoided my eyes while she spoke: "You never will get started on it, either, until somebody's dead."

The remark caught me off-balance. "You have a customer in mind for the mortuary?" I asked. "Or any reason for making a crack like that?"

She kept her face averted. "I've been through this before, and that's reason enough. Your memory's as bad as your manners."

"I can remember whatever's *happened* to me." I stalked to the fireplace, passing behind her as I crossed the room. "So suppose you explain that 'until somebody's dead' line."

"All right, I will." She stayed on her knees, but swung her body around to confront me. "Before your last novel you were going through the same dreary routine. Can't get started. Got a block. Can't get started. Got a block. Then one day you decided you had to have a change of scene, because Frank Steinmetz had invited you to pack into the Sierras with him. And the next thing I knew you were calling me long-distance from some sheriff's office and—"

"Why don't you say I pushed him off that ledge?"

"Because you didn't, and no one ever could've imagined that you did. But I will say that as soon as you got home you sat right down and began pounding away. No more 'can't get started,' no more 'got a block.' You didn't even bother to unpack."

"Frank's death was a shock that broke the log jam in my head. Ask any psychiatrist."

"Maybe so, but *I* couldn't've rushed into a novel after watching a friend die. And so horribly."

"Frank Steinmetz wasn't a friend of mine. I didn't really like him, in case you're interested."

"Then why'd you go on a crazy pack trip with him, just the two of you? With that guide who was drunk all the time?"

"Business. Frank was an important man."

"Frank Steinmetz? I can think of a dozen independent producers who were more important than Frank Steinmetz. And still are."

"He was important to *me*—at the time, anyway. You know damned well he'd tied up *The Red and the Black,* and how much I wanted the screenplay assignment, especially when I'd been drawing a blank with the novel. 'Until somebody's dead.' What's gotten into you, Polly, coming out with a fool remark like that?"

Polly picked up an unusually ugly *santo* and stared at it. "I'm sorry," she said. "I'm tired, that's all. I told you I was tired."

I opened my mouth, but nothing came out; there was nothing left to come. I'd done what I set out to do, and there was no use hanging around any longer. Polly paid no attention when I left the room.

I took my depression to the river terrace, where we watched the Río Maldorado and listened to its lulling sound, but without being lulled at all. After a while I wandered upstairs and halfway along the balcony to Jock's room. He sat on the edge of his bed, studying his own purchases, which he'd lined up on the counterpane. The newspapers they'd been wrapped in were scattered over the floor.

"Hi," he said, as I paused in the doorway. He hadn't thrown off his gloom, either. For once we were meeting on the same emotional level.

I leaned against the doorjamb. "You and Nan have a fight?"

"Huh? No, we didn't have a fight. Everything's fine."

"You never used to clam up on me, Jock."

"Yeah, but—ah, the thing was, she was writing to this Ohio joker, and she even had the gall to wave his picture under my nose. You should've seen it. A big blond slob. Buster Bloat. Freshman team offensive end."

"Bigger than you?"

"Not as tall. Heavier, maybe—but he won't be for long, you can bet your sweet arse."

"Who writes your dialogue? Someone from Grove Press?"

"Sorry, Father. I don't know where I picked up that word 'sweet.' "

Suddenly we both burst out laughing, and, laughter-flailed, our depressions escaped through the roof, fracturing their skulls as they did so.

"Jock, you've got to learn when you've got it made," I said. "You're in a perfect position to intercept a pass while Cousin Offensive's still running his pattern. Near as I can make out, it's a lovely high, soft one. She's floating straight into your arms, for God's sake, and you've got six long weeks to gather her in. And if you can't intercept this pass and lug it back to pay dirt, through a broken field, in six weeks, I reckon I'll have to trade you for a lost golf ball. But until then—" I gestured at the line-up on the bed. "You got yourself quite a group."

"Great, aren't they? Only twenty bucks for the whole lot. Sra. Gutierrez said I got a real bargain. I guess the guy did it because she and Mother bought so much other junk. Want to hear about 'em?"

It didn't matter if I wanted to or not. When Jock becomes enthusiastic, your smartest move is to make for the nearest storm cellar and hope that the tornado won't do as much damage as last month's did.

He had seven of the small clay figurines known as "pretty ladies." Four were from a place called Chupicuáro. These had elaborate headdresses and wildly slanted eyes, reminiscent of windshield wipers on a spree. The others, including a two-headed charmer, came from Tlatilco in the Valley of Mexico, and seemed to represent the final stages of elephantiasis. A couple of the figurines lacked a leg, and one of the Chupicuáro quartette had nothing below her navel but wishful thinking and air.

The clay females were flanked by four pieces of copper, shaped like blunt arrowheads and beaten so thin that they bent under normal breathing. Two others, looking like the business end of battle-axes for midget knights, were thicker, heavier, and by no means as finely beaten. According to Jock, these copper artifacts were as near to actual money as the pre-Columbians ever came. They'd also pounded gold into the same shapes, but most of those had somehow passed through the Pillars of Hercules in an easterly direction. The Conquistadors were not in the habit of leaving gold where they found it.

After Jock ran out of information I gave him some in return, about Levinson and his infernal machine and his willingness to have a companion while he sought for civilizations long since gone to earth. Jock's enthusiasm was tripled on the spot. "Can I go out with Mr. Levinson tomorrow morning?" he asked eagerly.

"I don't see why not, if you can find out where he lives and can get out of bed to make it there in time. Nine o'clock. Levinson's a good, pleasant man, from what I saw of him. And if you miss him, you can always make arrangements for Tuesday or Wednesday. In the meantime, what're your plans for that bedful of women and wampum?"

"Oh, they're the base for a general collection. Then later I'd like to specialize. Make sense to you?"

"*Eh*-uh. You know, I once upon a time started a collection of females, but I ended up specializing in your mother. I've never regretted it, either. As a matter of fact, I think I'll go tell her right now that I've never regretted it."

Jock followed me to the door. "Doesn't she know?"

"We have to keep reminding 'em," I said over my shoulder. I turned left, and behind me I heard Jock bounding along the balcony in the opposite direction. I couldn't figure out how he'd locate Levinson, but from past experience I knew damned well he would.

The *santos*, still waiting to be rewrapped, were where I'd last seen them, but Polly wasn't. I went back to the master bedroom. She lay on the ancient bed, gazing blindly at the ceiling. "Polly—" I said. She ignored me.

"I'm sorry, Polly," I said, before the silence had a chance to implode. "I had two rotten days without you, and they made me depressed. Damn it, when I get depressed I want everybody to join the Club. I'm really honest-to-God sorry, Polly. Please believe me."

She left me sweating for almost a minute, then sent a faint smile in my direction. "Most of our days've been good ones, Sam," she said. "We do better than we deserve, I guess."

If you've been married long enough, these rudenesses and roughnesses, such as Polly and I had been using to hurt each other, come with the house; suddenly they're with you, suddenly they aren't. I sat beside her on the bed, pulled her nearest hand toward me, kissed it, and put it back where it'd been. "Seems like I got in the way of my telling you," I said casually, "but I met our friend Flay-a-*chair*. Only his name's Fletcher, Thomas Flint Fletcher, and he comes from Vermont, and he's eighty-five years old."

"Eighty-five! Good Heavens! Can he walk and talk?"

"Honey, he can outtalk me if he tries, and outwalk me without trying. But what surprised me about him—and this'll be tough to swallow—it was for me—is that he was Father's company commander in the First World War."

"Oh, Sam, I don't believe it. That's not possible!"

"God's my witness, Polly. He was."

"Why, I—why, that's simply the most fascinating thing—coincidence—I ever heard of. Oh, Sam, if only your father could—"

"I thought of that, too," I broke in. "So I told the old boy I'd write Father and say I saw Captain Fletcher."

Polly, as soon as she'd gasped, exclaimed. "Sam, how *could* you say a thing like that to the poor old man? Your father's been dead nine years."

After a moment I said: "Don't worry about it. Fletcher's on his last legs. He'll forget."

"But you just made him sound healthy, with his walking and talking and all. What's the matter with him?"

I frowned at the palms of my hands. "He ran out of steam shovels."

"Oh, God!" Polly rolled her eyes toward the ceiling beams. "You've got me all tangled up."

"That's how I like you best," I said. "All tangled up. What're you going to do about it?"

She considered what she might do about it, then stretched, showed her teeth like a smiling kitten, and held out her arms to me. "Come here, Sam Culloden, damn you."

I came there, and we kissed each other. And after a while she asked: "You want to know something?"

"I'm not sure. I know almost as much as a man can bear, as it is."

"Remember me telling you that as soon as we got back from Tepectlán Angela'd take Lencho off someplace else?"

"I remember. As though it were yesterday."

"Well, I was right. The Gutierrezes are driving to Mexico City tomorrow morning early. They'll be in Cuernavaca, too. Angela hopes to stay away for at least two weeks."

"Did you drag me down on this unmade bed to tell me that?"

"What do *you* think, dirty old Sam?"

I thought she hadn't.

I was right, too.

❧ Five

Play That *Little* *Tune* on Your *Krafft-Ebing,* *Baby*

"Did you show my note to your wife?" Marian Delmore watched me carefully from across the coffee table in her wall-of-glass house. The light that was filtered through those sour-milk bricks reminded me of what reaches skin divers three fathoms down. Her racehorse legs were crossed and she was swinging one foot back and forth like seaweed in a changing tide.

"I only show Polly the passionate notes from women who want assignations with me," I said. "They keep her from taking her husband for granted."

The Delmore smile was automatic and minor. "What made you think I didn't want an assignation?"

"What makes you think I could've imagined anything of the kind?"

The smile was whisked off. "You're a difficult man, Mr. Culloden."

"Since you seem to know me well enough to comment on my character, you might as well call me Sam." Had she been twenty years younger, and I twenty years stupider, I might've replied to the message of that swinging foot; but I was already giving her more than I wanted to give her, and more than she deserved. "And now that you know me well enough to call me Sam, you know me well enough to tell me what I'm doing here, when I could be hunting for the grave of Benedict Arnold, which I do at the drop of a cocked hat—no matter where I am, or where he was buried."

"I want your advice, Sam. That's all." Her frequently lifted face was so taut that I could've played handball on it.

"Fire away," I said. "Don't leave me here in the dark." I checked up on the milky wall-that-was-a-window. "Make that a thick fog."

"You don't like this new little hideaway?" She uncrossed her legs as she leaned forward to open a marble box on the coffee table.

"Look, Marian—now that you've put us on an informal basis—I'm not the man from *Architectural Forum*. I'm Mr. Anthony Culloden, called Mr. Anthony by those who know him, a kind of two-legged ear—and you want my advice on something or other. Well, I've enough advice in me, covering every possible subject—and as long as I don't have to draw on it myself—to give any number of people conniption fits. In your case, I reckon the Something-or-other is Lalage."

"Yes, Lalage." Marian frowned at the cigarette she'd taken from the marble box. "She likes you, Sam. People've told me so."

This is where I came in, isn't it? I thought. Aloud I said: "What's she done this time? Set up housekeeping with an iguana?"

" 'Snake' is the better word."

That was the problem, then. And now that I knew what the problem was, I owed it to old copies of *Child Life* to see that Marian Delmore should sweat a little longer. "Eve made the snake scene first," I said. "But the ménage broke up when her husband came home early one year and caught her trying on fig leaves for size."

"This is a waste of time," Marian said, and snatched up a lighter from the coffee table. "I should've known. It's impossible for you to be serious." She tried to work the lighter. She failed.

"Not necessarily." I took the lighter out of her hand, flicked the wheel once, and lit her cigarette. "If it's high seriousness you're after, you can have it, all the way to the stratosphere. So let's open the ball, highly seriously, with a question or two from me. Such as: Why do you come to a stranger for advice about your own child? And:

Where've you been all these years, when she must've needed a mother? Dismasted and drifting?"

"Just what has that girl told you about me?" Marian's mercury bid fair to bust the thermometer.

"I had a map of the entire Delmore country after I'd talked three minutes with you," I said. "Your daughter's not involved." I got to my feet, if only to prove that two could anger as cheaply as one. "Too bad Maldita doesn't have telephones. This might've been done at a distance."

Suddenly I wasn't standing alone. "Please, Sam," Marian was saying, "let's not be at swords' points. I need your advice. But you have to be patient with me." It was amazing how quickly the anger had left her voice. The only explanation I could come up with was that it'd gone back for reinforcements.

"Sorry," I said. "It's been a bad couple of weeks, more or less, and I'm apt to be edgy—in the mornings especially." I sat down again. As soon as she'd followed my example I went on. "What're your present complications with—with Ugly, as I think you call her?"

She blushed. I had to look twice to be sure, but she'd actually blushed. "That's what Saint calls her. It's not very pretty, I'll admit, and I shouldn't've used it the way I did on the night of the buffet. I'd had a couple of drinks, though." She took a long drag from her cigarette. "So had you."

"Only because table-tipping works best in a haunted house." Before she began to question psychic phenomena I said hurriedly: "Never mind, let's get on with the problem at hand."

"Ah, yes," she sighed, "let's. Sam—and do be honest—what can you tell me about Mrs. Lancaster?"

"Nothing. I don't know a Mrs. Lancaster."

"She's been using her maiden name. Durwood."

"That's more like it," I said. "We've met."

"I thought so. Well, she was married to a man named Robert Lancaster, from Phoenix, Arizona. He's a builder who also speculates, and very cleverly too, in real estate. Perhaps he's not so clever where women are concerned but, women apart, he's made millions."

"They're good at that sort of thing in Phoenix," I said. "Or were." I helped myself to a cigarette from the coffee table sarcophagus. "But as for Mrs. Lancaster, or Miss Durwood, I can't tell you anything about her, for the simple reason that I don't know anything about her."

"You introduced her to Lalage."

"Oh, that. Well, we were all on this bridge, and you know how bridge friendships are. Once you're on land you never see the people again."

"Is she a Lesbian?"

"Who?"

"This Joy Lancaster. Durwood. Whatever her name is."

"If she were, it'd be a body blow to heterosexual relations." I lit my cigarette and I took my time about it. I used my own lighter, too, and as I returned it to my pocket I asked: "Thought of scratching Lalage lately?"

Marian must have been wondering what made her daughter itch, because a lot of seconds went by before she concluded that I might have information that'd been denied to her. "What do you mean?" was the way she put it.

"Oh, in case there's a Lesbian tickle," I said, as casually as I could, thinking: Play *that* little tune on your Krafft-Ebing, baby.

"What a horrible thing to say!" A regular chameleon, the Widow Delmore. She'd gone dead white.

"Not as horrible as finding it out for sure."

"Lalage doesn't even know what sex is."

"She went to school, didn't she?"

"A great many, but—"

"Then don't kid yourself. She knows what sex is. One school's all it takes."

The numbness that came over her while this idea sank in was almost visual. "Do *you* think she's a Lesbian?"

"Certainly not."

"But you just said—"

"All I did was suggest. Perversions were being tossed back and forth, so I figured they might as well be tossed in every direction. She's your daughter. It's your job to find out what she is. Not that you'd find out from her, of course."

For no other reason than that the cul-de-sac interview was becoming a drag, I'd given Marian the opening she wanted. She was through it before I'd had time to drop my dulled chisel. "Ah, you've hit on the real trouble, Sam," she said. "Lalage won't ever tell me a thing. We simply have no communication whatsoever. Why, I don't believe she even sleeps here any more. And so I've been hoping— I realize it's an imposition, but I *am* hoping—that you'd do me the great favor of finding out precisely what she's doing with Mrs. Lancas—Miss Durwood, that is. Will you do that for me?"

"No."

"For her, then. Lalage."

"I wouldn't even do it for myself. If you want a company spy, try old McDermott. He looks moldy enough to get a rise from it."

"Oh-hh-hhh . . ." With a dying-fall exhalation, Marian Delmore turned in her Favor-Asking Suit. The reinforced anger returned, and visible now for the first time was the I-Have-Several-Million-Dollars-Therefore-You-Don't-Count attitude that she'd kept in sable-covered mothballs since my arrival. She rose to her feet with a richness. "Thank you for coming here, anyway," she said. Every word was a stalactite.

I got to my own feet with the disarming simplicity of a man who plans to shock the Virginia House of Burgesses by bringing forward a few examples that George III might study with profit. "Not at all," I said. "This is my favorite way to spend a morning. You must've known that."

As I opened the door she said: "I'm going to send the creature away, you understand? There are places where they'll keep any number of eyes on her. And a net on her too, if they have to."

"And *quis custodiet ipsos custodes?*" I asked as I shut the door behind me. "You bitch," I added, addressing the nearest tree. Trust Old Slew-Foot Sam to make a limp exit via a Latin tagline. Latin to Marian Delmore, if it were anything, would only be what you

tacked in front of "-American" when discussing *bossa nova* rhythms.
Why did I waste my breath on the subtleties of a dead language,
when I had all that lovely mule skinner's Anglo-Saxon stored up in
me, the judicious use of which during the 1943–45 period had made
my life a charmed one?

No more than a tank of oxygen and three B12 injections were
required to get me across the Delmore patio and through the Delmore main house. Then I sat in the car until my sea-level heart
stopped taking offense at my heartlessness in bringing it with me to
this dishearteningly high plateau. As soon as I'd convinced myself
that the insurance company wouldn't have to take to biting its nails
and computers for another six months, or at least another sixty
minutes, I made up my mind to look in on the Durwood establish-
ment. But not to check up on Lalage. And not out of perverse
curiosity. Not, as a matter of fact, for any logical reason—except
that I had to go to the post office sometime before noon, and I might
as well do it the hard way.

◎ The cord I pulled rang a bell inside the prisonlike gates of the
Matthews *finca*. A wizened and somnolent woman, whom I took to
be the maid Juanita, eventually opened the door in the right-hand
gate and passed me through. Then a very tall young gringa, whom
I knew from experience to be Lalage Delmore and whom I greeted
as such, passed me all the way into the living room of the house.
There I found a turquoise-eyed divorcee named Joy Durwood sitting with a man I recognized, to his embarrassment, as Bruce Young,
a professor of American history (with tenure). He had his clothes on,
bless his academic heart.

"Why, *Sam!* Sam *Cullo*den!" Joy hurried to me, wrapped both of
her arms around one of mine and squeezed. "I'd about decided you
were lost and *gone*."

"*Eh*-uh, I thought it was time to come by and count bedrooms,"
I said. "Hi, Bruce. What do you hear from General Hooker's head-
quarters? The night shift all rosy and r'arin' to go?"

"I've been out of touch with Joe Hooker lately. He hurt his head listening to a battle." Bruce had climbed out of his embarrassment as quickly as he'd fallen in.

"I was going to give you *one* more day, you *wretch* you, Sam," Joy said, "and then I'd've—oh, yes, indeed I *would*." She tugged me toward Young. "What's your opinion of a man, Bruce dear, who gives you a really *ador*able present and then never shows his *face* again to get his proper thank-you-kind-sirs?"

"Sounds like a rotter to me," Bruce said.

"Not to mention a cad," I added. "Hooker wouldn't have me on his staff. 'Got to draw the line on caddishness somewhere,' he said."

"Who's this General Hooker?" Joy asked. "Is he in Vietnam, Bruce?"

"Sam knows."

"In Tokyo," I said. "He's masterminding the Rest and Recuperation bit and the International Date Line. A CIA type. *Our* CIA, of course, not Theirs. At least, I think it's ours."

"There you are, Joy. I told you Sam'd know. Sam's been shot at."

"I'm not surprised," Joy said sullenly. "Men ought to be *lazy* in the morning and not quite so *smart*. They're always trying to be so goddamned *clever* from nine to twelve. It's only after they've had that first *business* martini that they start being *lovable* again."

"I didn't come here to be clever," I said. "Not for free. Not when I get paid for it at home."

"You didn't *really* come by to count *bed*rooms, did you, Sam dear?" Joy hadn't bothered to detach herself from my arm.

"Well, strictly speaking, I wanted to see the damage the earthquake did. That was in a bedroom, wasn't it?"

"Yes, but that was *years!* It's been fixed *ever* so!"

"Is that a nice way of hinting you don't want me to see the bedroom?"

"But, *Sam,* you sugar *thing,* what's the—?" A hank of hair had fallen in front of one eye, and a quick toss of her head put it back where it belonged. A quick toss of a mental coin took place at the same time, it seemed, for now she clutched my arm tighter and said: "Of *course* you can see my bedroom. I'll even lead you there my*self,* just like old Daniel into the *lion's*. You'll excuse us a *few,* Bruce dear, won't you? And Lalage, you'd best check on the coffee. Juanita'll never learn *when* to turn things off, and I *swear* I can smell that sweet goddamned stuff burning *up*."

Then, having set in motion or immobilized everyone else who was present, Joy led me where Fate willed—out of the living room, down a dark and narrow corridor, through a gloomy and apparently empty room, and along another dark, narrow corridor which brought us, blinking, to the *finca's* master, and only usable, bedroom.

"*Here* you are, Sam dear," Joy said, with what was, I thought, relief, "the only *decent* spot in the en*tire*. The rest of it's simply un*bear*able, even the living room. I spend as much time as I *can* here, and *damn* the earthquakes."

I went forward a few steps. Around me was more space than any two retiring people could possibly need, unless they preferred running obstacle races over modern reproductions of Spanish Colonial furniture to eight satisfactory hours in the sack. The bedroom was, I calculated, forty feet long and twenty-five wide. It had a twenty-foot-high ceiling, too. The three-quarter-size twin beds were covered with navy-blue spreads, on each of which a copy of the design known as the Eye of God had been embroidered in muted and restful colors.

"I can't understand why we never met in Hollywood." Joy, addressing my back, could've been another woman. The inconsequential quality was gone from her voice; it had a different timbre. Delilah had returned to the painted couch, and the Sirens were back on their rocks. "I used to be on the Coast for what amounted to six or seven weeks of the year, and it was parties every night and double that on Sunday. You must've gone to parties now and then."

I strolled to the nearer of the pair of great windows opposite the beds. "Oh, now and then I felt a shotgun jabbing my spine," I said. "That's when I went."

Through the not-too-clean panes of glass I saw a brownish lawn forgotten by God, blotched with flower beds neglected by man. After thirty yards or so this glum and orphaned greenery was cut off from any hope of escape by the wall, which was also rebuffing the attempt of a line of scraggly trees to reach the sunlight.

A door, whose function I couldn't fathom, was set in the wall. In the United States I'd've taken for granted that it led to an incinerator area, but in Maldita, where the acme of cleanliness was to dump your slops in the Río Maldorado, that theory was self-exploded before I'd finished scrawling it on the blackboard. If the door wanted to be mysterious, however, it had my permission. I wasn't planning to bother it, coming or going.

"Joe Salvatierra said you worked at Metro. I don't see how you could help not running into my husband. Gorham Rangeley. I was married to him for six *whole*."

"No, I never met him—but then I only worked at Metro once in a great while, four times, maybe, in seventeen years. How is old Joe, by the way? I haven't met him lately, either."

"Who *has?*" Joy came close to hissing the word. "He's *such* a silly damned fool. I told him to stop neglecting his business."

I had no comment to make on her status as an adviser, so I continued my study of the terrain. Not far beyond the wall a hill rose up at an easy angle. It was crowned by a clump of squat, umbrella-like trees.

"Sam—you didn't come in here *just* to see the bedroom, did you? Or that *dreary* view?" There was impatience in her tone, which made me wonder why she hadn't joined me at the window, but which didn't persuade me to turn around.

"That Handsome Dan you arrived with, Joy," I said casually, "—you should've let him beat his own path to the bus station. Why didn't you?"

This was hardly the response she'd expected, so her reply was by no means instantaneous. After a while, though, she got around to saying: "He wasn't that kind of a man," which left me several miles behind where I'd started from.

The best defense is an attack, they say—a premise that used to cost the French several thousand men every so often. French casualties notwithstanding, I considered a discreet attack the better part of valor—in this instance, anyway—so I pressed on with mine. "Another thing that's bothered me," I said, "is that night you dropped in on the Gutierrezes. You acted as though I were a stranger."

Joy's reply came quickly enough this time. "How did you expect me to act, when you hadn't told your wife that we'd met?"

The view became empty of interest. I swung around. "How'd you know I didn't tell her?"

Her smile mocked me a little and pitied me more. No words went with the smile.

"Woman's intuition again, I suppose?" I said uncomfortably.

"Man's lack of it, *I'd* say." The smile hung on.

I didn't like what I was hearing, which was a not too indirect way of letting me know that my Mask didn't fit well. This was a train of thought I didn't enjoy being on, so before it picked up too much speed I hopped off the end of the caboose and heaved myself on an empty flatcar of a freight that was chuffing in the opposite direction. "That was a great night for intuitive women," I said. "I suppose you noticed?"

The smile's grip failed and it tumbled from her face, yet her answer was incisive—if a trifle oblique. "Joe Salvatierra's a fool, remember?"

"Give the Devil his due, though. He did help you get this bedroom put together again. Otherwise, you'd still be curling up on sofas or hard hotel beds or—"

"Lalage told you *that,* of course. She talks too much, our *little* Lalage, and without understanding a goddamned *thing.*"

"Why, Miss Durwood, honey, she worships at your shrine."

"All *over* my shrine." Etna was beginning to rumble faintly, far below the human landscape.

"When it comes to shrines, Joy, have you seen the rest of the Gutierrez house yet? Now *there's* a bed for—"

"The Gutierrezes're away."

"They'll be back within the week."

After a long time she said slowly: "You'd love to be able to read my mind, wouldn't you? Or even *think* you could?"

"Well, we do have a lot in common. For instance, did you ever meet Robert Taylor on the set?"

"Robert *Tay*—? What's *he* got to do with it, for Christ's sake?"

"For all practical purposes, nothing. But we have a great deal in common, Joy, you and I. So much in common, in fact, that half the time—intuition aside—I do know what you're thinking."

I turned back to the window and waited. Then I heard her say: "What about the other half of the time?" It had been a very short wait.

"Oh," I said, "the other half of the time I don't want to know what you're thinking. And, as you'd be the first to admit, I daresay it's just as well." I sighed. "Why do you call this a dreary view? I call it hot-blooded."

Again I waited, and the wait was longer until she said: "As for *you*, Sam Culloden, half the time you *frighten* me."

"And the other half?"

The clack of high heels in the dark corridor, progressively fainter, was an answer of sorts. A Valley of Dry Bones answer.

Rather than chase after her, which would've been an admission of defeat, I preferred to reconsider the door in the rear wall, on the basis of new evidence. For instance, I'd've bet a thousand dollars against a lead slug that the door was not only unlocked, but had been used, instead of the tatty tree I'd visualized, by a sated Sr. Sins on a recent Sunday morning. I'd've made a similar bet, too, that the door's hinges had been beautifully oiled, and by the hand of a master. I doubted if they even knew what a creak was. In fact, when a male hand eased the door open, those hinges probably hummed a lascivious little tune.

Other footsteps, recognizable by their floppiness as Lalage's, were approaching through the corridor. I crossed the room and we met at the doorway. "Want some coffee?" she asked. "Professor Young doesn't, but I thought you might."

I hadn't paid much attention to her eyes when I first arrived, but now I did. They were as wonderful as ever, but I noticed that they were cushioned on charcoal-gray crescent moons. Lalage, whether or not she was aware of it, was a very tired young woman. Oliver Culloden, Protector, who had taken off his lobster-tail armor, was pierced to the heart by those tired eyes. "No, thanks," I said. "Where I come from, only professional Hungarians drink coffee at this hour."

"It's not very good, anyway," Lalage said. "Juanita burned it again."

"How're things, Lalage?"

"And Professor Young'd like to ride to town with you, if you're going in."

"I am going in," I said. "But I asked you how things are with you."

"Oh. Fine."

"You ever go home these days?"

"I have to. My clothes're there."

"Along with your bed."

"I didn't mention a bed, did I?"

"Where do you sleep, Lalage? Here?"

That got me a shrug. "No, sometimes I sleep in cars." She giggled. "And sometimes—well it doesn't matter, I sleep badly wher*ever* I am. It's because I don't re*lax, Joy* says." Before I was aware of what she was doing, and with a quickness I hadn't suspected was in her, she disappeared into the corridor's darkness.

I studied the nearest bed and considered a plan to sit on it for ten minutes, brooding. I never went through with the plan, though, because it dawned on me that at least eight of the minutes would be spent either wondering why the bed was harder than it had any right to be, or trying to come up with the sort of lascivious little tune that might be hummed by a set of well-oiled hinges.

Eventually, and after not too many wrong turnings, I discovered where the living room had been all this time. When I stumbled in from the dimness Bruce was standing by the front door, obviously waiting for me; and Joy, who was curled up alone on a love seat in a corner, was not working very hard at sipping coffee. Lalage was nowhere to be seen, and the coffee smelled vile.

"Where's that adorable present?" I asked Joy. "I've heard so much talk about it."

"Oh, it's around someplace," Joy said vaguely. "*Such* a sweet thought, you Sam dear. And getting the *most* best care."

"Aren't we all?" Bruce Young said.

"Yea, verily, so it has come to pass," said unto him the Unrevised Version of Samuel Fraser Culloden.

◎ The drive into Maldorado began in an understandable silence. I was content to be quiet, and Bruce, although I could tell he had something he wanted to talk away, was keeping his mouth shut until he felt he'd mentally set up a proper approach to the subject.

I hadn't seen him for a week, when we'd gone to the Youngs for dinner, but at least I'd seen him. Other than that, this morning was the first time in ten days I'd stuck my head out of our mesquite gates. I hadn't even bothered to call on Fletcher. There was only one person I'd failed to avoid: the Man in my Mirror, a stranger.

Polly showed no concern over finding herself married to a semi-hermit. Her own life had fallen into a pattern of busy leisure, in which I was more an object than a force. A trickle of mail was arriving at the post office box she'd rented for us, and each morning she peeked into it before she did anything else in town. Every other day she'd buy food for the house in the big glass-and-iron public market, with side excursions to a bakery or a *farmacia* or the single shop that dealt in *ultramarinos*—this being the term Mexicans use to describe foreign or special foods, for which they charge the painfully high prices that a word of five syllables deserves. Sometimes she took Concepción with her, sometimes she went alone, and twice she and Helen Young frittered sunny hours away prowling the dustier corners of Maldorado. During the second of these scavenger hunts they'd stumbled upon a weird house whose lower rooms and inner courtyard were crammed with godawful junk, the stock in trade of a weird and godawful gringa crone, who called herself "Ramona," and who dressed like something left over from Doug Fairbanks Sr.'s *Mark of Zorro*. From Ramona's compost heap of artifacts and trinkets Polly and Helen Young had each plucked a worm-eaten painted chest of the early 1800's. They'd also paid an afternoon visit to the Pepper & Salt Ceramic Works. A gaudy little overpriced pot was the bitter fruit of that mistake, and no tears were shed when a clever bit of clumsiness on the part of Polly's husband Humpty-Dumptied the tiny horror off a mantel and down upon a cruel tile floor.

Jock meanwhile had been tramping the hills with Hy Levinson. The Treasure Tracer, even with its chromium fittings and quivering needles and constant click-click-click, had notably failed to turn the world of pre-Columbian archaeology topsy-turvy. They'd been led by its noises to dig holes all over the landscape, but their spadework had uncovered nothing beyond an oxidized succession of nails and metal *nada;* and Jock's original enthusiasm had certainly ebbed away.

In a backhanded manner, though, these futile field trips brought him and Nan Young together again. From pretending that Jock didn't exist she had gone into a state of fretful curiosity over this new interest of his, an interest in which she had no part; and this attitude quickly hardened into a raging resentment of his muscle-building hikes with Hy. She then put on full sail and scudded along the only sea lane left open to her—which was making herself more interesting to Jock than any other interest he might have. During the last four days, I gathered, she'd made this a full-time job; anyway, the hours that Jock spent with Levinson were quietly dwindling in number. One might've said, I suppose, that in her eyes Jock was, so to speak, the only game in town; and that, after all, a girl couldn't very well spend the rest of the summer with nobody to talk to but her *parents*—but one wasn't going to say anything of the kind. She liked the boy more than she was willing to admit, even to herself; and Jock, whose occasional gaucheries belied his basic good sense, was in careful love with her. If she ever were Humpty-Dumptied, I felt, it would not be by Charles Lockridge Culloden.

My own mood during this same period had been both settled and unsettling. I'd been floating in a dispassionate vacuum, neither depressed nor elated, automatically doing the correct thing at the proper moment, but not really doing very much at all. Most of the time was spent in reading. I'd even whipped through a couple of the books I'd brought from California. It had been a cold and therapeutic snowbank of days, in which I lay emptied of desire, and with but a single, growing regret—that I was neglecting old Tom Fletcher.

This was a piece of inaction even colder than the snowbank that held me. I had purposely put off calling on him, although for the life of me I couldn't say why. I was collecting my pay now, though, in the form of a parasitic host-devouring guilt, whose weight and bulk were becoming impossible to support. Less than an hour ago I'd been shocked to find, after I'd gone by Fletcher's place, that I'd unconsciously increased the car's speed while driving past. I knew that I *had* to see him again—but it was as though I'd lost my way and the world held no compass that hadn't been smashed.

While the last of these thoughts were high-tailing around in my head I had a nebulous sensation of the Gage house, off to the right, which went from cloudiness to concrete when Bruce said: "There's the nudist colony." Evidently he'd set his thoughts in satisfactory order.

"*Eh*-uh," I said.

"You've been there?"

I tacked to avoid a murderous pothole. "A man finds himself in queer corners sometimes," I said. "And you know I've been there."

"Sad but true. Polly told Helen and Helen told me."

"Why not?" I said. "It's the Age of Communications."

"And therefore an age that's hard to explain," Bruce said carefully, "since the people who live in it can't communicate worth a damn."

"The wires're down," I said.

"Away down," he said.

"Nevertheless, Mr. Morse," I said, "your message is coming through loud and clear. The great thing about the telegraph is that I can talk to you without seeing you."

"Amazing, isn't it?"

"Amazing. And if you'd just sniff the ozone, sir, you're sure to smell paper burning. Your message, sir, was on that very paper."

"Appreciate that, Sam. I really do. I never was in Joy's house before, you know."

"I know."

"I'd planned on a brisk morning walk, that's all, and—"

"I know."

"You bastard, Sam."

"I'm going to the post office. You want to go there, too?"

"No, when we hit the center of town you can let me off at the nearest clean corner."

"Why not the nearest Missouri Compromise?"

"Oh-*ho,* he wants to play in *my* yard, does he? You've heard what happened to the people who got off at that stop, haven't you?"

"Naw, suh, Mizztuh Bones. Whut happen to dem fo'ks whut dee-scended at duh Miss-houri Comperize?"

"Why, Uncle Butter, their fingers got burned, same as those telegraph messages. Sniff that fine ozone, Sam."

"You bastard, Bruce."

"Now we're even, you untrustworthy layman."

"You wouldn't talk to me that way if I had my comedian here."

I dropped Bruce off at a central but clean corner and went on to the post office. There were two letters for Polly in our box, and two for me. One of Polly's, which had been readdressed in Beverly Hills, was from her brother, Peter Lockridge, who was a little higher than the angels, but a little lower than the Ambassador, in the American Embassy in Athens. Her other letter, postmarked Mexico, D.F., was in the hand of Angela Gutierrez.

Of my own letters, the first contained a surprisingly large residual check for a downright bad television drama I'd done in a weak 1962 moment. The second, addressed to *Sr. Samuel Culloden, Domicilio Conocido, Maldita,* was from someone whose writing meant nothing to me—but only until I opened it.

Dear Sam, I read, *Expected youd be around but guess weve both been busy. Would like to see you once more before I leave. How about Saturday afternoon anytime after three? Probably the last chance. No word from Jamie. Wishing you the world, boy, T F Fletcher*

Well, I said to myself, that not only settles the old guilt, but also takes care of Saturday afternoon.

Before too many days had passed it had settled several other matters to boot, and taken care of a few more—in a lethal way, unfortunately. If I'd been aware of this at the moment I daresay I would've made for the tall timber. Once in a very great while it pays to be innocent, and I think this was one of those times.

But on the other hand, once in a very great while the tall timber makes for the man. And what does the robin do then, poor thing?

Why, he bides in the balm, to keep himself warm, and hides his head under his head, poor thing.

Especially when there's been no word from Jamie.

If He Tries Real Hard
He Can Cut His Throat
Before Sunset

Anytime after three, Fletcher had written; but I'd overstretched the elastic invitation. It was nearly five before I came walking along the old dirt road. This was strange behavior for a man who'd once broken his own world record in the Punctualathon, only to be disqualified, while still in the stadium, by the arrival of the Theory of Relativity. I'd stalled through a good part of the afternoon, doing things that didn't have to be done or hunting for things that weren't lost. Not until I'd run out of delaying actions was I reduced to a slow shuffle over the river. Meanwhile my demon-in-residence had been damnably closemouthed as to what lay behind this reversal of form.

The sight of Bruce Young's car, parked outside Fletcher's place, didn't help matters much by adding resentment to my emotional pot-au-feu, which was unsavory enough without more ingredients. For all I knew, Fletcher might be throwing a party. Even if he weren't, I had no proprietory rights in the man. But that didn't matter. What mattered was that Bruce Young was inside the hacienda; and, to make it worse from the Culloden point of view, inside before I myself was. John Doe, in the same position, perhaps would've headed back where he came from; but John Doe's demon-in-residence is merely a tired dress-extra from the old Dracula films. Mine is for keeps.

I finally ground to a halt, though, smack in the middle of the dowdy entrance. Fletcher's voice stopped me. He was singing. His tone was clear and he was on key. I listened, and "Coolness under fire" he sang:

> *Coolness under fire,*
> *Mentioned in dispatches*
> *For pinching the Company rations,*
> *Coolness under f-f-iiiii-EERRR—*

He held the last note for a long time, and then Bruce Young, less sure of the words, made it a duet for the chorus:

> *Whiter than the bloody dixie-lid,*
> *Whiter than the bloody dixie-lid,*
> *Wash me in the water*
> *Where you wash your dirty daughter*
> *And I shall be whiter*
> *Than the why-yy-yy-TWASH on the wall-lll-llll—*

I heard them as they slipped from the song into laughter, without taking the trouble to catch their breath. It was dollars to doughnuts that they'd been lapping up the Azteca, and by the bowlful. But other men's joy is the best of plagues; and before I knew it the virus had been filtered through my skin. I looked around and saw my resentment, tail between legs, making for the land where no bong trees grow. A big grin preceded me into Fletcher's little house.

They were sitting opposite each other at the round table, with an empty chair and an empty glass for me expectant between them. In the center of the table were two Azteca bottles. One was a dead soldier, the other three-quarters full. Fletcher pulled out the empty chair a couple of inches as soon as he saw me. "About time, son," he said. "I was worried you'd turned teetotal. Reckon you and the professor here know each other."

"Reckon we do." As I sat down I noticed a mild slackness around the Young mouth. "Pain all gone, Bruce?"

"Never to return," he said happily.

"The reason I'm late," I told Fletcher, "is that I had to listen to a slew of dead people complaining about how you'd waked 'em up with your loud singing and lewd ways."

Fletcher was already filling the empty glass; he might've had a gyroscope in his elbow, his hand was so steady. "The damned fools deserve to be dead," he said, "if they don't know the difference between singing and a history lesson." He pushed the brimming glass closer to me. "Down the hatch, Sam boy."

I tossed a swallow of liquid gold down the hatch, all the way to my keelson, and immediately regretted the dallying I'd done at home. "History lesson?" I said. "You've lost me there, sir. I heard the song, but I don't get the connection."

"Heard it before, you mean," Bruce said.

"No, as I was coming in. I never heard it before in my life."

"Poor Sam." Bruce shook his head sadly.

"Well," Fletcher said, "the professor appears to be a crackerjack historian, as long as he's talking about pants-down politics and the sorry results thereof. But he's still in the backstretch when it comes to the violent side—except, of course, for who beat whom and where they took the licking. Trouble with the professor is, he's never done time in any army, including the Salvation. Anyway, that song, in spite of its being careless enough to be somewhat outside the professor's particular period, is a by-God sidelight on history. Around fifty years ago it was a very popular hymn with what is now a sizable portion of the topsoil of Flanders, but which then was still on its feet." He glared at the empty bottle. "I mean the poor damned dead British Army, in the war you both weren't here for."

After a moment I said: "It's a good song. Too bad the Americans never had any then."

" 'Over There,' " Bruce said. "And 'Mademoiselle from Armentières.' "

" 'Over There,' was tin-pan-alley crap," I said. "And we got the Armentières number from the Limeys."

"That's right, we did," Fletcher said. "How'd you know that, Sam? Jamie tell you?"

"If he did, I don't remember. No, it's just that every so often I like to tear myself away from the fictions of daily life and read a few historical sidelights. I steer clear of the 1840–1870 period, though. That's when the politicians were too damned political and the wars were too damned cruel. And those rhetorical snow jobs that they rumbled out, from the rock-bound bottom of Hannibal Hamlin to the sun-kissed cheeks of John C. Fremont—my God!" While the hatch was engulfing more Azteca I slipped the old man a wink.

Bruce was disturbed; he hadn't seen the wink. "I thought you liked history, Sam."

It was too late to dismount. I'd have to ride the subject until it threw a shoe. "What's the use?" I said. "The way they write it these days, a man can't tell the good guys from the bad guys. And the more books he reads, the more mixed up he gets."

"If it gives you that much trouble, why read it at all?" Bruce asked.

"Because a red-white-and-blue-blooded American has to know his enemy, that's why."

Bewilderment was being added to Bruce's growing annoyance. "How is history the enemy?"

"Because the Great Society, if it wants to be really great, needs an enemy it can be greater than. The Russians're trying to act as though they lived in Des Moines, so they don't fill the bill any more. But history deals with dead men, so we've made *it* the enemy—which, in turn, makes it possible for us to blame all our present errors on the dead. I wouldn't be surprised to read one day that the motto of the United States had been changed to *De mortuis nil nisi malum.*"

"Honestly, Sam," Bruce began, "I don't understand—"

"You don't understand a leg pull, that's for sure." I patted his shoulder. "Forget it, ace. Pretend I'm still in the field house."

Bruce managed to mount three fifths of a grin, but couldn't bring it out to the corners. "We were having a fine historical afternoon," he said, "and then you had to come along."

"You can still have your fine historical afternoon," I said. "I brought an extra face with me. Play with your drink while I put it on."

"You're below water level there, professor," Fletcher said slowly. "Can't let that happen." He pushed the bottle of rum across the table. He was slow about that, too, which made me glance sharply at him.

"I suppose I should say I'll hate myself in the morning," Bruce said, pouring himself four thick fingers. "But I won't. No, I won't, no, sir." He then disposed of a finger and a half in the proper way, set his glass on the table, and surveyed me bleakly. "Now, Sam, what I want from you is a good definition of history."

"I don't think I can give one," I said.

"I gathered as much," said Bruce.

"Hold your horses," I said. "I can damned well try. Wait a minute." Then, after a thirty-second review of what I knew of the subject, what I didn't know, and what nobody else knew—including the ablest historians—I said: "This might work. As I see it, history can be reduced to a single narrow statement: Two men, both of whom had 'J.C.' for initials, and who believed themselves to be acting rationally, were killed by men who believed themselves to be acting rationally. There's your nutshell, Bruce. No need to tell you where to gather the nut to put back in it."

"Sorry," Bruce said, "but I distrust narrow statements."

"That's why I was dealing in broad particulars," I said mildly. "How's this, then? History's what the human race wants to think it did."

"A nice, neat aphorism," Bruce said. "Nice, neat—and hollow. I also caught an echo of misanthropy. Definitions should be dispassionate."

"All right, last chance. See how this looks in the mirror: History's the White Paper of mankind."

"Better, but it won't do. I like the irony, though."

"Why won't it do? It's nice, neat, dispassionate irony."

"But it's still an aphorism, Sam, and an aphorism's by no means a definition."

"My brain's getting a charley-horse. Let's have *your* definition."

This time he mounted a full grin. "What definition?" he said. "I can come up with fifty, but none of them'd hold water. Every last one'll have a gap somewhere."

"The hell with you, Young," I said. I turned to the old man, who was staring at his little shelf of books. "You been following this conversation, sir?"

"For a while," Fletcher said. "But when it slowed to a crawl I went ahead of it. Frankly, I don't give a whistling damn for all this nit-picking jabber about definitions, whether it's talked jabber or printed jabber. As far as I'm concerned, History's a very big and very lazy and very stupid man. It's now afternoon, and he's been trying ever since dawn to pull himself up by the bootstraps with one hand and cut his throat with the other. He's too stupid to learn that he can't pull himself up by the bootstraps, but he's just smart enough to know that if he tries real hard he can cut his throat before sunset. And he's trying real hard, believe me. He's doing his damnedest. That's all I've got to say on the subject, and I suggest we leave it at that."

We left it at that.

Bruce looked at his glass for a while and then lowered the contents considerably. I looked at my glass for a while and then lowered the contents considerably. Fletcher looked at his glass for a while and then lowered his eyelids all the way. He began to sing softly to himself:

> *Now he's on the peg,*
> *Now he's on the peg,*
> *Mentioned in dispatches*
> *For drinking the Company rum,*
> *Now he's on the peg—*

"On the peg," Bruce mumbled; and Fletcher went on:

> *Whiter than the whitewash on the wall,*
> *Whiter than the whitewash on the wall—*
> *Dish me in the water*
> *Where I ditched your dirty daughter*
> *And then I might be whiter*
> *Than the whitewash on the wall—*

"On the wall," mumbled Bruce. "On the wall. The whitewash on the wall."

The old man was silent. His eyes stayed closed.

"Wall," said Bruce. He chuckled for my approval; none was given. "Wa," he said.

While Fletcher'd been singing his Cato-like head had gradually sunk forward until his chin was on his breastbone, where it remained. He seemed asleep, but he wasn't. I had no proper standard of comparison, not having seen him this way before, but as near as I could tell the damned old fool was drunk.

Perhaps I should've worried about him; after all, his eighty-sixth birthday was less than a fortnight away. Instead I let a fresh anger cross the borders of my mind—and not as a mere reconnaissance in force.

It was a corps of anger, composed of resentments in divisional strength. I resented the presence of Bruce Young. I resented Fletcher's "last chance" invitation to visit him on what had become a nonsense songfest on an empty afternoon. I resented my own presence there. I resented the old man's lack of interest in me. I resented Bruce's semicollapse. I resented—Christ! I even resented my own resentment.

"Good God, it's five thirty!" Bruce's exclamation was so loud and sudden that I was startled.

Fletcher's eyes opened. "Wha'd you say?"

"It's five thirty, and I have to go home." Bruce stood up, as steady as though he hadn't drunk a drop. "There's a Japanese double feature showing in Maldorado," he told me. "*Rashomon* and *Woman in the Dunes*. I missed *Rashomon* and Helen missed them both."

"Will you give me a lift to our place?" I said. "Jock's got the car. I walked here."

"Glad to, Sam."

Fletcher rose to his feet when I did. He was controlling himself fairly well; it couldn't've been easy. "Both of you going?" he asked.

"Looks that way, sir," I said. "I told my wife—"

"Sure, that's the way it goes." He held out his hand to Bruce. "Glad you came by, professor. I enjoyed it."

Bruce shook the old man's hand. "So did I, sir. And I hope to see you again soon. Perhaps some day next week."

Fletcher blinked several times. "Not next week, no. Next week I—" The sentence trailed off. He blinked some more.

It was a loose ball, so I fell on it. "He's going to the States," I said to Bruce.

"Oh?" Bruce said. "I didn't know. Leaving tomorrow, sir?"

"According to the ticket."

"Alone?"

"Not for long. Somebody's meeting me."

"Well, I'll see you when you come back, then."

"Bet your life, professor," Fletcher said. "If not before." He put an arm across Bruce's shoulders and weaved beside him to the door.

My unshaken hand was clenched in a fist as I tagged along after them, more resentful than ever. Bruce went out of the house. Fletcher remained in the doorway, his back to me. "Have a good trip," I said flatly, and started to ease past him.

He reached out and grabbed my arm. "Sam boy—"

I waited, not liking it much.

He continued: "Come back later, Sam, if you can. Come back at eight o'clock."

"I don't think I can, sir."

"It's important to me, Sam."

I felt that if he didn't release my arm I might explode in his face. I didn't explode, though. As usual, I snuffed out the fuse and took the coward's way. "All right, I'll be back, sir. Eight o'clock."

"Bless you, Sam," he said. "I haven't been given time to put—"

I never heard the rest, whatever it was he was going to say, because he'd freed my arm and I was hurrying to catch up with Bruce.

"Nice old fellow, that Fletcher," Bruce said as we drove over the bridge. "I ran into him yesterday morning when I was taking a walk. Incidentally, I hope I didn't interrupt any plans you'd made—"

"No plans. None at all."

"That's good. I thought you acted strained there for a while."

"It's the altitude," I said. My resentments were making me laconic. I was also inwardly occupied with drafting a Culloden White Paper to prove that a drunken Fletcher had misunderstood what I'd said about coming back at eight o'clock. Actually, the only thing that might persuade me to show up there at eight would be to turn on the radio at seven and hear that it'd been an icy day on the Equator. This would make two solid reasons for my nonappearance. The other, of course, was that the *finca* had no radio.

The thought cheered me a little. "Polly might like to catch that show with you," I said. "I'm sure she missed both pictures. I know *I* did, so she must've too."

"Love to have her. How about you?"

"I don't go to films much any more."

"Really? But you've written a lot of them."

"Which is why I don't go to films much any more. Especially Japanese films. It's exhausting to watch all those Mifunes bat out gutturals with the flats of their swords."

Bruce eased the car onto our cobblestoned road. "I see your point," he said, in a tone that made it clear he saw nothing of the kind.

Neither did Polly. As soon as Bruce had asked her if she wanted to take in an Oriental double feature she needed less than four minutes to follow her face upstairs, repair the ravages of the day, and be off up the hill with him. She didn't even look back.

Lot should've had a wife like that. Orpheus, too.

◎ At half past nine the gates were still open and I was sitting in my usual chair in the patio. For a change, though, there was nothing on the table but an ashtray and moonlight and pencil-stub shadows of pepper leaves. The moon was nearly full in a cloudless sky, its pock-marked brilliance intensified in the high, clear air, and every powerful star dimmed by that white reflected power. Somewhere up the hill, on the other side of the main road, an overmongrelized dog had persisted in an idiot moon-directed barking for as long as I could remember.

Fletcher should've given me up as a bad job by now and gone to bed, which is what I'd've done in his position. I wasn't Fletcher, however. I was the man who hadn't turned up, who had no excuse for his behavior, and whose guilt had become very active in his mental landscape. This guilt was building me a one-cell prison, the thickness of whose walls were triple the width of the tiny area they enclosed. I was aware that my cell, when finished, would be too small for any pacing, so I grew more and more restless. But the only pacing that could ease my conscience would have to bring me to Fletcher's door, and it was now too late for such bitter mobility.

Movement of a less drastic sort was required though, and at once. I chose to turn on the gatepost lights—a pair of old carriage lamps whose wiring Weatherby'd somehow concealed. The lamps weren't really necessary at the moment, with so much moonlight bouncing around, but I saw no reason to disregard all that hard work by Edison, merely because the sky happened to be clear on a night when the moon was going for broke. Polly, too, would be coming home soon, glassy-eyed from four hours of Japanese fun-and-games, and she deserved a mild electric welcome. So might the long-overdue Jock, wherever he was.

The switch lay behind a thorny climbing vine that Luis had let get out of hand. As I felt for it I heard somebody running down the cobblestoned road with an urgency that made me think: O God! Jock's had an accident—

I tore through the vine and found the switch at the price of a mean scratch across my right knuckles. The lit lamps made a mere dent in the moonlight as an undersized boy of about twelve skidded to a stop in the gateway. Recent tears had left streaks on an unwashed face, and one dirty hand clutched a folded piece of paper.

"*Sr. Cuyodén?*" He gave my name the Mexican pronunciation.

"*Sí.*"

"*Para Usted, patrón.*" He thrust the paper at me and scampered back up the hill.

I took a deep breath, held it while I read the message, and exhaled with relief: the message had nothing to do with Jock. But then black waters were closing over my head: it had a great deal to do with me. All it said was: *Can you come to Tom's right away? Inskilling.* And all it meant was: Fletcher's dead. I knew this as surely as I knew it was a drop of blood from my scratched knuckles that fell on the word *you* and blotted it out with red.

⊚   Inside the hacienda gates three women and a man and the under-sized boy were standing by the doorway of Dolores' house. The *rebozo*-draped women were sobbing politely into their open palms, the man puffed on a cigarette in disassociated embarrassment, and the undersized boy was evidently too winded to take up his crying where he'd left off. From the dark interior of the little house a more substantial keening came through the open door, together with a muted chorus of several soothing voices. I listened to this for half a dozen heartbeats, then walked toward Fletcher's own house. The door was open, too.

I entered, I squinted, I hesitated: what I saw seemed hardly a death scene. A green-shaded oil lamp in the center of the table cast a narrow circle of light and mocked my powers of observation; until now I'd failed to realize that there was no electricity in the hacienda. Fletcher sat in his high-backed chair, and across from him was Dr. Inskilling. Both men were beyond the circle of light and their faces were more or less shadows, although I was able to make out that Fletcher's eyes were closed. The old man, in fact, was in almost the same position he'd held when Bruce Young's loud telling of time had startled him back from where he'd drifted. A pair of standing frames for photographs were placed in front of Fletcher. The bottles and glasses we'd used in the late afternoon were still on the table.

Inskilling twisted in his chair to see who'd come in. "Ah, Culloden," he said. "I thought you were George Simmons." He was holding a fourth glass. It had six or so ounces of rum in it.

"Had to walk," I said. I moved on tiptoe to the table, not taking my eyes from Fletcher, until I was close enough to him to be positive about his condition. A dead man sat there, and no mistake. Everything vivid had gone from the face. "When'd it happen?" I asked.

"Around eight o'clock, I'd say." Inskilling paused to sip some Azteca. "I got here at quarter to nine, not that it made any difference.

I didn't even bother to move him. Help yourself to rum, Culloden. This is the only wake Tom'll have."

I sat down and poured myself a few fingers. "Same glass I drank from this afternoon," I said listlessly. I raised the glass to Fletcher and tossed off a couple of the fingers. "Bruce Young and I were here."

"Your hand's bleeding, you know," Inskilling said.

I inspected the scratch. It was messy around the knuckles, but the mess was made by coagulated blood. Actual bleeding had stopped. "I went a fast round with some mountain greenery," I said. My eyes returned to Fletcher.

"I sent you that note," Inskilling said languidly, "because I thought you'd want a last glass with the old boy. And a last look, too. You wouldn't get one at the funeral. They nail the coffin lid down before the body leaves the house."

"The funeral," I said automatically. My gaze left the dead for the living. "*Eh*-uh, the funeral. What can I do to help?"

"Nothing."

"Nothing?"

"There's not that much to do. The only tricky bit is to fix it so he won't be buried until Monday, and that's something I can take care of. You see, according to local law the dead have to be buried not later than sunset on the day after death. It's a sensible law, of course, since the undertakers haven't the faintest idea of how to keep a corpse cool. So what I'll do is hang around until one or two a.m., then go into Maldorado, pound the undertaker awake, and tell him Tom Fletcher opted for a harp at twelve forty-seven. He'll yawn, give me a form to sign, and agree to deliver a coffin in time for a funeral Monday morning at a sensible eleven o'clock. Then tomorrow George Simmons'll persuade Father Macías, who's the local errand boy between Maldita and God, to let Tom be buried behind Santa Caterina, which is the local St. Peter's. It may take some dickering, because Tom was beyond religion, but George should be able to swing it. He'll catch Father Macías between Masses, because that's when he's most amenable. And Macías is rather afraid of George, for some reason, so he'll go along. Tom won't be buried in consecrated ground, naturally, but he wasn't a man to worry about being sunk in heathen soil."

"There'll be expenses, though. Who's going to pay for them?"

"Why, the bank—who else? You didn't think Tom was broke, did you? Last I heard, he had nearly forty thousand dollars, most of which was invested in Mexican deals that were bringing in from eight per cent to ten per cent interest."

"Well, certainly I ought to be able to do something—how about the sons? They'll have to be notified. I could do that."

Inskilling toyed with his glass before saying drily: "According to most people, they'll've been notified already."

"I don't get it," I said. And I didn't.

"Oh, I forgot," Inskilling said, "I didn't tell you the whole story. Well, the two boys've been dead over twenty years."

"What're you talking about?" I demanded. "Fletcher was taking a trip over the border to see them."

"He took his trip," Inskilling said. "He's over the Border."

I got it then. "Oh," I said. I went over and stood beside the high-backed chair and studied the photographs. One was of an Infantry lieutenant, the other of an ensign in the Navy. They were in their early twenties and there was a great deal of Fletcher in them—except for the eyes, which were soft and Latin. "Mere babies," was all I could think of to say. "Mere babies."

Inskilling sighed. "In April 1945," he said, "young Tom was a captain in Germany and Bill was a lieutenant j.g. on a destroyer off Okinawa. At precisely 6:13 on the evening of April 12 young Tom stepped on a mine as he got out of his jeep; and on the other side of the world a Kamikaze blew Bill's destroyer out of the water. It was terrible enough to have them killed on the same day, with the war nearly over—but to discover that they'd both died at the exact same moment was almost more than a man could bear. And, as it turned out, more than a woman could bear. Tom's wife went absolutely to pieces, mentally and physically. She was dead herself a year later. And after that, Tom—well, he's at ease now, I think, the poor old boy."

I felt a chill; obviously the old man was also looking at the photographs. I sidled over to my own chair, picked up my glass from the table, and finished my drink standing. "Who's the heir, then?" I asked.

"Oh, Dolores. Tom loved her, you know. He needed to have someone to love. The money, however—" Again he toyed with his glass. "I doubt if the money'll last long. Dolores is a generous old thing, but she has ten thousand hungry relatives, any one of whom is more than capable of whining her away from her last centavo. Culloden, you simply can't imagine how many Tresguerras live around here and're waiting to climb up her back. At the funeral you'll begin to get an idea, though. A sizable number of her kin'll be present, from great-great-grandmothers to yesterday's newborn baby."

"What about the gringos?"

"What about them?"

"They'll want to come to the funeral, won't they?"

"Culloden, you *are* a child. There'll be—just a moment—all of *five* whom I'd expect to attend. You. George Simmons. Hy Levinson. Lalage Delmore. Me. No more than that. Angela'd come, perhaps, but she's away."

"Make it eight," I said. "I'll bring Polly and Jock, and Bruce Young. And possibly Helen Young, and Nan."

"The more the—well, 'merrier' isn't quite right," Inskilling said, "but you know what I mean." He rose from his chair. "There's no point in your hanging around, Sam," he continued, using my given name for the first time. "I suggest that you help me shift the old boy onto the bed, so he'll fit easy for the undertaker, and then go home and put a dressing on that hand. I don't have a kit with me, and infection comes easy in this country."

I was delighted to take his suggestion. I gathered, from his greeting to me, that George Simmons would be showing up eventually; and I had no special desire to lay eyes on George Simmons before Monday morning, if then.

We toted Fletcher's body to the bed and stretched him out in a neat line. He'd stiffened considerably, which didn't bother me. There was a period in my life when my close friends, one after another, became instant dead men, and usually when I handled them they were in far worse shape than the late Thomas Flint Fletcher. None had made it to eighty-five, either. The oldest, as I remember, had been twenty-nine.

◎ On my way home I met Lalage, as she came down the slope from the bridge. She was carrying a square leather box, well worn, that must've been a hand-me-down from her mother. For any other woman than Lalage Delmore the box would've held enough cosmetics for six months of male-hexing. I couldn't imagine what Lalage was lugging in it; watercress sandwiches, maybe.

In the moonlight her face seemed more haggard, her wonderful eyes darker-circled, than when we'd talked so briefly at the Matthews *finca*. She showed some cheerfulness, though. I even was given a rueful smile as we stopped and confronted each other. "When I saw you the other day," she said, "I meant to give you back that poetry book, but I completely forgot. And I keep forgetting to bring it from Joy's. It's on the mantel over the fireplace in her bedroom. I must be losing my mind."

"Only sensible thing to do, these days. You on your way to Joy's now?"

"Oh, *yes!* It's a surprise, sort of. She doesn't expect me. And tomorrow I'll make break—" She stepped nearer and peered at me. My back was to the moon and my face was in shadow. "Are you all right? You look the same way you did when we were sitting on the stairs to my tower, and you—"

"I'm all right, Lalage," I cut in. "I'm fine, just fine." I paused for a heartbeat, then went on: "But Mr. Fletcher, he's—well, he's dead."

Those fairy-tale eyes opened wider and wider and her lips parted a little. She stared at me for a long time before she said, very faintly, "Oh." Her fingers relaxed, and the leather box fell. I caught it before it hit the ground. "Oh," she said again. "Dead." She swayed, then steadied herself. "When was it?"

"Couple of hours ago. He's in his house. Dr. Inskilling's there."

"I'll go see him," she murmured.

"No, don't," I said. "You don't have to. No point in it. Don't."

"Thank you." She lowered her gaze. "Because the thing is, I'm afraid of looking at dead people. Even Mr. Fletcher. Ever since my father. When they—"

"You just hurry by his house and go and do what you want to do," I told her. "I shouldn't've said anything about it." I slipped my scratched hand behind my back. She hadn't noticed the blood yet, and I didn't intend that she should.

"Poor, dear Mr. Fletcher. Once he said to me—" She shook her head and the motion threw off one of the tears that were beginning to slide down her cheeks. She swallowed, then managed to ask: "Is the funeral tomorrow?"

"No, Monday. Eleven o'clock. At that church on the—Santa Caterina's."

"I'll be there. Can I be with *you?*"

"Sure. Want to come to the house first?"

"I'd rather meet you at the cemetery. And we'll stand side by side, you and me."

"I'd like that," I said. "Very much. Pretend I'm your father."

She put her free hand out and I thought she was going to take mine. But then she let her hand fall and walked away. "Thank you for—" She didn't turn around. "Telling me," floated, a whisper, through the moonlight.

I started up the slope to the bridge, unaware that I'd just talked to Lalage Delmore for the last time.

◎ Jock and the station wagon were still among the missing when I got back to the house. Our bedroom was dark, though, which meant that Polly was home and asleep. I was neither sleepy nor anxious to wake her by treating my hand in the bathroom, so I went out to the river terrace. My hand would keep.

I leaned on the stone wall and studied the moonlit Río Maldorado, letting myself sink into a kind of trance until once more I became aware of running feet—across the river, for a change.

The runner was Lalage Delmore.

She could only be coming from the Matthews place and Joy Durwood, but she sped along as though the abomination of desolation were at her heels, and it made for a terrible fleetness. As she reached a point opposite me she was less than forty yards away, over the river, and I opened my mouth to shout to her. But, God help me, I didn't shout—and then she was gone forever, around a downstream bend.

I wonder now what difference it might've made if I had called her name and she'd heard and stopped and poured out her heart and let me comfort her.

None, I'm afraid. No difference at all.

Probably she wouldn't've stopped. And even if she had, poor, lost pitiful girl, it wouldn't've made any difference. Not one goddamned bit of difference in the world.

PART THREE

THE FUNERAL
GAMES

"I remember once, when something went wrong with me, being told—like the wounded knight in the tourney who said, 'I thirst'—being told, I say, in the words of the King, *Bois ton sang, Beaumanoir, et tu n'auras plus soif.*"

❀ One

A Poopdeck of Starbucks,
Blanched with Despair

I was standing under an old pepper tree in the cemetery, watching four men lower a blue-painted coffin into a narrow grave. The ropes that they were using seemed too worn for the job, but the men were adroit from years of practice. The pepper tree had lived a long time and reached a great size; and, although it had been planted outside the cemetery, some of its gnarled, sympathetic limbs extended well within this northwest corner of the crumbling wall. A shy zephyr wandered through a few thin leaves near my head and stirred them into whispers. Susurrant bees were farming the higher branches.

It was no day to be dead in.

The morning had fused the best of spring and autumn, due to a short hard rain between midnight and sunrise that had excited the earth and polished the air to an uncorrupted clarity. The mild sun was content to make more vivid the muted colors of the landscape and sharpen the outline of every solid form—even the tired Maldita-Baroque bulk of the Church of Santa Caterina. To the east, beyond the church, each of the small hills that rolled like waves toward and over a hidden Maldorado had its own shade of green; and the higher hills in the distance, for the most part bare rock, were elegant variations on a basic gray that, through some subtlety of stone, gave the impression of a private lithic spectrum.

This beauty made me twice as sad as I would've been in a drizzle, under a gunmetal sky; and the odd thing was that the sadness hadn't hit me until now. My trance on the river terrace had been triggered by guilt, not grief, while the Sunday just past had held little of emptiness or much sense of loss. I'd regretted Fletcher's death, certainly, but within limits suitable for someone I'd met only recently and seen but three times. Had I known and loved the old man for years, or had he been young and cut down in his prime, I would have viewed his death through darker eyes. As things were, though, he had gone out of my life still much of a stranger, and his own life had lasted far longer than mine would.

But these were the thoughts I'd had yesterday; and this was a glittering today, and a man was going into the ground.

It was hardly a funeral at all, although it had started like one—with Fletcher's arrival on four men's shoulders, nailed in forever and followed by half the native population of Maldita. Yet his grave had been dug in the most remote corner of the cemetery, at least fifty feet from any other grave and in earth which, I presumed, they hadn't gotten around to consecrating. Father Macías failed to appear, nor did I see anyone who even resembled a priest.

There was no burial service, either, in the accepted meaning of the term. All that Fletcher was given in the way of godspeed he received from George Simmons. An awkward moment came—while the coffin, tilting a bit, waited on one of the piles of earth that the gravediggers had thrown up—when nobody seemed to know what to do next. Then George walked over to the coffin, raised his hand above it in a kind of blessing, and said: "*Nunc dimittis servum tuum, Domine, secundum verbum tuum in pace. Quia viderunt oculi mei salutem tuam, quam parasti ante faciem omnium populorum.*" He raced through the Latin as though he were in a hurry to catch a train. This speed was balanced somewhat by the clothes he had on—a rather tight-fitting black suit, and a white shirt, tieless, but buttoned at the neck anyway. It occurred to me that the Latin words were more suitable for Simmons himself than the late Thomas

Flint Fletcher, but this was hardly the time to look a gift canticle in the mouth. It was more than the old man would've otherwise had spoken over him, at that.

The coffin hit bottom. The ropes were withdrawn. The four men took up their shovels. The first scoop of earth struck the coffin lid. And a moaning came from the Maldita crowd.

They'd been pretty quiet until then, allowing themselves a few muffled sobs, but nothing serious. Something in the hollow sound of earth on wood brought the tragic business home to them at last and gave them a chance to show their appreciation. It was, I guess, the next best thing to getting a good, close look at a dead face. They went about their keening politely, though, and with a fair amount of formality. Nobody shrieked. Nobody swooned. The moans all came from eight strategically placed women, who'd probably been chosen by lot.

The work of filling the grave was swift, mechanical, and void of any interest, so I began to pay less attention to the hole in the ground and more to the people in the graveyard. There must've been a hundred natives, most of them female, grouped beside and behind old Dolores in a prevalence of black and Tresguerras. Every *rebozo* wreathed an impassive square face, and even Dolores of the High Decibels held her dry husk stolidly erect. Either she'd cried herself out long since, or she was afraid that any untoward show of sorrow would bring on a raging and rapacious sympathy from her hyena-like kin.

Inskilling had been correct about the number of Tresguerras who'd attend the planting of Thomas Fletcher. There was so much family resemblance in the press around Dolores that it made my head swim. Too, some of them were so decrepit that I felt they'd be back here within a week, toted and horizontal. Several mothers, surely of various ages although they all could've passed for sixty-two, were pouching very young babies in folds of their *rebozos;* and one of these fresh-whelped critters, its tiny red puckered phiz swathed in filthy flannel, couldn't have been more than nine hours old.

Inskilling's calculations had been off, however, concerning how many gringos would be at the burying. So had mine, as a matter of

fact. He'd said five; I'd said eight: eleven were standing around.
Among them were four Surprises.

Of the unsurprising people present:

Polly, first, was at my right, and prettier by far than anyone ought
to be in a graveyard. There'd been no question of asking her to come.
Although she hadn't met Fletcher, she took it for granted that I'd
be at the funeral, and even before I'd finished telling her about his
death she announced that she'd go with me.

Next to her, *Jock* shifted restlessly from foot to foot, staring at the
sky with eyes that matched it in blueness and vacuity. When I told
him I wanted him at the cemetery he'd mumbled something about
a plan to go out with Hy Levinson and his Treasure Tracer, but he
agreed to complete the Culloden family picture when I made it clear
that Hy Levinson would certainly want to see Tom Fletcher into the
ground. Jock wasn't too enthusiastic, of course; but even if he'd
tried to worm out of the affair I wouldn't've let him. Ever since he'd
stumbled away from his bed on Sunday noon he'd been keeping his
mouth shut about where he'd been and what he'd been doing so
late on Saturday night. His remark about "just wandering around"
was a haphazard explanation, and a sullen one to boot. Nan Young
hadn't been with him, because she, too, had gone to the Japanese
films. Therefore Jock's wandering around had been done, I hoped,
alone.

Bruce Young stood at my left, by himself. His daughter had never
been to a funeral and, according to him, was afraid that if she went
to one she might decide she liked them—whatever that meant. The
down-smiling Helen, on the other hand, had refused point-blank
to go. Bruce looked worn and yet tense. His condition could've been
due to a few rough hours, presented to him by his generous wife and
centering around the subject of his own unnecessary attendance.

Across the grave from me, *George Simmons* concentrated on the
four workmen and the job they were doing. His lips moved slightly,
as though he were counting the number of shovelfuls of earth it
would take before the hole stopped being a hole.

Hy Levinson, wearing a wrinkled brown suit and giving the impression that he didn't belong in it, leaned against the northern wall

of the cemetery, apart from everyone else. His huge hands were clasped behind him and he dug little holes with the toe of one Wellington boot—a lonely, gentle, friendly man, every line of whose body revealed the misery he may have thought didn't show.

Dr. James Winters Inskilling bore his poker-faced self like the most urbane and bored of generals, wearily reviewing second-rate troops for the thousandth time. It occurred to me that in his day he'd very likely walked behind scads of his late patients to one vault or another. I reminded myself to check up on his past sometime, just for the devil of it.

I then turned my attention to the Surprises.

Mrs. Ransom McDermott, I had to admit, didn't seem at all out of place; and I should've known that funerals would be her favorite spectator sport. She had on a black gown that undoubtedly served her for a dress uniform on these delicious social occasions; and although she was as bejeweled as she'd been at Marian Delmore's buffet, now the stones were obsidian or onyx or whatever else there is that is black and semiprecious. Her little beady obsidian eyes, so incongruously set in her broken pendant of a face and darting onyxlike everywhere, hadn't missed a trick since the arrival of the coffin.

It was more of a surprise to see *Jefferson Gage*—coatless, tieless, sandals on his bare feet and grease-spotted beige chinos covering his skimpy hams—off to one side in the middle background. He was leaning against a rusty iron railing that gave rectangular protection to somebody's maudlin funeral monument and disassociated remains. I didn't understand what the railing was doing there, unless it was to keep picnic parties off the plot on the Day of the Dead, and I didn't understand what Gage was doing on the railing. He had arrived clutching a spiral-top stenographer's notebook in one hand and a pencil in the other; presumably he wanted to make notes on a Mexican burying-bee for some present use or future reference. But as soon as he planked his buttocks against the wrought iron he forgot all about the tools of his trade and spent the next thirty-five minutes, while they packed Fletcher away, in contemplating the top of the pepper tree and trying to touch his nose with the tip of his tongue.

I searched for the rest of his family, but he'd evidently left all his open-minded females back at the Fun House. I took it for granted that Rose Gage and her happy babies were spending the morning wisely—in needlepoint, say, and the singing of hymns.

A greater surprise was given me by a brace of women who were clutching a brace of bouquets—and it was a double-barreled surprise, to say the least. That they should've come at all struck me as odd enough, but that they should've come together nuzzled the fantastic. The older woman was somewhere in her sixties. I'd never seen her before, but I recognized her instantly as the *Ramona* from whom Polly had bought the painted chest. The old dutch's face was layered with enough make-up, ineptly applied, to satisfy a Port Said whore, and her flour-sack figure, costumed for a 1918 Toby Show version of *In Old California,* had the airs and graces of a blood pudding.

The younger woman, who wore a simple Galanos dress in a somber pattern that might've been designed for chic summer mourning, shouldn't've been *Joy Durwood,* but that's who she was. What she was doing at Tom Fletcher's rites, what lay behind her choice of a companion, or what song the Sirens sang when they hid themselves among women were, though puzzling questions, not beyond all conjecture. But I conject right poorly in company, so I paid slight attention to Joy while Tom Fletcher was trying on the world for size. Anyway, to glance at her was to take in Ramona as well, and my eyeballs weren't in shape for that sort of grotesquerie while the sun was still shining. Joy's interest in the proceedings had the proper balance, neither retreating into boredom nor advancing into morbidity; but this attitude, unfortunately, gave no aid in the solution of a number of problems, the least of which was her physical presence.

But the greatest surprise was *Lalage Delmore*—and the surprise was that she wasn't present at all. She was the one person I was sure would come to the funeral. Inskilling, who knew what he was talking about, had said she'd be there; and she'd told me the same thing herself when we'd met near the bridge. Again and again I tried to spot her. She was so tall that she'd've been hard put to escape my searching eye, and the fact that she did escape it meant that she wasn't around.

By the time the grave had been filled and the four men were tamping down and rounding off the mound of earth that the coffin had displaced I was aware that my sadness had been generated from a subconscious brooding on the absent Lalage; and to it was added a worry and fear that increased until the four men, their work finished, walked off with their shovels and ropes.

There was an uncomfortable and uncertain silence before George Simmons cleared his throat and announced to the gringos: "It's finished now. May he rest in peace." Then he said, directing his words at the crowd from Maldita: "*In nomine Patri et Filii et Spiritus Sancti. Amen. Terminado.*" He started to make the sign of the cross, but caught himself in time. A few of the Maldita people pushed others aside to toss small bouquets on the grave. Meanwhile a sizable group encircled Dolores Tresguerras, filling her ears with quick, liquid, low pleading words.

I turned to Polly. "Well—" I said hesitantly.

"What a strange service," she said. "Nonsectarian with a vengeance."

"Look, Polly, I think I'll—" I was about to say I was going for a walk instead of returning directly to the *finca,* but before I could finish the sentence Ramona was upon us, peering up into my face with myopic intensity.

"Ah, Sr. Culloden!" she exclaimed, in a squeaky voice that might've been bounced off some tenth-rate ventriloquist's dummy. "*He querido* to meet *Usted! Su* wife is so *chula—y simpático,* too. *Con* such good *gusto. Muy!* Oh, *muy!*"

God, I thought, it's worse than I expected. Aloud, I said: "You don't mean it."

"This is Ramona," Polly said. "Where I got that charming chest."

"I thought as much," I said, and smiled at the weird old thing. "Ramona—what *uno* wonderful *nombre.*" If you ever find yourself in Naples, Bonnie Prince Churlish, pretend that you're on the Tower of—Hoot, mon!—Babel.

"*Sí,*" said Ramona, clutching my arm, "*pero* it's not my *verdad* name. *Eso* is a *secreto.*"

"*Yo creo* in secrets," I said. "*Nada* like 'em." I bobbed my head at

Joy, who'd come over after taking her time about laying her bouquet on the grave. " 'Morning, Miss Durwood."

"Good morning, Mr. Culloden. *Mrs.* Culloden. We met at the Gutierrezes, didn't we? Are they *away,* Mrs. Culloden? I haven't seen them in I don't know *when.*"

"They're in Cuernavaca," Polly said. "I had a letter from Angela last week."

"Oh? Did she say when they'd be *back?*"

"Around the middle of the month sometime. But nothing definite."

"Oh, *dear!* I'll *never* see the rest of their lovely house, *will* I?"

"Haven't you seen it yet? I thought Angela said you—"

"I haven't seen *any* house," Joy said hastily. "Not a *single* house in Maldita, except the one I'm in. And I've met so few *people.* I never, *never* thought I'd be so *lonely* down here."

"You knew Mr. Fletcher, though," Polly said.

"Would you be*lieve* it, I never even *met* him. He's Ramona's— *was* Ramona's old, old friend."

"*Sí, sí,* for *muchos* years," Ramona squeaked. "He bought many *cosas* from me, *hace* a few *años,* my *querido* Mr. Fletcher. Tomás Fletcher."

It was only then that I discovered a pair of males were missing. Jock and Bruce Young had tiptoed off like a couple of Starbucks avoiding the spoken thoughts of Ahab. Jock was going out the cemetery gates with Hy Levinson, and Bruce had vanished completely. I got set to follow their example.

"What it was," Joy said to Polly, "I happened to go into Ramona's *funny* little shop this morning, *first* thing. I was hoping she had one of those *sweet* painted chests—but she'd sold the *very* last two she had, wouldn't you *just* know it? Well, she asked me where I was *living,* and when I told her Mal*dita,* she—"

I didn't hear the rest. Sam the Second Mate had also stolen away, making it a trio of Starbucks. The open sea lay dead ahead and it looked like clear sailing for the *Pequod.*

"Sam?" Polly called. "Where're you going?"

"Something I have to do," I called back. "See you at the house." I neither stopped nor waved.

I stopped outside the gates, though. Gage had pulled a pack of Delicados out of his pocket wrong end up, and was bent over, gleaning. If I hadn't skidded to a halt I'd've slammed into his rear view and knocked him head over hump muscle.

"Damned Mexican cigarettes," he said, straightening. "Want one, Culloden?"

"Not right after a funeral, no. It's a profanation." I started down the undulant street that led to the main road.

Gage hurried after me as soon as he'd lit one of his damned Mexican cigarettes. "What's your religion, hey?" he asked. "Rose was wondering."

"Surprised she'd take an interest. I'm a Cynocephalite."

"Never heard of them. You putting me on?"

"It's a kind of Aegean Zen, if that means anything to you."

"Oh, sure it does. Sure. Zen, hey? That's different. Lots of good points in Zen." He yanked the freshly lit cigarette from his mouth and tossed it against a house. Three little brown-bottomed boys immediately appeared from nowhere and tore it apart in a fight for possession. "Not much of a funeral," Gage said.

"What can you expect on short notice? You know how it is in small towns."

"I do now, but I didn't before. That's why I came. I had this feeling there'd be riots, what with them dumping an atheist in a Catholic cemetery."

"So you came alone? Because there might be a riot?"

"Nah, Rose wanted to come, and so did the kids, but I put my foot down. A man has to, hey? Rose is very sensitive, and she'd bawl. And then the kids'd bawl and there'd be a hell of a racket."

"You wouldn't've heard them in a riot."

"Culloden, I'd hear those bare-assed babies in a boiler factory. When're you coming around again, hey?"

"Hard to say. I've been working."

"Not all the time, though. Rose said she saw you up at the dam. Right?"

"I was doing research."

"Yeah, there's that. I need a lot for my book, too."

"What's your book about?"

"Ah, this and that. That's a beautiful wife you got, Culloden. How old is she?"

"I never thought to ask her, to tell you the truth." We'd reached the main road. "But I'll let her know you said she was beautiful. Meanwhile, give my regards to Mrs. Gage."

I'd taken only two steps east when Gage said: "You don't have your car down here? I thought you did."

"I walk as much as I can. My plethora, remember?"

"Ah, sure. Incidentally, you don't happen to have an extra dictionary around, do you? Maybe we can work some kind of deal."

"I even forgot to bring one for myself. Stupid of me, wasn't it?"

"Ah, those things happen," he said, and sighed. "Well, that's the old Gage luck for you." He touched his forehead with his index finger in a feeble farewell gesture. "See you around, Culloden. Watch yourself, hey?" He slouched off.

◎   Something was wrong at the Delmore place, although I couldn't pinpoint what gave me the feeling. There were no cars in the parking area and no people standing outside the massive brass-bossed entrance doors, so perhaps this lack of activity had more than a little to do with it. But it went deeper than that: the very air wasn't right.

It was shortly after noon on a day of notable clarity, and yet as I approached the main house along the Delmore private road I seemed to be seeing its gray stones through a cobweb curtain. I was also struck with a sense of emptiness—an impression of such force that it was nearly vocal, crying out that no car had ever stood in the parking area and that no living person had ever lingered outside the door. Nor was this phenomenon new to me. At the moment, however, my brain kept the secret of where I'd experienced it before.

When I was within a few yards of the door the atmosphere suddenly became normal again, as though I'd been walking through a four-dimensional wall that had been set up by mistake in a three-dimensional world.

An antique chain dangled from a hole at the left of the carved façade; I tugged at it and heard a bell clang, faint and solemn, somewhere within the house. No one came to the door, though, and after a while I gave several more tugs to the chain. Again the bell clanged dimly; again I waited; again no one came. So I got mad: after all, Marian Delmore kept enough servants to staff a small hotel. I intended to see Lalage, one way or another, too, and I didn't want to be thwarted by the Applied Carelessness learned at the Maldorado Normal School. I grabbed the huge door handle, which was cast in the form of a laurel wreath, to see if I could rattle it right out of its socket.

To my surprise, it turned. I pushed, and the door gave inwardly. It wasn't locked.

I paused briefly in the entrance hall, heard nothing anywhere in the house, and then headed for the living room—from which I could go on to the terrace and the vast expanse of the Delmore patio. Perhaps that's where everyone was, I thought—out by the artificial ruin in Lotus Position, with Flents stuffed in their ears.

A man was at one of the living-room windows, staring out across the dappled patio. His back was toward me, and the room was so wide that it wasn't easy to recognize him as Francis St. Albans. When I did, it made me more angry. "Doesn't the bell in this mausoleum get answered these days?" I demanded.

St. Albans glanced over his shoulder at me, then turned away without replying.

I started toward him. "Where's Marian?"

"Gone," he said in a conversational tone. His gaze remained fixed on the patio.

"What happened to all the servants?"

"Gone."

"To the funeral?"

"I don't know. There won't be any funeral."

"What the hell're you spouting, St. Albans?" I'd reached his side. "I came to see Lalage. Where is she?"

"Lalage's dead."

I grabbed him by the shoulder and swung him around. "Look, I had all I ever want of your brand of humor the night I met you. If you don't give me a straight—"

His face was abruptly filled with such fury that I thought he was going to spring at my eyes with claws unsheathed. I dropped my right foot back, bracing myself automatically, but he burst into tears, sank to the floor, and buried his face in his hands. "She's *dead*, God damn you!" he moaned through his fingers. "God damn you, I *said* she was dead!"

What I'd seen on his face hadn't been fury, but rather such a flood of emotion as to surpass the expressive capabilities of any human being.

I felt neither shock nor surprise. I suppose I was too numb to feel anything at all, including pity for the sobbing St. Albans. Anesthetized to the point of nonchalance, I went over to the nearest of three sofas, sat down, lit a cigarette, and waited for St. Albans to get bored with playing his private Wailing Wall game. He took his time about it, naturally. However, little by little the shaking and sobbing subsided, until finally he wiped his eyes with a previously sodden handkerchief. "I'm sorry," he mumbled. "I'm not a very steady person—when things—happen—things like—" He raised himself from the tiles and sagged into a wing chair not more than a furlong away from where I sat. "I'm *really* sorry."

"I'm waiting," I said.

"Waiting?"

"For the story."

"Oh." He sniffed. "They found her this morning in her tower." He blew his nose. "Excuse me. But she must've done it Saturday night."

"Done what?"

"Taken the sleeping pills. A whole bottle—fifty or sixty, at least. Marian didn't even know she had them."

Why should she? I thought. Marian didn't even know she had a daughter. "Where is she?" I asked.

"Marian?"

"Lalage."

"Oh." He licked his lips, then patted them with the handkerchief. "Marian's driving her to Mexico City."

"You mean, driving the *body?*" If I hadn't been shocked before, I was now.

"Yes."

"For God's sake, why?"

"Because she doesn't want her buried here, she said. She wants her cremated. They have cremation in Mexico City."

"Wait a minute," I said. "According to my AAA Guide, there's a Customs checkpoint between here and Mexico City. How'll she get by that?"

"Oh, Marian doesn't care 'pooh' about Customs men. Anyway, they only want to see your car papers."

"They'll also see Lalage, this time."

"No, they won't. Lalage—Lalage's locked—Oh, dear *God!*—" St. Albans' mouth quivered. "—locked in the *trunk* of the Mercedes."

"How is it you know so much about it?"

"Because I helped." He closed his eyes, frowning. "I *had* to. Marian sent all the servants away, and then I helped her with—" Water was seeping from behind his shut eyelids.

"Is the tower open now?"

"Marian—she locked that, *too—!*" he wailed, then promptly burst into tears again.

"Well, I'll be blistered," I said to the tiles at my feet. While I let what I'd heard sink in I drew one toe back and forth, a couple of inches back and forth, along the rough edge of a tile. Before long I grew weary of St. Albans' blubbering. "Why don't you knock it off, Mary? The only reason you're bawling is, now you've got to find another girl to insult."

He pushed in some of the stops, muted his grief, and glared at me. "That's a cruel and—" He sniffled. "—vicious thing to say." He sniffled again. "How dare you talk—" Another sniffle. "—to me that way?" A fourth sniffle. "I *adored* Lalage." He blew his nose and, save for reddened eyes, was back to what passed for normal in his set.

"Sure," I said. "I heard some of your adoration at the buffet."

"Why, you don't think I *meant* that, do you? I was merely amusing

Marian, who was in one of her bitchy moods. And besides, I wasn't myself. Phil had me absolutely furious. I could've said *any*thing."

"You came pretty close," I told him.

"Are you going to make me pay for that for*ever?*" He was ready for another whirl at weeping.

I stood up. "No, but save the tears for the next crocodile caucus. Or whoever else drops in, since you're holding the fort here."

"I'm going, too," he said, getting to his feet. "I can't bear this house any more."

"Fine. As long as you don't try to leave with me." I made for the doorway that led to the entrance hall.

"Why do you have to hate me?" St. Albans whined. "Lalage didn't."

I paused in the doorway. "What makes you so sure?"

"Did she ever say anything rude about me to you?"

"Maybe she didn't have time," I said.

"*Well*, she had time to tell you she loved *you*. If she'd hated *me* she could've told you that, too."

"Where'd you find out about—?" He'd stopped me cold there.

"About Lalage loving you? Why, she told me herself. She came to see me the morning after you upset that table. And I said I thought it was wonderful, because you weren't like the other dreary men around here. But now—" The water was gathering strength again. "Oh, *now* I wish I'd said something else, because what you really are is a bully! Oh, a *horrible* bully! A bull in a china shop, *that's* what you are! So leave me *alone*, do you hear?" He hunched forward and returned to his bellering.

I left him alone. I was halfway to the entrance door when I heard him cry out: "Oh, *poor* Lalage! Oh, poor—sad—lost—lonely—*girl!*" The words came thickly through his hands, but each one was a dagger in my heart. I'd used them myself about Lalage.

With the door open, I hesitated before going outside. I was aware that whatever else might be wrong with Francis St. Albans, his grief for Lalage was, indeed, sincere. He must've been very fond of her in his own way; otherwise he couldn't've described her as he had. And Unsympathetic Sam Culloden, as usual, was dying of his own special hoof-and-mouth disease, in the final stages of which the patient sticks his hoof in his mouth with enough force to break his neck. I was tempted to return to the living room and offer St. Albans whatever comfort a bull could offer a china shop. I didn't, of course. Once you've wrecked his shop, the dealer doesn't want your business.

I left the Delmore house and laid my course for home, in spite of a gray mental cloud off the beam to port, a cloud that had me in its awesome power. After all, there was no one else around who could even haul out the topsail reef-tackles. The whole damned ship's company was stumbling about the stern of the vessel—a poopdeck of Starbucks, blanched with despair.

◎ Joy Durwood's car roared up from our road and turned away toward the bridge when I was still two hundred yards off the reef. She didn't see me, which was just as well. I didn't want to see her, either—at the moment. Later I would, though. I had quite a few matters to discuss with old Joy.

In the patio Polly was tidying what remained of glasses and bottles and ice buckets and teapots after two women had had highballs and one woman tea. I walked toward her, saying: "Entertaining the Durwood woman and her raffish friend, eh? *Muy,* oh, *muy.*" I shook my blanched head in despair.

She smiled. "Isn't that Ramona a screech?" she said. "She has an old parrot that talks the same way. I forgot to tell you."

"Tell me about the Durwood woman before you forget," I said.

The smile faded. "I may've been wrong about that one, Sam. She's had more than her share of problems, but I think she's harmless in the long run. Terribly silly, but basically harmless."

"What caused the problems? Men?"

"That, and her silliness. Wasn't it ever thus? Sit down and have a drink and I'll tell you all about it."

"Don't want to sit down. Don't want a drink, thank you."

"Why not? Where've you been?"

"At Delmore's. Lalage was supposed to be at the funeral and didn't show up."

"But that has nothing to do with you. She probably forgot."

"No, she joined the Club herself. Committed suicide Saturday night."

"*Sam!*—You're joking!—No, you're *not*. You're not. *No!* Oh, my *God!*"

"*You* sit down, Polly, and I'll tell *you* all about it. Not that there's much to tell."

She sank into an *equipál*, and I told her what I knew. Indeed, it wasn't very much—especially since I left out Lalage's connection with Joy and the request Marian Delmore had made of me. When I'd finished Polly went upstairs and I walked out on the river terrace and looked up at the sky. The rain that would hit Maldita later on was forming its battalions off to the east, but overhead the sky was clear and blue.

It was also empty. The apprentice god was gone, and gone forever.

His place, I knew, would be taken eventually, but not by another apprentice. No, whoever moved in, to act in his stead, would be a mature master craftsman—and not necessarily a god.

❈ Two

In Case You Don't Know It,
Your Needle's Stuck

"Hell is Tomorrow, understand?" I gasped to a goat-nibbled bush, "and Yesterday's what gets you there."

Oh, I was in a delightful mood, gamboling over the hills on the other side of the river, while pleasant thoughts like that ricocheted around in my skull. Fletcher had told me that I'd take some hillside walks, but I hadn't believed him; on the contrary, I'd thrown the idea over the bullpen fence as soon as I'd caught it. Yet here I was on the morning after his funeral—an out-of-breath human delta for sweat, laboring up the fourth or fifth or nth incline of an eternity of hills; a Sisyphus still alive, whose stone was the very atmosphere he lurched through.

Barely twenty years had been unraveled since I'd sworn on a stack of contour lines that never again in my life would I do any overland foot travel. My combat boots, at first hand, had taught me the topography of a huge and deafening hunk of Europe; and my future plans didn't include a Master's degree in Pedestrian Studies of the Physical Features of the North American Continent. But my future plans (c. 1945) hadn't taken into consideration my mental state on this particular morning (c. 1966). If I'd hung around the *finca,* being pushed against the wall by memories of the mortal events of the weekend, I might've dissolved like wax in the sun. It was better to do something exhausting, and to the point of utter exhaustion. So when one news straight came huddling on another of death and death and—then Sam the Ram Culloden went butting across the Maldita hills until his horns were splintered and his strength was that of a May fly.

I'd begun this stampede by following the bridge-side limit of Fletcher's hacienda to the jacaranda grove, then swung left along the hillside and the smashed rear wall. I paused at the gap where I'd first met Fletcher to study the sloping expanse of ruins that the battered stones encompassed. The two little houses inside the main entrance had their doors shut, and even the flimsy gates were closed. Either Dolores wasn't receiving that day or she'd gone to earth in the den of one of her hundred foxy relatives. The path through the street of grass was still visible; I wondered how long it would be before new grass erased it.

From where I stood I could see another definite path, running up and down the hills in an easterly direction. It might've been made by shepherds, but I didn't think so. Fletcher had undoubtedly worn it flat over the years; an old man tends to stay on a route he's established by trial and error, meanwhile avoiding all detours. I stayed on Tom's Way too: the difficult path itself was detour enough.

It was also a man killer, as I learned before long. My hazy original intention had been to slog to the hill behind the Matthews *finca*, then scramble down, slip through the well-oiled door in the wall, burst in on Joy and, regardless of whom she might be entertaining and what lubricous form the entertainment might be taking, find out what lay behind Lalage's last haunted dash from the Second Circle of Hell. But by the time I'd spoken to the nanny-gnawed bush the mere idea of survival put all immediate thoughts of Joy Durwood back in the trunk.

I supposed I was on the hill that reared its round head halfway between the Matthewses' cold home and the late Tom Fletcher's place. The site didn't matter that much, though. What really mattered was that I had to sit down for a while, wherever I was, and convince myself that I hadn't reached the end of my tether. My heart and lungs doubled up with laughter at the arguments I put forth, and kept right on tossing strings of Chinese firecrackers at each other. But eventually, thank God, they decided that perhaps they were on the wrong calendar and that it wasn't really the Fourth of July. When they let their joint stick of punk fall I snatched it up, lit a cigarette with it, and relaxed enough to allow myself a short goat's-eye view of Maldita.

It wasn't my day for scenery, and there wasn't much to see if it had been—roofs here, a stretch of river there, a few rods of road somewhere else, a crumbling church directly below me, and clumps of trees in all the places where clumps of trees should be. Although little round hills are pretty, when you've seen one you've seen them all—a statement which also covers stretches of rivers.

My breathing had more or less become the breathing I remembered, and my heart had stopped hitting my ribs with a sledge hammer, when I spotted a distant brace of birds. They were far beyond Maldita to the north and they were beating heavily east. At first I thought they were *zopilotes,* the Mexican buzzards, but then I decided they weren't. All the other *zopilotes* I'd ever seen had been swinging in lazy circles over their moribund next meal, whereas these two birds were flying in a straight line and, as it seemed, wingtip to wingtip. They were anything I chose to make them.

I chose to make them great-bodied northern geese, sent by Somebody from Somewhere to bear the soul of Lalage Delmore to the place it wanted to be—and therefore I told them in a firm, clear, telepathic voice:

> *Gray goose and ganer,*
> *Wap your wings togidder*
> *And bear ye her fadir's daughter*
> *Owre the ane-strand river.*

The message had no sooner been sent than they veered as one bird to the northeast. I watched them until too much blue haze came between us, then rose to my feet with a sigh and moved along.

I was pleased to find, as I reached the clump of trees on the hill overlooking Joy's oversized bedroom, that I was still in pretty good shape. Possibly this was because I hadn't been forcing my pace as I'd done before the birds hove into sight; but, whatever the reason, I'd gotten my second wind. Nevertheless I waited for a few minutes, leaning against a stunted tree, before plunging down the bare slope to the *finca*'s rear wall.

The door in the wall was locked. I hadn't expected that.

I also hadn't expected to do what I did next—hurry around to the main gates and yank the bell cord.

The wizened Juanita seemed to have set up light housekeeping just inside the gates. The small door swung open on the instant and she peered out at me, pursing her bloodless lips.

"*Quisiera ver la señorita Durwood,*" I said.

She made a clucking sound with her dry tongue. "*Lo siento, señor, pero la señorita no está en la casa.*"

"*¿Dónde está la señorita, por favor?*"

"*No sé, senor. Se fué.*"

"*¿ Á Maldorado?*"

She shrugged. "*No sé, señor. Se fué.*"

"Well, *gracias* anyway, you dumb bitch," I said. "And in case you don't know it, your needle's stuck."

"*De nada, señor,*" she said, closed the door in my face, and went back to her light housekeeping. That was that, then.

On the way home along the old dirt road I met a small flock of sheep, driven by an adolescent boy who was probably a *nouveau riche* third cousin of Dolores Tresguerras. He was so busy reckoning up his cut of the Fletcher loot that he wasn't paying attention to his sheep. They came toward me in a panting mass that blocked the road.

I stepped aside, watched them pass, and felt a contemptuous kinship with them. After all, human beings are sheep, too; but it just so happens that they're sheep with fangs. Every so often a shepherd is found with his throat ripped open, although the sheep never seem to gain much by this act; and when it's reported to other shepherds they're inclined, and quick, to change the subject.

The boy stopped dreaming about double-entry bookkeeping long

enough to toss me a *"Buenos días, patrón,"* which I ignored, if only
to prove to myself that I was still in a delightful mood.

"Oh, you've hurt your hand!" I heard Lalage say behind me.

I spun around. She wasn't there, of course, and I should've known
it. The gray goose and gander were bearing her into the Celtic mists
at that very moment, and even Lalage Delmore couldn't be in two
places at once.

Or so I thought then.

◎ "How was your walk?" Polly asked. She'd been about to get
into the station wagon as I came through the gateway. Concepción
and a big empty basket were already in the back seat.

"A bore," I said. "But let's call it a necessary bore."

"Did you meet anyone?"

"Strictly speaking, no. You're off to market pretty late, aren't
you?"

"I had a visitor. Joy Durwood."

"Oh? Why?"

"No reason, really. She was off on a trip and she wanted to say
good-bye. Funny that she should take the trouble, though, isn't it?
We don't know each other that well."

"Where's she heading? Cuernavaca?"

"She didn't say."

"Probably hasn't made up her mind yet. Well, I'm going to take
a shower, wash some of this sweat off. Where's Jock?"

"Haven't seen him since breakfast. Anything you want in town?
A paper?"

"No, thanks. I'll be going in myself this afternoon. They don't get
in until after three."

"That's right, I forgot."

Polly slid into the car and I made for the exterior staircase. A light
blast on the horn came when I'd nearly reached the top.

"Another thing, I forgot, Sam—" Polly was leaning across the front
seat, calling up at me from the half-opened window on my side of

the Ford. "A boy came with a package and envelope for you. The envelope's too thick for a letter, whatever's in it, and the boy ran off before I could ask him who sent them. On the coffee table in the living room."

"Thanks. I'll look at 'em later."

I had a cold shower, which helped a lot, and changed my clothes, which didn't help much but didn't do any harm, either. The big Band-Aid I'd put on my scratched hand had become somewhat the worse for wear in the course of the morning. I took it off and didn't bother to slap on a fresh one. The gash was coming along fine; and, after all, I wasn't planning any bare-knuckled fights in the next few days, nor did I intend to be using a grindstone for a punching bag.

The package was small, wrapped in manila paper and tied with brown twine. The envelope, of the kind offices use to hold triple-folded typewriter-size stationery, was white and bulky. On both envelope and package *Sr. Culloden, por mano* had been neatly written. Written by Thomas Flint Fletcher, as a matter of fact.

Some people might have opened the envelope first; I opened the package. Inside a thin cardboard box and placed between two layers of cotton was a piece of blue silk on which white stars were scattered. With it was a substantial chunk of metal. The metal was gold-finished and had a laurel wreath in green enamel enclosing a five-pointed star. Below an eagle beating its wings the star framed a bust of Minerva, around which ran the phrase United States of America. The phrase seemed vaguely familiar to me. The eagle clutched a bar that said Valor, an uncommon word these days, archaic but not yet obsolete. Metal and blue silk together added up to what is known to the trade as the Congressional Medal of Honor. On the reverse I read that it had been awarded to Capt. Thomas F. Fletcher, 312th Regt., 26th Div., who had done whatever had to be done to earn the thing at a place called Démence-sur-Fosse, France, on September 21, 1918.

I'd never seen a Medal of Honor, so I gave it a good going-over before I got around to opening the envelope. It was a letter, in spite of Polly—nine precisely written pages folded to cover a pair of one-thousand-peso banknotes. Fletcher had dated it *18 July 66* in the upper corner of the first page—just over two weeks ago. That would make it the day after my Sunday visit to the old man, the one that had been interrupted by the Iscariot brothers, Judas and George. I lit a cigarette, leaned back on the sofa, and started to read:

> *Dear Sam, I dont expect to finish this letter today but I want to begin it now because I honestly dont know how much time is left. Im up to snuff for 5 or 6 hrs every day, so I guess Im mighty lucky, but not if I dont take advantage of it. I forgot to ask you if youd met Jim Inskilling. Anyway, if you have Ill bet he said I walked in my sleep even when I wasnt sleeping. Im not a sleepwalker though, as Ive told Jim many times. When my mind is clear its as sharp as it ever was. Maybe sharper than theres any call for. Jim & I know considerable about each other, including some of the things that arent so good, but neither of us knows whats really going on in the others head even though hes a Dr & Ive seen enough to last a dozen lifetimes. But when I say I honestly dont know how much time I can count on Im being a mite dishonest, because when a mind & body have been together as long as mine have theyre able to get word to each other about whats going on & whats likely to happen. Except that they dont buddy up like that until a man has walked away from the steam shovels for good & is alone by himself, alone. Most men never do leave off watching the steam shovel, though, & then one fine day its Bang! Gone! & a new eye at the knothole. Which is the nature of the beast. So when I told you I wasnt sure but that I could pinpoint the day Id be leaving this Vale I was whitelying. The way I feel Ive got less than a month left in me. A double birthday party would be a real blowout beano but I dont think Ill be available & surely not for my official 86th. Fact is, I dont suppose Ill be with the minority much beyond Aug 2 or 3. Sam, you know what this Trip Im taking is. Youre not such a damned fool as to miss my meaning, so you must be too polite to dwell on the*
>
> *But here Im being a damned fool myself rambling on & on. Id best tell you right out that its a dead man writing to you & that when you get this letter Ill be six feet under. But please dont have any queer feelings as you read, because Im not having any as I*

write. Instead I see myself sort of looking over my own shoulder while I put the words on the paper. Maybe thats what Jim means when he says Im a sleepwalker. But a spade isnt ever a spade to a Dr. Its a pickmattock or probably some fancy Greek word. Now Im wandering again. Bad as my old bitch Dolores. But quieter. Must must stay on the path &

Sam boy, Im sorry you had to do all the talking yesterday when you didnt want to & Im sorry I didnt tell you a little about myself when you wanted me to. It was one of those mornings when I felt good for another ten years or so & thought I had all the time in the world. Which I dont. So I shouldve told you something about my life, but not everything & not only because its been such a long long life. I suspect that you didnt tell me all about you either, which is as it should be. The worst things about ourselves we put into brackets & write in invisible ink. Of course we all know what the worst things are but we never find out how many of them somebody else has done unless theyve caught him. Also I didnt know how much Jamie told you about me. Im not even sure how much I told him, as far as that goes, but whatever I mightve told him & he passed on to you would only bring you up to 1918 & that adds up to a weedy patch of weekends. To me its at least ten centuries at lea

Six grades of schooling was all I ever got where the woodbine twineth & whatever else I learned I dug from the living world. The Fletchers were too damned stubborn to move from the piece of Vermont theyd originally shot out from under the Indians, even though they harvested more rocks than anything else. My father married late. Wounded three times in the War of the Rebellion. Seven Pines. Chancellorsville, Cold Harbor. Went in as a private soldier, May 61, mustered out a limping major June 65, & never really believed in anything again. He used to say Americas clock was stopped by the concussion of the Fort Sumter bombardment & when they tried to get it going again it ran so fast that you were well into tomorrow before youd even lived through today. I didnt go along with him then but I do now & Im glad hes not around now to see what the republic turned into. I dont envy you either, stuck with living another twenty or thirty or forty years. Although perhaps you wont, through no fault of your own. Well, Ive strayed over the crest again havent

I was 18 when that fool thing with Spain started & full of being 18 I went & joined the navy. My father was against it & we had an argument, so I ran away from home & never saw him again. He died in 1899 & I guess that when he saw the 20th century coming he just said Be damned to it & turned his face to the wall. He was a good man but bitter because he & his country had gone to the whorehouse of war together & lost their innocence together but the difference between him & his country was that he wanted the old innocence back & his country didnt even know it was gone. He always hated the GAR & well he mi

I dont think your father was bitter though. Not Jamie.

When I got out of the navy, that was in 1904, I was in real good shape as far as money went since Id had six years of staying sober & doing good with the dice & having a lot of friends who thought they could fill inside straights. Went partners then with an old Bluenoser named Swasey, Capt John Swasey. We bought this hermaphrodite brig the Rosetta Tyne, sailing out of Halifax N S with Swasey as master & me as mate. She was old so got her cheap. Sailing vessels were on their way out by then, whatever new came down the ways was screwdriven. A fine trim ship & for 11 years we sailed her from Newfoundland to the Falklands & the N Atlantic to the British Isles. Wasnt there for her last voyage, Feb 15 thats 1915, because broke my leg day before she sailed from

Poor old dear was torpedoed & went down with all hands 700 miles WSW of Lands End. Johnny Swasey too, the damned bastard Huns killed Johnny. I was crazy mad & as soon as I had a pair of sound pins I enlisted with the Limeys. Glad to have me too, second Ypres had just been fought. I was with the British lucky as hell, all through the Somme & everything else without a scratch, nothing worse than trenchfoot until Aug 17, when the Yanks

But you know all that. Jamie wouldve

About Jamie & me, the day we

After the Armistice I fixed it so I got out of the army in France.

Thats where they found me, thats where they left me. Still had a lot of money too. The Rosetta Tyne had done us well all those years if it wasnt for poor old Johnnys last voyage. I stayed in Europe, France mostly until 24 not doing much of anything outside of being alive & liking it. Emilie Larrou, a French girl, was who I married in 1919 & we had 2 sons, Tom Jr in 20 & Bill in 22, after my father.

    But you know about the boys dont you you know about the boys
    Dont you know about the boys dont you dont Rambli

    In 1924 America was complacent & rotten & cheap & a country I didnt recognize, half the people crooks & the other half idealists with power. Theyre the worst kind, idealists with power, give them time & theyll bring the world down around our ears. Its the good men always do the most damage in the end. Meanwhile back then theyd given us prohibition. I dont like to see pleasure made illegal & liquor is a pleasure unless a mans a goddamned fool. Im not ashamed to admit I went down to Halifax & made some arrangements with some friends & did what I could to strike a blow for Liberty. Only a sideline, but I didnt get caught or hurt or any poorer. Had other things going for me too. An importing business mainly. Had friends from the old days damned near to Tierra del Fuego. For instance I came to Mexico the first time in 05, did a favor for Chavez-Truebas father that long ago. 61 years. God its hard to believe, it was so very

    But I wasnt seeing enough of Emilie & the boys, I was out of the country so much you know about the boys dont

    1929 Summer I pulled in my horns because I missed Emilie & the bo I

    I got bored with business in the summer of 29 & besides I didnt like the way the wind was blowing the country. So I quit Sold out Retired. With plenty of money, not yet 50 yrs old. Just in time. A few months later all the trimmers got trimmed & all the biters got bit. Then we traveled, the whole family & took it easy & enjoyed the sight of each other. Lived where we felt like, only where we wanted to stop for a while. Two years in France. Two more yrs in San Francisco. Two Great Years in a Sussex house with beautiful grounds where Tom & Bill once but youve heard about the boys them dont you

I bought a fine old farmhouse in the Berkshires, 1936 & thats where it all stopped the bastards the Huns got to us again in 41 Tom was a senior at Amherst & Bill a sophomore at

24 July 66

I feel better it wasnt so bad dont know the time but guess Ill write some more to you Sam boy you

Remember what I wrote before so I dont have to read it over do I

Why didnt you come back sooner than this Youre still not here & I wanted to say things to you very much & tell you what I never got a chance to tell my own

In the morning it was A spring morning all over the world

Emilie died in her sleep with a sad little sigh during the night before Christmas 1946 & all through the house

There were presents nobody got they werent under the tree We hadnt had a tree since The presents grew dusty poor dusty pre

I died 1 July 16 I died 21 Sept 18 I died 12 Apr 45 I died 25 Dec 46 I died

I am 4 people No, 5 I am 5

I sold the house I gave most of the money to her people in France Emilie her people I was alone I had no people Anywhere I kept some money for myself I came here Ill remember the date in a where did

30 July 66

Listen, Sam boy, its 7 oclock, but you wont be back. I know you wont, & theres not much time. My head was fuzzy a while back but now its clear & God how fast the clock is running. Still in a way Im glad you wont be here at that last wrong moment. A man has the right to go out of his life alone.

Now, with this letter Im sending a medal for Jamie, which I

*want you to mail to him. You will, wont you? Its his medal, well &
truly earned, & be damned to what the government says. Jamie
wasnt concerned about saving any damned government, only a
few friends. Because governments are Always but friends are only
once if that.*

*All Major Lathams fault, regimental adjutant, also wrote all the
citations. Didnt believe enlisted men ought to get anything higher
than DSC. Son of a bitch wore pincenez all the time, tin hat sat
square on top of his head. Maj Josiah P Latham. County assessor
in uniform.*

*I dont honestly recall what Ive said in this long letter but there
isnt enough time to reread it & still go on, so if you find Ive repeated myself here & there please excuse me. I hate people who
ramble on & on, always have.*

*It didnt work out the way it should have did it? Our last talk,
that is. There was so much I wanted to say to you & maybe some
advice I couldve given. About so many things, advice I intended
to give my bo intended to give other people when the time came,
what Id learned in this endless life. I didnt mean other people then
I meant but you know about my boys dont you. Jim Inskilling
wouldve told. Wish I could see Jim again, hes serving his time even
now but hes nobodys fool, No. Dont lose touch with him, son.*

*Oh I wish how I wish Jamie had written by now. Hes had time,
even with these damned slow crawling Mexican mails. Unless hes
sick. I hope to God thats not the reason, that hes not sick. But now
theyll send the letter back when he writes because I*

*But youll explain everything when you send him the M of H
wont you? Yes I dont worry about that, son*

*Sam I forgot, the enclosed money is for that birthday party we
shouldve had together. I want you to give the party anyway & I
know you dont need this money but I wouldnt enjoy the beano
if you didnt take it & use it. On Aug 13, as you suggested even if
the 13 turns out to be a Friday. Ill try & make it myself, one way
or another but if you dont see me around dont go looking for me.
Invite anybody you want & ask Jim to lend you a hand. Hed love*

to. *Maybe invite the whole blasted Maldita crew. Jam the lot in a
bottle, push the cork in & then watch what happens. I bet you
youll get a*

Better finish this up I blanked out just then. O Sam I wish

*Well, now Ill finish this letter & put it where theyll be sure to
find it, in my chest at the foot of the bed. With the package that has
the medal. Then Ill sit down with my boys & have a word or two
with them. I wont give them advice though, too late for that.
Theyre their fathers advisers now, Or will be in just a minute*

*A last word Sam, Hold the hills. Avoid the valleys, son. The
valleys theyre where the floods hit Where all men drown. Love &
thanks to my Jamie &*

*Oh Luck & Luck to you Sam & much love, the last, from some
dust*

T F Fletcher

◎ After I'd read the final page I avoided the valleys for a considerable space, holding the sofa, while every clock in the world stopped working and left my heart as the only arbiter of time. Eventually a faint ticktock, inhuman, came from somewhere and made me lean forward. I put the medal back in its box and redid the package, reversing the manila paper so that a clean surface met the eye. I stuck the package in the inside breast pocket of my jacket, along with the one-thousand-peso notes. At the fireplace I crumpled the letter and envelope into a shapeless mass, set fire to it, and watched it burn black. Then I descended to the patio.

There I did nothing, with complete success, until I heard the noise of an automobile braking downhill toward the gates. It wasn't the Ford. This approaching motor had asthma, and it stopped with a wheeze just outside the wall. I strolled over to the center of the gateway and found myself face-to-radiator with a beat-up delivery truck. It had no advertising on its side panels, it looked older than the cobblestones on which it stood, and it was obviously stuck together with piano wire and spit. The driver was a grizzled old chunk with a mustache right out of Emiliano Zapata. He leaned from the window and asked cheerfully: *"¿Sr. Cuyodén?"*

"Sí."

He said something I didn't understand, got out of his seat, went around to the back of the truck, and then came toward me toting a cardboard carton that had the Azteca trade mark printed on every side.

"¿Dónde, señor?" he wanted to know.

I pointed vaguely at the patio tables. *"Sobre la mesa, por favor."*

He walked to the nearest table, set the carton down carefully, and made for his truck again. As he passed me he said: *"Adiós."*

"Wait a minute," I said. *"Momentito."* He was about to climb onto his seat, but he waited, still cheerful, while I put a sentence together in my head. Eventually I spoke it, one slow word at a time: *"¿Hay que pagar algo por este cajón?"*

"No, señor," he said, and then went on in a spate of Spanish that left me behind with the second syllable. Fortunately, I'd already established, from his first word, that there were no charges on either the carton or its delivery. I fished in my trouser pocket, caught a wrinkled piece of paper currency, and handed it to him. It was a one-hundred-peso note. I could hear his happy progression of shouted thanks even over the motor's death-bed groans as he backed the old truck, against all natural laws and most technological rules, up the hill again.

I sat at the table by those twelve well-housed bottles of rum and admired the beautiful parallel lines of the carton that contained them. I may not have written to Jamie, but Fletcher's letter to Chávez-Trueba had gotten through, and no mistake. A temptation to tear open the carton for a formal rum-tasting ceremony was building up a full head of steam. I tried to put a damper on the boiler fires by reminding myself that this would be a more criminal act, under the circumstances, than tunneling through to a Fort Knox vault on Charles de Gaulle's birthday—but I sensed a lost cause. As a growing boy I was given a New England conscience for everyday wear, but in the past few years the thing has always seemed to be at the tailor's, having its sleeves lengthened or a new zipper put on the fly.

Polly let me off the hook in the nick of time when she eased the station wagon into the patio. She strolled across to me while Concepción lugged the loaded basket up the stairs to the kitchen. "No mail," she said. "Not a scrap." Her eyes went to the beautiful carton. "What's that?"

I told her what it was and where it came from and how it happened to be in our rose-girdled patio. Her reaction was sadness, and sadness was something I hadn't expected. But then—women cry at weddings.

"Isn't it a shame?" she said. "The poor old man died before it arrived. Now you can't thank him."

"Don't be too sure," I said. "Remember, the show must go on. And if the stage is dark we'll have the actors speak louder, that's all."

"Whatever that means."

"It means that the birthday party will take place on schedule."

"Whose birthday party?"

"Mine. On the thirteenth."

She gave a quick little laugh. "Why, Sam, you've never had a birthday party in your—" The quick little laugh was replaced by a big slow raising of eyebrows. "Did you say 'thirteenth'? Your birthday's the *nine*teenth."

"I'm having a joint one with Fletcher. His is the eighth, so we're splitting the difference."

"Sam—" Polly's tone was low. "Mr. Fletcher's dead."

"I know that, damn it. But his last request was that I give the party anyway."

"You didn't tell me."

"The letter didn't come until this morning. You saw it."

"That *was* a letter? I thought it might've been an inventory of somebody's house. Or a section of newspaper. Or—well, something. It was thick enough."

"He wrote large. I guess his eyesight gave out, toward the end."

"What else did he say?"

"Not much. He could've been ga-ga when he wrote it, too."

"Where's the letter now? Upstairs in the *sala*?"

"*Eh*-uh, but carbonized. I burned it."

"*Burned*—? Oh, Sam, for Heaven's sake, why?"

"God knows." I shrugged. "Maybe I've been reading too many spy novels."

Polly mutely studied the top of the carton for a moment, then said: "I suppose you burned the package, too."

"No, I let it drift down the river. It was empty, by the way."

"Empty?"

"Empty."

She tightened her mouth and stared down at me. "I'd've liked to have seen that letter, Sam. You might have saved it."

I nodded glumly. "I'm sorry, Polly. I simply didn't think." Then I left off being glum and continued: "The party'll be for the Delmore girl, too, in a way. She liked birthday parties. Incidentally, did you hear any mention in town about what happened at the Delmore place?"

"I didn't see anyone in town," she said in a level voice. "Whom do you plan to invite to this party of yours?"

"Everybody. All the gringos, that is. That's what Fletcher wanted."

"Are you planning to give it here? In the Weatherby house?"

"I'm not sure."

"Well, I'm sure. Find somewhere else, Sam. I don't like the idea and I don't want any part of it."

"Now, Polly—" But she was already on her way to the staircase, so I choked back what I intended to say and let her run clattering up to the balcony. There are more things loose on the surface of the earth than women can understand, even if they should be given ten per cent of eternity in which to achieve understanding and, to begin with, had an inclination toward the achievement. Obligations to the dead are one of the things. Living men, another.

◎ In Maldorado that afternoon I sat in the restaurant by the newsstand and sipped a beer and combed very carefully through the *News* and three other Mexico City daily papers. These last were in Spanish and were three hard rows to hoe, but I managed to stumble through them after a fashion. I was hunting for a headline, even a one-column headline, which would announce that the Customs men on the road to Mexico City had nailed Marian Delmore.

I found nothing, of course.

When I'd completed my study of the papers I strolled along to the post office and mailed the medal to my father, addressing it to the last place he'd lived.

I knew that the American postal authorities would forward it to him, wherever he was. They always do. Even when your name used to be Jamie. Even though you betrayed the ones who loved you most.

Three

He'll Amass Messmates Wherever He Goes

A tiny flirt-tail canyon wren stopped poking out insects near the top of Inskilling's wall and went into a "*Chew*-ee, *chew*-ee, *chew*-ee!" as Inés stepped from the pool. I kept my mouth shut, but my silent appreciation of what I saw was certainly more thorough than the bird's. Inés wore a black one-piece bathing suit, with buttons that worked running nearly to her navel. It managed to convey the essence of Woman better than the most immodest bikini that ever bit into a buttock. She was long-legged, high-breasted, slim-waisted and proper-hipped; and her wet hair hid, almost by accident, most of her back while reflecting the late-morning sun. It was a pleasure to watch her proud animal carriage as she took that sleek anthropomorphic body around the end of the pool. When she came to where Inskilling and I were stretched out she smoothed the wrinkles from a big white towel at poolside, smiled shyly at me, and lay belly down on it. Her skin was live gold on the towel's dead white.

The canyon wren went back to work, and I said languidly: "Jim?"

"Ummm?" His nose was pointed at the sky and his eyes were closed below dark glasses. He had on a pair of trunks but he hadn't been in the water, being content to let the sun lend a fillip to the tan he already had. He was in damned good shape for a man in his mid-fifties.

"The birds and the bees and the beasts," I said. "Do you suppose they see the man-made world as a kind of Heaven? You know, with all the creature comforts we have? Plus which, we don't have to worry about being gobbled up every time we step out of the old warren or nest or hive."

"More than likely," Inskilling said. "Why shouldn't they? It's a step upward for them. And the fact that the angelic orders consider our world a terribly run-down Coney Island means nothing at all to the lower animals. What gave you that far-fetched idea, Sam?"

"No excuse. Lying in the sun makes me stupid, I guess."

"Lying in the sun, my friend, stokes the old fires. The young fires, too, as far as that goes."

"What about the fires of early middle age?"

"Those aren't fires. They're holocausts." Inskilling finally gave his head permission to loll toward me. "The best solution, by the way, would be to have the party here." His eyes were invisible behind the glasses; his face, as usual, showed no expression. "Then your wife's stuffiness won't matter."

"She's being female, not stuffy," I said. "When the chips're down she'll be with me. But before we carry your last suggestion any further, remember that I'm here merely for advice, not to involve you completely."

"Tom wrote you to ask me to lend a hand—or so you claim. Very well, that's what I'm offering to do."

"A hand, yes. But not two arms and a leg."

"Let's not be dreary, Sam, please. The more I brood about the possibilities of this affair, the more charmed I am by the—well, let's say grim prospect." Inskilling swung his legs in my direction and sat up. "Tom said to invite every gringo in Maldita, didn't he?"

" 'The whole blasted Maldita crew' was the way he put it."

"And a very mild way of putting it, too, in the light of some of Tom Fletcher's other comments on his dearly beloved neighbors. You've met them all, haven't you?"

"*Eh*-uh. Between fifteen and twenty-five people, depending on whether you want to count children as people."

"I always count children as people," Inskilling said. "It gives them that sense of false confidence, so necessary later when they become either businessmen or buinessmen's wives. But let that pass. You'll invite the whole blasted crew, I trust."

"Well, everybody I've met. But some people are away—the Gutier- rezes and Joy Durwood, for instance. And then—"

"Oh, Angela'll be back. The thirteenth's ten days away, remember. But where did Miss Durwood go?"

"*¿Quién sabe?*" I said.

Inés heard me speak Spanish, raised her head from the cradle of her arms, and smiled at me again. I tried to locate the talkative canyon wren. It was nowhere in sight.

"Perhaps she'll find her way home in time," Inskilling said. "I hope so, anyway. She's far too well-done a creature to go slumming through Mexico in that junior-size British limousine."

"And then there's Marian Delmore," I said.

Inskilling glanced at the golden Inés. "Yes, I heard about what happened. Marian won't be gone long, though—I promise you. She may even be back now. And I doubt very much if she'll be in mourn- ing or capable of refusing an invitation."

"That's just it. I'm not sure I want her."

"Now, don't be a child, Sam, of course you want her. Why, Marian'll be the party's *pièce de résistance*. She might even end up as the catalyst. No, make that the anticatalyst."

"Is that the end-all we want, an anticatalyst?" I asked.

"Every good Maldita party has at least one," Inskilling said, "and often two or three." He wasn't joking, either; his tone told me that, although his face gave no clue. "But they're not necessarily first-rate," he went on, "which is what our dear Mrs. Delmore would be—taking into consideration her most recent activities. And as it wouldn't faze her a bit to find herself the arch-anticatalyst, I find the prospective presence of Marian Delmore infinitely pleasurable. Oh, very much so."

"You could be right," I admitted. "In fact, you probably are.

Fletcher must've known what he was talking about. He suggested in his letter that I jam the lot in a bottle, push the cork in, and watch what happens."

"It'll require very little pushing," Inskilling said, "and very little cork. Has it ever occurred to you, Sam, that in a city which—*teems* is the word, I think—with millions of God's images, a New York or a Los Angeles, you may have only twenty friends?"

"Make it an anticatalytic six," I said.

"The number isn't important. The really telling thing is that they're your friends and you've drawn them in the Anthill Lottery. But on a dead limb like Maldita you're forced to associate with the other gringos, no matter how many, who've picked this place in which to return to fetal position. And you play with them not out of choice, but because—as the joke has it—there's no other wheel in town. Meanwhile, and this is the double zero on the wheel, you loathe them. Oh, two or three may become your friends, through desperation if nothing else. As far as the rest are concerned, however, you'll go to their parties, along with other people who loathe them, and they'll come to yours, along with other people who loathe you. A Maldita party is a Night of the Sharp Knives. There's not an unscarred back within a dozen kilometers."

"I believe it," I said.

"Well, don't worry, we'll do Maldita better than Maldita deserves. We'll plan it so the party'll run from twelve noon until twelve midnight—or until the swimming pool becomes a rendering vat, whichever happens first—giving the guests an unbelievable gift of hours for happy backstabbing. Agreed?"

"Agreed," I said.

"Very good. The high whine of knives being sharpened is grating on my ears already. Now, there's a hotel in town, the Conde Azul, which can do a decent catering job if you catch the chef sober and give him sufficient time. I'll handle that, and handle the chef, too—even if it means getting him drunk. I'll also arrange for some boys who've heard about hand washing to see that the guests are fed when they're hungry. And I'll get the Conde Azul's barman's brother to mix the drinks. He's actually better than the Conde Azul's barman, but he's younger—and if there's anything worse than a lobotomy in Mexico, it's being a younger brother who does his older brother's job better, but without having a job of any kind himself." He looked at Inés again. "And I think I'll put my lost-wax Chalco delight here to work as hostess. The last couple of weeks she's become much too lazy. Lasciviousness enters into it somewhere, too. I realize it's been a dull summer, but that's no excuse."

"And what do I do?" I asked.

"Why, invite," Inskilling said. "And invite. And invite. And invite."

◎ Invite I did.

It might've been out of a fading twitch of guilt or out of sheer unfaded devilment, but my first invitational call was on the St. Albans–Payne ménage. They lived a half mile nearer Maldorado than we did, in a sprawling square little pile that was built at one end of a short, sunny ridge, across the main road from the river. Its walls were nearly obliterated by a rank pointillism of bougainvillaea which, if nothing else, proved that God had anticipated Georges Seurat.

My knock on the door was answered by Payne, a pencil transversely in his mouth and a liquid-stained sheet of paper in his free hand. His hair lanked down along each pale cheek; in many a latter-day set, he could've passed for a well-dressed maggot. He showed no surprise at the sight of me. "Well, *yes*," he said, sounding as though I were somewhat late but for all that expected. "Do come in, won't you?"

"Now that you've brought it up, I will," I said.

"Saint's painting like a mad thing," Payne said. He closed the door quietly behind me. "And I've written the *wild*est little satire—a perfect bush-baby poem. I just this second finished."

"That's a relief," I said. "I'm a person who's never been in Porlock in his life. If I'd interrupted you—*Oy veh!*"

"Would you like to hear it?" he asked.

He'd failed to glove the Porlock reference, which had then rolled into short left field for a single—although the official scorer called it an error. Payne couldn't've cared less, of course; his own poetic tradition probably went into the dark backward and abysm as far as 1923. "Depends on the length," I said.

"Oh, it's very short, very, only six baby lines."

"In that case, shoot," I said.

"I call it 'Vietnamby-Pamby,' and it's based on a nursery rhyme Eulalia—she's my mother—used to sing when I was a tiny child."

"Bang away, Lulu," I said.

Payne banged away; and what I got was:

> *"Ride a cracked hearse*
> *To the Tonkinese coast*
> *To hear Uncle Sambo quote chapter and verse—*
> *Finks at his fingers*
> *And tanks at his toes,*
> *He'll amass messmates wherever he goes."*

The straight face I'd been keeping wasn't enough; Payne was waiting for praise. Not criticism: *praise.* So I did what I could. "Nice," I said. "Especially that Uncle Sambo bit. I'm glad you managed to slip in the racial question. You had me worried there for a minute."

"You don't think it's too *obscure?*"

"No more obscure than our Vietnam caper."

"Oh, *yes!*" he exclaimed. "That's the very thing I want to get across. I'll tell Saint we have a visitor. Wasn't it *ghastly*, that buffet at Marian's?"

"I don't know," I said. "I wasn't there." He didn't hear me, though; mainly because he'd already left the room.

The decor of the *sala* I was in had to be seen to be believed. The style and period were Late Fruitcake, and there were more stripes laid on the various drapes and fabrics than Justine would've picked up even if she'd been able to dodge the lightning. The Zebrasville abattoir, that's where I was. Pretty soon I felt myself becoming part of an Op Art Happenstance, so I tried to concentrate on simple, recognizable objects. I started with a pair of chairs that flanked the fireplace, if only because they were wooden and stripeless—but it turned out they had problems of their own. Each had been carved in the shape of a curling-up human hand, with the polished palm as a seat and the polished fingers serving for a chair back.

I needed something simpler than that. Fortunately a desk by one of the windows came into view just then. It didn't pretend to be anything but a desk, in spite of sporting a few too many curlicues in the corners for my bare-boned taste. I went so far as to recognize an object on it—the letter opener with the jade handle that had figured so prominently in the threats St. Albans shrieked through the Delmore house darkness. On the blade *Tu Corazón y Mi Amor* had been engraved, none too well; but, whatever the thing lacked in workmanship, in sentiment it was last-ditch Mexicana.

St. Albans came into the room, wagging his Payne behind him. He had on what I took to be his painting costume—a jump suit whose smeared front, were it not for the buttons, could have been framed and sold as a middle-period de Kooning. He didn't seem overjoyed to see me, but at least he didn't fall into a shrieking fit, which was a step in the right direction. "I'm getting ready for a *show*," he said, flexing his eyebrows.

"Sorry," I said. "I should've realized you'd be working. But I wanted to invite you both to a party."

The St. Albans' attitude changed for the better immediately. "Oh, a *pahr*-ty?" he chirruped. "How *lahrv*-ly! At your *finca*?"

"And when?" followed quickly from Payne.

"The thirteenth," I said. "But not at my place. At Dr. Inskilling's. You know him, don't you?"

"Well, by reputation, yes," St. Albans said. "*Every*one knows the Old Black Doctor by reputation. Oh, we've met, now and again, but we've—"

"—never been where he lives," Payne chimed in, "and we're *dying* to see it. They say it's so—"

"Phil, *please,* I'm talking," St. Albans said, and burbled on to me: "Oh, that fan*tas*tic slave-girl, that Inés Injun who's all the time kissing Old Black Doctor's feet—isn't she the *end?* Such a great willowy, *butter*-y, strong, slithery, naughty *snake!*" He clapped his hands together out of self-imposed excitement. "I just would give *anything* if she'd model for me. And do you know how I'd pose her? Can you *guess?* On a *motor*cycle, my dear. Naked. Stark, staring *nude.* There's this boy in Maldorado who has the most divine old Harley-Davidson. Can't you just see those long bronze naked vicious legs, straddling a battered old Harley at every which angle? Lordy, the thought leaves me breathless! Injun-Gal Bare-Bottom, akimbo on the Twentieth Century!" He thought about it, then got his breath back. "Would she *be* my model? Would you ask her?"

"I don't even have enough Spanish to ask her to pose with her clothes on," I said. "Have you tried Mrs. Gage, though? She ought to—"

"*That* one!" St. Albans sniffed contemptuously. "Is *she* coming, too?"

"I haven't invited her," I said.

From my tone St. Albans gathered that I had no intention of inviting her, either. "That's *so* wise of you," he said.

"Why are you having the party?" Payne asked.

"Kicks," I said. "Nothing but kicks."

"The only *poss*ible reason," St. Albans said. "Oh, it ought to be the larkiest thing!"

"Not to mention interminable," I said. "Doors open at twelve noon."

"In Maldita," Payne said, "that means 'come at one.' "

"Or two," said St. Albans.

"Or any time at all," I said. "And, while we're at it, what's this reputation Inskilling's supposed to have?"

St. Albans stared blankly at me before he said: "You mean you haven't heard? Why, he ran just about the biggest abortion ring in the whole history of Chicago. The papers were full of it three or four years ago."

"I seldom read anything but the sports news," I said. "And when I do I try to avoid items datelined Chicago. Was he convicted?"

"Certainly not!" St. Albans giggled. "He'd made *much* too much money."

"But he can't practice medicine any more," Payne said. "Not in the States."

"Pooh!" St. Albans blew out some of his recaptured breath. "As if *that* worried the Old Black Doctor."

"I didn't say it did," Payne murmured.

"You never say anything, *really*," St. Albans said. "Anyway," he went on, "he *did* keep a lot of awful people from having their double-awful babies, and that means a great deal these days. Don't you agree?"

Since he was speaking to me, I had to give him some sort of reply. "I'm the most agreeable soul in the world," I said. "You ought to know that." And I made for the door.

A few minutes later, as I found myself leaving God's bougainvillaea behind me, I realized that there was one thing, at least, that I liked about St. Albans. He hadn't asked me to look at his work.

◎ What with one thing and another, I invited the McDermotts by note. Pepper and Salt got the same treatment, what with one thing and another.

◎ The interior decoration of Ramona's courtyard could only have been done by the Collyer brothers. A frazzled and molting parrot, perched on the neck of a dressmaker's dummy that hadn't been used since the bustle went out, blinked a bloodshot eye at me and yelled: "Go home, niece! Go home, niece!"

"Bugger off, Beaky," I told him, "unless you want to try for no feet."

"*¡Muy, oh, muy!*" The dirty bird began to bob his raddled head up and down. "Go home, niece! Go home, niece! *¡Muy, oh, muy!*"

Then, breaking the spell, Miss Capistrano Swallow of 1909 popped up from behind a pile of unidentifiable pieces of rusty iron. A regular little Jill-in-the-box, our Ramona. "Ricardo, Ricardo! *¡ Tu stop esto vile hablar!*" she remarked to the parrot. She then stumbled around, over and somewhat in between the heaps of junk until she found

herself, with considerable surprise, peering up at what she thought
was my face; and which was, unfortunately. "Ah, Sr. Culloden," she
whispered, "*me gusta* to *ver* you, truly *verdad. Sí,* very *mucho. Muy,*
oh, *muy.*"

"*¡ Muy, oh, muy!*" the parrot echoed, pirouetting awkwardly on the
dummy's neck. "Go home, niece!"

Ramona glared at her bird. "*Yo* mean *lo,* Ricardo," she said, with
a fluttery attempt at firmness. "*Detente* that *malo* talk, *tu* terrible
pájaro." She then gave me a grimace that I guess was meant to be a
grin: "Now, let's *hablemos* about *nosotros. Quiere* some *te* with
mí? Uno spot, *señor?*"

I couldn't very well tell her that the last thing I wanted was tea
with her, but I could tell her why I was there and that I was in a
hurry. So I did, and then hit the street as fast as I was able.

Meanwhile I left her thrilled to the marrow of whatever bones she
still had. I don't think the poor old side of beef had been invited
to a real, live party since the Maxixe died the Death.

The fresh air felt shamefully good, once I'd escaped from Ramona's
courtyard. It was quite a while before I could get enough of that
fresh air. Or could get my wits back, for that matter. I'd felt a touch
of vertigo during the short time I'd stood among those trashy step-
pyramids, and—

Well, I was nearly to José Salvatierra's Volkswagen agency, where
I planned to do a bit more inviting, before I realized that the parrot
hadn't been saying "Go home, niece!" at all. The word he'd used,
every damned time, was "*Cojones!*"

Muy, oh, *muy.*

⊚   The Salvatierras would come. So would the Youngs. And so, on
long second thought, would Polly Lockridge Culloden.

⊚   Hy Levinson was hard to pin down. Early every morning he
lugged his infernal machine out to some obscure odd corner of the
landscape until rain or darkness sent him loping home. I tried twice

to catch him, but I was either too late in the morning or too early in the afternoon. The third time I played it cute and drove to where he lived during a downpour. He was in.

His house, about the size of Tom Fletcher's, was divided into a pair of small rooms instead of being a single large one. I didn't see where Hy slept, but the front room, which also served as a kitchen, was a regular hoorah's nest of thick unreadable books, magazines, newspapers, unwashed dishes, canned goods, and rock specimens. The Treasure Tracer lay at ease on an oilcloth-covered day bed, resting from its labors.

We drank coffee and talked about Fletcher a bit and listened to the dwindling rain outside and decided to call each other Sam and Hy. After a while I told him about the party and he thought it over, his big fingers drumming on the table, until he got around to saying: "In the days when I was young and entitled to enjoyment I was never a man to party. For that you need girls and there I was too uncomfortable, too stupid with the use of the hands and feet, for the girls to show interest. Even in my best twenties, Sam, the girls each and every looked the other direction. My mother—you should have heard her, the way she carried on about such a shame. To be Jewish and a bachelor yet is not a good thing to be. It's like you're sick in the head, and people give you funny looks. In my whole life long maybe four parties I went to, and it was no pleasure, any of them. But this party of yours is different. For Tom I will go. For your double birthday I will go. For Lalage I will go. But, one question—"

"As many as you want," I said.

"No, the one only. To leave when some people get too drunk, this is all right?"

"Sure," I said. "I may leave then myself."

"You, I don't worry about," Hy said. "But me, I don't like it to see men and women make fools of themselves."

We talked some more after that, about nothing in particular. It was then, however, that it occurred to me Hy'd had an air of expectancy about him ever since I'd arrived, as though he were waiting for me to bring up a subject and I'd failed to do it. But it wasn't until the rain had slackened and I'd said I'd better be getting home that Hy put his expectancy on the line. "Didn't your young Jock tell you?" he asked.

"About what?"

"The find. The big find."

"He didn't tell me a thing. Did you make a big find?"

Hy chuckled. "A good keeper of secrets, the boy. I said to him, don't let the word get around—but I didn't say keep it from Papa." He chuckled again and leaned back happily in his chair. "More than a week ago it happened, the big find, and all because of the boy. And the books are all proven wrong. Here there was a real culture, maybe even a blended culture. But the blending I can't be positive about until more of the artifacts are located."

"How was it all because of Jock?"

"It was like this, Sam. There was a small hill and the boy, he wanted to try the Treasure Tracer half the way up it, and when I remarked that such places are where the books say you don't find anything, young Jock he asked me wasn't I trying to prove the books as being wrong. So this made sense. So I went up with him and the Treasure Tracer, and the boy said maybe to try *here,* and I did, and then with no waste time the needle began to—" He pulled himself to his feet. "Better I show you," he said. "One minute."

He returned from the bedroom carrying a cardboard box from which he took a shaped piece of beaten copper. He showed it to me as he reached the table. "This is what made the needle to jump," he said. "The first of the artifacts we dug up. It's money, what the old cultures used for money."

It was in the form of an ax and reminded me of the "money" Jock brought from Tepectlán. "Yes," I said, "I've seen others like it."

"Many have been found, I know," Hy said, "but never in Maldita or even in the whole State of Nuevocegado." He put the box down on the table and pushed it toward me. "Here are the other big finds. Tell me what you think, Sam."

I leaned over the box and saw five other examples of the copper "money" along with four—five—six—seven of the "pretty lady" figurines. "Believe me, Hy," I said with some difficulty, "I honestly don't know what to think."

And I didn't—not right then and there. For what Hy's Treasure Tracer had led him to not only resembled the artifacts that Jock had bought in Tepectlán—they *were* the actual artifacts themselves.

◉ I didn't face up to Jock until the next morning, after Polly had gone to market in the car. He'd slept late, and when I entered his room he was sitting on the edge of his bed, not completely awake, trying to put his feet into his slippers and not having much luck. He saw me and yawned. " 'Morning, Father," he said.

"I'd like another look at your base for a general collection," I said.

"Huh?"

"Don't tell me you've forgotten. The pre-Columbian stuff you got in Tepectlán."

Suddenly his drowsiness was gone. "They're not here," he said. He rose and walked barefooted toward his bathroom.

"That's right," I said. "They're not."

At the bathroom door he turned and faced me. "I suppose old Levinson showed you what he found," he said sullenly.

"*Eh*-uh," I said, "and now you're going to set him straight on exactly what he did find."

"What's the use?" Jock shrugged. "The old joker's had his kicks. It's done now, anyway."

"It's also going to be undone, little friend—in jig time, and by you."

"Suppose I don't?" He was clenching and unclenching his right fist; inadvertently, I hoped.

"Well, Jock," I said, "you're too old to be spanked. But I reckon you're old enough—God knows you're big enough—to get the living hell beat out of you, once and for all. And if you don't think I'm just the fella that can do it, you high-arsed son of a bitch, here's your chance to find out."

The young face became salt-white, the big fist relaxed. "I—I don't want to fight you, Father," he mumbled, avoiding my eyes.

"Then you'd damned well better square things with Hy Levinson," I said. "Apologize, or whatever else has to be done. You set the problem and now it's up to you to solve it. Make your choice, boy: fix or fight." I left him, a growing giant with the face of a ghost, standing openmouthed in his bathroom doorway.

◎ For reasons best known to myself I invited George Simmons by note. I also invited the *adult* Gages by note, for reasons best known to myself.

◎ "You don't know why she did it?" Marian Delmore, her racehorse legs uncrossed for a change, watched me carefully from across the coffee table in her wall-of-glass house. As she spoke she was opening the marble cigarette box.

"I don't," I said, "I truly don't. If I knew, I'd tell you, Marian. And I wish to Heaven I did know. Cigarette?"

The marble box was empty.

"Thank you." She pulled a Kent from the pack I offered, saying: "When I'm away the girls get careless." She studied me as I extended my lighter. "Are you going to say I did a wicked thing?" she asked.

I lit her cigarette and, before I sat down again, one for myself. "Disturbing, maybe," I said, "but hardly wicked. Illegal, though— isn't it?—as far as the Mexican bureaucracy's concerned."

Her answer was a shrug.

"The thing that disturbs me, I suppose," I went on, "isn't the deed as much as the method."

Marian blew out some smoke with great force. "You talked to Saint, obviously."

"Saint talked to me, let's say."

"I'll admit that the method was improper," she said. "But I really had no choice. And at least the girl had a decent cremation. The cemeteries here are the most awful boneyards. Anyway, it's over now."

"*Eh*-uh," I said, "it sure is."

"You expect me to have feelings of guilt, don't you?"

"I don't expect you to have any feelings at all," I said.

"Strange, your talking that way, Sam—considering that you're the most emotionless man I ever met."

"I like that remark, Marian. What's it based on?"

"Observation." She jabbed her cigarette out on the marble ashtray that matched the box. "And reflection. If you'd done what I asked you to do about Lalage, she might've—"

"Had a change of heart?" I broke in. "No, not a chance. It was in the cards for her to go, and she went."

"How can you say that, and still say that you don't know why she did it?"

"What I mean is, she'd reached the point where as simple a thing as stubbing her toe could trigger the action. But where I draw a blank is in the fifteen or twenty years that led up to the toe stubbing."

"I gave her every advantage, Sam. She was strange, that's all. And even you would have to admit that she wasn't an attractive girl."

"She had great charm. And beautiful eyes."

"Yes, the eyes." A shadow swept across Marian Delmore's taut face: perhaps it signified regret, more probably a fleeting jealousy. "I grant you the eyes. But no woman gets very far on a single good feature." She rose and began to pace the room in an oddly manlike way. "I might as well be frank with you, Sam," she said. "I think Lalage's far better off as she is. She'd've led a very unhappy life." When I made no reply Marian stopped her pacing and stared at me. "You have no reaction to *that?*" she asked. "Coming from the girl's own mother?"

"No reaction," I said. "In fact, I'm inclined to agree."

"Then what's all the fuss about?"

"Fuss?"

"Didn't you come over here to stir something up?"

"On the contrary. I came to invite you to a party."

"A *party?*"

"That's right, on Saturday the thirteenth. I'm giving it with Inskilling, at his place. Beginning at noon and going on forever."

Marian startled me with an abrupt barking laugh, barren of humor.

"You invite me to a party—knowing that I've just lost my only child?"

I nodded.

"And that I'm officially in mourning?"

I nodded.

"And that my grief is limitless?"

I nodded.

"In that case—" She laughed again. "I'd be delighted to come. And thank you for inviting me."

"Not at all," I said. I put out my cigarette and stood up. "And now I'd like to ask a favor."

"Yes?" She'd crossed to a delicate desk that was tucked away, wobbly and lost, in a corner.

"I'd like to see Lalage's room."

Marian glanced quickly at me, then started to scribble in an appointments book. "Her things've been taken out. There's nothing up there except a bed and a table and a chair."

"I just want to look at the room."

"Very well." The scribbling continued. "I'll take you up in a—"

"*Alone,* if I may," I said. "And you won't have to wait for me. I can find my own way to the car."

Another brief glance in my direction. "Oh, go ahead, Sam, if you must. The tower's unlocked."

"Thanks."

As I walked toward the door she said: "I detest Dr. Inskilling, of course, and he detests me."

"*¿Cómo no?*" I said. "It's the Maldita syndrome."

Each of the steps to the tower was a couple of inches higher than steps have any right to be, so by the time I'd mounted to the head of the staircase I was winded and feeling dizzy. I waited until my equilibrium came back from lunch, then entered the room that Lalage had left for good.

It was indeed bare, although it did contain a floor lamp, a bureau and a wastebasket that Marian had neglected to mention. A door hung open to reveal an empty closet. The table's three shallow drawers had been pulled out enough for me to see that they contained nothing. The wastebasket was clean. No pictures hung on the walls, nor even a mirror. The room's stripped impersonality was more depressing than any shoddy single in an eighth-rate hotel. As soon as I was in it I wanted to be out.

Somehow I couldn't leave, though. I sat in the chair and leaned my elbows on the table and gazed off at the hills, diminishing westward, one after another, until they melted down into a plain. At first it was so quiet in the tower that I could hear the ticking of my wristwatch, and then—

"I'm coming to the party with you," Lalage said behind me.

I kept my eyes on the western hills. "I'm glad," I said. "I was hoping you would."

"My mother'd say I couldn't." Lalage giggled. "But I don't care what my mother says. Not now. Not any more."

"About time, too," I said.

"Past time," Lalage said, then: "Don't turn around."

"What makes you think I would?"

"You started to."

"I never *start* to turn around, Lalage," I said. "I either turn around or I don't. Will I see you at the party?"

"Maybe. Since I love you."

"Still?"

"Yes."

"Why?"

"Because you drive very fast and wear pink paper hats. Did you know a girl named Lalage?" She seemed to have moved further off.

"In a way, yes."

"Where is she now?" Then Lalage answered her own question, in a voice grown much fainter: "*Long gone . . .*" It was the lowest of whispers. "*I'm afraid . . .*"

I turned around then, and fast. And faced an empty room.

Beyond the open door there was a sibilance of leaves.

Bendable Anywhere,
and Down Here to Rust

The Inskilling-Culloden party sequence could open, I suppose, with a 270-degree panorama shot, made as the hands of a clock on Central Standard Time join at twelve noon on a mid-August day. In such an opening the pan would cover an area of twenty thousand square feet, give or take a cubit, and the scene would begin at the front of Inskilling's big house as an adolescent boy, bearing a silver bucket of ice cubes, uses a thin shoulder to push himself past a screen door. The camera would stay on this boy as he makes his way to the temporary bar—a trestle table, draped on three sides by a ground-touching cloth. As the lens skims this outdoor bar, which is set up in the center of four tall avocado trees, the audience cannot avoid seeing that several dozen glasses, of various shapes and sizes, have been arranged lip down at one end of the table, while at the other are virgin bottles of Mexican-made rum, gin, vodka, tequila, vermouth, soda water, and Coca-Cola, together with shakers and stirrers and lemons and such. Between the temporary bar and an ancient soft-drink cooler in which unchilled bottles of beer are embedded and cooling in shaved ice, flanked by cartons of still-warm beer and Peñafiel, stands a twenty-year-old named Paco, who wears a white open-throated shirt and black trousers and who is the unappreciated brother of the Conde Azul bartender. Across the trestle table from him the audience would note a delectable pre-Columbian creature, listed among the members of the cast as "Inés," and wearing the same patriotic and desire-inspiring costume that brought her to fame in an earlier film by the same producer, entitled *Cocktails at Angela's,* which failed at the box office because people weren't going to pastorals that particular week. With her would be James Winters Inskilling, sometimes referred to as the Old Black Doctor, and a nonentity named Samuel Fraser Culloden, invariably described as the Aging White Zero, whose wife would appear later in the reel, prettily disguised as "A Guest." This group, seemingly frozen in Time and Mentality while each reviews his private version of the wild doings they had last Ash Wednesday at Marienbad, would spring into a lackluster kind of action with the arrival of the ice bucket; and out of the corner of its collective eye the audience might perhaps watch two glasses as they are set in front of the gentlemen and gape as a bottle of Azteca appears miraculously from under the cloth-veiled bar. Then the inexorable camera would swing beyond the avocado trees to reach the pool, around which ten metal tables, each shielded from the sun by a huge canvas umbrella running through a hole in the table's middle, each with its complement of four metal chairs, and all rented from the Posada del Conde Azul as part of the catering service, are placed in a haphazard way. Every table top holds a saucerful of peanuts and a saucerful of sunflower seeds. Were a narrator's voice accompanying the sequence, information would be passed to the audience that (a) hot hors d'oeuvres will be offered from two thirty on; that (b) the full Posada Azul buffet will be ready at four, along with a more substantial portion of the Posada's clean-handed manpower; and that (c) until then three boys, one of whom had just been seen bringing the ice bucket from the house, would attend clean-handedly to the guests' more pressing needs, at least as far as nuts and drinks are concerned. Then, narrator or not, the camera would pan to the gate that leads into the Inskilling patio, where it would hold—precisely at the moment when a bell clangs outside.

But the Inskilling-Culloden party sequence will not open that way. Instead, a fade-in to a group shot at the bar will do to start the ball rolling—if only because that was how the party began for me.

◎ Inskilling finished helping himself to Azteca and said: "Why were we waiting for the ice, Sam? A man who'd put ice in rum like this would shoot his mother down."

"Well," I said, "if she raised him to put ice in rum like this, the old girl deserves to be shot."

"Granted." Inskilling lifted his glass. "Here's luck to the party. May she never abort."

I nearly choked on his last word, remembering what St. Albans had told me. I didn't choke, though—not with my mouth full of Azteca. And then the bell sounded. Inskilling looked at his wristwatch. Inés looked at Inskilling. I looked at her.

"That makes us official," Inskilling said. He nodded to Inés, who walked toward the gate. "Somebody must be terribly lonely," he said to me as we watched Inés threading her way among the tables at one side of the pool. "I didn't expect our first guest until at least twelve thirty."

"Is that usual?" I asked.

"With the Mexicans, yes. You might even call it jumping the gun. But you never know what gringos'll do, especially if you're a gringo yourself. For instance, I'm never quite sure how I'll behave from one day to the next." He sighed and made a clucking sound inside his mouth. "Oh dear," he went on, "see what Inés let in. 'For they went at large like horses and leaped like lambs.' Happy now, Sam?"

I watched Rose Gage come through the gate. She was followed by Jefferson Gage, who was followed by Alpha, Beta, Gamma, and Delta Gage, in descending order. "Hell!" I said.

"Not happy now, Sam?"

"I didn't invite the damned kids."

"Never mind. As long as we keep them out of the house they won't be any trouble."

"What'll they do if they get inside? Wreck it?"

"No, but they might drag one of the smaller and weaker bus boys into a bedroom and—" He shrugged off the rest of the sentence.

"Mybe we'd better keep Mama Gage out of the house, too," I said.

"No," Inskilling said slowly, "Papa Gage's the one to watch. He's a regular goat, Papa Gage is."

"Oh? I had him down as merely a lush."

"That plastic Pan shouldn't be left alone with any female over the age of six." Inskilling spoke in a whisper without moving his lips. "And I don't think the female is even required to be human." His voice abruptly became normal again: "Ah, Mrs. Gage. Gage. So glad you could make it. And how thoughtful of you to be so prompt. Sam and I were afraid we'd have to put up with each other's company for another hour or so." His face was, as always, expressionless; but certainly somewhere inside him a demon was doubled up with delight, laughing so hard that its horns smoked.

◉   Americans are a sad and folksy crew. They're sad when alone and pale with anxiety to get together with other Americans and be folksy; but as soon as they find themselves surrounded by real, live folks they slip into a chalkier pallor and a deeper sadness. This glum truth impressed itself on me, and not for the first time, while I acted my role of half-host. The on-the-dot Gages seemed to have broken the dam, for a flood of fresh arrivals was pouring through the gate even before the dam breakers had a chance to wet their whistles; the McDermotts, Pepper and Salt, George Simmons, Ramona, Polly with the Youngs, the Salvatierras, St. Albans and Payne.

For a week and a half I'd Invited; now for an hour and a half I Mingled. I Mingled at the bar, I Mingled by the gate, and finally I did my Mingling among the tables that rimmed the pool. It wasn't easy, either. At Marian Delmore's buffet I'd been drunk when I zigzagged across the paths of the ten or twelve people in Maldita I'd be most apt to like; this sunny August afternoon I was sober and surrounded, with certain exceptions, by people I didn't care for at all. Sobriety presents a number of problems to its practitioners, not the least of which, politeness aside, are a necessary suavity and a patience for small talk.

I did what I could, within my limitations. I moved smooth and I talked small and I tried to make myself as amusing as, say, a Deaf Smith County preacher. If I failed, the failure could be blamed on my never having been a preacher. Or in Deaf Smith County.

My memory, for reasons I prefer not to fathom, has fixed that early segment of the party in snippets of dialogue, as dull scenes lifted from a nonepic film or a singularly undramatic play. It might be called *In My Father's House There Are Many Unheated Mansions.* And then again, it might not; the title's too long for any known marquee. But, whatever name the thing goes by—

ACTUS PRIMUS. *Scaena i.* CULLODEN *solus. Enter to him* McDERMOTTS.

McDERMOTT. Why didn't you say it was your birthday in the invitations you sent us?

CULLODEN. Well, it's not exactly my birthday. It's—

MRS. McDERMOTT. Someone said it was your birthday.

CULLODEN. Well, you know how people talk.

McDERMOTT. In Maldita, yes. Terrible. The most terrible gossip. I've lived a long time, mind you, but I don't think I've ever—

MRS. McDERMOTT. How old does this make you, Mr. Culloden?

CULLODEN. How old does what make me, Mrs. McDermott?

MRS. McDERMOTT. Your birthday.

CULLODEN. But it's not my birthday.

McDERMOTT. He just said it wasn't his birthday, Joan. Not precisely his birthday, that is.

MRS. McDERMOTT. I know what he said, Ransom. But if it *were* your birthday, Mr. Culloden, how old would you be?

CULLODEN. How about forty-six? That sound right?

MRS. McDERMOTT. Why, you're a mere boy, aren't you?

CULLODEN (*his suavity askew for the moment*). Only when I'm around mere girls, Mrs. McDermott.

McDERMOTT. Well, Culloden, I'd say you're right at your peak now. Mind you, I'm no psychologist, but I recall reading that a man reaches his peak in his mid-forties. Intellectually, mind you, not physically. He reaches that earlier. I mean, by his mid-forties a man's learned and assimilated all he's ever going to learn or assimilate. From then on he spends the remainder of his life in consolidating and refining the knowledge he's accumulated to that point.

CULLODEN. I hope not, sir. I've learned so little that I'd dread to have my brain pensioned off and put out to pasture before I—

McDERMOTT. Oh, you've learned far more than you think you have, I'll wager.

CULLODEN. No more than three things, I'd say. That I'm sure of, I mean.

MRS. McDERMOTT (*smiling*). Only three? Goodness, that's not many!

McDERMOTT. Three things are a great many, Joan, if you're sure of them. Most men, mind you, are fortunate to—

MRS. McDERMOTT. What three things, Mr. Culloden?

CULLODEN. I'd rather not say, Mrs. McDermott. You'd think them silly. And besides, it's not my birthday yet. I might come up with a fourth by then.

McDERMOTT. I'd be interested to hear them, Culloden. Curious, too. It's not often—

MRS. McDERMOTT. Oh, let the man talk, Ransom! How can he tell us what they are if you won't let him get a word in edgewise?

CULLODEN. Very well, Mrs. McDermott. But please remember that although they may sound silly to you, I consider them not only as my personal discoveries, but I also let them serve as rules of conduct.

McDERMOTT. Good, good.

CULLODEN. Yes. All right, the first is: All human labor consists of picking something up and putting it down someplace else; and it makes no difference whether it's a lug of peaches or an idea.

The second is: The quiet night and the quiet head are both full of noises. And the third is: No matter how long or how much you bite your nails you can never make one of them smooth again. This last, incidentally, is known as Culloden's Law of Digitidynamics.

McDERMOTT (*dubiously*). Well, yes . . .

MRS. McDERMOTT. When exactly *is* your birthday, Mr. Culloden?

McDERMOTT (*looking off*). I can't understand why they haven't put that Ramona woman away.

Scaena ii. POLLY & *the* YOUNGS. *Enter to them* CULLODEN.

CULLODEN. Where's Jock?

POLLY. Why, I thought he came over here to help you.

CULLODEN. To do what, for God's sake?

POLLY. Whatever you've been doing, I suppose.

CULLODEN. Well, he hasn't shown his face here. It's so long since I've seen him I forget what he looks like.

NAN YOUNG. He told me last night he'd meet me here.

CULLODEN. Did he say when?

NAN. No.

HELEN YOUNG. He never does.

BRUCE YOUNG. Is it true, Sam, this rumor that you've inherited some fine old rum?

CULLODEN. Maybe. But the will's still in probate.

BRUCE. That's a lie.

CULLODEN. So it is. And I suppose you want some, don't you, Bruce? Can't wait to curl your little pink tongue around it. All right, go to the barman and tell him Sam sent you. And meanwhile point your finger under the table. That's where it's stashed.

Scaena iii. CULLODEN *solus. Enter to him* ST. ALBANS & PAYNE.

ST. ALBANS. I'm *furious* with you, Mr. Samuel Culloden.

CULLODEN. Nice to see you keeping in character, Saint.

St. Albans. I *mean* it. You invited those sloppy, soppy Gages after you promised me you wouldn't.

Culloden. I don't remember promising you that.

Payne. You did. I heard you.

Culloden. Well, I won't argue the point. It just goes to show how perfidious males are, doesn't it?

St. Albans. All I can say is, if they try to talk to me I'll snap my fingers in their faces.

Payne. So will I.

Culloden. Suits me, boys. I'll pass the word around.

St. Albans. I hope you *do*. If I'd suspected for a single moment that those creatures were coming, I'd've—(*claps hands together quickly several times*) O-o-o-ooooo! Will you *look* at that Inés Injun thing over there by the house! Isn't she just the *outré*-est *bizarrerie* you ever saw?

Culloden. Just the.

Scaena iv. Culloden *solus. Enter to him* Pepper & Salt, *in tandem.*

Pepper. It's a great relief to everybody that you've made up with Saint.

Salt. Oh, yes, we're very pleased.

Pepper. He needs all the friends he has, these days. You know, don't you, that he was in a literal state of shock over what happened to Marian?

Culloden. Funny, I thought it happened to Lalage.

Salt. Yes, it did, it did! We all said—

Pepper. Oh, it was sad about the girl, I agree, but you can't claim that it was unexpected. People in Maldita who knew her saw the handwriting on the wall *there*, all right. The real trouble is, though, that many of Marian's friends don't understand her at all. They think they do, but—

Salt. Elizabeth does, though. Don't you, dear?

Pepper. I think so, yes. But let's not discuss it now.

Salt. Oh, I hadn't the least in—

PEPPER. I've been wanting to ask you, Mr. Culloden. How did you like the *olla?*

CULLODEN. *Olla?*

PEPPER. The one your wife bought from us.

SALT. The pot.

CULLODEN. Oh, the little pot. I found it very interesting. You have no idea. And I arranged it myself—put it, that is—in the spot where it's most effective.

PEPPER. Really? How clever of you! Is interior decoration a hobby with you?

CULLODEN. It used to be. (*glances at his empty glass*) And may be again pretty soon.

Scaena v. CULLODEN *solus. Enter to him the* OLD BLACK DOCTOR.

INSKILLING. Any heads fallen in your lap yet, Sam?

CULLODEN (*shaking his own head*). Reckon the owners don't know me well enough.

INSKILLING. More likely they've decided you're too closemouthed. They hate to have their gossip wind through an ear drum and then hit a dead end. Anyone you invited who's failed to appear?

CULLODEN. Three or four, maybe. But you know who I miss? Old Angela. And don't ask me why.

INSKILLING. I miss Angela, too. But cheer up, Sam. I left a message with her cook, saying that if she got back today, and if she didn't feel too tired, then she should drag herself and Lencho over here before the funeral baked meats were cold.

CULLODEN. Is the cook expecting them back today?

INSKILLING. She didn't know anything about anything. But then, Angela's cook is about as stupid as a human female can be. The fool girl'd had three babies before she was made to realize that a different, not to mention *in*different, man had put each one in her. She'd been praying to the Virgin for children, you see, and she thought that the prayers had worked. Christ, even a dormouse has more sense than that—although a dormouse can't

whip up a delicious *huachinango Veracruzana,* more's the pity.
Stay unbloodied, Sam.

Scaena vi. CULLODEN *solus. Enter scurrying to him* RAMONA.

CULLODEN. Ah, so there *Usted* are! I have a compliment for you.
Mr. McDermott told me you were the most fascinating *mujer*
he'd seen in years.

RAMONA. Did *él?* That *chulo* old *hombre? Muy,* oh, *muy. Y* he *es*
so *alto. Y* dignified, *también.* Oh, *tengo que* talk *con* him *ahorita!*
Perdón me. (*exits, still scurrying*)

CULLODEN (*cheerfully*). Go home, niece.

Scaena vii. CULLODEN *solus.* JEFFERSON GAGE *nosing around.*

GAGE. Sorry about Rose, Culloden.

CULLODEN. Oh, are you? Why?

GAGE. Ah, it's the way she's acting. Real sullen. Didn't you notice?

CULLODEN. Sorry. Must've been looking the other way.

GAGE. Yeah, you must've. When we got here she hardly spoke to
you.

CULLODEN. What's wrong with that, *hey?* Hell, everybody else is
speaking to me too much. It's overspeak, Gage, pure overspeak.

GAGE. Sure, that figures. Anyway, Rose's been grouchy ever since
we got up this—(*calls o.s.*) Hey, you *Gamma!* All you girls!
What you doing in the pool with your shoes on? If you want
to play in the water, take 'em *off!*—(*to Culloden*) Damned
kids, always crazy to strip. I wanted to leave 'em all home, tied
up to clothespoles, but Rose, she—Ah, the hell with it. How
about a little talk about writing for pictures, Culloden? You
said we'd have one, that day you came to the house.

CULLODEN. Did I? It slipped my mind.

GAGE. That's because your mind's on this book, hey? Me, I get
forgetful when I'm working, too. So who can I get in touch with
in Hollvwood who'll fix it for me to get something out there?

CULLODEN. Beats me. The way it usually is, they see something you've done that they want and then they get in touch with your agent.

GAGE. I don't have an agent. I mail out my own stuff.

CULLODEN. Then they'll get in touch with you, as soon as they see something of yours that they want. How many books've you published?

GAGE. Well—uh—since you put it that way, none. But I'm working on one now, though. A doozer. It'll make 'em all sit up and take notice.

CULLODEN. Well and good. Meanwhile, have you published anything?

GAGE. Ah, sure, lots of stuff. You know, fiction. In the men's mags.

CULLODEN. Men's mags? Oh, I get it. *Esquire* and *Playboy*—magazines like that.

GAGE. Yeah, sort of. But more like the smaller men's mags. *Adam*, say. *Knight*.

CULLODEN. Now I catch on. I was wondering why I hadn't run across your name. Probably it's because I don't see those magazines very often. I like to read in Study Period, you know, but they're not the right shape to fit into the *Atlantic Monthly*, which is what I want the study-hall teacher to think I'm reading. But never mind my problems, Gage; and to tell you the truth, without an agent you're licked before you start, as far as the Coast's concerned. If I were you, I'd put Hollywood out of my mind. Go East, young man, and wilt with the country.

GAGE. Yeah. You got an agent's name you can give me?

CULLODEN. Half a dozen, if you want. Not on me, though.

GAGE. That's okay. No hurry. By the way, you ever tried peyote?

CULLODEN. Not in so many words, no.

GAGE. Maybe you'd like to try some, hey?

CULLODEN. I doubt it. I still haven't caught up on my glue sniffing.

GAGE. Ah, that glue stuff's for kids. Listen, this guy I know came through from Texas this week. Brought me more goddamned buttons than I can use from now till Christmas. The way I see it, you and your wife could come over tomorrow and the four of us'll have a peyote party. What we do, we put the buttons in the Waring blender and get all the juice out. That way you don't have to chew the crummy pulp for twenty, thirty minutes. How's it sound, hey?

CULLODEN. Ginger-peachy, except that the model I'm driving now has built-in LSD.

GAGE. The hell with that fancy stuff. Listen, peyote right from the button is roughing it, know what I mean? And I bet your wife'll —(*he stares o.s.*) God *damn!* What the hell are those bare-assed babies doing? (*yells*) You, *Alpha!* Hey, Gamma! All of you girls! I said take your *shoes* off! I didn't say take *everything*— (*exits at a dead lope*)

Scaena viii. CULLODEN *solus.* INÉS *sola. They pass each other.*

CULLODEN (*smiling*). ——!
INÉS (*smiling*). ¿——?

Scaena ix. CULLODEN *solus. Enter to him* GEORGE SIMMONS, *somber.*

SIMMONS. Do you have the feeling that Tom's here with us?

CULLODEN. Not yet. Try me later.

SIMMONS. People seem to be enjoying themselves, but I somehow can't get into the mood.

CULLODEN. That's all right, George. Neither can I.

SIMMONS. So you have a sense of someone missing, too? Someone who's not here and should be?

CULLODEN. Sure. Every day of my life.

SIMMONS. *Do* you, you really? How very strange. Tell me, Sam, were you in Normandy during the war?

CULLODEN. Normandy, no. Every place but.

SIMMONS. Where, then? Italy?

CULLODEN. Italy, North Africa, Sicily, France—the whole bit. Italy was the worst, I guess, although all of them were thirty kinds of crap.

SIMMONS. Did I tell you I was a chaplain in Normandy until—
CULLODEN. You didn't tell me, but I figured you were.
SIMMONS. You did? What gave you the idea?
CULLODEN. How the hell do *I* know?
SIMMONS. I understand. You *felt* it. Were you wounded?
CULLODEN. Twice. Once in the butt and once in the calf of the leg. More painful than anything else, not that it matters. And both times from eighty-eights, not that they matter much any more, either.
SIMMONS. My wound doesn't show, I'm afraid, but I was—
CULLODEN (*quickly*). Excuse me, George, my wife seems to be— (*exits, in several directions*)

Scaena x. POLLY *sola. Descends to her* CULLODEN, *deus ex machina.*

POLLY. Sam, I'm beginning to worry about Jock. You don't think he might've been—
CULLODEN. Polly, I'm beginning to worry about you.
POLLY. About me? For Heaven's sake, why?
CULLODEN. Because you're beginning to worry about Jock. Relax. He'll get here in his own good time.
POLLY. You were worried before.
CULLODEN. No, I wasn't. I was curious, that's all. By the way, has anybody else but me told you you're the prettiest woman here?
POLLY. Only three other men, so far. But it's early yet. Things going smoothly?
CULLODEN. So far. But it's early yet.

Scaena xi. CULLODEN *solus. Enter to him* INSKILLING.

INSKILLING. Would you say we're steaming along, Sam?
CULLODEN. *Eh*-uh, at full speed. Except that nobody's gotten around to tying down the whistle.
INSKILLING. Marian Delmore'll do that.
CULLODEN. I suppose so. If she ever gets here.

INSKILLING. Don't underestimate our Marian. The Queen of the Anticatalysts knows when to come sweeping in.

CULLODEN. Yes, but when?

INSKILLING. Frankly, I haven't the faintest idea—which is as it should be. Otherwise the pleasure might go out of it. (*gazing across the patio*) Look at them, Sam! Aren't they wonderful?

CULLODEN. I guess so, in a grim sort of way.

INSKILLING. I have a pet name for them, all these gringos. I call them the Iron Crowd—bendable anywhere, and down here to rust.

CULLODEN. That'd make sense, if you and I weren't down here, too. Doesn't that make us part of the Iron Crowd?

INSKILLING. Don't be dull, Sam. You and I've been through a private Bessemer process and now we're steel. We may not be stainless, but we're steel, for all that. Highly polished, too.

CULLODEN. I see. But what's our purpose in Maldita? To set shining examples?

INSKILLING. Exactly. And isn't it a shame that we're making such a mess of it?

Scaena xii. LUZ SALVATIERRA *sola. Enter to her* CULLODEN.

CULLODEN. Deserted again?

LUZ. No, José has gone to the bar for new drinks. He is there. (*points*) See him?

CULLODEN. At the moment I prefer to be nearsighted. You're drinking along with him?

LUZ. Yes, but not very much. I do not drink very much.

CULLODEN. I know.

LUZ. You know? How is it that you know?

CULLODEN. Because you look like a woman who doesn't drink very much.

LUZ. That is not a good answer. At different times I look like different women. Many different women, thinking many different things.

CULLODEN. Not to me, you don't.

Luz. Then you do not know me very well.

Culloden. Do you want me to know you very well?

Luz. No.

Culloden. Life is better now, isn't it?

Luz. What do you mean, life is better? Was it bad?

Culloden. That's the impression you gave me, the last time I saw you.

Luz. Oh, yes, the last time you saw me. At the restaurant, no? I was not feeling well that afternoon. I said many words that I did not mean. It was from not feeling well. Did you believe those words I said?

Culloden. Not if you don't want me to.

Luz (*confused*). Do not believe them, please. *Por favor.* They were words only. I was—

(*Enter to them one* Salvatierra, *a cup bearer*)

Salvatierra. And who may this handsome couple be? Why, one of them is my wife, and the other is—yes—no—yes, it *is* the host! I'd know him anywhere. Culloden's the name, right?

Culloden. Hello, José. Who's minding the store?

Salvatierra. Are you kidding? Nobody's minding the store. I sent 'em all home and the store's closed till Monday. Here's a trade secret for you, Sam: cars aren't bought on a weekend, not even a Volkswagen. And you know why? Because María has spent most of Saturday afternoon watching her friends take their *niños* for a ride in their shiny new sedans, after which María has spent all of Sunday yelling at Juan about why can't Sr. and Sra. Juan have a shiny new car like their friends, until finally Juan yells at María, "Okay, okay, I'll *buy* a car—only let me get some sleep." And then on Monday, if Juan's got any money, he goes and buys a car. And if he hasn't got any money, on Monday he goes and borrows enough so that he can buy the car on Tuesday. —And meanwhile, what've you two been talking about?

Luz. ———.

Culloden. Oh, Luz has been nagging me to buy her a car on Monday, but I told her I couldn't. "We're not married," I told her. "It wouldn't look right, and people would talk. And besides,

I'm a gringo and can't get a loan. Not even on a Monday in Maldorado."

Scaena xiii. CULLODEN *solus, bemus'd, his Skull in his hand.*

CULLODEN. *He who would probe the body of this world*
Should learn the trade through self-evisceration:
Prod his own brain pan first; configurate
His spleen in papier-mâché, perhaps, or mud;
Bone up on gonaducts; and goose his liver
According to his lights. Who'd probe his time
Must auger through the hummock of himself
And, like some camera'd archaeologist,
Use flash in that Etruscan tomb, his heart.
Then let him, if it's worth the shovel, dig.

(Exits, toward an abyss, as

THE CURTAIN GOES UP.

❦ Five

But a Lack of Bamboo
Leads to Vulgarity

I didn't see Jock and Hy Levinson when they came into the patio.
They hadn't bothered to clang the bell, the gate had been left open,
and I was facing in the wrong direction anyway.

As a matter of fact, I was facing St. Albans and Payne, who were
trying to play a very one-sided version of the old Do-You-Know?
game, this particular scrimmage taking place over a frost-bitten field
of New York City artists. Both of them were astonished to learn that
the painters they mentioned, together with their work, meant absolutely nothing to me. "But Billy Sidewinder," St. Albans said, "you
simply must've heard of Billy-boy, or seen reproductions of his paint-
ings. Why, just last year the Guggenheim bought three, and *Time*
reproduced them in color."

"The name sounds vaguely familiar," I said. "Perhaps that was the
week I read *Time* last year." I didn't bother to mention that I knew
one New York City artist very well indeed, but he lived in a cold-
water, walk-up stupor on the wrong side of the Guggenheim. He was
neither rich enough, nor notorious enough, for St. Albans to have
met him.

"You've been to the Guggenheim, haven't you?" Payne asked.

"*Eh*-uh, but the damned ramp made me airsick. If God had intended man to spiral down the interior of a building, He'd've given Frank Lloyd Wright talons."

Payne giggled. "I've heard that's what He *did* give him."

St. Albans giggled, too. "Well, He certainly gave them to Billy-boy Sidewinder. Billy's the most frightful sadist you could imagine, and it shows in his work, in the cutest ways."

"I'd call him romantic," Payne said. "And you've called him that, ducky, thousands of times. I've heard you."

"Phil, what I mean is," St. Albans said, "Billy-boy's a *romantic* sadist." He smiled at me in a sado-romantic way. "He has these mad fantasies, Billy-boy does, regular Ogre-Giant fantasies, and he always paints himself into them."

"As a knight," Payne added. "A plumed knight."

"But in black armor, naturally," St. Albans said. "Because Billy sees himself as the boy who owns the tower where the Princess is in prison."

"Prince," said Payne.

"Oh, pooh, Phil!" St. Albans sniffed. "It's all the same, one way or another, once you're thrown in a dark dungeon. You've read the Marquis, haven't you, Cully-boo?" He pronounced "Marquis" in the English manner.

I didn't like his calling me "Cully-boo," any more than I liked his talking to me at all. I let it pass, however. "Which Marquis is that?" I demanded. "I left my Debrett under the bed."

"Why the Marquis de Sade, who else?" St. Albans exclaimed. "Don't tell me you haven't read him?"

"Oh, sure I've read him," I said. "Years and years ago. I can remember myself, as a kid, wishing they'd get Rube Goldberg to illustrate *The 120 Days of Sodom*."

St. Albans wasn't really listening. "What do you think of him?"

"Rube Goldberg? A great man."

"No, the Marquis de Sade."

"I think he must've been a bore in conversation."

"Why, that's something *no*body's ever said before, to my knowledge. Phil, do you—?" But St. Albans'd chosen that moment to look past me, and so lost the thread of what he was about to say—replacing it immediately with another thread from his spindle, "Ah, here's that great big luscious *child* of yours, Cully-boo. With Gentle Hyman, meek and mild."

It was then that I turned and saw Jock and Hy Levinson standing uncertainly inside the gateway.

"You've met Gentle Hyman, haven't you, Cully-boo?" Payne asked.

"A couple of times," I said, "yes."

"Well, I give you fair warning," St. Albans said. "Don't *ever* go along with a meek man's meekness. He's fearfully smug, deep down —because he knows that in the end he's going to inherit the earth and that you, ducky, are a cooked goose."

Jock's eyes met mine, as though by accident, before he located Nan Young, who was being talked to by Jefferson Gage between the avocado trees and the wall. Without even a nod to his father, Jock headed for Nan. Hy meanwhile remained by the gate and seemed to shiver in the breeze of chatter that blew toward him from the pool.

"Why did you invite *him?*" Payne demanded.

"For the best of all possible reasons," I said. "He doesn't own a Harley-Davidson. Excuse me."

Hy saw me coming, smiled and held out his hand. My metacarpals could've done without the handshake, but they lived through it. "He's a good boy, Sam, your Jock," Hy said immediately. "And he made a cleaned breast of it to me. Don't punish him, please, Sam."

"Don't worry," I said. "People punish themselves far worse than other people can punish them. I'm glad he told you what he did, Hy, although I'm sorry it was you he did it to. Let alone did it at all."

"Sam, believe me, there is sorrow enough in the world without us adding more over small nothings. This was a prank we might do, you and me, if we was young boys ourselves. But there is one thing your Jock wants, that I should keep the artifacts. This is not right. They're his, bought with his own money he earned. Sam, I want you to tell him he should take them back."

"I'll tell him no such thing," I said. "You keep them, Hy. You've earned them, a damned sight more than Jock has."

"You don't mean that, Sam."

"I do mean it, Hy."

He dropped his eyes, scraped the ground with his shoe, and frowned. "Well, I'll talk again with the boy," he said.

"Come on and have a drink," I said. I took his arm.

Hy freed himself from my grip, gently. "Forgive me, Sam, but I'm not staying. I only came as company for the boy and to give you a present." His face grew bright again. "Real floods they don't have here any more, but the the big flood of 1896 was only the last of many. Twice in the 1700's the place was hurt bad with these old floods. And then was the revolutionary troubles, a hundred fifty years ago. The people buried their things and maybe they never came home alive to dig them up again. I knew this from books, but it didn't mean nothing. That is, until the other day it didn't mean nothing. The day before yesterday, to give the exact date. Anyway, I walked along the river, away down the stream. Walking only, Sam. I had the Treasure Tracer with me, but not even turned on. Then I sat for a while where I guess was years ago the bed of the river, that shifted. And for no other reason, but for something to do only, I switched on the Treasure Tracer, right where it was laying on this old sand there. Sam, it begun to click like a crazy man, never before so loud. So what could I do? I dug. Look at this, Sam—"

From the pocket of his shirt he pulled a piece of tissue paper that was folded to form a small rough square. When he put it in my hand it felt heavier than something that size had any right to feel, but after I'd unfolded the tissue paper I realized that it had every right to feel heavy—because it was a gold coin, dated 1761, and as unworn as the day it was minted. "Well, I'll be damned, Hy," was all I was able to say. "Well, I'll be damned."

Hy was beaming. "Carolus Three, it says on the front, but it stands for Charles. And it's for you, Sam, the coin."

"Oh, no, Hy. Thanks, but no. I can't accept anything so valuable. This must be worth—" I tried to return it to him, but he pushed my hand aside.

"Worth maybe two hundred dollars U.S., this Maldorado man told me," Hy said. "For the eight-*escudos* coin, which is the value of this one. He showed me the worth in a catalogue, the Maldorado man, he's a part-time dealer. And for the four-*escudos,* as much as five hundred dollars U.S."

"Please, Hy—keep it for yourself."

"To give back again a present is not polite," Hy said stubbornly. "And you think maybe this was the only one was dug up? No, Sam my friend. A sum total of thirty-seven was dug up, in what was maybe a leather bag once upon a time. Twenty-one of these eight-*escudos* and sixteen of the four-*escudos,* enough money to buy everybody in Maldita a Treasure Tracer if I wanted. So please keep it, Sam, or I'll get mad."

I sighed. "All right," I said.

"That's better. I only wish Tom was still here, so I could give him one."

"I wish he were, too, Hy. He'd've been mighty happy for you."

"That I know," Hy said. "Well, good luck, Sam. I came to the party, like I said. And to see you. These other people—" He gestured toward the conversational groups around the pool. "—to me it's no pleasure to mingle with. And now back to work. Even though it's already a good year if I never traced with the Tracer again." As he went out through the gateway he said: "Oh, I also gave a coin to the boy. A four-*escudos.* He will grow up to be a good man, your Jock."

I rewrapped the coin but kept it in my hand while I walked to where Jock and Nan were. Gage had wandered off, perhaps to check on whether or not his daughters had shucked their clothes again.

I didn't beat around the bush with Jock. "Thanks," I said. No more than that, but he understood me.

"I don't deserve any." His eyes were steady on mine as he spoke. I liked their steadiness.

"If I didn't think you did I wouldn't've thanked you. Here." I gave him the tissue-wrapped coin. "Go buy yourself a Spanish prisoner." Then, before he could protest, I turned to Nan. "You understand this shorthand talk?" I asked her.

"No, Mr. Culloden. Not a word."

"One of the pleasures of being a male," I said, "—and mark this for future reference, Jock—is that you get a chance to confuse females."

I winked at Nan. "*Eh*-uh," I went on, "almost a tenth as often as females get to confuse males."

Nan laughed. "That's more like it, Mr. Culloden."

"Meanwhile, Jock," I said, "if I were you I'd find my mother and say hello. She's been worried about you. She's afraid that you may've run off with the wraggle-taggle gypsies, O."

"That's me, sure enough," Jock said, grinning. "I run off with every gypsy I run into. Come on, Nan." He took her hand.

As he led her away Nan asked: "Are there actual gypsies in Mexico, Mr. Culloden?"

"Except that they call 'em *gitanos*," I told her, "there's one in every Mexican heart."

I watched them stroll from me until I was interrupted by Lalage. She said: "I know you."

It was the interruption I'd been waiting for. I didn't answer her directly, though; and when she added, "But you don't know *me*," all I did was nod my head to show her she was wrong.

◎ By three o'clock voices were louder and restlessness was rampant in the patio, possibly due to the fact that the hot hors d'oeuvres, which should've shown up at two thirty, were still in the Inskilling kitchen. And by three o'clock I'd been sufficiently inept to have gotten pinned against the trunk of a pepper tree by the dreary McDermotts, who had each absorbed enough alcohol to set them off on their favorite subject: The Great, Universal, and Perhaps Galactic Communist Plot. "It's a crying shame J. Edgar Hoover's so old now," McDermott boomed into my ear. "If he'd run against Kennedy—and I'm not saying Mr. Nixon isn't a fine man, mind you—Mr. Hoover would undoubtedly have been elected. And J. Edgar would have come down like a ton of bricks on all these beatnik Commies. He wouldn't've let them parade their long hair around the campuses of our best universities, not for one minute. No, sir!"

"And that's not all, Ransom." Mrs. McDermott grabbed the torch and tucked it into the feathers of her right wing. "Mr. *Hoover*'s Army wouldn't be shirking and kissing Red Feet in Vietnam, the way they're making Our Poor Boys do now. Mr. Hoover'd *use* the Bomb on Vietnam—and on Red China, too, before Those Chinamen use It on Us. If Uncle Sam *has* the Bomb, He ought to *use* It. That's what *I* say. Don't you agree, Mr. Culloden?"

"It would save a lot of Our Boys' Lives, mind you," McDermott chimed in.

What could I reply to these idiots? She'd spoken of an *Uncle* Sam. But if I talked to them for a century, beating my gums twenty-four hours a day for a hundred bloody years, I'd never be able to prove to them that Uncle Sam, as a personification, had somehow turned into *Aunt* Sam—a timorous old WASP maid, convinced that Communists were stacked like cordwood under her gold-trimmed mahogany bed, sleeping with a tommy gun on the night table, and, every so often, waking up to fire a burst at what she thought was in the bedroom —including a couple of nephews who'd run in to see what the screeching was about.

If the bell outside the open gate hadn't clanged just then I might never have escaped the McDermotts. But the bell did clang. My God, how it clanged!

Every eye that could focus swiveled around and fixed itself on the gateway.

The clanging stopped. A silence began. And then the Queen of the Anticatalysts appeared in a puff of Pucci.

The silence liked the view so well that it wanted to stay awhile, but it looked so shabby, poor void, that it was sent packing within five seconds by several conversations who recalled that *they*'d been the first settlers in the Inskilling wilderness.

The Great Red Spot in Mrs. McDermott's heart was being occulted by the moon of Marian Delmore. "Bold as brass," she said with grim delight. "I don't see how the woman can do it—come to a party, with the daughter she killed hardly cold in the grave."

"Now, Joan," McDermott said mildly. "The girl committed suicide. And she was cremated, not buried."

Ah, I thought, how nicely precise the legal mind—even when it's over the hill.

"Marian Delmore killed Lalage as surely as if she'd struck her down with an ax," Mrs. McDermott said. "Don't you agree, Mr. Culloden?"

Whether I agreed or didn't was none of her business. "Sorry, Mrs. McDermott," I said. "My mind's still on China. Funny, but what you said about the Chinese and the Bomb—you used a capital 'B,' didn't you?—reminded me of a proverb, I think Tibetan, that might have some bearing on the case: 'A lack of meat makes one lean, but a lack of bamboo leads to vulgarity.' Worth thinking over, wouldn't you say? And now, if you'll forgive me, I'm supposed to be one of the hosts. A Greeter and Mingler."

As I left them I heard McDermott mutter, before I was out of earshot: "Curiously disjointed person." I swapped him mutter for mutter. Mine was: "Goddamned old bores." I hoped he wasn't out of earshot, either.

I may've had a half-formed idea of giving Marian an official welcome to the fold, but while I was weaving my way through the talkers by the pool I saw the Old Black Doctor coming in on her starboard bow and St. Albans and Payne approaching from port. I believed three fireboats more than sufficient for a reception in such a tiny harbor, so I instantly heeled over and set my course for the house.

The *sala* was empty. I sat in front of the fireplace, which was also empty, and tried to keep my mind empty, too—if only to match the atmosphere of the room. For a good ten minutes nobody, and nothing, disturbed me—including my empty glass. Then Inskilling entered from the patio.

He was nearly across the *sala* before he noticed me and stopped. "Dodging issues, Sam?" he asked.

"Catching my breath. What's left of it."

"Marian's here."

"*Eh*-uh. I saw the show. Reckon I'll talk to her later."

"Take your time. Give the guests a chance to tell her how well she looks and how bravely she's bearing up. To her face, of course. Behind her back—brave, good-looking woman—she won't hear—*feel,* I should say—a thing, knives being silent. Now I've got to roar into the kitchen and tell those hotel boys, to their pimply faces, that if they don't have the hors d'oeuvres out there before I count to *diez* I'm going to take a rusty scalpel and use it where it'll end any plans they may have for future fun and adult *machismo*." The Old Black Doctor then strode through a door that opened on a corridor of bedrooms, and which eventually would bring him to the kitchen.

He covered the distance in jig time, too. He'd hardly left the *sala* when a couple of busboys, toting trays of hot something-or-other, raced from the corridor and out into the patio. A moment later the third busboy followed their example.

Inskilling appeared again. "This is really Inés' job," he said. "I told you she was lazy."

"Where's Inés now, Jim?"

"Oh, last I knew she was talking to that bobtailed St. Albans and his unwashed mignon. I presume she's safe enough, in company like that, except for having to listen to St. Albans' terrible Spanish accent. But I doubt that the dear girl would understand him, even if his accent were good."

"Just as well for her," I said.

"Just as well," Inskilling said. If he'd caught the nuance in my remark he must've decided to drop it at once. "Did you manage to snatch anything from those trays as they went by?"

"No."

"You made a mistake. That wolf pack of antiques will've gobbled every last one by now."

"That's life," I said. "What else is new on the Rialto?"

"New? Nothing. Everything's old. No, wait a minute—George Simmons seems to have slipped through God's fingers again. He's not only drinking Oso Negro vodka and pretending it's water, but he's also making what we used to call a pass—of sorts—at Rose Gage."

"He's had a fling with her before, hasn't he?"

"Don't be naïve, Sam. That's why I said nothing's new, everything's old. George's trouble, you know, has always been women and booze—although he's been dodging the sauce for over a year now. Can't imagine what knocked him off the wagon. Well, Sam, don't fire until you're sure the whites of their eyes're white." With that, Inskilling pushed open the screen door and became a part of the murmuring patio.

It was quiet in the *sala* for a while. I smoked a cigarette and threw the sizable butt in the fireplace. I was getting ready to take my own chances in the patio again when—

"George's God isn't the Man Upstairs," somebody said. "George's God is the Man Caught in the Elevator Between Floors."

For half a dozen heartbeats I didn't know who was speaking. Then I realized that it was Thomas Flint Fletcher. "Oh, you finally got here, did you?" I asked. "I'm glad, sir—very glad."

"No, he isn't here," Lalage said from near a window. "You only think Mr. Fletcher's here."

"I'm the best judge of that, child," I told her, and went to face the music in the patio.

◎ "What do you mean, you have a bone to pick with me?" Marian Delmore, two thirds of a drink in her hand, watched me carefully from across an empty tray that had held hors d'oeuvres. We stood beneath one of the canvas umbrellas. I'd found her, alone somehow, in the center of a kaleidoscope of people.

"It's what you told me I was," I said. "How can you call me emotionless? Didn't I disrupt that buffet of yours, for God's sake?"

"Oh, that was a simple overt act. Meaningless. But you *are* impulsive."

"Impulsive and emotionless at the same time? Sorry, Marian. The terms don't dovetail."

"You know better than that, Sam. You're not a fool."

"I must be," I said. "Only a fool would commit an overt act in the dark."

"How about an arcane act in the dark?"

"Those're for a higher type of fool," I said casually. "An Argus of fools." Then I realized that she'd spoken with an odd lilt in her voice that I found unattractive; nor was I in the market for innuendos that afternoon. "Or are you referring to a specific arcane act?" I asked her. "By some definite person?"

"I don't know," Marian said uncertainly. "I don't. I'm beginning to think they're all dark. Oh, Sam, I feel so—" She stopped talking, but not before the lilt slipped through again. It wasn't what I'd thought it to be on first hearing, but more the tone a woman's voice takes when she's on the point of tears. Her hand, I noticed, was trembling. Ice clinked faintly in the glass she held.

"Do you feel sick, Marian? Want to go inside and lie down?"

She shook her head dumbly, then managed to say: "No, I'm not sick, no. But thank you. And it's only that—Oh, Sam, I've tried so hard to—" Again she broke off, but for a different reason; and instantly and neatly tucked any dangling emotions back under the mask of her face.

The different reason, calling itself Mrs. McDermott, was all at once standing at my elbow and saying: "Marian *dear*—I haven't had a chance to ask you about the cremation. Was it difficult to arrange? Ransom's convinced that this black-tie Communist government does everything it can to discourage decent people from—"

Mrs. McDermott had long since discouraged a black-leg Culloden misgovernment from being anywhere near her, so by then I was off and running. Therefore I never found out what the Mexican government does to discourage "decent" people—whatever *they* are. A backward glance over my shoulder, though, showed me that Marian Delmore was her ordinary frigid self as she chatted with the old ghoul. I couldn't see Mrs. McDermott's mug, but I could imagine the sparkle in her death-haunted eyes as she drank in the details of the Mexico City crematorium.

My legs, which occasionally get around quite well without any help from my brain, were taking me toward the house again, and I might've let them lead me into the *sala* for a second visit if I hadn't met George Simmons and Rose Gage outside the screen door. I wasn't in the mood to share a *sala,* or anything else, with that pair. Rose had on a skimpy dress, of the sheerest silk, and it was obvious that nothing lay between the gossamer frock and her Earth Mother body.

I smiled benevolently at them both. "To what green altar, O mysterious priest," I asked Simmons, "lead'st thou this heifer lowing at the skies?"

Simmons' eyes were cloudy, his lips wet. His hand, resting on the screen door, didn't give him enough support to keep him from swaying. "Rose wanted to see the house," he said. "I'm going to show Mrs. Gage the house. Any objections? Jim doesn't mind."

"Neither do I," I said. "Not treating the girls, too, Rose? Where are they?"

"Ask my husband," Rose said. "He was the one who wanted to bring them. Come on, George. There's not much time before we eat." She pulled his hand free of the door, opened it herself, and pushed him into the house ahead of her.

For a little while I remained where I was, letting my imagination hang out, and then decided it was time to look into the Azteca situation again. While I was tucking my imagination back where it belonged, however, Jefferson Gage, at a queer trot, rounded the corner of the house that was farthest from the gate. He was holding one hand over his nose and upper lip, and there were flecks of blood on his scruffy beard. He passed in front of me and hurried along the front of the house, unnoticed. Alpha, Beta, Gamma, and Delta were playing near the gate, or—and more likely—placing a satchel charge. Gage kept his hand pressed against his middle face while he herded the four girls into the gateway and outside the Inskilling walls before the bewildered babies knew what he was doing.

I walked to the corner from which Gage had appeared and gazed with mild curiosity across the expanse of rear patio. The area itself was empty of people, but beyond a chiaroscuro of fruit trees and flower beds I spotted Inskilling and Inés near a small building at the far end of the patio. This was a combination tool house and potting shed that also contained a cot for the gardener, who doubled as a night watchman when the Old Black Doctor was out of town. I couldn't hear what Inskilling was saying to Inés, but the words had to be harsh: she suddenly sank to the ground, sobbing. I turned away, embarrassed, and loped across to the bar. "Sam sent me," I told Paco, and held out my glass.

Paco winked and ducked under the table, coming up with a glass that now contained three thick fingers of Azteca. I was taking it from him when Inskilling arrived on the scene, his face as blank as ever and his own glass empty. He gave it to Paco. *"Lo mismo, Pacito, por favor,"* he said. "Getting hungry, Sam?"

"I don't know yet," I said. "They haven't told me." I waited until Paco went under the table again. "What happened, Jim?"

"Happened?" His voice was noncommittal. "When?"

"A few minutes ago. I saw Gage go off with his kids and his bloody nose, and then I saw you and Inés—" I left the sentence dangling.

Until Paco delivered his booze Inskilling had nothing to say, but after he'd taken a substantial gulp he said: "What happened, Sam, was that our goaty friend got Inés in there, and down on the gardener's bed, and when I showed up he had his hands—well, I popped him one and sent him packing. Dirty little slimy man."

"You'd think his own wife'd be all he could handle, wouldn't you?"

"No. Certainly not. Gage could be locked in a bedroom with fifty howling nymphomaniacs and he still wouldn't be satisfied. Satyriasis, that's his problem and cross." He allowed himself another swallow of rum. "And sometimes I wish it were mine, instead of the one I have. Inés, you know."

"How is she a problem?"

"She's too innocent. She's so damned innocent that any man she's met ten minutes ago can do anything he wants with her—and to her." He looked off across the rear patio. "I don't know, but perhaps I ought to auction off this pre-Columbian collection of mine. It only contains one piece, but that piece is very, very rare. You interested, Sam?"

"I would've been, twenty years ago."

"Come, now, Sam—you're not that old yet."

"No, but I've been married nineteen years."

"And you're still faithful?"

"Still, and always."

Inskilling studied me with somber amazement, then patted my

shoulder. "Someday, my boy, and somewhere—somebody's going to raise a statue to you." He drank off the rest of his rum. "And now I'd better get poor innocent Inés up on her feet and dry-eyed." He set his glass down on the tablecloth. "And then we'll see if we can find her pants," he said as he started back to the tool house.

I mulled matters over and eventually decided that, since it seemed to be an *in flagrante* afternoon, I might as well get into the act—so I strolled over to the main house and went in. I passed through the *sala* and on into the long corridor, off which four bedroom doors opened.

The door to the second left-side bedroom not only hadn't been locked but gaped a few inches, as though the former Father Simmons and the present Mrs. Gage had wanted to make things easy and explicit for casual passers-by. There wasn't anything I had to do except push the door open all the way and beam in on them. "O Attic shapes, fair attitudes," I said, "excuse me."

Rose Gage quit work. "Can't you see we're busy?" she gasped without rancor from where she lay under a concentrative Simmons.

"Sorry, Rose," I said. "It's these cheap eyes I'm wearing. I only wanted to tell you that Jeff's gone home and taken the kids. *Bon voyage,* George. Bless this food to our use and us to Thy service."

I made the sign of the cross—in reverse, I'm afraid—and shut the door, trying the latch to make sure it had caught. Then I went, whistling, back outdoors.

◉ Simmons disappeared from the party before the *comida* was served, but nobody commented on his absence. In fact, I doubt if anyone except Peeping Sam Culloden—I can't answer for Rose Gage—noticed he was gone; and I certainly didn't worry about his going. I figured that his exploration of the house—or, shall we say, Rose—had sobered him enough for his normal sense of guilt to come galloping home and, still booted and spurred, harry him over the river to a place where he could grovel on the floor, begging for mercy, at the feet of his non-Turkish but cruel master, the Agenbite of Inwit.

In at least one way I could appreciate Simmons' choosing to vanish. The *comida,* which was to have been on the tables at four o'clock, wasn't delivered until after five; wasn't served until five thirty; and then wasn't enjoyed, when eaten, by people who had either drunk too much while waiting to be fed or were out of sorts due to semistarvation. The four extra men who had brought the food and drink in a battered pickup truck, and who were waiters from the Posada—where they outnumbered the paying guests—must've stopped on the way to Maldita and dallied an hour or so for a soccer game or a gang shag. By the time it got to the tables the ham was cold, the turkey was dry and curling, and the white wine was worse than lukewarm. The wine also turned out to be a cloying sweet sauterne instead of the *blanco seco* Inskilling had ordered. All in all, it was as unsatisfactory a meal as I've had since I was taken off C-rations.

The McDermotts didn't wait to have coffee before they excused themselves and skittered off to their Slumber Room where, I suppose, they sat around in their bathrobes, guzzling Alka-Seltzer and nibbling Tums. Ramona also belched off home, complaining in two languages, neither of which was recognizable, that she had to feed the foul-beaked Ricardo; and Pepper and Salt cleared out, with the apology that Saturday night was shard-combing time around the Olde Oaken Kiln.

Several other people, including Polly and St. Albans, were getting around to a testiness, but the Old Black Doctor soothed these ill-fed malcontents with an announcement that a Surprise was in store for them: *mariachis* were coming. These were from Fuerte and were considered to be the best group in the State of Nuevocegado. Brandy was then brought out, huge candles were made ready to light the grounds, and the reassured guests began to circulate uncertainly among themselves in the last slanting rays of the sun. The weather, unlike the Posada Azul crowd, had not played us false. There wasn't a cloud in the sky. The night would be warm and clear.

I'd joined Bruce Young at a table, to begin with, and then we'd both watched in helpless fascination while Rose Gage, in a wrinkled dress, and Ramona, in a wrinkled face, had come to take *comida* with us. Their presence made the bad meal even more of an agony than it was at the other tables; but when Ramona finally bubbled away to her parrot and slag heaps the situation eased somewhat. Or so I thought. Rose, as I saw it, had only one thing on her mind and, when she couldn't drag the conversation around to that overblown subject, was inclined to quietness. It also occurred to me that right then she might have been a trifle on the sated side, to boot.

Be that as it may, after Ramona had gone birdward Bruce and I sipped a not-bad brandy and fell into a comfortable discussion of history and its ramifications, during which Bruce also fell head over heels into every generalization he could think of—together with a few I thought of myself—quite forgetting, in the brandy's warmth, the Young distaste for generalizations.

"—When it comes down to that," he was saying, although I no longer remembered what *that* was, "it's taken men several hundred years to recover from the shock of learning that they're not the center of the universe. So now they spend every waking moment that can be spared from the—" He hesitated, drank in Rose Gage, and went on: "—from the contemplation of women, in an attempt to prove that their original calculations were off."

"Maybe," I said. "But don't forget, you five-cent Gibbon, that in the Western Hemisphere we're spending an inordinate amount of time trying to figure out why the twentieth century is still paying for the eighteenth."

Bruce never got to gather in that onside kick, because Rose Gage —a member of the opposing kicking team, whose regular position was split-end—snatched the ball in midair and cut with it toward the sidelines. "I liked what you said then," Rose told him. "About contemplating women. That was a good image."

"Was it?" Bruce flicked his eyes at me, then down at his pony of not-bad brandy. "I hadn't noticed."

"You never brought him over," Rose was speaking to me now. "Why not?"

"He has his own car," I said. "And his own wife, too, when you come right down to it."

"I should hope so," Rose said. "Every man should support a

woman." Her attention returned to Bruce. "Marriage is an economic necessity. But Sex—why, Sex belongs to everyone. Isn't that true?"

"Well," Bruce said nervously, "that depends on what you mean by 'sex.' Right, Sam?"

"You're the definer, Bruce." I leaned back in my chair. "Get down to business. Define."

But he never was given a chance to come up with a definition, not even edgeways. "You like to contemplate women, don't you?" Rose was asking before he could get off the ground.

"Well—er—yes," Bruce admitted. "Every man likes to con—"

"You have your car here, don't you?" Rose was asking.

Bruce stayed on the ground. His reply was an insecure nod.

"Then I know a place we can go," Rose said. She glanced at me. "The three of us. And we'll screw. The three of us."

"*Scr*—" Bruce's mouth opened and shut, opened and shut, like that of a fish thrown up on a bank.

"Did you ever try a Sex Sandwich?" Rose leaned forward in her chair and lowered her voice a little. "What it is, you two'll be the slices of bread, and me—I'll be the meat."

"Meee-e-*ut*—?" Bruce seemed ready to choke to death or bolt for his life. But then he gained control of himself long enough to look wide-eyed at me, as if asking: *Is she drunk?* She wasn't, of course. No, Rose was cold sober; give her credit for that. She had no need of alcohol because she had no inhibitions.

When I shook my head at him Bruce didn't know what to do. So, for the sake of doing something, he drank the rest of his not-bad brandy and tried to stare past the blatantly desirous Rose. This was a tactic that would get him nowhere, as I had learned by experience. I'd tried it myself the morning when, wearing nothing but a smile, she'd first swum into my ken.

"Or we can take your car, Mr. Culloden," Rose said to me. "There's all that space we can use with the back seat down."

I appreciated her formality in calling me "Mister," but nevertheless I was starting to rummage through my brain in search of a reconditioned excuse when Bruce mumbled: "Sam—?"

"What is it, Bruce?" Drowning men. Straws.

He pointed a quivering finger toward the gate and I followed the finger's unsteady line—to discover that the *mariachis* from Fuerte weren't going to be the only surprise of the evening. Not by a long chalk.

Joy Durwood was ambling toward us in the twilight.

And behind me Lalage was leaning over and whispering in my ear: "I think I'm happy now. *So* happy."

I knew what she meant, too—and it had nothing to do with the usual definition of "happy."

❦ Six

With No Help from You, You Old Cully-Boo

The *mariachis* came with the dark. There were six of them, although I'd've taken oath that under the silver threads of their sombreros I counted seven mustaches. On occasion they'd wander around the patio, strumming their inlaid guitars and singing their nasal love ballads, but they preferred to be handy to the tequila, so they sensibly left their instrument cases as near to the bar table as they dared. They were pretty good, I guess, as *mariachis* go—but to me the guests were more entertaining.

Through some error on the part of G-2, word quickly got around that Joy, returning from her trip, had almost run over Geoge Simmons as he staggered across the bridge. She had reined in the Jaguar, had talked with Simmons long enough to hear him croak that he was coming from a Filthy Party at Dr. Inskilling's, had left him to race to the Matthews *finca,* had whipped off her traveling costume, had bathed, had perfumed herself, had slipped into something more comfortable, and had then roared around to the Inskilling pad. Her Seventh Cavalry arrival had saved Professor B. Young and, on a secondary level, Mr. S. Culloden from a fate worse than Fate—a deed which wasn't mentioned in dispatches.

Anyway, Joy's appearance on the Old Black Doctor's threshing floor caused a sudden readjustment of positions. Some of the guests who were sticking out the party found themselves with friends or wives or lovers from whom they'd been separated for as much as nineteen minutes. I, for instance, gladly sagged into a teetering chair next to Polly. I'd been so derailed by my recent jump-the-track encounter with the Rosy Coozy Express that I'd've been content to sit beside my pretty, neglected wife, inventing details of my meeting with Robert Taylor, for the rest of the night—or even until the drab expanse of Culver City had returned to the dust from whence M-G-M came.

Not that I didn't keep an eye on Joy Durwood: I did. In fact, every so often I'd switch from one eye to two, which made me see her as inexplicably three-dimensional. She was pleasant in greeting people she'd met and carefully modest when introduced to strangers. She even said brief but pleasant things to me, which I carefully and modestly gave back to her. After all, we were the oldest of friends, having met several times before; and the conversation I really wanted to have with her could wait until I caught her alone—preferably in a room where curses and screams would be muffled by walls sound-proofed with sixty-nine canvases from the understanding hand of Guillaume, Marquis de Sidewinder. Surely at this stage of the game Polly couldn't brood about any earlier moments I might've had with the Durwood woman. Joy and I *had* met, and Polly knew we had. But what Polly didn't know, and what I was only now beginning to realize myself, was that I hadn't *truly* met Joy Durwood. In fact, I—

"Is your father alive?" Lalage whispered.

"No, but he's dead. Amounts to the same thing, though."

"What about his son?"

"Nobody here by that name," I said. "Is there?"

"Ask *her*," Lalage said.

"Ask who? Ask her what?"

"Ask *Joy*. Ask her *why*."

"Mind if I pick my own time, child?"

"What'd you say, Sam?" Polly's eyebrows were raised.

"Sorry, darling. Counting unhatched chickens. Didn't mean to make so much noise."

"Chickens?"

"Forget it."

"Maybe we'd better go home. You've been drinking too much."

"No, I haven't. I've had damned little all day. Blame it on the altitude, and throw in old age."

"A horrible age," said Lalage.

"I'll throw in no such thing," Polly said. "But if you must talk under your breath, please talk about something worthwhile. Not chickens."

"Yazzum, Miz Cullyden, ma'am," I said, after which I managed to keep my mouth shut—helped by a sudden vertigo that grabbed me by the pineal gland and then took its own white time about letting me go again. A buzzing in my brain began low and rose in volume until, unlike the melodrama heroine who was trussed and being trundled toward the hell noise of the saw, I chose the Easiest Way, said "Yes, dear Villain, anything you wish," and went completely blank.

I also went thoroughly blind, but without bothering to close my eyes. Just before I reached up and snapped off my immediate surroundings I fixed a few tableaux in my mind to carry me through the intermission. Bruce Young, still shaky, was sitting where I'd left him, with the armor-plated Helen in my vacated chair. The *mariachis* had formed a semicircle around a table at which Joy, Inskilling, Inés, St. Albans, and Payne were huddled uncomfortably while the latter two did their best to talk to Joy above the throb and quiver of Mexican vocal cords. At the other end of the pool Marian Delmore was chatting with the Salvatierras, and Rose Gage was head to head with, of all people, Nan Young and Charles Lockridge Culloden. The last thing I recall, before I went drifting away from that flaccid capsule, my body, was telling myself that I ought to check on the Gage-Young-Culloden trio: any seminar given by Frau Doktor Gage was for graduate students and Ph.D. candidates only, and under no circumstances to be audited by young things not yet matriculant. *Eh-uh*, Rip van Culloden was thinking, I'll look into that situation as soon as I—

"*Sam!*"

"Huh?" I switched the world on again, starting with Polly. "Oh, sure, I'll go right over and break it up."

"What're you talking about? Break *what* up?"

"Why, didn't you say to—?" I blinked in bewilderment. The trio no longer existed. Jock and Nan were gone from view, and now it was Rose Gage, rather than Marian, who was with the Salvatierras.

"I asked you to get me a rum-and-soda," Polly said. "The waiters seem to've all gone home. What did you think I said?"

"I—my mind was on something else."

"It must've been. You've been glassy-eyed and gaping at nothing for over ten minutes."

"That long? I don't believe it." I had to believe it, though, because of the way the human elements in the immediate landscape had shifted. Marian Delmore now stood alone in the shadows by the screen door. Joy Durwood was walking along the side of the pool and using a smile as a link boy to light a path to José Salvatierra. Inés was hemmed in by St. Albans and Payne, who were bouncing words off her like hailstones but without the need to raise their voices—the *mariachis* having gone back to the bar to take a break and lap up some tequila. There was no sign of the Old Black Doctor.

"Please, Sam," Polly said petulantly. "A rum-and-soda."

I jumped to my feet. "Sorry, darling. No sooner said than done." I picked up her glass and made for the bar.

"Remember," she called after me, "*three* ice cubes."

The music men were taking up the entire front of the bar table in a dress rehearsal of the old lemon-and-salt-and-tequila routine, and I practically had to bring up the artillery before a sombreroed traitor opened a sally port and let me through. Paco grinned, said "Sam sen' you, no?" and pushed a four-finger glass of Azteca into my free hand. He'd obviously been keeping it ready for my next appearance in his neck of the woods.

"Well, bless your warm, wise, worldly heart, Paco," I said. I gave him Polly's glass, told him what to put in it, and then faced around among the jostling guitarists, intending to sip rum and survey the action until pretty Polly's drink was put together. I only had time for one sip, though.

Then the night began to come apart.

It happened at the far end of the pool, at the table where Joy had joined Rose Gage and the Salvatierras. Joy had been talking to José while Luz, between them, unhappily drummed on the table with her red nails. Then Joy, smiling like a Cheshire cat, spoke to Rose. I don't know to this day what she said, but her words made José Salvatierra laugh, and their effect on Rose Gage was, to say the least, amazing. Perhaps the words themselves were meaningless, and Rose—who'd been jockeying for position, *à la* Aretino, all evening—was merely fed up with, not to mention overwhelmed by, the unfair competition of two beautiful women. One alone was sufficient to cramp her open-and-aboveboard style.

Anyway, whatever lay behind the act, Rose languidly left the table and strolled to the edge of the pool. As she did so her hands went behind her and worked absentmindedly at the zipper of her silk dress. She slipped out of her sandals, studied the water for a moment, then bent and, with a single smooth skin-the-cat motion, peeled the silk sheath off over her head, tossed it aside, and stood naked. Joy and the Salvatierras became figures of stone, with eyes of stone fixed in stony fascination on the flowing lines of the Gage buttocks.

"*¡Ay, mira!*" the *mariachi* next to me gasped. "*¡Mira, mira! ¡Ay, ay, AY!*" And then they were all gaping at Rose, and a couple of them were whistling, and everyone else in the patio had discovered what was going on.

Rose didn't rush matters. For a while she seemer content to stand and let candlelight flicker over and flatter that tanned-blonde, Earth Mother body. Finally, however, and slowly, as though she were tired, she brought her arms up from her sides like wings, until she was in the same attitude she'd taken the morning I met her, when she mentioned her love of the Mexican sun. She held herself like this while fifteen seconds took fifteen years to tick away, then tensed and dove into the pool. She didn't cut the water cleanly, though; indeed, she made quite a splash.

The drops had no sooner spattered down than the *mariachis* came out of their collective trance and ran as one man for the pool, with Paco barking at their heels. Blasé Sam Culloden, however, who'd not only done a hitch in the Gage country, but had done it in full daylight, recalled that Polly was the errand you forgot while you stopped to watch the streamlining—so he pushed himself away from his private knothole, added some Peñafiel to the drink Paco hadn't finished making, polished off the rest of his Azteca, and toddled toward his thirsty wife.

She evidently wasn't as thirsty as she'd thought. She also wasn't where he'd left her.

Polly had, in fact, joined forces with the Youngs. "What's all that about?" she asked as I arrived with her rum-and-soda. "That topless-bottomless bit in the pool?"

"Beats me," I said. "Training for the Olympics, maybe. You got any ideas, Bruce?"

He shook his head feebly. But Helen Young, as always, had some ideas. "Exhibitionist Amazons aren't in the textbook," she said, "so my husband doesn't know anything about them."

Rose was now floating on the surface, belly up; and Inskilling had appeared from somewhere and, as near as I could make out, was telling the bulged-eyeball *mariachis* to locate their instruments and strike up a tune—Handel's *Water Music,* say, as scored for electrified guitarists.

"What *is* in the textbook, Helen?" I asked. "I've always wondered."

"No matter what's in it," Helen Young said, "when the clothes come off, the Youngs go home. How do you feel about leaving, Polly?"

"Why not?" said Polly. "It's been a long day. Where's Jock, Sam?"

"Last time I saw him," I said, "he was talking to—"

"He walked Nan home," Helen interrupted. "He's going out early in the morning with that Levinson man, so he wanted to get to bed early."

It was just as well that she'd cut in on me, although that wasn't why my sentence'd trailed off. What had made me clam up was the sight of Marian Delmore holding the screen door open for Joy Durwood and then following Joy into the house.

"I'm glad there's one sensible Culloden," Polly said. "I suppose you're not coming, are you, Sam?"

"You know I can't. I'm co-host. Have to stay here until the last gun's fired."

Helen Young glanced toward the pool. "How about the last torpedo?"

Polly sighed. "Helen, dear," she said, "I'm not worried about that, so don't you be." She took hold of my sleeve, pulled my face down to where she could reach it, and kissed my cheek. "You damned old fool, Sam," she whispered, "it was a terrible party, but I love you anyway. Don't stay too late, darling. You know how grouchy you are if you don't get enough sleep." She squeezed my biceps and picked up her purse. "I'm ready, Helen," she said, "if you are."

I stood by the gate and waved good-bye to Polly and the other two and watched them get into the Young car and listened to the motor as Bruce drove off much too fast. It was only after the gasoline-engine sounds had faded that I realized I was still holding Polly's rum-and-soda. The sensible thing was to stay by the gate and drink it; and, since I'm hung up on the sensible thing, within limits, that's what I did.

St. Albans and Payne, arm in arm, weaved up to me before I was halfway through indulging in the sensible thing. "And what are *you* doing, Cully-boo?" St. Albans asked.

"Reliving my childhood," I said. "Can you think of a better place?"

"Wasn't it *fun?*" he asked. "Don't you wish we were *all* children again?"

"Eu-eu*lal*ia," Payne mumbled. "Eulalia dearest-earest-eeriest."

"Miss Payne is *so* drunk," St. Albans said happily. "And do you know *what,* Cully-boo? The most *mar*velous thing! Inés Injun's going to sneak off and *pose* for me! Tomorrow I'm going to see that boy in town about his Harley-Davidson, and day after tomorrow Inés Injun'll be on that motorcycle bare-bare-*bare*-bottom *nekkid!*

And with no help from *you*, you old Cully-boo." Before I could duck he'd reached out and pinched my ear lobe. Then he steered Payne through the gateway.

After they'd gone I polished off Polly's drink, set the glass on the ground, and chewed ice cubes while I considered my next move. To amble along to the pool and coach Rose Gage in the backstroke— which was my first thought—didn't offer enough of a, as they say, *challenge;* nor, since there was nobody within several hundred miles with either the money or the authority to make a deal, could I sell Old Rose as a cut-rate, flesh-tinted nuclear submarine, Model Mark LXIX, suitable for the navy of any Central American country or for possible use by the overthrown and fleeing Strong Man of last week's CIA-approved *junta.*

What I really wanted to do, of course, was catch at least the final quarter of the Delmore-Durwood game. It must've started by now; they'd certainly been in the house long enough. But somehow the feeling that what Marian and Joy said, or did, to each other was none of my business, at the moment anyway, held me back for a time. I also kept telling myself that, after all, neither team was Ivy League; and if I did see the end of the game it would have to be while standing behind one team's goal line, which meant I wouldn't see very much of anything.

Suddenly the screen door swung open and Marian Delmore stepped out into the patio. She glanced around the area once, as though looking for someone, before walking directly toward the gate —and, incidently, me.

"Leaving?" I asked as she approached.

"Oh!" Marian was startled until she recognized me in the half-darkness. "Yes, Sam, I'm leaving. I was wondering where you were."

"Did you have a nice talk with the ex-Mrs. Lancaster? I saw you go in with her."

"We talked, yes. Where's your family?"

"Gone home. Where's Miss Durwood now?"

"I wouldn't know. Are you leaving, too?"

"I have to listen to the mermaids singing, don't I?"

Marian's eyes darted to the pool. "Not necessarily."

"I guess I'll stay on for a while longer," I said.

"I'll give you a lift."

"I'm sure you would. But I—"

"I *want* to, in fact."

"Thanks, but no, Marian. I'm one of the hosts, remember?"

"Of course. Good night, Sam."

"Good night, Marian."

She continued on to the gate, stopped, and turned toward me, her face heavy with troubles and confusions. She seemed about to speak again but changed her mind and, with a sigh, passed beyond the wall.

"Good night, Lady, good night, sweet Lady, good night, good night," Lalage whispered from the shadows. "At least, that's what my mother'd say. So would apprentice gods."

"How about master craftsmen?" I asked her.

"What are they?"

"You'll see, child, you'll see."

I left the vicinity of the gate and strode to the house, ignoring the Salvatierras, who were staying the course come hell or low water; ignoring Rose Gage, who was trying to see how far out of water she could raise her *mons Veneris* while floating sacrum down; and even ignoring certain thoughts of my own, which were suggesting I do something other than what I intended to do.

The *sala* was empty. So was the corridor. But the door that earlier had brought me face to back with a double-backed beast was still open, and from beyond a second, closed door to the right of the bed came the sound of a water closet in labor. One of the night-table lamps was on. It couldn't've been more than twenty-five watts, but it lit up the room sufficiently to reveal that the Gage–Simmons bed had been tightened and tidied since I'd seen it in action; and it also lit me sufficiently for Joy Durwood, coming from the bathroom, to recognize Sam Culloden.

She accepted my presence with aplomb. "Why, you Sam *thing*," she said, hesitating by the bed, "have you come in here to rape me? No, I guess not. You left the door open."

"Not any more." I swung it shut behind me.

"Then you *have* come to rape me." The possibility seemed to interest her.

"Why should I?" I wanted to know.

Joy pouted and sat down on the edge of the bed. "That's a *rude*," she said.

"First things first," I said. "I haven't had a chance to talk with you all evening. How was the trip?"

"Oh, hot and wet and *dull*. But mostly *wet*. Every night, wher*ever* I was, it rained *buckets*."

"Where were you?"

"Oh, Mexico City. Acapulco. *Places*."

"Acapulco? It's out of season there now, isn't it?"

"That sweet little goddamned *ocean* isn't out of season. And if there was anybody I *wanted* to see, I *saw* him. Them. Her. *It*."

"Did you hit Cuernavaca, too?"

"Cuerna*vaca?* Oh, I looked in, coming and going. *So* hot, Sam dear."

"Didn't you stay overnight?"

"Why, of *course,* it's such a *lovely*. All those flowers *every*where."

"And if there were anyone in Cuernavaca you wanted to see, you saw him? Them? Her? It?"

"But there *wasn't* anybody. I don't know a *soul* in that goddamned *rain*forest."

"Nothing worse than being alone in a strange hotel room on a wet night, is there, Joy?" I sat down beside her.

"That's better," she said. "*Ever* so. Has it rained much *here?*"

"Only when I wanted it to."

"Oh, you old *Sam* thing! Did you arrange for this *perfect* night?"

"*Eh*-uh. Had to make up for how horrible most of the guests are."

"Who'd you invite last year?" Lalage asked from the other side of the bed. "Where did you have the party?"

Joy was patting my hand. "I'm glad you didn't say *all* the guests. Why, that Frankie's the cutest little *wiggle*-worm I *ever*."

"Frankie?"

"Francis St. Albans."

"Oh, Saint. They call him 'Saint.'"

"*I* call him *Frankie,* and he and his friend are the *dear*est little baby *weirds.* Why didn't I meet them be*fore?*"

"I guess because the goalie has to stick close to his goal," I said. "How'd you like Marian Delmore, by the way? You hadn't met her before, either."

Joy swung around toward me, all seriousness. "Oh, *Sam*—Sam *dear*—wasn't it the most *ghastly* thing, what poor Lalage *did* to herself? That's the *true* reason I ran off, you know. When they told me, I simply had to go *some*place—Oh, I just *had* to!" Biting her lip, Joy faced away from me again.

"What did you think of Marian?" I was being quietly persistent.

"Lalage's *mother?* I didn't like her at *all.* She's *strange,* haven't you *no*ticed?"

"Can't say as I've been that close to her. How do you mean, strange?"

"Why, *you* know—*strange. Different* from. And those funny *crazy* questions—! Sam, I was *afraid* of her. She literally *fright*ened me."

"So do I frighten you," I said. "That's what you told me, anyway."

"Oh, that's not the *same!*" Joy cried. "But with Mrs. *Del*more— Sam, she made me *sick,* physically *ill.* I threw up *all* over that *bath*room in there. *Such* a mess. But *please* don't say *I* did it, will you?" She waited until I'd shaken my head, then went on: "Oh, I realize how up*set* the woman must be, but she *prac*tically accused me of being a *dyke.* Can you *imagine,* you Sam dear—*me* a dyke?"

"My imagination's pretty good," I said, "but not that good."

"You're teasing me," Lalage said from a corner. "But I'm used to being teased. I live with my mother, and—"

"—she liked to tease you morning, noon, and night," I said "*dulce ridentem.*"

"What was that?" Joy asked.

"Nothing," I said. "Part of a quotation."

"It's sometimes he's thinking of lots of things at once," Lalage said, "and the wrong words come out."

"And, Sam, that's not the *worst* Mrs. Delmore accused me of," Joy said unhappily. "She blames *me* for what her daughter did, the silly—"

"Blames you?" I broke in. "Now why in God's name should she take that attitude?"

Lalage laughed sweetly from somewhere in the room. "Oh, you're *teasing* again."

"I can't *imagine*," Joy said.

"Well, Joy, I can't imagine why, either," I said slowly. "But it's an attitude I can take myself, and without too much effort."

After a chill silence Joy said: "*Can* you, Sam?" The inconsequence had gone from her voice. "Can you *really*?"

"Don't you know I can, Joy?"

"I don't even know what you're talking about." She rose from the bed. "And neither do you."

"I know that Lalage was seen running away from your house, as fast as she could leg it, on her way to empty the pill bottle."

"From *my* house?" Joy glared down at me. "Seen by *whom*?"

"A man named Culloden was out on his river terrace."

Joy parted her lips and sucked in air through her teeth. "And the stupid girl *told* you she was running from my house?"

"Lalage didn't tell me anything. All Lalage did was run."

Some of the fury left Joy's face. "Then you *don't* know what you're talking about, do you? You couldn't see where the girl was coming from. And my house isn't the only goddamned one on that side of the river, don't forget that. She could've been running from those other people—that stripper in the pool, and her husband—the *Gages*."

"She never went near the Gage place. She didn't like the Gages."

"Or maybe some Mexican dragged her into the bushes."

"Or maybe something happened at your place that broke her heart," I said. "Something that hurt enough to drive her to suicide. How about putting it that way?"

"How about dropping the subject?" Joy went to the door, opened it, and smiled at me. "Or how about my confessing that, yes, she *did* come to my house, uninvited and unexpected—and that her heart was broken when she discovered a person named Culloden and me entertaining each other in the most *shame*ful fashion?"

"Don't talk nonsense, Joy," I said. "I saw her from my river terrace, remember?"

The Durwood smile broadened and became triumphant. "Oh, you old Sam *thing*," Joy said, "you're the one who ought to remember you're not the only *male* Culloden in town.

I was off the bed and aiming for the door as soon as she sauntered out of sight, but then I got control of myself and did nothing more than follow her along the corridor and through the *sala.* I was going a little faster than she was, though, and when she went out into the patio and stopped short, I was so close behind her that I nearly slammed into her spinal column.

Joy had jammed on the brakes to avoid a collision with three people who were chatting a few feet beyond the screen door. One of these was Dr. James Winters Inskilling. Another, fat and exhausted, was Angela Ammon DeKalb Pierce Gutierrez, *née* Wade. And the third, who was staring greedy-eyed at Joy as though he were Coronado and she were every gold and glittering street of the Seven Cities of Cíbola, was the true, the good, the beautiful Lencho Gutierrez, a former great fan of Robert Taylor.

Angela carefully ignored Joy in order to give me a wan nod. "Well, Sam," she said, "as I was just telling Jim, perhaps we shouldn't've come. Everyone's gone home, it seems."

I didn't feel like counting noses to see how many guests remained, but Angela's first statement was certainly correct. At one point in the early afternoon I'd wished very much to have Angela present, but now I knew better; and the reasons for my change of heart, both of them, were then and there giving a demonstration that explained why my heart had changed. Even after they'd guzzled the love potion, Tristan and Isolde could never have stared at each other with such nude and open desire as the gorgeous Joy Durwood and the ravishing Lencho Gutierrez.

"Hi, Angela," I said with an effort. "And never mind that talk about everyone having gone home. If you'd come any earlier, you'd've run into all the wrong people."

◎ Less than half an hour later I was going home myself, slipping through the gateway and pursued by certain Furies that I needed to dodge. I suspected that I wouldn't be able to dodge them, unfortunately—inasmuch as I was the bugler who'd waked them to begin with. They also seemed to have developed a taste for my triple-tonguing.

However, they weren't pressing me closely just then; perhaps the party had exhausted them, too. In fact, I didn't realize how much had been taken out of me by ten hours of Mingling until I'd reached the end of the Inskilling road and hobbled west along the highway. Subconsciously, though, I must've been aware of my weariness; otherwise I wouldn't've stolen off as I had—without saying good night to a soul, and leaving the Old Black Doctor to hold the frayed bag.

But exhaustion wasn't the half of it; I was mentally upset as well. Joy's intimation that Lalage had caught her and Jock together, playing any one of a hundred grim sexual games, grew more and more unbearable the longer it pressed on my brain. I tried to convince myself that Joy was lying, and that whatever Lalage had seen to send her racing home through the moonlight had nothing to do with a young Jock Culloden. And yet—

And yet he'd been out until all hours that same suicidal night, and the next day had come up with a misty, vague story as to where he'd been and what he'd been doing. And yet—

And yet it was a situation in which I simply couldn't imagine him. It was, God knew, easy enough to visualize a naked male body joined with Joy's, but none of the naked male bodies had the face of my son. Every damned body was faceless, in fact.

So, no matter what I thought, it all came down to a basic premise that was as nebulous as Jock's story had been. Joy had cruelly set me a problem that, in the long run, would turn out to be no problem at all—but which, problem or not, had no imaginable solution.

I hadn't gone thirty yards along the highway before a motor turned over, headlights were put on, and a car that had been parked under some trees was driven out onto the macadam and quietly drew up alongside me. It was Marian Delmore's Mercedes.

"I've been waiting for you," she said.

"I can't imagine why."

"I told you I wanted to give you a lift, Sam."

"I don't mind the walk, honestly. It's good to be alone for a change."

"*Please,* Sam. There's something I must tell you. Something about—"

I hesitated. Since noon I'd had more than my share of humans and their inhuman complications. Too, I found the suppressed agony in Marian's voice unpleasant, and I was glad I couldn't see her face very well. Nevertheless, what Joy had intimated was a persistent drum roll in my skull—and, for all I knew, the Something that Marian had to tell me might have considerable bearing on the case. Anyway, this had turned out to be my night for grasping at straws. "But a lift only as far as the house," I said. "I'm too bushed to be driven over the whole State of Nuevocegado."

"Just to the house, Sam. I promise."

"Okay, then." I walked around the rear of the car and got in beside her.

Marian drove at a steady clip, not too fast, not too slow, and in a silence that was even steadier than the speed of the car. I waited to be told whatever it was that she wanted to tell me, and the longer she held her tongue the shorter my temper became. I kept it in check, though, until without bothering to use the brakes she swung the Mercedes into the Delmore private road and I was thrown against her. As soon as I'd drawn myself erect again I took my temper off the leash and let it range the interior of the car. "God damn it, I meant *my* house!" I yelled. "Not your mausoleum, for Christ's sake!"

Marian kept her eyes on the narrow, twisting road. "I'm sorry, Sam, but this—this thing I—it's too important to be discussed in a car."

"The hell it is!" I said. "Nothing's so important that it can't be discussed in a car." I reached across, switched off the ignition, and jerked the key out of the lock. "And this is the end of the line," I growled.

Marian shifted into neutral and the Mercedes coasted to a stop. "I can't talk about it here," she murmured, eyes still fixed straight ahead. "And I won't." She extended her hand, palm up. "Give me the key, Sam."

"No. First tell me this thing that's so important."

She shook her head in sudden violence. "I've changed my mind. It's too disgusting. Too *horrible.*"

"For me to hear? I doubt it, Marian—not after some of the crap they've tossed at me today. Joy Durwood, for instance, told me that—"

Marian twisted in the seat, grabbed my jacket, and hauled my face close to hers. Her eyelids opened so wide that I thought her eyes would fall out. "What *did* that creature say?" she demanded. "What did she *say?*" Spittle flecked my cheeks.

"It's too disgusting," I said, mocking her, "too horrible." Then, for no reason, I added: "Surely *you* know what she said, Marian—if anybody does."

She did her best to shake my head off. "I *don't!* I *don't!*" she screamed. "*Oh, God, what did that bitch creature say?*"

I grabbed her forearms, tore myself loose from her hands, and shoved her hard against her side of the car. "She said I should walk the rest of the way," I told her. "And that's what I reckon to do. Good night, Marian."

She made a lunge for me as I got out, and I nearly shut the door on her wrist. "Here's the key," I said. I tossed it on the floor of the back seat. Then I walked fast toward the highway.

There were no developments until I was getting close to the road that led down to our *finca.* I heard the Mercedes before I could see it. Tires squealed as Marian cornered her heap around the bend behind me, and the headlights cut a swath across the landscape. They missed me, however; I'd had time to get off the macadam and throw myself flat against a convenient stone wall. The Mercedes, holding to the crest of the highway, went past me like expensive thunder.

I was on the point of turning into our cobblestoned road when the silence was shattered and the night shaken by the sound of a great crash. I'd heard a number of automobile crack-ups in my time, but I sensed a lethal difference in this one. What reverberated through my ears wasn't exactly the crunch of metal rending metal. It was more like—well, more like metal smashing, and being smashed by, marble. Marble female torsos, say.

Abruptly I understood what I'd heard. Marian Delmore had driven right off the Maldita bridge, taking several of the statues with her into the Rió Maldorado's hard-rock bed.

"Do you suppose—?" Lalage was asking from over my shoulder: "Do you suppose that she had this fantastic idea that if she drove fast enough, and closed her eyes real tight, that she'd leave her and everything—?"

I didn't quite get Lalage's drift, but I figured I might as well humor her. "I suppose," I said. "*Eh*-uh, I suppose. Good night, Lalage."

There was no answer from over my shoulder.

Polly couldn't've heard the crash. She was asleep when I got to the bedroom. Funny about the Weatherby *finca;* he built it in a kind of dead spot in the air. Why, it had you thinking that maybe Jack Weatherby was a master craftsman, and not an architect at all.

PART FOUR

THE SURPRISING PRIZES

—*tuam amicam uideo, Calidore.*

                        —*ubi ea est, opsecro?*

—*eccam in tabellis porrectam: in cera cubat.*

✿ One

As Soon as I Push Frank Steinmetz off the Ledge

I was sitting under the same old pepper tree in the patio, listening to the big black bird assault the morning with Martian music. One of the books I'd brought from California—a fine study of the city of Rome, in which such buildings and monuments as remained were used as points of departure for historical and humanistic digressions—lay open on the hide-topped table, but its pages were having a devilish hard time when it came to holding my attention. At first I thought this was due to the blatting of Uncle Too-ra-loo-ra in the branches overhead, but when the bird finally flew off, after wrapping up his performance with an imitation of a cussing contest among four Marseilles fishwives, the resulting silence made it clear that the only distractor present was a once-avid amateur of history named Samuel Fraser Culloden who, let it be admitted, had more than enough to distract him without any aid from the aviary.

Even before the bird took a powder my own recollections of Rome impinged on the pages before me. I was seeing myself on the Via Veneto as a spring afternoon faded, toying with a Cinzano outside Doney's while I inspected the swelling crowd of passers-by—beauties and uglies, talents and zeros, saints and scavengers, tourists and beats.

This daily spectacle, unfolding in an area limited by the Via Sicilia and the Via Boncompagni, resembles the surge of supernumeraries at the rear of the stage in *Aida,* when Rhadames trots home in triumph after all those exhausting evenings over brandy and war maps at Desert Force GHQ. If the strollers should suddenly burst into song it would seem the most natural thing in the world. The faces of these peripatetic Romans are liquid, their voices are liquid too, and their expressive arms, flung every which way as conversational emphases, embrace nearly three thousand years of survival on their murderous long peninsula.

Yet being a Roman these days, I thought, is no more than an accident of birth. The descendants of the original tribesmen were all but extinct by the time the Galilean water was changed to wine. The swords of Pyrrhus slew them in myriads, Carthaginian Hannibal hewed down whole armies, and in hundreds of no-quarter battles in dozens of mean little countries the hot sands absorbed their life blood in laconic drops. Exigencies of empire took care of the few who were left after the gang got around to avenging Caesar; and meanwhile from every backwater cove and deforested mountain of the Mediterranean the living fruits of conquest, either as slaves or ciphers, ripened and rotted in the overblown City. South of the Alps then came Vandal and Goth and centaur-like Hun, chopping the men and bedding the women and toppling the houses and bending their knees at last before still another new deity, until the volcano called Italy blew apart in a lava of ignorance, ruins, and God. A final thin trickle of this lava, this sauce of two millennia, runs with its piquant taste and indefinable flavor down the Via Veneto every pleasant afternoon.

I am fascinated to watch these Romans loaf past Doney's, because I sense that I am seeing not men and women alive like myself, but the full history of mankind; and in every face is something of my own history, my own thoughts, my own emotions, my own life and my death to come. Each of us is many people in one, a huge, breathing nest of Chinese boxes. We open one Self to find another waiting, the successive Selves becoming ever more compact until we reach the innermost box of all, our very core of being, where we find—

Well, all too often we find that the last tiny box is empty, in which case we have wasted our time—as God has wasted His. But no matter: it's the luck of the draw.

The Via Veneto curves down past the Capuccini Church to end at the Via del Tritone, where a mottled marble river god is poised in a vacuum of belief among the man-choking Vespas. The ceiling and walls of the Capuccini vault, in which I once spent an unsettling hour, are decorated with the bones of dead Capuchins. The chandeliers are cobwebs of tibia and femur; and a use is found even for the phalanges that are sifted from the soil of the graveyard that is also the floor of the vault. Vertebrae and ribs, woven outward from cracked pelves, form great gray-brown intricate flowers high on the walls, and between them sag complete monkish skeletons, wire-supported, each skull carefully cowled in dust-weighted cloth. The monotony of stained and disarticulate bones is only now and then broken by the cranium of what might have been a child, or a midget lay brother, or perhaps a monkey that made the scene by mistake. With a dozen tables and a little work the place would be a dead ringer for one of the better restaurants in Hell.

"Hell!" I said aloud. My cigarette, sticking to my lower lip, had removed some skin as I'd pulled it free.

The minor pain brought me back to what passes for reality and made me wonder what sun-heated chain of thought had dragged me into the Capuccini vault. It didn't make sense for a man, presently rusticating in one foreign country, to project himself into another foreign country and his own past. I'm generally incapable, however, of either explaining my thoughts or understanding their import—which is what I get for having opened so few of my own nest of Chinese boxes.

Yet when it comes to self-analysis most human beings are in the same boat. And self-analysis *is* a boat. We sail toward the landfalls of the Inward Islands, over a well-charted sea, only to find ourselves becalmed in a pea souper that girdles the world and intends to hang there forever. So men must be basically phlegmatic, basically incurious and basically resigned—or we would all leap overside and go plummeting down to unfathomed and currentless canyons.

"Plummeting" was the word that tidied the chaos in my head. Marian Delmore, clasped in folding steel, had gone plummeting to her death nine days before. I'd tried to avoid thinking about it, but now my subconscious had bulldozed me there by a tricky and round-about way. The boneyard that bemused me on that hot August morning wasn't below the Via Veneto at all; on the contrary, it lay up behind Santa Caterina where, two weeks to the day after Thomas Flint Fletcher was buried, Marian Delmore's smashed carcass went into the ground not far from where Tom was a-cold.

I hadn't gone to Marian's funeral. Indeed, I hadn't left the patio since I'd walked home from the party—not even to inspect the damaged bridge. The details of the accident were given to Polly and me by Jim Inskilling, who looked in on us the next morning.

In common with most tiny Mexican towns, Maldita has a *delegado,* who is a combined mayor and chief of police, the office being appointive rather than elective. The *delegado's* main duty as mayor is to collect money for the street lights, and his main duty as chief of police is to keep his relatives out of jail. His symbols of office are usually one empty desk, one cobwebbed cell, and one inefficient policeman.

The Maldita *delegado,* a man named Ruiz, had come to Inskilling's *finca* around midnight, which was a couple of hours after the accident had happened, saying that *la Señora, la viuda de Delmore* had unfortunately driven her fine foreign automobile off the Maldita bridge and—*¡Qué lástima!*—appeared to be dead. Sr. Ruiz would be eternally grateful if the eminent Dr. Inskilling would give a definite opinion—but off the record, since he no longer practiced medicine officially—as to whether or not *la Señora, la viuda de Delmore* was indeed dispossessed of life.

When Ruiz turned up Inskilling's guests had gone and he was sitting alone by the pool, wondering whether to go to bed with Inés or simply go to bed. He felt neither sorrow nor regret at Marian's reported death, although he was pleased that Ruiz's request had relieved him of having to decide if he should sleep with frills, or without. He followed Ruiz to the bridge in his own car.

The Mercedes had taken three female statues, their pedestals, and most of the east railing into space with it, and lay crumpled in upon itself, driver-side down, among fragments of stone and marble in the middle of the Río Maldorado. Its trajectory had carried it an amazing distance from the bridge to where, Inskilling judged, it had hit hood-foremost and then rolled over two and a quarter times before it came to rest in low and sluggish water.

Inskilling had arrived to find the scene lit by a small bonfire and a weak flashlight, with forty or so morbid spectators lining the banks. The flashlight was being waved back and forth by the inefficient policeman, who leaned against the exposed underbelly of the Mercedes, his blue pants rolled up to his knees and his laced-together shoes draped over one shoulder, getting grease from the drive shaft all over his back while he presumably kept a loot-mad crowd at bay.

"Nobody knew whether Marian was alive or dead," Inskilling told us. "Being Mexicans, of course, they preferred to think she was dead. The car was a complete wreck, curling back on itself as though it wanted to touch its heels with its forehead—but by some freak the doors were jammed shut. Not only that, but the glass in them wasn't broken. It was this three-ply safety glass. The policeman had tried to smash it with the butt of his pistol, but he'd stopped when it occurred to him that the pistol might smash before the glass did. I waded out to the car with my shoes on—it was cheaper to ruin a pair of shoes than to step on a broken bottle—and tried to look through the window with that impossible flashlight. I could dimly see Marian doubled up in some water. I got the *delegado* to order some men on the bank to come and push the car upright, and when they'd set it up on what was left of its wheels I finally had a decent view of Marian. Her door was stuck, too, but I could get my head inside the open window. She was very dead—and had been, I daresay, since the car struck the bank. And—well, I won't go into details, but Marian's last affair was a violent one, and with a steering post."

Polly had already closed her eyes. Now she gasped: "I don't want to hear it!"

"That's all there is," Inskilling said cheerfully. "Except that Ruiz had to send to Maldorado for an acetylene torch."

"Strange," I said. "The doors should've sprung open forward in an accident like that."

"As far as strangeness goes," Inskilling said, "what made her swerve off the bridge? And where on earth was she going?"

Polly, who'd opened her eyes, couldn't imagine where Marian could have been going. Polly's husband, who hadn't shut his eyes and who is always running into distraught females or Illinois tourists on bridges, perhaps could have thrown a weak-batteried ray of light on the ultimate destination of *la viuda de Delmore*—but master craftsmen are not in the habit of giving away trade secrets to every Tom, Dick, and Polly who pops up. Polly's husband therefore shook his buzzing head in bewilderment and said: "Maybe God knows. Sam Culloden sure doesn't."

"And why was she going there, wherever it was?" Inskilling asked. This question also came apart upon hitting the south bank of Culloden ignorance.

The Old Black Doctor visited us again after Marian's funeral. It had been held on the following day, a Monday, at four p.m.—and it had not been a smashing box-office success. Mrs. McDermott had come, expectedly—but with Mr. McDermott, for a change. Pepper and Salt had showed up, too. Pepper had acted bored about the whole thing, although Salt had been clever enough, or smart enough, to strain a tear or two through a miniature handkerchief. And St. Albans and Payne had been present, fidgeting uncomfortably through the entire business of getting Marian underground. Lastly, Angela Gutierrez had put in an appearance—alone and, according to Inskilling, extremely down in the mouth.

"Incidentally," Inskilling said, "a brace of Maldorado policemen arrived during breakfast this morning. They wanted to know what might've happened at the party that could have some bearing on the case. I said it was an especially quiet gringo party—chaste, if not downright dull. How about you, Sam? Anything occur to you?"

"Offhandedly, no," I said. "But how is it they didn't call on me? Wasn't I co-host, or something?"

"Well, since they'd heard it was my party, I didn't bother to disabuse them. And they weren't overconcerned, as it were." Inskilling sighed. "I still can't imagine where Marian was going, or why."

"Where was Lencho?" Polly asked.

"Why, at my house, I suppose. The Gutierrezes came very late to the party. You'd already left."

"No, Jim. When Angela was at the funeral, I mean."

"Why, I—" he began, then thought better of it. He got to his feet. "I really don't know," he said. "It could be that he doesn't like funerals. Not that I blame him. Children, I'll be going home now, or Inés'll think they buried me with Marian."

I walked to his car with him, and as he slid behind the wheel I asked: "Where was Lencho, Jim?"

"Now, where do you think he was?"

I nodded. "Didn't waste any time, did they?"

"Poor Angela," he said. "She's been afraid of something like this."

"*Eh*-uh," I said, "and well she might. How's Inés, by the way?"

"Fine, all things considered." He switched on the ignition. "Why?"

"No reason," I said. "I just like to see everyone I know in good health and happy."

"Oh, sure," Inskilling said as the motor came to life. "Sure you do, Sam. You should've been a doctor." He eased the car through the gateway.

Some other results of Marian's death were told to Polly by various Maldita gringos whom she met in the Maldorado market, and these she dutifully passed on to her vegetating husband. A couple of lawyers from Cleveland arrived in a rented Mexico City limousine on the day after the funeral. They stayed at the Delmore *finca* for forty-eight hours, and then left as quietly and luxuriously as they had come. It was rumored that the *finca* would be put up for sale. Meanwhile most of the Delmore servants were paid off, with bonuses. A maid was kept on to dust the rooms of the several houses, along with a gardener who'd double in brass as a watchman.

"I'm coming around to your viewpoint, Sam," Polly said pensively one rainy night when we'd gone to bed early.

"Which viewpoint's that?"

"Remember our second night here, when you were being disagreeable about Maldita? And I said I liked it—or would, if you'd let me?"

"And I did let you, didn't I?"

"In your way, I guess—yes. But I'm not sure I like it as much now. Not the way I wanted to, anyway. It's a town that—wouldn't you call it an *unlucky* town?"

"For some people, maybe. Not necessarily for us. Jock wouldn't call it unlucky."

"I wonder. He's been acting funny the last few days."

"That doesn't mean anything. You know how boys are."

"No, I don't know how boys are, even when the boy's my own."

"How about husbands?"

"Oh, I know a little about them, if they're my own." She sighed. "And you're not happy either, darling."

"What gives you that idea?"

"Oh, the way you hang around the patio and pretend you're not at loose ends. You've given the book up entirely, haven't you?"

"The Hollywood novel? I suppose so. But I'm working another one out in my head, believe it or not, and some fine day I'll start putting it down on paper. As soon as I push Frank Steinmetz off the ledge."

Polly's hand sneaked under the sheet and began to stroke my chest. "Please, Sam, don't let that silly thing I said prey on your mind."

"Who said it was preying on my mind? If a murderer has talent he doesn't need a conscience."

"Dear old Sam. Come over here and kiss me good night."

"Indeed I will, me proud beauty. And I'll take all night to do it."

Although I'd passed off Polly's remark about Jock, it had been perceptive; the boy *was* acting strangely. More and more of his time was being spent in Sarah Weatherby's workroom, where he lay on the sofa and read her modern poets and avant-garde novelists by the hour—not with any manifest plan or purpose, but as if these books were a means to keep his mind from matters more grim.

Yet whatever was troubling Jock was minor compared to what

troubled his father—or so his father hoped. Joy's innuendo still stuck in my craw, and I couldn't dislodge the damned thing. Major surgery might be necessary before I could breathe freely again. It would have been easy, of course, to sign myself in at Durwood General Hospital, where excision, although painful, would be quick; but master craftsmen don't have a Group Hospitalization Plan, and I'm too young for Medicare. Besides, accommodations at Durwood General are the worst in any hospital south of Hudson Bay; the eighty dollars-a-minute private rooms there are a scandal. Oh, I'd appear at Durwood General eventually—I was positive of that—but I'd be driving a metered meat wagon, and it'd be as First-Interne-Through-The-Door. Until then, though, minor surgery was in order, and minor surgery consisted of a gentle probe of Jock Culloden's wound.

The morning after I'd spent an inordinate and delightful amount of time kissing Polly good night I paid a call on a sofa in Sarah Weatherby's workroom, which was occupied just then by my long-drawn-out son and several short-drawn-out novels. One of these he seemed to be reading. As I stepped through the doorway he laid the open book across his belly and said: "Hi."

I glanced at the title. It was *The Deserted Painting*. "What's the story?" I asked.

"Beats me. It's a drag. You know, hard to follow."

I sat in the swivel chair by Sarah's desk. "What I can't understand, Jock, is why, with all the hidden gold and unconcealed girls in these parts, you've been tucking yourself away and pretending to read this junk." I jerked my head at the bookshelves.

"But I *have* been reading it, Father."

"Why, for God's sake?"

He was slow to answer, and when he did it was with a question of his own: "Where're we going to end up?"

"Who?"

"All of us."

He'd given me a narrow opening and I took it; I might not get a wider one. "You mean people like you and me, and your mother, and Nan, and Joy Durwood?"

"Yeah, the world in general." He studied me in mild bewilderment. "But why'd you mention Joy Durwood?"

"No special reason. Don't you like her?"

"She's okay, I guess. I've only met her a couple of times. Haven't
really talked to her."

I reached in my pocket for a cigarette. "She's a mighty good-
looking woman," I said.

Amusement slid into his eyes. "Hey, what're you trying to do—
fix me up with someone old enough to be my *mother?*"

The lighter was flaming a foot below the cigarette. There are an
infinite number of things in this world that I don't know and never
will know—but I have a fair understanding of my son and, at that
moment and forever more, I knew that Joy Durwood had lied in
her teeth, or tried to, with her insinuation about the other male
Culloden. I finally got around to lighting my cigarette, blew some
smoke at the bookshelves, and showed Jock that I too could answer
a question with a question, as well as he could and any day in the
week. "Where are we going?" I asked. "The whole bunch?"

"I just don't know, Father. But I'm bothered by the possibilities."

"General or particular?"

"Both. But in particular as they affect me."

"Worried about college?"

"That's part of it. Maybe I should've entered this fall, instead of
next year."

"We've been through this before, Jock. Seems to me we agreed
that you wouldn't enter until you were eighteen."

"Yeah. A year's an awful long time, though."

"Don't kid yourself, buddy. And by then you'll've gotten a lot
smarter, and a lot stronger, and you'll've filled out a lot."

"Well—there were all those football scholarships I was offered."

"We've been through that before, too, haven't we?"

"Yes, Father, but—what I mean is, some people think I'm smart
enough and strong enough right now to—"

"Jock, as I told you, no college or university that throws athletic
scholarships around like confetti is worth a hoot in hell as far as

education goes. And I can afford not only to send you to any college in the country, but I can also afford the mental luxury of sending you where they spend more on faculty salaries than on stadium upkeep. However, since you're set on playing football, I insist that you wait until you're coordinated enough so that they won't be telephoning me late some Saturday afternoon to say that—"

"*I* know. To say that this three-hundred-pound freshman linebacker is very sorry, but he just broke my neck. Okay, Father, I'll buy your reasons, and you don't have to go on. But—" *The Deserted Painting* fell to the floor as Jock sat up. He let it stay there. "—I can't help it if I feel restless, can I?"

"No, of course you can't. And if you didn't feel restless, at your age, I'd be a worried man."

"And you don't object to my having my own thoughts?"

"If you didn't I'd be even more worried."

"Me, too." Jock bent and scratched his ankle. "Well, then, this is what I've been thinking. Why don't we kill two birds with one stone? Why don't I spend the next couple of years in the Army and get that out of the way?" He paid attention to his ankle while he spoke, which was just as well; he wouldn't've liked the expression on my face.

I finally was able to say: "Kill two birds? Or one Culloden?"

"Aw, it'd only be a couple of years of training. They don't send you anywhere."

"Who told you they don't send you anywhere?"

"Some joker in Beverly. I forget who."

"Did this same Beverly joker also remind you that they don't take boys under eighteen?"

"I could pass for eighteen."

"Sure. And when I found out you had, I'd take the recruiting sergeant who passed you and tear him apart, chevron by chevron. Get this straight, Jock, once and for all: I don't want you in the Army. I repeat: *I don't want you in the goddamned Army.* Not this year. Not next year. Not *ever*."

Jock continued to concentrate on his ankle, but a flush had found his cheeks. "I don't know why you're so upset," he mumbled. "You spent enough time in the Army. And they didn't have to draft you, either, according to you."

"That's right. Because I wasn't much older than you are now, and even more of a damned fool. I'll say one thing in my own defense, though: In 1941 we had a reason for fighting. I'm not saying that the reasons that led up to 1941 were good, or that the whole thing couldn't've been avoided if we hadn't spent the previous fifty years electing second-rate men to high office. But democracies unfortunately have a built-in distrust of the first-rate—the citizens of any given democracy being instinctive second-guessers or, as you'd say, Monday morning quarterbacks. Anyway, the tenth-raters who make up all but an infinitesimal percentage of the American electorate find it easier on their limited brains to second-guess second-raters. Be that as it may, in 1941 we were attacked—so I joined up. The Japanese had given us a Cause, and Americans like to Believe in a Cause before they push the plunger. And so off we went—probably the last American Army that'll ever Believe in a Cause, no matter if the United States outlasts Armageddon—while behind us the second- and third-rate men in business suits sat around conference tables and doodled us into a fifth-rate future. The country that the Army of the United States came home to wasn't the country it'd left. Pretty soon we discovered that America intended to stay on a war-economy level, and that the men in business suits had somehow warped a good many Beliefs and twisted others completely out of shape. For instance, to have 'Freedom' meant to have your freedom considerably curtailed. And 'Freedom' had to be 'Defended,' it seemed, by American troops and air bases all over the world—with a little 'Free' saber rattling tossed in, now and then, just to keep the game honest. After a while they let it leak out that it wasn't America we were 'Defending,' but the 'Free World,' for Christ's sake. Someday I'd like to wander around Washington and ask a few of the fourth-raters in business suits exactly what the 'Free World' is—but I'd hate to be hanging until I got a sensible answer. However, and according to the newspapers, we're 'Defending' the hell out of the 'Free World' in Vietnam right now. Yes, sir, we're keeping South Vietnam out of

'Communist Control.' *Hoooo,* boy! That's our new bogeyman—the Red takeover. Jock, Russia and the United States are nothing but two chained dogs, barking at each other at a distance. One's saying: My *bow-* is better than your *-wow;* and the other: My *-wow* is better than your *bow-*. And meanwhile a lot of promising boys're getting their heads blown off in a rice paddy between the kennels. Well, you're not going to end up in two pieces in any rice paddy, not while your heroic and bemedaled old man's still on his feet and sassy. I trust you get my message, son."

Midway through my tirade he'd raised his head to stare at me in awe. Now he laughed self-consciously. "Sure I get it," he said. "It damned near knocked me down. I didn't figure on making you mad, Father."

"You didn't," I told him. "And—keep this in mind—when I'm really mad I don't say a word. A man lives longer that way."

"I'll buy it," he said. "The hell with the Army."

"And the hell with the fancy M-16," I said. "So—how does your immediate future stand? You and Nan had another argument?"

"No, sir. But I think we ought to taper off a little. I like Nan, and she likes me, but these things can get complicated before you know it. She probably'd be glad to get married tomorrow, but I couldn't, and I don't want to. There's no sense in getting in over my—*our* heads, is there? Far as I'm concerned, we ought to cool it a bit."

"She go along with the idea?"

"She hasn't even heard it yet. I'll ease her into it by degrees."

My turn to laugh had come, and there was no self-consciousness in my laughter. "You're pretty smart now, boy," I said. "I dread to think how smart you'll be in a year." I rose, tousled his hair, and went out on the river terrace.

This abortive probing of Jock, which had turned into a dreary monologue on my part, took place on the morning before the book on Rome led my thoughts to the Maldita boneyard. Now, as I sat alone in the patio—Polly having taken the Ford to town and Jock, I supposed, having gone off to cool it with Nan Young somewhere—I had no one to talk to except myself. We're such old and complementary friends, me and I, that we can sit for hours without saying a word to each other; but at the moment, and while keeping my silence, I was inwardly as restless as Jock had been twenty-four hours ago. The racketing fantail bird had temporarily quieted my private mental noises with his mindless public ones, and now that he'd beat his wings toward Birdland I discovered that I missed his black presence and raucous sounds. I was in need of some company—and it didn't much matter what kind.

God, however, takes care of drunkards and Cullodens. I got what I needed almost immediately, and in an unexpected form. A faint gasoline-engine snarl became audible at the top of the cobblestoned road and changed its voice to a banshee wail as whatever machine it came from careened down the hill toward the patio gates. Then a decrepit Harley-Davidson motorcycle, with St. Albans fighting the handlebars and Payne riding pillion, bounced through the gateway and skidded to a kind of halt. Until St. Albans remembered how to cut the motor the thing sounded, in the narrow walled area of the patio, like a Panzer division on maneuvers, with three burros in heat thrown in.

"Ah, *there* you are, Cully-boo!" St. Albans shrieked. "Sitting and reading your life away, aren't you? Old before your time, aren't you? Is *this* where you've been hibernating since that Old Black Bear party?"

"Far as I know, *eh*-uh," I said. I went over to them and kicked the motorcycle's front tire. "This the man killer you borrowed in town?"

Payne quit riding shotgun to flex his thin legs on the patio stones. "We didn't borrow it," he said. "We bought it."

"Yes, Cully-boo, it's our own dear little Harley-Dee." St. Albans caressed the phallic tip of the right handle bar. "And our own dear little Hellish-Angelic costumes. How do you like them?"

To tell the truth, I hadn't noticed their costumes. For the past decade or so the dress of the neo-Neanderthals who call themselves motorcyclists has become so outlandishly standardized as almost to seem part of the vehicle itself. St. Albans and Payne looked no different, sartorially, from a thousand other hog jockeys. They wore tight black leather jackets above tight black jeans that fitted tightly around calf-high black Wellingtons. Even the glass in their goggles was so dark that seeing must've been difficult. The only accouterments that I missed were crash helmets—or perhaps surplus Wehrmacht coal-scuttle jobs, swastikas included. "Why, you're more beautiful than Jupiter and Venus in the skies," I said.

"These black jacks are merely tempos," Payne said. "Saint's having some others made."

"*Blinding!*" exclaimed St. Albans. "Coo, *gaudy!* Like nightmare rainbows, Cully-boo. But now we have to wear these because we're in mourning for Marian."

"Touching," I said. "Thoughtful and touching."

"Just till the end of the month, though," Payne said. "Then we'll go *wild.*"

"Cully, you weren't at Marian's funeral." St. Albans wagged a forefinger against a button on my sleeve. "*Shame* on you."

"I wasn't at Marian's accident, either," I said. "How about a belt?"

"*Sweet,* but I have to drive," St. Albans said.

"It's all he can do to control dear old Harley-Dee *sober,*" Payne said. He went over to the wall and began to smell roses.

"I gathered as much," I said. "And as for the funeral, I've made it a lifelong rule never to attend more than one a month. Marian timed hers badly."

"Oh, how *right* you are!" St. Albans tossed his head. "How right you *are!*"

"Tell him what happened, Saint," Payne piped indistinctly from the wall. His nose had found a home in a rosebud.

"Should I?" St. Albans was looking at me as he spoke.

"Why not? Isn't he our own dear little old Cully-boo?"

"*Some*times. But—Oh, well" St. Albans inhaled a double-strength gulp of air. "I was going to paint Inés Injun, Cully-boo—remember?"

"That's right," I said. "And on the dear little old Harley-Dee."

"Oooo, you're *cute.* Yes, you *are.*" St. Albans availed himself of some more air. "But Marian was thoughtless enough to have herself buried on the afternoon Inés Injun was to come, and the Old Black Doctor *had* to drag that lovely, slithery snake along to the funeral with him. But of course we were there, too, so nothing got done—

although I *did* slip a note to Missy Butter-bottom to come pose the next afternoon. So what could one *expect* but that even before break-fast the next morning she skulked over, moaning that the Old Black Doctor'd found the note and was in a dead-pan *fury* about it and now she wouldn't be able to pose at all. She'd only come over because Old Black-Dee had gone to Maldorado to see his lawyer about some silliness or other, and she had to go right back. That's what she *said*, anyway. *Well!* Cully-boo, I was a writhing mass of flibberty-gibbets until I asked myself what Billy-boy Sidewinder would've done, and—"

"That's what Saint did!" Payne squeaked from a rose.

"Oh, didn't I *ever!*" St. Albans crowed. "And—*please*, Phil, don't interrupt—before she knew what was going on I had that Injun gal stripped and astraddle old Harley-Dee just every *which* way. Would you believe it, Cully-boo? In less than twenty minutes I took seventy-two snaps of that bare-bottomed, wide-apart sugar baby. They're simply *utter*-gutter. I'm fantastically good with a camera, you know."

"And he's painting from the pictures, Cully-gully." Payne had returned from the roses. "Or will be."

"What's holding him back?" I asked. "A model-release?"

St. Albans and Payne exchanged glances and giggles. "No, the *room*ies," St. Albans said when his face was straight again. "The naughty roomies who've moved in on us. Joysie brings him there all the time."

"Joysie?" He could've been talking about some visiting queen from Newark, Poith Amboy, or Joysie Siddy.

"Little old Joysie-Dee *Dur*wood, honey," St. Albans said.

"She and little old Lencho-Gee done went and druv us out of house and home," Payne chimed in. "Such dirty old *naughties,* up there oozin' and squoozin' at each other mornin', noon, and night. Our sheet bills'd be tremendous in a *civilized* place."

"You knew about them, didn't you, Cully-boo?" St. Albans asked.

"Oh, sure. And I'm glad they found a better hideaway than the bus station."

"Little old Angela's going right out of her gray cells," Payne said.

"She thinks they're humping up in the hills. It's the most fun since Senator McCarthy."

"We've got to go, Phil," St. Albans said. "Suppose you come mount little old Senator McHarley-Dee."

Payne swung a leg over the rear wheel and settled on the pillion seat. "You forgot old Cully-boo's present, Saint."

"Oh, I did, didn't I? I must be going out of my gray cells, too." St. Albans clucked his tongue like a contented hen as he reached inside his Black Leather Temporary Mourning Jacket. "That's because those two humpers interrupt my work. But it's in a good, wicked cause, isn't it? Yes, in*deed*-y." He pulled a fat five-by-seven-inch envelope from the Mourning Jacket and shoved it at me. "Here you are, Cully-boo. Don't open until Christmas—or until we're gone. Bye-bye, you old Cully-boo." He stamped his foot on the starter and the Panzer Division was back again. Then St. Albans raised hob with the throttle, Payne yodeled a barely heard "Bye-bye, Cully-boo-hoo-*hoo!*" and they shot through the gateway like a jazzed-up Polaris.

I should've guessed what the envelope contained; I think I did, instinctively. There were seventy-two enlargements of a naked Inés exposed on the Harley-Davidson at maybe a score of angles—each degrading, all obscene. Yet in every one her beautiful face was full of a puzzled resignation, as though she were thinking: I don't understand this, but it's what these nice gringos want, so I have to oblige them.

I didn't give the pictures a careful study; I'm not even sure there were seventy-two. I thumbed through the lot in a hurry, then took them upstairs to the *sala* and burned them in the fireplace. Together with the Fletcher communiqué, they gave the chimney more summer work than it'd had since the house was finished.

A single photograph had somehow slipped under the andiron, and I only noticed it when the others were flickering into ash. As I pushed it with my toe into a dying tongue of flame I saw that Inés' two-dimensional eyes were fixed on mine and she was saying: "What are you waiting for, Sr. Culloden? Don't you realize it's time to act?"

A master craftsman gets messages from the damnedest people, and in the damnedest ways. If I'd been more of a master and less of a craftsman I might've been given this message in person. But it wasn't really that crucial, I thought, at that particular time of day. Yet a few hours later I got it again, by God. The whole message. And in person.

Not from Inés, though.

❃ *Two*

Where the Ski Jump Curves Back in an Immelmann Turn

"Mind if I take a walk?" I asked.

"Darling, now? It's late and it's dark." Polly was curled up at one end of the living-room sofa with a thin little number from Sarah Weatherby's library. "And it might rain again." It had rained in the late afternoon.

"I doubt it. The moon's out. Anyway, I'm feeling jumpy and I want to work it off. Damn it, Polly, I haven't stuck my nose outside the patio in ten days."

"Poor Sam, maybe you're right." She yawned. "But don't get run over. And don't wake me if I'm asleep when you get back."

I kissed the part in her hair. "Don't figure to be out that long."

As soon as I'd started up toward the main road, my hands in my pockets, my chin almost touching my chest, I felt better—but not much. Ever since the Harley-Davidson had snarled away I'd been serving as a funnel for a private maelstrom. Inés and the indignities she'd been subjected to, innocently or not, had something to do with this, but she wasn't the pinpoint in the depths to which the whirlpool sucked my every thought. That infinitesimal tollgate was under the control of some Customs officials named Angela, Lencho, and Joy.

Inés, in the last analysis, was Inskilling's duty payment, not mine; yet I couldn't shake the belief that the overcharges on the other three people were somehow the fault of Culloden Optimus Maximus, an uncivil servant who'd given over his ancient and honorable thunderbolts in favor of some lightweight stuff he'd pinched from Eros' quiver. C. O. Maximus meanwhile was learning that Eros' stuff wasn't as light as it looked; the weight was making him sweat— plus which, the damned shafts were nose-heavy.

I'd nearly reached the highway when a car, driven at a higher speed than the disintegrating surface made advisable, flashed past to the west. It was a station wagon, and big enough to be a Buick station wagon; and the driver, who seemed to be the only person it it, could've been Lencho Gutierrez. But it was so dark, despite the young moon's efforts, that I was by no means certain of the car's make and model, let alone the sex of the driver. I had Gutierrezes on the brain, that's all.

Nevertheless, the moon was bright enough for me to see the edge of the macadam as I turned right toward Maldorado, although as I ambled along, my hands still in my pockets, I kept my eyes fixed on the ground immediately ahead of me. I didn't trust the weak moonlight *that* much.

I can't explain why I took the direction I did. The motions of master craftsmen, it must be understood, become to a great extent instinctive. The mind is responsible for these movements, of course; but in the empyrean, where the most exquisite of master craftsmen live, mind and motion prefer to operate in separate areas, meeting briefly on occasion, but not remerging fully with each other until the masterpiece of craftsmanship is finished and carted from the shop.

On this particular nocturnal ramble, for instance, the Culloden Mind and the Culloden Motion didn't make contact until I found myself standing at the head of the Gutierrez road without quite knowing how I got there. Mind paused long enough to suggest to Motion that it might be fun to pop in on Angela and read the tea leaves, or something. Then Mind flitted off.

A single car, the Ford 200, came dimly into view under the semi-useless lights of the parking area; perhaps it had been Lencho I'd seen on the highway, late for an assignation with Joy and tooling the Buick hell-bent toward her. Angela might very well be alone in the house, and miserable. In that case, she'd be in need of a friendly ear in which to complain or a friendly shoulder on which to weep. I walked on to the wall of the *finca*.

The narrow gate hung open and I squeezed through it into the arcadelike patio, to find that the main door to the house was also open. This struck me as odd. Maldita doors are always shut at night, but not, as one might think, as a protection against burglars. Maldita natives are honest; mosquitoes, alas, are not.

In spite of the door being open, I stood outside the lighted living room and knocked; only when a second knock went unanswered did I go in, saying: "Angela?" I waited, then spoke her name louder: "*Angela?*" Again no response. I hesitated, surveying the *sala,* uncertain as to what I should do. Off to my right the dining room was dark, but at least one lamp was on in Angela's office. Not that she was in there, of course; she'd've answered me if she were.

But master craftsmen are a stubborn lot. They never take for granted the things that should be taken for granted. I sent my Hesitation Suit back to Western Costume and crossed to the office doorway.

I'd been wrong, it turned out, about Angela not being in there. She was.

Until a moment like that happens, you're never sure what your first thought will be. In this instance my first thought was: Old Lencho sure had a damned good reason for driving fast, by God.

Angela lay face up on the floor, her feet toward the bathroom. One leg was drawn up slightly, the knee bent outward and the slippered foot pressed against the calf of the other leg under the long white *muu-muu* housecoat she was wearing. Her head was thrown back, her eyes were saucerish, and she was staring up at me openmouthed as though about to upbraid me for walking in unannounced and catching her like that—with a score of holes in her housecoat, and the fabric red with what had oozed from the holes, and St. Albans' jade-handled letter opener driven to the hilt behind her collarbone, the silver pommel just touching the lobe of her ear. She undoubtedly would've complained, too, of the terrible mess on the floor around her.

◎ I'd never expected to see emotion of any kind on Jim Inskilling's face, but when I told him about Angela his expression, had it been photographed, might've served to illustrate Shock in a primer for actors. I'd gone directly to his *finca* from the Gutierrez place, instead of galloping to the police by myself. My Spanish was so sketchy, for one thing, that by the time I'd made the cops understand that there'd been a murder they'd've thrown me into a rat-gnawed cell as the prime suspect; and for another thing, I'm happiest if the nearest cop is three precincts away, off duty, and asleep.

We drove to Angela's in the Old Black Doctor's car, as soon as he'd regained his composure and refitted his Mask. Nothing had changed during my absence except the blood around the body, which shone somewhat more dully in the lamplight. Inskilling viewed the thing on the floor as he would have a medical-school cadaver, trundled in for dissection. He made no effort to examine the wounds, either, although he did squat down to study the protruding jade handle. "Where'd this come from, I wonder?" he said, speaking aloud but asking the question of himself. "It's not Angela's."

"Looks like a letter opener I saw at St. Albans'," I said.

"You sure, Sam?"

"I can't be, until I see the blade. The one at his place has *Tu Corazón y Mi Amor* engraved on it."

"Interesting. But—" Inskilling stood erect again. "Well, we'll let Ataudado worry about that. I'll go rouse him now, I think. Nothing else to be done."

"Ataudado? Who's he?"

"Head of the Maldorado police. This one's over the *delegado's* head—Ruiz can read about it in the papers. Ataudado's a former Army colonel and still uses the title. He's a slob but, as policemen go these days, he's not too difficult to deal with. And at least he's honest. His family's well off, so he doesn't have to play around with bribes."

"He speak English?" I asked.

"Very good English. Come to think of it, Sam, this is going to hit the colonel where it hurts. He and Angela were old friends, you know. In fact, the word is that they had an affair about thirty years ago on the Riviera—at Cannes, to be exact, where Angela was recuperating between husbands. Ataudado also had something to do with persuading her to build down here. You don't mind holding the fort for a while, do you, until I show up with the law? Not that I'm worried about Lencho coming back, but somebody else might wander in. I'll be as quick as I can."

"No, I don't mind, Jim. But how long will you be? Twenty, twenty-five minutes?"

"At this time of night?" Inskilling glanced at his wristwatch. "I'd say an hour, anyway—maybe more."

"Why? The cops coming out on Pogo sticks?"

"No, but Ataudado's sure to be in bed. And first he'll want to call Fuerte and have them put out an all-points for Lencho. And then he'll want to alert the local paper—and the Fuerte papers—and, in this case, the Mexico City papers, too. A rich gringa's been murdered, don't forget—and that means a publicity landslide for the police. And then finally Ataudado may even get around to letting his own men in on what's happened. Thoughtful of him, wouldn't you say?"

I walked as far as the wall with Inskilling. As he stepped sideways through the narrow gateway he paused to ask: "Are you certain that Lencho was alone when he drove by you?"

"I wouldn't swear to it," I said. "And on the witness stand I couldn't even swear it was Lencho."

"Well, don't worry, it's not your problem," Inskilling said, slipping free of the gateway. "Or mine," he added as he strode toward his car.

I didn't know whether it was his problem or not, but it damned well wasn't mine. The problem I did have—which wasn't much of a problem, at that—was a private matter, and nobody else's business. S. F. Culloden, Ltd., Master Craftsman by Appointment, whose specialty was constructing master craftsmen, would handle everything in person—cunningly, acutely, and without any help from apprentice gods. Or former physicians.

◎ I returned to the living room and smoked a cigarette and let myself get increasingly restless. Part of my restlessness had me hearing whispers that seemed to emanate from the bathroom, and when they grew loud enough to drown out the noises in my head I got up and went to the office door and glared across the shell of Angela at the bathroom beyond. The whisperers, instead of being quelled, came up with more sibilances than ever.

The lights in the bathroom were also on—which I hadn't noticed before. There was no reason why they shouldn't've been on; there was no reason why they shouldn't've been off, either. Be that as it may, Professor Samuel Moriarty, the bane of Baker Street and all it stood for, decided to check the bathroom, and all *it* stood for, at first hand.

An awkward hop got me over Angela's shapeless red throw rug, and as soon as I was in the bathroom the whispering stopped. There were traces of water in the tiled bottom of the big sunken tub and a few drops on the floor proper. A towel the size of a Sibley tent had been carelessly draped, still damp, on a wall rack set in bronze lions' heads. Possibly Angela, coming from a bath, had flung open the door to her office to find Lencho & Letter Opener, Inc., a firm that dealt in Ultimate Services, open for business and committed to the hard sell. Yes, possibly. But—

I sniffed the air like a pack of bloodhounds. The bathroom was permeated by a faint odor, unusual and yet familiar, that had me working my nose this way and that in an effort to locate the source. At last and, I suppose, logically, I centered my investigation on the water closet. As there were probably enough fingerprints about the room at the moment to satisfy the Bertillon experts of six cities I used a Kleenex tissue to keep my whorls from the cover of the toilet seat as I lifted it. The smell was stronger then, although the toilet bowl held nothing but clear water; it had been flushed by the last user. When I lifted the seat itself, though, I saw flecks of a pale, indefinable substance at the rear of the bowl near the hinges.

I sank to my knees, put my nose as close to the bowl as I dared without retching, and inhaled deeply several times. Pretty soon I smiled, gently lowered seat and cover again, and climbed to my feet in contentment. The hunt for the Grail was over. What I'd smelled had been human vomit.

A more practiced hop carried me past the former Angela on my way to the living room. I was feeling much more bouncy as I blended a second time with the sofa—for I now had two dovetailing facts on which to brood. Until my trip to the bathroom I'd only had one— those many overkill holes in Angela's nice white housecoat.

I lit another cigarette, and no sooner had I shoved the lighter back in my pocket when the whisperings started up. But this time I let Whoever was whispering whisper away to his bloodless heart's content. The hell with avant-garde whisperers, in or out of bathrooms, I thought: I'm sick of shy ectoplasm.

◉ Colonel Rafael Ataudado was so fat that he had trouble clasping his hands behind him as he paced the Gutierrez living room, grumbling under his breath. He had the face of a swollen, shaved, and swarthy owl on the body of a uniformed hippopotamus. Yet he was extremely light on his feet, and behind his pouches and dewlaps were faded X rays of the handsome man he must've been in the early 1930's. The room was crowded with policemen and detectives and photographers and reporters and a number of effaced men whose duties seemed undefined but who spent most of their time getting out of Ataudado's way. It was now well past midnight and, since shortly after the colonel showed up, the scene of the crime had taken on the colors and confusions of a madhouse run by the inmates.

Ataudado had arrived with Inskilling, in the ex-doctor's car, before anybody else. "We have not met, Mr. Culloden," he said as he approached me in the patio, his hand extended. "I am Colonel Ataudado, and I cannot bring myself to gaze upon the body of a dear old friend. Is the door to the—the *room* shut? And if not, would you be so kind?"

I was so kind on the instant, after which Ataudado, who obviously knew his way around the house, led us into the dining room, switched on the lights, used his wheezing bulk to overwhelm an astonished chair at the head of the table facing the door, and gestured for us to join him. I sat with my back to the regimented *santos* on the sideboard, across from the Old Black Doctor.

"Ah, a sad night, Mr. Culloden," Ataudado said. "Sad for you, doubly sad for me. And I am responsible, broken fellow that I am. If I had not *begged* my bewitching old friend to build a house in Maldita she would still—but *no!* He would have destroyed her, that Gutierrez, no matter where she lived. You knew my dear Angela well, Mr. Culloden?"

"Not too well," I said. "I've only been here six weeks. But I liked her, and so did my wife. She made a trip to Tepectlán with Angela."

"True, my old friend was always buying *santos* there." Ataudado glanced at the sideboard and sighed. "But they gave her no help when she needed them, did they, those wretched holy opiates?" The sideboard received another, angrier glance. "Although I must take one figurine home with me, as a souvenir of Angela. Or perhaps to burn, depending." He turned to Inskilling. "I am not happy tonight, Jimmy. I am not pleased." His wrist watch caught his attention and he snorted. "*Todavía los hideputas no han llegado.* Ah, Mr. Culloden, the Mexican police leave much to be desired, no?"

"Couldn't tell you, colonel," I said. "I've never had any dealings with them."

"You're a fortunate man," Ataudado said. "Or were, until this *noche triste.* Ah, this sad night! Did my old friend ask you to visit her?"

I shook my head. "I was just taking a walk and thought I'd see if anyone was home."

"At what time was this?"

"Oh, nine thirty, quarter to ten."

"A strange hour to go walking, Mr. Culloden."

I didn't cotton to the way he talked. He managed to undercoat the simplest statement with a threat. "A damned strange hour, colonel," I said. "And now I wish I hadn't gone walking."

"And *I* wish, my dear friend, that you'd taken your walk an hour before. Then you might have—" He left the sentence unfinished while he pulled a pack of Filtrons from his pocket. "However," he went on, "you did see Gutierrez driving his car toward Fuerte, which is of great aid to us. Otherwise we might be hunting him in all directions."

"I thought it was the Gutierrez car, colonel, but as I told Doctor Inskilling, I'm not sure. It was very dark." I took the cigarette he offered me. "Thank you."

Ataudado waited until Inskilling had refused a cigarette and he had pulled one free for himself before saying: "I have absolutely no doubt that it was the Gutierrez car, and that they were both in it— that *cabrón* and his *puta*. But they will not get far. Not far. You'd heard about what they were doing, of course?—Ah, *gracias*." He leaned toward my lighter.

"Lencho and Joy Durwood, you mean? I'd heard rumors, but that's all. I never saw them alone together." I lit my own cigarette.

"My dear friend," Ataudado said, "even murderers dislike spectators when they make love." He grimaced as though a picture of a bloodstained, love-making Lencho had been shoved in front of his nose.

"According to St. Albans," I said, "they used his place for their bedding down."

Ataudado snuffled and blew out smoke. "This is the same St. Albans, Jimmy, whose letter opener may be in—in the *room?*"

"It would appear so," said Inskilling.

"Bub-bub-bub." Ataudado made thoughtful drowning noises and flicked an ash on the floor. "Very interesting, even if it infuriates. An addition, my friends, that complicates a basically simple—uh, death. I know of this St. Albans. A *cabrón,* of the most hideous sort. And his friend. *Otro cabrón,* no less hideous. When my men report from the Matthews *finca* I may send them to sweep up these hideous *cabrones*. Or I may dispatch other men sooner."

"You sent men to the Matthews place?" I asked.

"Routine," Inskilling said.

"Exactly," Ataudado wheezed. "Mere routine, Mr. Culloden. To see if the *puta*—whore, if you will—left anything behind when she and Gutierrez the unspeakable—" A high whine of sirens, increasingly loud, shut him up. He listened to the sound, frowning in such a way that his fat-enmeshed eyes nearly vanished. "And here are my own damned *cabrones*," he announced presently, "making all the wails and noises I ordered them not to make."

We sat in silence while the sirens died out, to be followed by shouted commands in Spanish and the clatter of heavy-shod feet in the patio. Then came a closer babble, as the vanguard of police and newspapermen burst into the living room. Ataudado called out sharply, and beyond the doorway the feet became silent and the voices still.

A young lieutenant of police with the eyes of a deer and a jaw like an anvil entered the dining room and stood at attention while Ataudado dressed him down at length. I don't know what the colonel was saying, but his words made the lieutenant wince as though winds of gale force were beating against him. When Ataudado finally ran down, the young man almost fell over himself in his eagerness to return to the living room and whatever duties he had there. Ataudado then gazed mildly at Inskilling. "If you will be so kind, Jimmy," he said, "please go into the *room* and watch those police doctors carefully. I must not have any rudenesses committed on the person of my dear old friend. And remind them that Colonel Ataudado wishes them to be quick. I cannot move about comfortably until the *room* is tenantless."

After Inskilling had gone Ataudado and I lost contact temporarily. Voices and shuffling feet and an occasional cough could be heard in the living room, and every ten seconds or so the doorway would fill with light as some photographer used a flashbulb. Then Ataudado cleared his throat and said: "*Cenicero,* please, Mr. Culloden," indicating an ashtray that was out of his reach and which he hadn't been using. I pushed it over to him. He crushed out his cigarette and started to drum on the polished table with five fat fingers.

Both of us were startled when a sport-shirted man with a Speed

Graphic popped into the dining room and scurried to the end of the table opposite Ataudado. "*Con su permiso,*" he said abruptly, hauling his camera up to eye level and aiming the lens at the colonel. Ataudado bellowed at him, pounding the table with his drum hand. The man shrugged, smirked, and trotted back where he'd come from, the picture untaken.

"I advised that interloper that I wasn't yet ready for photographs," Ataudado told me soberly. "Later, I said, when I am less sad, more composed."

The remark didn't seem to require an answer, so I didn't give him one. It wasn't long before his attention wandered to the *santos* on the sideboard. He studied them one after another, squinting until his tiny eyes vanished between folds of pink flesh. At last he murmured: "Mr. Culloden, would you be so kind as to hand a discomposed fellow the fifth—no, *six*th figurine from the right in the second rank?"

I went to the sideboard and pointed. "This one, colonel?"

"Please."

It was the San Ysidro they'd passed around the circle on the floor the night we'd had drinks with Angela. Actually the figure wasn't what I'd've called Spanish Colonial. It wore a round hat with a wide, flat brim and was more reminiscent of an Amish farmer than a Catholic saint. I brought it to Ataudado and sat down again.

He inspected it impassively and from various angles. I was beginning to think he'd forgotten my presence when he asked: "You will stay in Mexico how long, Mr. Culloden?"

"I've rented the *finca* for a year, colonel. Let's put it that way."

"Yes. And this sad event will not encourage you to leave?"

"I don't think so," I said slowly, "no."

"Bub-bub-bub." He rubbed his thumb on the base of the figure. "Are you not one of these *norteamericanos* who dislike their own country?"

"On the contrary, I like the United States."

"Like, but not *love*?"

"It's gotten too big to love," I said, "and too jam-packed. But I'm fond of the place. It's a kind of deadly Disneyland, where the ski jump curves back in an Immelmann turn and the children don't laugh unless the clown breaks his leg."

"Yes, my Mexico, too, is a Disneyland," Ataudado said, still paying attention to San Ysidro, "but not deadly—and this makes my Mexico different from the rest of the world. In other lands men are executed for murder and politics; that is, for the improper use of weapons and the improper use of states. Perhaps we Mexicans were like that once, my friend, but no longer. Now we are almost too civilized. It is next to impossible for a murderer, no matter how brutal his crime, to be executed in Mexico today. Even this Gutierrez, when he's caught, will manage to avoid execution, on the plea that the crime was unpremeditated, that he killed my dear—that he killed his wife in a fit of pique." Fat fingers drummed on the table again, and Ataudado continued cheerfully: "However, he may not be able to avoid being killed while attempting to escape, once he is in my hands. No, I don't think Lorenzo Gutierrez will be able to avoid that. No." Ataudado chuckled and patted the *santo*'s wooden backside. "I will keep this little man as a souvenir of my dear old friend," he said, and put the figure in his voluminous pocket.

San Ysidro's head stuck out above the flap; his worm-eaten eyes could watch whatever went on as the night ran its course.

◉ From the moment that Inskilling, followed by another lieutenant of police, reappeared in the dining room to announce that the body had been removed, I became a monolingual spectator. All conversations, except for the brief exchanges I had with Ataudado, were in Spanish. I therefore stayed close to the Old Black Doctor, who did the necessary interpreting for me. The dialogue from here on is thus not first-hand, but rather the Gospel According to St. James—as heard from the Apostle's own lips.

The new lieutenant, who had the eyes of a striking snake and no chin to speak of, carried the letter opener in a handkerchief.

Colonel Ataudado wouldn't touch the weapon when it had been laid on the table before him. He stared at it with distaste. "Is this the letter opener you may have seen, Mr. Culloden?"

"That's it, Colonel." On the blade was *Tu Corazón y Mi Amor*.

"Thank you. Lieutenant, take three men and pick up the gringo *cabrones,* St. Albans and Payne. They live in Maldita."

"Yes, sir, I know the house. There've been reports."

"I shouldn't wonder. Anyway, I want them jailed on any charge that seems applicable."

"I can think of several, sir."

"And when they're in jail, keep those two *hideputas* away from the other prisoners. They are hard-working, misunderstood men—the other prisoners. I refuse to have them corrupted."

"Yes, sir."

"And remove this exhibit." He waved at the letter opener. "It offends my sense of justice."

Ataudado waddled into the living room in the lieutenant's wake, with Inskilling and me tucked behind his bulk; now that Angela's mortal coil had been wound in an ambulance he had no qualms about being near where she had lain. Four or five cameras banged away at him as soon as he came from the dining room, nearly blinding us with their flashes. The Old Black Doctor and I retreated to the wall while Ataudado posed by the sofa and the photographers took his picture until their thumbs were calloused. Meanwhile a dozen reporters were barking questions at him like a pack of wild dogs.

This savage attention did for Ataudado what a pair of Adler Elevator Shoes might have done for Napoleon. He seemed to grow taller as his ego expanded. When one of the reporters left the group to ask me: "You found the body, *señor?*" the colonel brought him back into line by snapping: "Leave the gentleman alone, man. He has had a sad night."

The press conference was interrupted by two patrol-car cops who reported on the Buick station wagon. It had been found, abandoned, on the roadside nine miles west of Maldita and about four and a half miles east of Highway 69, which ran south from Fuerte. The ignition key was in place, the engine was warm, and the car seemed in good running order.

"Any blood on the seat?" Ataudado asked.

"No, sir, no trace of blood. Or anything else."

"Including Gutierrez and the woman, eh? What happened to *them?*"

"The Fuerte police have search parties out, sir. They think they're heading for Fuerte."

"Damn them, they're not out of Maldorado jurisdiction yet." Ataudado summoned the deer-eyed, anvil-jawed lieutenant. "I want every available man out hunting those beasts. The search will start at Highway 69 and work back toward the car they deserted. Quick!"

The lieutenant double-timed out of the house.

"What about the Buick, sir?" the second patrol-car cop asked.

"Leave it where it is. I'll take a look at it later." After they'd gone, Ataudado shouted at me: "Maybe those *carbrones* aren't home, Mr. Culloden. Maybe they were waiting down the road to pick up Gutierrez and his gringa whore. Maybe now they're in Durango, the four of them."

Then, without waiting for a reply, he started his pacing.

Only twice did he stop. The first time was when the Gutierrez servants were brought in—two young women and a thin, coughing, middle-aged man. They were all scared out of their wits to such an extent that they hardly knew their own names. Ataudado in exasperation ordered them to be put in jail until their memories improved. It would, he said, be no hardship on them; with one employer dead and the other a fugitive, they were out of work anyway. So they were led off, the cook shrieking: "I don't want to go to jail! There's no church in jail, and I'm such a religious woman! With three tiny babies who'll starve!"

"And thirty-seven fathers who'll see that they don't!" Ataudado muttered. He resumed his pacing.

The second halt came when a burly police sergeant entered unsteadily. "And where have you been, man?" Ataudado demanded.

"At the *finca* of the Durwood woman, sir. To see if she left anything."

Ataudado shoved his own face so close to the sergeant's that their noses almost touched. "She left a lot of liquor, didn't she?" he bellowed. "And you stayed until you'd drunk it all, didn't you? All the thieves in the world aren't behind bars, are they, Sergeant?"

"We didn't steal any liquor, sir," the weaving sergeant said. "She gave it to us."

"*She?*"

"The Durwood woman, sir. She was in bed."

"Bub-bub-bub. In *bed?* Bub."

"Yes, sir. Asleep."

"*Asleep?*" This information made Ataudado himself unsteady for a moment. "How do you *know* she was asleep? Because she told you so?"

"No, sir, we went right into the bedroom. We didn't know she was there. And she thought we were burglars. She screamed, sir."

"And—?"

"And then she put on the light and saw we were police and asked us what we were doing." The sergeant momentarily closed his eyes. "She don't wear nothing in bed, sir. A beautiful woman, sir."

"Never mind that. What did you tell her you were doing?"

"We said there'd been a murder, sir, that Gutierrez had killed his wife, and she said, 'Oh, God, God, *God!*' —three times, just like that. Then we thought she was going to pass out. She was holding the bedclothes against her, like this—" The sergeant placed his clenched fist high on his chest. "—but then they fell down and we saw her ti— well, sir, then she grabbed them up again and asked Sergeant Gómez to please bring her a drink from this cabinet there. So he did, and then she drank it, and it made her feel better, so she told us to have a drink, too. And we did, and then she told us to have another, and then she had another, and then she made us have one more. And then she begun to cry and carry on and say we couldn't leave her because this Gutierrez was a monster and he'd be coming to kill *her,* too. So I left Sergeant Gómez with her—he's the one who speaks English, sir—and now I'm reporting to you, sir."

"Gómez is with her now?"

"Yes, sir, Sergeant Gómez. Far as I know, he's with her."

"He'd better be, Sergeant—or it'll turn out to be a sad night for both of you. Get back there, *hombre,* and put some clothes on her, and take her in to—No, take her to *my* house. Hold her there until I can talk to her."

"*Your* house, sir?"

"You heard me, *hombre*. Jump, now!"

The sergeant jumped—and Colonel Ataudado resumed his pacing, back and forth, wall to wall, while people scampered out of his way. As he walked he mumbled to himself. Not many words, and even fewer phrases, were intelligible—according to the Old Black Doctor. At one point Ataudado was heard to say, "Bedclothes . . . beautiful . . ." and, at another point, what sounded like "fat old bachelor . . ." But a single sentence came out of him clearly, and with the force of a shotgun blast: "It's indecent of her, not to be mixed up in it—even if she isn't!"

This sentence, when dissected, didn't make much sense. Neither did anything else that was going on, in fact, until Ataudado glared at me and said bleakly: "If you will be so kind, Mr. Culloden, you may go home now. It has been a sad night for us, in many ways. If I should need you, I will pay you a visit at your home. *Hasta luego,* Mr. Culloden."

After a mumbled good night to Inskilling I got out of there fast. Not too fast, though. It doesn't pay to break into a run when you're surrounded by the fuzz. No, that's when it's smart to be dignified and to move at your stateliest. I therefore had the stately dignity of a gold-in-the-hold galleon as I went past the two cops who were guarding the patio gate—past several others who lounged by the parking area, keeping the Morbid Set of Maldita at a respectful distance from the house—and past the Morbid Set itself. The Set's mute and white-faced members examined me in detail as I moved through them toward the main road. They were awed by the Culloden grandeur, and some of them regarded me as an object of wonder— Halley's Comet, for instance. Others, however, although also regarding me as an object of wonder, put me on a more earthly plane—as a fellow who'd killed a gringa, say, and who'd managed to fool the police.

✇ Three

A Woman Who's Stabbing You
Ends Up Arm-Weary

"Sam, we've got to!"

"I swear, I didn't expect you to carry on so."

"And I didn't—couldn't ever—imagine you'd be so insensitive, so utterly cold."

"I'm not. I'm being realistic."

"Realistic, my foot! If you were you'd be thinking of your family and—"

I red-dogged that play in a hurry. "What the hell do you *think* I'm thinking about?"

"I don't know. Nothing. Yourself. Or this latest book you're going to write. That's it, probably. You ought to be full of inspiration, now that Angela's been mur—"

The unremoved breakfast dishes rattled and jumped as I brought my open palm down hard on the table. Polly rose several inches in her chair; if the suddenness of my act hadn't startled her, the noise certainly had. She stared at me in alarm, her pretty lips still slightly parted by the word she hadn't finished saying.

"Not again," I said. "Not that again, Polly."

A sigh worked its way through her parted lips and her body gave over being tense. "No," she said—and her own voice was calmer, "not again, Sam." She set Jock's empty coffee cup back on its base; my table pounding had knocked the thing on its side. "But that doesn't change the way I feel," she went on. "I can't stay in Maldita. Not after this."

I'd made a mistake in waiting until Jock had eaten and gone before I told Polly about Angela. I'd thus let her see herself not as my wife and equal in things and events, but as a second-class associate, a sackable employee who'd been given, almost as an aside, a frightful piece of information. She was shocked by my news while being humiliated by my casualness. If I'd waked her as soon as I'd come home and confided everything that had happened she might've reacted as a confidante, stunned perhaps, but at the same time a sharer of my ordeal. Unfortunately she'd been asleep when I slid in beside her, and by then my own exhaustion had pushed me off the ledge.

At least I'd kept my mouth shut until Jock was out of the house. It was bad enough to have Polly running scared without the added complication of an exhilarated Jock Culloden thrown in. He'd learn of the murder soon enough; probably from the first articulate gringo he met.

"I wish you'd give me your reasons, Polly," I said.

"For wanting to leave Maldita? Good God, Sam, isn't a murder reason enough?"

"There's a murder of one kind or another committed every week in Los Angeles, but all the time we lived there you didn't r'ar up and yell, 'I can't stand it, let's get—'"

"Los Angeles has millions of people. But this—"

"Is a small town, I agree. But, without being able to quote statistics, I'd be willing to bet that there's a murder a week committed in Maldorado, too. That hot Spanish blood'll do it every time."

"What I was about to say, when you butted in, was that this is the murder of a friend, and by her husband. *You* may not care, Sam Cul—"

"Don't talk that way. You can't be sure Lencho did it."

"Don't be a fool, Sam."

"Honey, the evidence is all circumstantial. They might have quite a time proving him guilty—once they've caught him, that is."

"That's where you're wrong, Mr. Blackstone. Ransom McDermott told me that in Mexico you're guilty until you can prove yourself innocent, and while you're trying to prove it you can stay in prison for years. For your whole life, even."

"Well, they still have to catch old Lencho," I said. "And perhaps a better suspect'll turn up before then."

"How can you call him *old* Lencho, as though he were a friend of yours?"

"Beats me, darling. Force of habit."

"Sam, if you're playing around with the idea that getting me to believe somebody else killed Angela will make me feel any better, you're double wrong. Because all that'd mean is that anyone in Maldita could've killed her—some horrible man who's walking around free and unsuspected and who's perfectly capable of killing again."

"Now you're the one who's being the fool, Polly. Who else in Maldita had a motive except Lencho? You must've heard that he and Joy Durwood had a thing going."

"Yes, I did—and not from you, either, in case you're interested." She put her forearms on the table, leaned toward me, and spoke very seriously. "Listen, Sam," she said, "a few days ago I told you I thought Maldita was unlucky. I can weather somebody being killed in a car wreck or committing suicide. But murder's the last straw. Maldita's more than unlucky, Sam—the damned town's got a curse on it. I want to get out."

"Well, I don't."

"You're just being perverse."

"No, I'm not. Polly, I came here to work, and I'm going to work. Whether I've adjusted to what's happened here lately needn't come into it—but I'm adjusted to this house and I know damned well I can work here, once I get started. However, if you feel that your surroundings're too much for you—well, then—" I left the rest of it hanging in the air, on the off chance that Polly would be put on the defensive by the unspoken suggestion.

And she was, to my relief. "Is that a hint for me to leave?" She was trying to bridle. "And take Jock?"

"I didn't hint anything, darling," I told her. "You're putting words in my mouth. All I had in mind was that you and Jock might want to see more of the country. Mexico City, for instance. For a week. Ten days. Two weeks. Something along that line."

She thought about the possibility, then said: "And what will you do while we're gone?"

"The same thing I'm doing now, only more so. I might even make a beginning on this new book. Especially since I won't have any distractions."

"You won't have a car, either."

"You worried about my being fed? Concepción can take the bus into the market. And so can I, to go to the post office."

Polly liked the feel of the material, but she hadn't yet decided to buy the whole bolt. "I'm not sure Jock and I could manage a trip like that ourselves."

"The Youngs might like to go along. Why don't you ask Helen? I'll bet she'd jump at the chance."

"And I'll bet she wouldn't," Polly said.

"Ask her and see."

"No, she'd say she thought of it herself. That's what I meant." She rose from the table, and I knew I'd won. "I'll go into town now," she murmured.

"If the Maldorado paper's put out an extra, get me one, will you?"

"Maybe, if I see one." Polly paused in the doorway that opened on the balcony. "But I don't want to read what's in it. And I don't want you to tell me." She went out on the balcony.

"Don't worry, I won't. It's a deal." She didn't hear what I said.

◎   When Polly returned from Maldorado it was nearly noon and I was warming the pigskin of my usual *equipál* in the patio. She waited until Concepción had carried the full market basket up to the kitchen before she got out of the car and came over to where I was sitting. "Well," she said, "I saw the Youngs."

"And?"

"You got what you wanted. We're all going down to Mexico City for a week."

"Darling, it wasn't what I wanted. I thought it'd relax you, that's all."

"Never mind, Sam. We'll be using the Young car. Leaving first thing in the morning."

"There's more space in the station wagon."

"You can't be without a car for a week. Don't think I'm keen on this trip, though. I'm not. But it's better than nothing, and certainly better than spending the next week here."

"What'll you do about a hotel?"

"Helen and Bruce're calling about one from Maldorado this afternoon." She went to the exterior staircase and paused at the bottom. "And they'll be over for a drink at five."

"How about a paper? Did you get one?"

"Two—Maldorado and Fuerte. They're on the front seat." She went up the stairs and into the kitchen.

The papers, when I brought them back to the table, were full of the murder—as I'd expected. The Fuerte *El Diario* even had an eight-column photograph of the body above the masthead, which had been lowered to half-staff for the occasion. I had sufficient Spanish to realize, though, that the reporters were about as inaccurate as sane men can get. One paragraph informed me that the body had been found by a Sr. Samul Cuyoden, a retired architect who had a lavish estate in Maldita. There was no mention at all, that I could find, of a Miss Joy Durwood.

◎   The rest of the day was a bore. Jock controlled himself during *comida,* out of deference to his blood-shy mother, but as soon as we'd left the table he dragged me into his bedroom and pumped me and pumped me and pumped me. I couldn't escape for an hour, and even then I had to plead a nonexistent headache.

Later in the afternoon, when the McDermotts came calling, I used the same dodge. *"Me siento como la mona,"* I told Concepión, who'd clumped into the living room with the unwelcome news that they were below. I was lying on the sofa. Polly had usurped the master bedroom while she decided what she could tote to Mexico City in the way of wearables; and Concepción, as a woman who knew women, had preferred not to disturb her and had come to me. I had no desire to meet the murder-avid eyes of Mrs. McDermott then or at any future time, so I passed the word to her—through Concepción, and by means of three verbs and twenty-seven gestures—that the finding of slaughtered females was a most exhausting avocation, and I was therefore completely incapable, as I would be for the next six months, of entertaining the McDermotts with a dissertation on the finer points of body finding.

Still later, and in spite of the bottle of Azteca I brought out, the visit of the Youngs didn't come off too well—perhaps because I *had* brought out the Azteca. Bruce arrived with the Mexico City papers, which he'd picked up in town along with reservations at the Hotel Sor Juana Inés de la Cruz, on the Reforma—but they contained nothing from the Maldita murder front other than short rehashes, telephoned in by Fuerte and Maldorado stringers, of what I'd already read locally and at length.

But Old Academic Bruce, after he'd guzzled some strong-water, couldn't resist leading me out to the river terrace, man to man, where he took a pontifical forty-five minutes to expound, through broad statements and narrow generalizations, Professor (with tenure) Young's theories on What Lay Behind the Sad Death of Angela Gutierrez. This monologue ran on far too long for even a dictated Ph.D. thesis. I finally told Bruce that if he had no deeper comprehension of the events of 1840–70 than he had of what'd happened in the last twenty-four hours, he'd be smart to resign his professorship and devote himself to drag racing. He didn't take this comment kindly.

Indeed, from then until Helen led him off, Bruce was more civil to my rum than he was to me.

Not that I could blame him.

◎   At eleven the next morning I'd been alone for an hour and enjoying it shamelessly—an attitude sufficiently un-American, had I dared to appreciate this solitude anywhere north of Laredo, to have alerted both the HUAC and the Son of HUAC. A carful of Cullodens and Youngs was rolling toward the quiet excitements of Mexico City while a bodyful of Sam Culloden, anchored in a sunny patio with the last of the books it'd brought from California— Christopher Smart's poem, *Jubilate Agno*—was glorying in its aloneness.

In this human-hive world of government by euphemism, where the tiny bit of life we're allowed is lived by innuendo, it is true that power corrupts—although never as much as the desire for power. A less familiar truth is that nothing on earth is more powerful than a solitary man, at ease in a landscape he's chosen, who knows exactly what he wants to do and has the means and ability for the doing. This was an of-that-moment description of me; and so I was content to bask in the sun and let my dynamos build up a Power. I had the solitude, I was loose in my emotional landscape, I was aware of what had to be done, and I had the crucial paraphernalia. The Time, the Place, and the Opportunity were still to be determined—that ultimate Trinity whose descent from the skies would be revealed at the proper moment. The awaited Revelation would come as it had in the past, I thought, by degrees. Perhaps in the form of another Trinity—of Messengers cleverly disguised and pretending to be what they weren't. And it was likely, too, that at some point I'd hear a chorus of advising Voices. The secret of the power of the Solitary Man is that he is never, *never* Alone, no more than the callous Universe is.

For the time being, though, nothing was required of me other than to wait, to be ready, and to recognize the Messengers when they came. As a result I wasn't disturbed that day until around five o'clock in the afternoon; and then I disturbed myself.

I'd had *comida* and taken a nap, and when I woke up it was because a bayonet of curiosity was pricking the small of my back. Perhaps my subconscious had looked forward to a visit from Colonel

Ataudado or, at worst, a couple of his underlings. Although I didn't especially want to be swept into a two-days-later investigation of Angela's death I couldn't avoid a rickety interest in whatever developments had reared their ugly heads since I'd cleared a passage for myself through the Morbid Set of Maldita.

Even so, I had no desire to drive into town and buy six different newspapers, all but one in Spanish, then sweat out such information as they could offer. I also had no particular desire to drive into town, period. The Solitary Man keeps to his known and personal acres.

Yet I had to know what had gone on lately; and—fortunately— the local Unholy-Water Font should be able to fill in my gaps. So I heaved myself off the bed and made for the *finca* of Dr. James Winters Inskilling, hoping to God he'd be there.

He was, as it happened—by the skin of my teeth. As I swung the Ford in from the main road he was driving out, and I blocked his way. Inés sat clinging to him, and there were suitcases on his car's rear seat. I left the motor running as I got out and walked over to his window. "Well timed," he said. "Saves me from stopping at your place."

"You off somewhere, Jim?" My eyes were on Inés, who smiled at me while she and I talked at great length with each other—instantaneously, and without a word passing between us.

"Yes, worse luck," the Old Black Doctor said. "A long weekend at the Rancho Guadalupe—the Bandera place, up above Fuerte. I don't think you know them, Sam. Anyway, it's a *compleaños* for their youngest daughter, and I'm the girl's godfather, don't ask me why. We'll be back Monday—Tuesday morning at the latest. Everything all right?"

"Far as I know," I said, "except that I don't know much. What's on the stove at Ataudadosville?"

"Oh, the usual guff. Threats and promises, with the accent on the former. No sign of Lencho yet, although the National Pawnshop's about the only place where he hasn't been reported as seen. Wait a minute, though—there's one bit of news. They've pulled up the pansy bed."

"Pansy bed?"

"The field of festering lilies, let's say. Anyway, they've deported St. Albans and Payne. Drove them to Fuerte this morning and put them on a plane for San Antonio. They should be wandering around Texas right now, trying to figure out what in the name of Jean Genet hit them."

"And the stuff in their house? What happens to that?"

"I don't care. Do you?"

"Hell, no," I said—although I did care about the ultimate disposition of seventy-two 35mm. negatives.

"As for our friend Joy," Inskilling went on, "I'd say she had the Evil Eye on Ataudado. I saw him this morning and he's still holding her under protective—shall we say?—custody at his house, and—"

"Still, Jim?"

"Certainly, Sam—and don't be childish. It's a perfect place for the pleasanter forms of interrogation. But, like all good things, it's going to end."

"Is he jailing her?"

"For the last time, Sam, don't be childish. He's releasing her to her own little bed tomorrow afternoon, which—"

"Which means she'll get out of the country fast."

"I doubt that, somehow. More likely she'll sleep for three days. After the interrogatory fun-and-games Ataudado put her through— or vice versa—she'll need the rest. And now, Sam, if you'll shove that overgrown, overchromed circus wagon you're driving into its idea of reverse gear, Srta. Photogenic and I'll be on our way to the wilderness northwest of Fuerte."

"Sure, Jim. Have a good time. *Hasta luego,* Inés." I started toward the Ford.

"I always have a good time," Inskilling said. "Even when I don't have a good time."

It wasn't until I'd backed the station wagon all the way to the main road and swung right, letting them head west before I did, that what the Old Black Doctor had meant by "Srta. Photogenic" hit home. The Maldorado cops might find a lot of curious material when they rummaged through odd drawers and corners of the St. Albans–Payne *finca,* but seventy-two 35mm. negatives wouldn't be part of the loot. No, sir, by Hippocrates, they certainly wouldn't.

I couldn't imagine, as I took my time driving home to my own joint, how anyone had been able to pin an abortion rap—and in Chicago, of all places—on Dr. James Winters Inskilling, who didn't practice medicine any more.

◎   A day later, almost to the minute, the first Messenger showed up.

Actually he'd been present for some time before I sensed he was there; but I was asleep when he came, and he was much too polite—contrary to what I'd once thought about him—to disturb another man's siesta.

The master bedroom was in semidarkness; in more ways than one this had been a strange week. For instance, it was now Friday and, although the rainy season was supposed to be at its height, there had been no rain since the previous Saturday afternoon. The waters of the Río Maldorado were hard put to wet its stony bed; and this had been a wiltingly hot day, reminiscent of a New York City August or a Los Angeles mid-September. When I stretched out for a nap I had good reason to draw the curtains—and even then I'd had trouble in falling into a sticky sleep and more trouble staying in it.

Sometime later I more or less opened my eyes to find myself lying unenthusiastically on my back. The pillow under my head was coated with the very latest in sweat. I sat up, neither effectively alert nor completely awake. As my feet touched the floor I had a peripheral view of a black bulk between the bed and the triptych of mirrors on Polly's dressing table. I turned toward it, and in my direct line of vision it became a familiar pale form in the pallid light. The only extraordinary thing about it was the revolver in its right hand. "Well," I said matter of factly, *"buenas tardes,* Lencho."

"Yeah," Lencho Gutierrez said, "the same to you. I need some help, man."

He was a far cry from the beautiful Lencho of two weeks before.

His clothes were torn and stained, his eyes red-rimmed and sunken, his cheeks dark with stubble. But this wasn't why my mouth hung open, any more than because he had a gun in his hand. What had come in on me from the side was the sound of accent-free American English as it arrived from the Gutierrez mouth. After a while I was able to say: "All the help you can get, I reckon."

"And from you," he said.

"*Eh*-uh." I bent and put on my shoes. While I was tying them I asked: "Where'd you pick up English so fast?"

"I was born and raised in Los Angeles, for Christ's sake. Where'd you think I picked it up?"

"Okay," I said, "I'll give you all the help I can. As soon as—" I rose and walked toward him. "—as soon as you give me the gun."

Lencho pointed the revolver at my solar plexus and took a step backward. "Stay where you are," he said. "One more won't make any difference."

"The hell I will." I kept on coming toward him and he finally stopped backtracking. His fingers relaxed around the butt when I reached out and took the thing away from him. It was a short-barreled .38 Smith & Wesson Police Special. I spun the cylinder, saw that every chamber had a cartridge in it, and tossed the gun on the bed. "No need to threaten me, Lencho," I told him. "I know you didn't kill her."

He put his hands on his cheekbones and rubbed them up and down before saying: "I was right, then, coming here. Jesus, I didn't know whether to bust in on you or those faggots. Goddamned smart to pick you."

"Smarter than you think," I said. "You'd've bored a dry well with St. Albans and Payne. They've been kicked out of the country already."

"Yeah?" He mulled the statement over and decided it made sense. "Not soon enough, though—that's the hell. But, listen—what made you so sure I wouldn't pull the trigger on you?"

"It's this way, Lencho—an old Robert Taylor fan wouldn't gun down an unarmed man. An old Peter Lorre fan, maybe. If you'd been a Peter Lorre man I might've cooled it."

"Yeah," he said, "yeah." He went over to the dressing-table bench and slumped down, letting his head droop. "Christ, I'm beat," he mumbled.

"That's no lie," I said. "Want something to eat?"

"Only thing I don't need right now is food. I was in your kitchen already." He forced himself to look at me. "But what I *do* got to have is some dough. Tonight. I got to get out of here tonight." His head sagged again.

"Not the way you are, though," I said. "How about some sleep first?"

"Can't. No time. Got to get moving by nine."

My watch read 5:03. "I'll wake you at eight," I told him. "Come on." I pulled him to his feet and guided him toward the bed.

"Can't. I—" He was aware of the mattress beneath him. "Got to—" And he was asleep.

◎ At eight o'clock I tiptoed into the bedroom. I was sure I'd have a hard time waking him, but I'd barely touched his shoulders when he was sitting bolt upright, blinking his eyes. Three hours of sleep seemed to have done as much for him as twelve would've done for me; most of the fatigue had left his face and he was infinitely sharper than when he'd hit the sack. "That's what I needed," he said. "Yeah."

"Well, we might as well go whole hog, Lencho," I said. "Go on into the bathroom and take a shower and shave. My robe's on the back of the door and the shaving stuff's on the shelf. You'll see it."

"I'd like to talk about getting me out of here first," he said. "If it's okay with you."

"It's okay with me. How much money can you get by with?"

"As much as I can get. Not just for myself, though. There's this guy in town who'll get me to Tampico—if he thinks it's worth it. I got family in this little place near Tampico. My old lady's family. Her brothers're all fishermen there, and they'll get me across the Gulf to Cuba or—you know, Santo Domingo."

"Well," I said, "I scraped together all the cash in the house while you were conked out. It comes to two hundred fifty-three dollars in American money and just under eighty bucks in pesos. Figure three hundred thirty in dollars. But if that's not enough you'll have to hang around until I can get to the bank in the morning."

"No, that ought to swing it," he said, "yeah." He went toward the bathroom. "I'll pay you back sometime," he said.

"Forget it," I said. "I never saw you before in my life. Reckon I never will again, either."

While he showered I laid out some shirts and socks and under-wear that weren't so large he couldn't wear them. There was also a pair of black Levis that had beat the sanforization rap at the factory and had shrunk a couple of inches all over when washed. It turned out that they were a perfect fit for Lencho Gutierrez.

The bathroom door was thrown open. "Hey, come on in," he called. "Let's talk while I shave."

I went in and sat on the toilet seat. Lencho stood in front of the mirror over the washbasin and began to lather his face. The damp towel he'd used was wrapped around his middle. He hadn't bothered to wear the robe.

"What's this no-spik-English jazz?" I asked him.

"Yeah, how about that?" Lencho said. "That's a kick I hope I've seen the last of. What happened was, I was hanging around Acapulco —and you got to really scratch for bread down there, the competi-tion's that stiff—when I first got together with Angela. She was spending some of the loot she took off this guy Pierce she was just divorced from. The money wasn't enough, though—she hated the guy even more than she liked the money. Hell, Pierce'd fixed her somehow so she hated every American in the world. Anyway, this beach-stud friend of mine had been trying to get in, and he did fine so long as he talked Spanish, but then he had to show her how good he spoke English. *Boom!*—Out. That's when *I* moved in. But, Christ, I never thought I'd get stuck with Spanish for four years. That's a long time to walk a tightrope."

"Well," I said, "you're back on the ground now."

Lencho stopped lathering his face for a moment. "I don't like it, though. I didn't want it this way." He finished with the lather, then said: "I meant to ask you—how'd you know I didn't do it?"

"Simple. It wasn't the kind of job a man'd do. Too many wounds, too much wasted effort. That's why a woman who's stabbing you ends up arm-weary."

"A woman, huh?" He was ready with the razor. "Joy Durwood, maybe?"

"*Eh*-uh," I said. "Joy Durwood."

"Yeah, I guessed it was her, the goddamned bitch. I was over there last night—you know, to where she's living. I couldn't've killed Angela, but I sure as hell was going to kill that bitch. There was nobody home."

"They've got her in town."

"Jail?"

I shrugged. "Protective custody." I couldn't very well tell Lencho precisely what kind of protective custody, let alone admit that she was already out of it and back doing business at the same old stand; to give away secrets like those would mean I was infringing on my own patent rights.

"The bitch'll get out of it somehow," Lencho said. "Anyway," he went on, shaving as he talked, "that was the worst mistake I ever made in my life, getting mixed up with that chick. Hell, it was worse than getting hooked on horse. One look at her and I was *gone*— dig?—and I had to be banging her all the time. Every chance I got. Any place. I couldn't get enough of it. I'm not saying I haven't done a lot of cruddy things, understand? There's plenty of bum in me. Even after I married Angela I managed to bang some chick once in a while—but it was the old Wham-Bam-Thank-you-ma'am jazz. I made sure Angela didn't find out, either. Hell, all I had to do was play it cool a few more years and I'd be set up for life. Like *rich*. But with this cruddy Joy I flipped, man. And Angela got wise. Christ, how could she help it? The chick and me were practically banging each other on the old girl's lap. So she told me, Angela did, loud and clear: quit or get out. I tell you, that brought me around, fast." The sentences were coming from him one at a time, between strokes. "What I mean, a bang is a bang, but some morning a guy's going to reach for that little black book. And I wasn't so dumb as to toss away being loaded tomorrow just for a bedful of loose change today. So what did I do? I went and told that bitch it was all over. And then, goddamn her, she made sure it damned well *was* all over. I keep asking myself: Man, why did you *tell* her?"

"Why did you run?" I demanded.

"Yeah, that's another dumb thing I did. That's a smart bitch, that Durwood chick—she must've known I'd take off. And she knew I went in for the mail every night about the same time, so that's when she did it. So there's no mail at all, and I go in to tell Angela and— Jesus! there she is, dead on the floor. The next thing I know I'm burning up the road ten miles from here. Well, I think maybe I'll drive back to Maldorado and call the cops—but then I remember I don't have any alibi. Nobody saw me in town. There wasn't even anybody in the post office. And by now somebody's probably found Angela. So I sit there in the heap and try to decide what to do. Finally I get this idea that if I leave the heap where it is the cops'll think I chickened out and made for Fuerte on foot, cross-country. Okay, I leave the keys in the heap but take the pistol—Angela always liked to keep one in the glove compartment. And then I cut cross-country, all right—back to Maldita. It turns out to be the safest place I could be—except that I got to get a long ways away from here, and damned soon. So then I remember this guy in town who'll get me to the coast if the price is right. And then I remember you, and I think maybe you'll let me have the dough. And so here I am."

"The quicker you get someplace else, the better," I told him, and then described Colonel Ataudado's threat to kill him while attempting to escape—supposing, of course, that he fell into the colonel's fat hands.

"Ah, that Ataudado—that *mother*," Lencho said. Then, surprisingly, he grinned. "I think I'll like Cuba a lot, yeah."

"What about papers? You'll need some kind of papers, won't you?"

The grin was turned on me now, and he went on, softly: "You think Gutierrez is my *real* name, man?"

I let it go at that.

◎   Lencho slumped low on the seat beside me as I drove into town, giving me quiet directions and finally having me pull up by a narrow alley that ran up from Calle B. Juárez near the Maldorado Normal School. I'd already given him the money. Now he told me to wait, slipped from the Ford, and disappeared into the black alleyway. For nearly an hour I sat in the dark car and smoked cigarettes and did what I could to keep my mind empty. Then at last a man popped from the alley's shadows and scuttled around to my window. I recognized him as the trucker who'd delivered the case of Azteca to me. He handed me a scrap of paper through the half-open window and immediately darted back where he'd come from.

I switched on the dashboard light and read what had been scribbled on the paper: *Everything okay. Thanx. L.* Then I started the motor and drove home to Maldita—and, I might add, to a meeting with the second Messenger.

◎   It was a Headache, that second Messenger—the worst I'd ever had. It put every inch of my skull in an unbearable vise as I was on the point of climbing into bed. Tighter and tighter and tighter bands were crushing the agonized bones. Screaming License or not, I ended up yelling and writhing on the floor.

And then, as suddenly as it had come, the Headache was gone.

Or had it gone? As I kneeled at the side of the bed, trembling in my sweat, I was unable to escape a belief that the Headache was still very much with me. Perhaps the Messenger had decided it wouldn't be in the best interests of the Message to let Pain, however pure, make a gibbering ruin of its host.

Four

The Fly, Whose Health
Is the Honey
of the Air

I was thinking:

> *She walks, the lady of my* Let Gage,
> house of Gage rejoice with the Cacifer a small
> curious meretricious beast *Delight*
> Where is the Simmons-matrix of the rose Who
> Swole my part a way, who maid me dye all Let
> Joe, house of Salvatierra toy with the Urbigot a
> transitional position Nurse, O *muy*
> Larva's lame, I saw Id go o'er the Let Lala, house
> of Ge run with the Dulceloquax, a crane
> immune to poison'd arrows Hurl'd dark Durwood
> Into the scheme beneath 'er As of old
> Appalled her pranging nougats too too late
> And all his timbers shivered into silence
> *A shepherdess of sheep*
>   She walks?
>   Then let her

—using "let" to mean what Hamlet meant when he took off after
the ghost, of course. *Whinny tuck oaf huffed err thug, Host?* 'At's

roight, me old cock-sparrer, and she's a jeopardess of sleep, she is, gorblimey....

I had to quit thinking that way, though—and at once; a man's thoughts're apt to take off, too, and in the wrong direction, when he's sitting by himself in a patio on a hot, windless night, with the still world glowing below a moon three days from the full, while he waits for a Visitation. The Final Visitation. The last of the Messengers.

Lencho Gutierrez by now ought to've been safely tucked away among his numerous uncles, who lived somewhere near Tampico and were hell on fish. Even the asthmatic delivery truck of my Azteca-carton acquaintance should've been able to cover the distance in the more than twenty-five hours that'd passed since I'd left old Lencho in his care. There was a chance, naturally, that the moribund truck might've broken down in an inhabited place that could be damaging, not to mention dangerous, for the fishermen's nephew; yet I had no doubt but that in such a situation he'd use the Smith & Wesson—on police, if he had to, and on himself as a last resort. However, that was something I'd have to discover in tomorrow's paper—or, and more likely, Monday's.

My Headache seemed to have been tucked away safely, too. Nevertheless, I couldn't get rid of the feeling that it was ranging my attic even then, after temporarily stuffing the accompanying pain into a mothballed trunk. As long as I behaved myself the pain would remain there, but if I should try to improve on my status as Message receiver, the lid of the trunk would instantly fly off and I would be—

I *was* behaving myself, though—patiently sitting in the moonlit patio and awaiting a third Messenger. I was, in short, a Man of My Time who was conforming to the time of the man his time had made him, a not-too-intellectual, not-too-conforming American of the Last Days—yet capable of a conformation, when the spirit twitched, to whatever dry nonsense Conformity desired him to conform to.

Although I'd've liked to hear a chorus of advising Voices, it was getting late; and meanwhile the common-sewer Río Maldorado wasn't clean enough to support a Spanish Colonial version of Aristophanes' claque of batrachians. This was a pity, all things considered; only a frog chorus, to my mind, can bounce the right echo off the ruined sets among which this morally wrecked century spews out its unsavory lines. We're all actors in a closet drama where Man has been changed from a Prince of the Mind into a Frog of the Groin. This metamorphosis is due to the enchantments of a thousand-eyed, thousand-eared, thousand-handed devil's dam—who also answers to a thousand names, none of them utterable on pain of Pain. And the interminable dull play in which we overact out our lives deals with Man's search, that doomed-to-failure Search, for the blind, deaf, limbless, and nameless Princess whose kiss, so it's said, will return the poor wretch to his true shape.

Neither as a performer on the stage nor as a spectator huddled coughing in an orchestra seat will I have anything to do with that damned Play. I am a variorum edition of the First Folio of Man—the Changeling Unchanged, the Primary As Before. Indeed, I'm unique in being a Frog who's been turned into a Prince; and I want nothing other than to be a Frog again. But only a kiss from a beautiful female Frog will turn the trick—and the mouths of Frogs are incapable of kisses. All I can do, then, is to go on thinking my lily-pond Frog thoughts while my Enchanted Prince legs lead me this way and that in an alien landscape, while my batrachian mind takes me to—

"Then we'll set a Man to watch," Lalage said from the roses. "Dance over my Lady Lee."

"Ah, you're back, are you?" I asked her.

"Back, yes," she said. "Don't you dare look this way."

"I wasn't going to."

"You always say that." I heard sweet laughter. "But then you don't ever look, do you?"

"You know it, Lalage. Do you still love me?"

"Why, that's part of why I'm back. I had to tell you the funny thing that happened. You see, I had this feeling I was living in my own future. There was one Me here, doing what I was doing, and another Me off in the past someplace, watching herself do it."

"Which was the nicest You? The one here or the one in the past?"

"The one in the past was terribly happy about something. Something that hadn't happened yet, but that *had* happened just the same. She was happier than I've ever been, my mother says." Laughter came again from the roses. "Or ever could bear to be. So thank you for the life, and for where I slept last night."

"Where did you sleep last night, Lalage?"

"Nowhere, my mother says."

"Is she with you?"

"Who?" Now she spoke from the portico behind me.

"Your mother."

"My mother's dead." She sounded fainter. "Is yours?"

"I don't know, Lalage. I never asked her."

"I did," a male voice boomed. "I asked her and she said No."

"Who's talking?" I demanded. "Who's that?" It was a voice I recognized and yet couldn't place. I couldn't pinpoint its source.

"Why, you wanted us, didn't you?" Lalage whispered. "You've been expecting us for days. All of us."

And then I knew that the chorus had come on stage. The advising Voices were present. "Yes, but who spoke then?" I said. "What man?"

"Feller from Démence-sur-Fosse, France." Thomas Flint Fletcher was chuckling over my shoulder. He then said to someone else: "It's a wise child that knows his own father, eh, Jamie?"

"This is a dumb one, Cap. Doesn't know his." The new voice wasn't new at all; it had been with me all my life, until lately. I'd heard my father, and it made me speechless myself.

"Reckon not," Fletcher said. "Reckon he didn't even know you'd gone west. Told me you were fine and dandy. Had lots of color, he said."

"Well, Cap, that wasn't an out-and-out lie. Those undertakers painted me up till I looked like a two-dollar whore. Hell of a way to treat a man who was just getting his second wind at the age of sixty-three. If I'd known they were going to put lipstick and rouge on me I might've changed my mind about dying. Except that I didn't have much choice in the matter. Sam'll tell you. Won't you, Sam?"

"Tell what, Father?"

"About the pillow. Tell Cap what you did with the pillow."
I twisted around in the *equilpál,* but they were too quick for me. The patio was empty. "Pillows're what people sleep on," I said.
"Or sleep under," my father said from somewhere else. "You've met my son, haven't you, Cap? You've met my son, haven't you?"
"Now and again," Fletcher said, "but maybe too late. He's a good boy, Jamie. Leave him alone."
"I've always left him alone, Cap. Always let him go his own way."
"You let everybody go their own way," I said, "unless it was some woman you were chasing."
"You've been listening to your mother too much, Sam."
"Not half enough. Where is she?"
"Who?"
"My mother."
"I don't know. I never asked her."
"God *damn* you, Father!" I exclaimed, and found I was beating my fist on the hide-topped table.
"Not yet, Sam boy, not yet." Fletcher's voice was conciliatory. "And, Jamie, take it easy. We were talking about something else, weren't we? And I still can't understand why it didn't reach you."
"The medal? I'll tell you, Cap. The reason it wasn't delivered is because Boston's gone to hell—lock, stock, and codfish."
"Reckon so," Fletcher said. "Just like the rest of the world."
"Except Démence-sur-Fosse," said my father, "which was a suburb of hell to begin with."
Fletcher chuckled. "By God, that's so, Jamie. You ever go back there after the war?"
"No. Never wanted to, either."
"Wonder what it looks like now?"
"Pretty much the same, I'd say, Cap, although I suppose they must've policed it up some and carted off all the dead Heinies. How many'd they tally after that counterattack? Ninety-two, wasn't it?"
"Call it ninety-two and a half, Jamie, considering how big that lieutenant was."
"God, yes!" my father said. "When he fell on me I went out like a light. Did twice the damage to me that the arm wound did. He—"

"Do you have to go through that story again?" I cried. "I've heard the damned thing a hundred times!" I couldn't bear the thought of listening to it once more—how a concealed German machinegun, firing from a shattered copse on a shell-blasted rise of ground had killed, wounded, pinned down, or driven back the remnants of Fletcher's company; how my father had bellied around one flank, wiggling below the shredded trees, and, at the price of a piece of lead in his upper right arm, had grenaded the machinegunners into Valhalla; how he'd been unable to operate the machinegun himself when the Germans mounted a counterattack, and had been joined by Capt. Thomas F. Fletcher, who'd cheerfully hosed down two depleted companies of Bavarian Guards until they'd broken and run, leaving all those dead behind them; and how, when the presumed corpse of a gigantic Guards lieutenant had returned to life, lumbered into point-blank range, and aimed to blow open a considerable portion of Captain Fletcher's head with a slug from a 9mm. Luger Parabellum pistol, Sergeant Culloden had managed to rip apart an even more considerable portion of the lieutenant's guts with a snap shot from another 9mm. Luger Parabellum, which had come to him along with the machinegun nest, using his left hand— and immediately thereafter had been knocked unconscious and nearly smothered to death by the Guardsman's jackknifing body. "And you weren't sent here to tell stories!" Again the table quivered under my fist. "You came to advise me! *Advise* me!"

Silence fell for a brief space, then I heard Fletcher say: "Advise you about what, Sam boy? That's news to me."

"News to him, too, like as not, Cap," said my father. "And it wouldn't be advice about pillows. He knows all there is to know about pillows. Don't you, Sam?"

"And all about you," I said. "And your women. Where are they now, your women? That stable of women?"

"Oh, in whistling distance," my father said lightly. "When I want them they're with me."

"And my mother?"

"She's around someplace, I suppose.—Beautiful girl, Cap. Too bad you never met her."

"Well, Jamie, the way Sam's carrying on, I'd say he wishes *you*'d never met her, either."

"The boy's jealous, Cap. Always was, always will be. The truth is, Annie Fraser loved me till her dying day."

"That was when she died in her heart," I told him, "and it happened a long, long time before she died in the flesh."

"Like you, you mean?" my father asked. "Because you're dead, Sam—as dead as if somebody pushed you off a ledge or covered your face with a pillow or stabbed you a dozen times or pressed something hard against your throat or—"

I fought my way to my feet through the heavy air and staggered across the patio, trying to locate my damned old father through a crimson membrane. "What's this about throats?" I yelled. "What's all this lying talk about throats?"

"Ask your mother," my father said. "She's so smart and pretty." He seemed to be above me now, but never in the place I grabbed for.

"You damned old bastard!" I howled. "Just let me get my hands on you and I'll teach you all about throats!" I was circling the patio, blindly clutching at emptiness.

Then I thought I heard Fletcher say: "All right, Jamie, I reckon he's mad enough now." I'm not positive I heard him say that, though, because suddenly a thousand invisible throats were cleared together, and somebody kicked my feet out from under me, and I went sprawling.

Beautifully disguised as an earthquake, the third Messenger had arrived.

◎   I lay curled on the tiles until the tremors winked out in a final jiggle. A silence followed, so profound that I could hear my heart thudding in my rib cage, and so implosive that when a dish at last made up its mind to fall and break in the upstairs kitchen it was like an exploding mortar shell. Then all the dogs of Mexico began to bark.

A loosened chunk of mortar dropped from somewhere high on the wall and rustled down through the bougainvillaea. I got to my feet, feeling calm now and under control, although annoyed at having been knocked galley-west by the rolling earth. I blamed it on the Indian-type moccasins I was wearing. They had neither soles nor heels and were hardly suitable for wear while flailing around in a patio. Thus the earth heave had caught me off balance.

I was mounting the exterior staircase on my way to the kitchen when Luis came out of the river terrace tunnel at a trot, waving a flashlight and chattering to himself. He saw me and directed the chatter in my direction, meanwhile raising his pitch. I couldn't understand a word he was saying, but I supposed it concerned the earthquake. He chased up the stairs after me.

I flicked the wall switch as I entered the kitchen, but the room stayed dark.

"*No hay luz, señor,*" Luis said, pushing past me. "*No hay electricidad.*"

"*Lo creo,*" I said.

The public utilities of Mexico are so operated as to compel their consumers to take precautionary measures, if only as a form of self-protection. Weatherby had flashlights stashed all over his *finca,* and Polly and I'd already used them twice, along with candles, when thunderstorms had done the dirty to the Maldorado power station, such as it was. Now I took the kitchen flashlight out of a drawer in the storage cabinet and joined its beam with Luis's while we checked up on possible damage. Two plates had been shaken from a shelf by the stove, but everything else in the kitchen seemed to be undisturbed.

The other upstairs rooms were also in order—save for a few tiny lumps of plaster from the ceiling that had sprinkled the living-room rug. I saw no cracks in the walls nor any other hints of structural weaknesses. Jack Weatherby had put himself together a mighty resilient house, and I couldn't imagine why Polly should feel worried about earthquakes while we were in it. The place'd take on an earthquake and siege simultaneously and not even bat an eyelid.

After we'd checked the portico under the house and found it in good shape I walked with Luis to the river terrace. He pointed at the doors of the workrooms and asked, as I gathered, if we shouldn't inspect in there for cracks. *"No, hombre,"* I said, *"yo buscarélos. Vaya Usted á su casa. Buenas noches y muchas gracias."* I watched him climb over the upstream side of the wall and take little mincing steps down the forty-five degree triangular stone buttress that gave outside support to that corner. I waited until he'd meandered along the bank to his house, then examined the workrooms and found them both undamaged. *Let Polly, house of Lockridge bless with the Spider, his warp and woof, his subtlety and industry, which are good.* I put the flashlight on Sarah Weatherby's desk and sat on her sofa in the dark and tried to smoke a cigarette. But it tasted like wormwood; and I had a great deal else to do. The Strategists had evolved a Plan, and now it was up to the Tactician to carry it through. Especially that masterly craftsman of no-quarter tactics, Samuel Fraser Deerfoot, the Crow scout.

◎ The moon gave me precisely the amount of light I needed as I eased myself down the buttress and waded the Río Maldorado. My moccasins got wet, but it didn't matter; that's why I'd worn them. I'd evidently sensed, when I put them on, that this was the night they'd be needed.

The old dirt road was deserted, of course. Everybody in Maldita was home counting candlelit walls and hoping they'd add up to four. *Let Thomas with the Badger bless God for his retired fame and privacy inaccessible to slander.* I ran across the ribbon of road, climbed over some stones that had been a shop, outflanked a tree-sized cactus whose spines could mangle an inattentive man, and mounted the nearest hillside.

Crests of hills can be dangerous at night, and never more so than when the moon is near, at, or just past fullness, making a man silhouetted against the sky almost as good a target as he would be in daylight. Although in this instance I was the projectile rather than the target, I hadn't forgotten my years of life-or-death training. A dozen or so yards below the summit I stopped and looked out over the dark and shaken town. *Let Samuel, the Minister from a child, without ceasing praise with the Porcupine, which is the creature of defense and stands upon his arms continually.* The dogs were still barking, and from where I was they sounded much louder. If someone had been standing with me then and had taken notice of my cocked head and alert attitude he might've thought I was listening to voices. I wasn't, though; not any more. The voices were silenced and gone away, and now they wouldn't return for years. Even Lalage's voice. Even hers. And we hadn't been given a chance to say good-bye.

Anchor-headed Scorpio curled above me and attempted to sting the moon that was dimming its lesser stars. The venom spread throughout Space as I turned from the Maldita I couldn't see and moved in a generally eastern direction along the slope of the hill. Pretty soon I descended to and went over a minor saddleback that was a bridge to the next hillside. This hill I circled, keeping below the crest as before. *Let Angela bless with the Scorpion, which is a scourge against the murderers.* I traveled fast. Once I paused to check my wind and discovered I wasn't even breathing heavily. My heart was taking it easy, as well. I started off again, at an increased pace.

Murderers—was that the right word? Wasn't it *murmurers?*

Yet what's the difference, in the end? Murmurs kill too. Not so abruptly, however. Slow poisons.

At last I reached the hill whose top I'd been seeking, a hill crowned with a clump of squat trees, which rose green-tufted to a vantage point behind the Matthews *finca*.

I'd come up the slope from the south, so I wasn't able to see the house, caged in its own high walls in the river valley below, until I'd climbed to the cock's-comb of trees and stared down at the higgledy-piggledy ramble of rock and masonry.

For a moment I failed to realize that the place was oddly out of whack, due to the moonlight-made array of confusing shadows among the angles and ridges of the whitewashed roof. *Let George, house of Simmons humble himself with an Ape before Almighty God, who is the maker of variety and pleasure.* Yet something was not as it had been when I'd viewed the damned *finca*, and from the same elevation, with the sun beating hard on us both. And then I saw what was wrong, and the knowledge made me dizzy, and I had to cling to the nearest unbrellalike tree.

The Matthewses' economy had finally paid off. Joy Durwood's bedroom no longer existed.

The wall in which the two arched windows were set had fallen toward the hill; and the interior wall, against which the bedsteads rested, had collapsed, although not as completely, into the bowels of the house. The bedroom floor now lay under a dire blanket of stone, plaster, and tiles, ribbed with ceiling beams that extended through the debris in a tangle of splintered wood. *Let Joy bless with the Dragon, who maketh his den in desolation and rejoiceth amongst the ruins.* If the former Mrs. Rangeley, the former Mrs. Someone-or-other, the former Mrs. Lancaster lay under that rubble, I thought, she could only be lying there in death. Tears, of their own accord, came to my eyes.

I blinked them back, in time to catch a gray, feeble movement in the ruined room. Distance and moonlight made vision deceptive, but it seemed to be the size of a human hand and forearm.

I wiped my eyes and looked again. I hadn't been deceived; the weak gray waving was repeated. The Devil was still taking care of his own. And then Samuel Fraser Craftsman, who wasn't averse to a spell of caretaking himself now and then, if the price were right, was running hell-bent down the hill. Joy was there, for sure, and alive. *Let Lorenzo bless God with the Caterpillar—the minister of vengeance is the harbinger of mercy.* Every time. *Eh*-uh.

I was picking my way over the cast-down wall when she cried out in a fairly strong voice; no identifiable words, but a terrified demand for attention. It wasn't the sort of noise that a badly hurt person forces out of his lungs. At the same time I could see, from my newer, lower line of sight, the gray hand waving weakly from the other side of a huge fallen beam.

"Coming!" I shouted. "Keep your shirt on—I'm coming!" I was in the collapsed bedroom now and I was pleased to note that there wasn't much dust or powdered mortar or anything else that would hold a footprint. Nevertheless, I was careful where I stepped.

Joy lay on her back with the entire right side of her body pressed against what had, an hour ago, been a "reproduction" of a supposed Spanish Colonial sofa. It had stood, I recalled, between the windows and faced into the room. Now it was a wreck. One of the ceiling's two great support beams, the roughly squared trunk of a tree that measured at least twenty inches to a side, had crashed on the sofa and crushed it, meanwhile holding Joy inescapably pinned within a constrictive triangle of beam, sofa, and floor. The wood dug into her abdomen from sternum to pelvis, forcing the flesh at least an inch lower, but without damaging it. That was all there was to see of Joy, incidentally—dusty, sweat-streaked flesh. She'd had no shirt to keep on in the first place. The police sergeant had spoken from experience when he told Ataudado the Durwood woman wore nothing in bed.

I bent over her. "What happened, Joy? Did you sneeze?"

"Oh—Ah, Sam, it's you—Oh, thank God! I've been calling and ca—Oh, Sam, Sam—I—" She began to weep with relief.

"Easy now," I said. "Easy, Joy." When she was heaving less I asked: "Are you hurt?"

"I—don't think so, but this—this thing on me—" She tried to push the beam away. "It's hard for—me to breathe—all that weight."

"Maybe I can lift it off," I said absently.

"Oh, yes, Sam—please lift it off."

"In a minute. Soon as you tell me who was with you when Lalage came here that night."

She stared at me, openmouthed, and then shook her head drowsily. There was dust in her hair. "Oh, God, Sam, not now—I—don't ask me that now—lift the beam, Sam—please!"

"When you tell me who was with you. And I want the truth."

She shook her head again, this time so violently that I should've been able to hear bits of mortar grind into her scalp. But her screaming would've made it impossible to hear. "It was Marian!" she shrieked. "*Marian* DELMORE!"

"And what were you doing that Lalage saw?" I was calm. I was inexorable.

Joy closed her eyes and gasped several times for breath and then she told me what Lalage had seen. It was so perverse that she could only have been telling the truth. *Let Marian bless with the Silkworm —the ornaments of the Proud are from the bowells of their Betters.* And when she'd finished telling me what I wanted, and didn't want, to hear she said faintly: "Now please lift the thing, Sam." She kept her eyes closed.

"I'll try," I said. I went around the sofa to where the higher end of the beam was a foot or so off the floor. And I did try to lift it—but not very hard. I couldn't've budged that half-ton of wood if I'd been a quartet from Muscle Beach.

"It's not moving," Joy moaned.

"Well, I did my best," I said as I came back to where she lay. "Guess all I can do now is say good-bye forever."

"Sam, no—Please! Get someone, for God's sake! Get—people to help—"

"Can't," I said. "Everybody's out of town. Lalage's out of town and Marian's out of town and Tom Fletcher's out of town and my father's out of town and Angela's out of town and—"

"You're *crazy*, Sam!" She screeched. "You're a MADMAN!"

I was ashamed to be in the company of a woman who'd let herself be carried away by emotion like that. I didn't complain, though. No, I went on with what I was saying, in the same reasonable tone: "—and Lencho's out of town. *Eh*-uh, poor old Lencho, too. And there's this point that's been bothering me lately. I know you excused yourself and went to the bathroom and stripped before you killed Angela, and I know you washed the blood off in the shower afterward. But what I'm not sure of is whether you vomited before or after. Which was it, you old Joy thing?"

She got to screaming again then and wouldn't stop, and it was nothing but pure noise. It was such pure noise that it grated horribly on my nerves—and anyway I was getting tired of noise and moonlight and sweaty whores. And Lalage had told me she loved me, and when a woman tells a man she loves him he damned well has to go to bat for her, even long after the game is lost and beyond any rally, even when he's stepping in against a spitballer. I figured I owed Lalage a little something, if only because she saw things in me that weren't there.

I fell on my knees by Joy's head and put my hands on her shoulders. She kept screaming in this ridiculous way and her unpinned arm came at me with a claw on the end. I had to rest my left shinbone on it.

Let Lalage bless with the Butterfly—beauty hath wings, but chastity is the Cherub.

◎ I was shocked, back home on the river terrace, to find I had Hardy's poems with me. I didn't remember taking the book from Joy's bedroom, but I supposed I must've seen it later, on the mantel. Anyway, I replaced it in Sarah Weatherby's shelves, then went upstairs with the flashlight I'd left on her desk. The lights still weren't working. I didn't get sick until I saw the toilet bowl.

As I climbed into bed I thought: *Let Culloden, house of Cards bless with the Fly, whose health is the honey of the air*—and then I started to cry, because the line ends: *but he feeds upon the thing strangled, and perisheth.*

Pretty soon, though, I quit feeling sorry for myself. It was more fun, much more fun, simply to relax and fall asleep.

❅ *Five*

Coming Out as Smooth
as Meat from a Grinder

Monday morning was beautiful—the most beautiful morning, I think, that I've ever seen. It had rained Sunday afternoon and evening, and the air was washed and cleansed. So was I; I had to be. A man can't fully appreciate a gorgeous day unless he mirrors Nature in himself and is in tune with the Age in which he lives. On that exquisite Monday morning I was a mirror, and I was in tune.

Sunday had been a delicious and lazy day, save for the hour when I went into Maldorado—it was between nine and ten a.m.—to telephone Polly. I knew that she'd hear about the earthquake, or read an account in the *News,* and I didn't want her to spoil her trip by worrying about me or the *finca.* The Maldorado telephone office was closed, but there was a *farmacia* near the market that had a booth. I put the call in from there. On my way I noticed practically no earthquake damage in Maldorado. The Mexicans had learned to build tough, too.

It was too early for Polly to have seen a paper, but she was relieved to hear my voice and by my assurances that everything was fine. Even the lights were working again, although I couldn't say when the break, or breaks, in the lines had been repaired. Polly'd offered to return to Maldita by train that night, but I convinced her that there was no reason for her to do so. I failed to mention that I had a surprise for her. I didn't want her back until the surprise would be worth the surprising. I wanted it to be a real surprise.

What it was, of course, was that I was beginning the novel, which I would dedicate to the twin culture heroes, and deservedly so, of the Age—Philoctetes and Caliban. I couldn't start it right off the bat on Monday morning, as I'd planned, because I wanted to work on the patio and I had to wait for my favorite table to dry out. While I was waiting I strolled around the river terrace and fooled with possible first paragraphs and titles and all sorts of matters like that. Once I found myself wondering when they'd trip over Joy and whether or not I'd done a good job of covering my tracks. I didn't brood on this for long, though. I'd covered my tracks very well indeed, and the maid should've tripped over that old Joysie thing shortly after she showed up for work at seven.

Now it was nearly eleven o'clock on this unbelievable Monday morning, and the novel was actually under weigh, and I was reading the few lines I'd done of the first page. They didn't add up to a great deal, but they caught the spirit of the story and—more important —I felt that what followed, until the end, would be coming out as smooth as meat from a grinder.

What I'd typed was:

I was sitting under an old pepper tree in the patio, at one of those round, hide-topped tables whose design hasn't changed since before stout Cortez hit the beach, trying to put down some ideas about the thing I wanted to do. There was an open notebook on the table, but my mind was shut and locked. I felt ill at ease and uncomfortable

I poised my fingers above the keyboard. All I had to do from now on was punctuate and keep going

, and I was damned if I knew why

A NOTE ABOUT THE AUTHOR

HARRY BROWN was born in Portland, Maine, in 1917 and grew up there. He studied at Harvard, and before World War II worked briefly for both Time *and* The New Yorker. *While in the Army he was attached to* Yank *and later transferred to the Anglo-American Film Unit. After the war he concentrated on film writing for many years. One of his screenplays,* A Place in the Sun, *written in collaboration with Michael Wilson, and based on the Theodore Dreiser novel* An American Tragedy, *won the Academy Award for the Best Screenplay of 1951. He has also won several poetry prizes. His play* A Sound of Hunting *was called the best of the 1945–6 season by the late George Jean Nathan.*

Mr. Brown is the author of a number of books of poetry and fiction, among them A Walk in the Sun *(1944),* The Beast in His Hunger *(1948), and* The Stars in Their Courses *(1960). He lives in Mexico with his wife and son.*

A NOTE ON THE TYPE

This book is set in Granjon, a type named in compliment to Robert Granjon, *type-cutter and printer—Antwerp, Lyons, Rome, Paris—active from 1523 to 1590. The boldest and most original designer of his time, he was one of the first to practice the trade of type-founder apart from that of printer. The face was designed by* George W. Jones, *who based his drawings upon a type used by* Claude Garamond (1510–61) *in his beautiful French books. "Granjon" more closely resembles Garamond's own than do any of the various modern types that bear his name.*

The book was composed, printed, and bound by The Book Press Incorporated, Brattleboro, Vermont. Typography and binding design by Betty Anderson.